THE FOURTH WATCHER

ALSO BY TIMOTHY HALLINAN

THE
FOURTH
WATCHER

TIMOTHY HALLINAN

WM

WILLIAM MORROW

An Imprint of HarperCollins*Publishers*

THE FOURTH WATCHER. Copyright © 2008 by Timothy Hallinan. All rights reserved. Printed in the United States of America. No part of this book may be used or reproduced in any manner whatsoever without written permission except in the case of brief quotations embodied in critical articles and reviews. For information address HarperCollins Publishers, 10 East 53rd Street, New York, NY 10022.

HarperCollins books may be purchased for educational, business, or sales promotional use. For information please write: Special Markets Department, HarperCollins Publishers, 10 East 53rd Street, New York, NY 10022.

FIRST EDITION

Designed by Laura Kaeppel

Library of Congress Cataloging-in-Publication Data has been applied for.

ISBN 978-0-06-125725-4

08 09 10 11 12   OV/RRD   10 9 8 7 6 5 4 3 2 1

For the Choys:
Gerald, Colleen, Gerald Alexander, and Michael

And, as ever,
for Munyin
who holds the thread

PART I

SMALL CHANGE

Three-Card Monte

P oke Rafferty has been on the sidewalk less than five minutes when he spots the tail.

Three of them, all male. One ahead, two behind. Taking
their time, no telltale urgency. All relatively young and dressed to fade:
one white T-shirt, one red T-shirt, one long-sleeved black shirt. Pants
of that indeterminate color produced by years of hard laundering, a
sort of enervated second cousin to beige.

The clothes aren't much help, but they're all Rafferty has: no conspicuous physical anomalies, no scars, no rap-inspired dreadlocks, no
tattoos, no bleached hair. He's looking at a trio of standard hands dealt
out of the Thai genetic shuffle—short and slim-waisted, with the black
hair and dark skin of the northeast. Three everyday guys, out on a
choreographed stroll, doing a pretty slick version of the barre rotation:
changing places at random intervals, the man in front casually crossing
the road to the far sidewalk and drifting back, replaced moments later
by one of the pair behind. A rolling maneuver, like a deal in three-card
monte.

The guy in the black shirt is what Arnold Prettyman calls "the flag." He's wearing reflective shades, he walks funny, it's too hot for long sleeves, and it's too sunny for black, even at 10:30 A.M. So either Rafferty is supposed to notice him or he's not very good.

Prettyman's First Law of Espionage, drummed into Poke's head over the past couple of weeks: Always assume that the other guy is good.

So. Take score. Moderate foot traffic, average for an early weekday morning in an upscale Bangkok shopping district. Stores just open, offering lots of nice, big, reflective display windows, useful to both the stalkers and the target. The sun is still low, so shadows are long, which can be either helpful or deadly around corners. The usual blast-furnace, wet-blanket Bangkok heat, heat with an actual *weight* to it that frequently takes Rafferty by surprise even after more than two years here. It changes the way he dresses, the way he breathes, and even the way he walks. The way everybody walks. It shortens the stride and makes it pointless to waste energy lifting the feet any higher than absolutely necessary; all the effort goes into moving forward. The result is what Rafferty has come to think of as the Bangkok Glide, the energy-efficient and peculiarly graceful way Thai people have of getting themselves from place to place without melting directly into the sidewalk.

Unlike the other two, whose glides are so proficient they might as well be ice-skating, the guy in the black shirt moves like a man wearing cast-iron boots: heavy steps, a lot of lateral hip action. He looks like Lurch among the ballerinas. The man has, Rafferty finally recognizes, a clubfoot, so put a check in the physical-anomaly column after all. The clubfoot is housed in a black architectural structure half the size of a *tuk-tuk,* the three-wheeled taxis so ubiquitous in Bangkok. So here's Black Shirt, aka *Tuk-Tuk* Foot; him, Rafferty can spot.

Okay, he can spot him. So what?

Thought One is to lose Black Shirt first. Reduce the opposition numbers and then worry about the others. Thought Two is to stay with Black Shirt and try to lose the others, on the assumption that he can spot Black Shirt anytime.

But.

The men who are following him probably expect him to proceed from Thought One to Thought Two. Of course, they might know he'd realize they'd expect that, and they'd revert to Thought One. That's what Prettyman would probably do in this situation.

Or is it? And is there a Thought Three that hasn't even come to him?

Rafferty feels a brittle little arpeggio in his forebrain, the opening bars of the overture to a headache.

A long time ago, he learned that the best course of action, when you're faced with a difficult problem, is to choose one solution, at random if necessary, and stick with it. Don't question it unless it kills you. Okay. Lose Black Shirt and keep an eye on the other two.

The flush of comfort that always accompanies a decision recedes almost immediately at the thought of Prettyman's Second Law. There are usually more than you can spot.

Moving more slowly than the flow of foot traffic, forcing the trackers to lag awkwardly, Rafferty passes the entrance to a five-story department store, one of the newly cloned U.S.-style emporiums that have sprung up all over the city to serve Bangkok's exploding middle class. He pulls his followers out of position by moving an extra twenty steps or so past the polished chrome of the revolving door, as yet unsmudged with shoppers' fingerprints. Then he stops and searches the glass for reflected movement while he pretends to be fascinated by whatever the hell is on the other side of the window. He counts to five, turns away, takes two steps in the direction he's been moving in, then decides that whatever was in the window—on second glance it seems to be women's shoes, of all the stupid fucking things—is indispensable after all. He reverses direction abruptly, seeing the pair behind freeze at the edge of his vision and then scramble to separate, and goes back to the store entrance, moving quickly and decisively, trying to look like a man who's just spotted an irresistible pair of high heels. Pushes at the revolving door.

Cool air like a faceful of water.

He finds himself in the cosmetics department, where a hundred mirrors point back at the door he has just come through. In the closest one, Rafferty watches White T-Shirt come through the revolving door, snap a quick, disbelieving look at the mirrors, and keep right on going until he's outside again.

Rafferty is practically the only customer in the store. Half a dozen hibernating saleswomen gape at him. One of them shakes herself awake and says, in English, "Help you, sir?"

"I've got a terrible problem with . . . um, tangling," he says, tugging at his hair and keeping his eyes on a mirror that frames the two men talking in the street behind him. White T-Shirt with his back to the door, Red T-Shirt displaying dark skin and a pimp's thin mustache. Lots of gesturing.

"You hair okay," says the woman behind the counter. She employs the unique Thai-style selling technique; the chat is more important than the sale. "You hair pretty good." She squints dubiously. "Maybe too long, *na?* Maybe cut little bit *here.*"

In the mirror Rafferty sees Red T-Shirt lose the argument on the sidewalk and push the revolving door. "I'll come back tomorrow," Rafferty says, shoving off from the counter. "Before I brush." He walks quickly through the cosmetics department and boards the store's central escalator.

Standing sideways as the escalator's sole passenger, he watches Red T-Shirt do some broken-field running between the counters to catch up, and then Rafferty turns and takes the rest of the steps two at a time.

Turn right at the top of the escalator, move at a half run through a voluptuary's forest of mannequins wearing impractical underwear the colors of extinct tropical fruits. The women's-underwear department borders the housewares department, a broad expanse of gleaming white marble and porcelain meant to awaken kitchen envy in female shoppers. Rafferty stops at the first of a long line of gleaming stainless-steel sinks, complete with a homey assortment of washed dishes in a drying rack, and grabs the squeeze bottle of detergent, hoping it's not just a prop. It is reassuringly heavy. Without looking back, he pops the top and spews a long zigzag of clear, thick liquid on the tile floor as he retreats up the aisle. At the far end, he waits until Red T-Shirt has found his way through the glade of underwear. Once he is sure the man has seen him, Rafferty turns and breaks into a full-out bolt. He is rewarded by the distinctive sound of running feet behind him, then a cry of despair followed by a clamorous crash as some display or another goes down. A glance over his shoulder shows him Red T-Shirt at the bottom layer of a heap of broken dishes, flailing to get his hands and feet under him on the slick floor as shopgirls come running from all directions.

The down escalators take Rafferty in easy stages to the basement, which is positively arctic. Housewives on the verge of hypothermia paw listlessly through piles of bargain clothes. At the far end of the sale area lurks an ersatz McDonald's, complete with its own frightening clown. Beyond the bright plastic tables, their chairs bolted gaily to the floor, a set of tiled steps leads up to the sidewalk, and Rafferty takes them in two springs.

Hot air again. Hot pavement through the soles of his shoes. Traffic noise.

Lots of pretty women wearing bright colors. No White T-Shirt; he's almost certainly watching the entrance. No Black Shirt. Red T-Shirt is probably flat on his back picking slivers of crockery from his hair.

Rafferty slows, debating the wisdom of turning the tables and grabbing one of them for a brief conversation. He is weighing the pros and cons as he makes a right into a side street and the little man with the black shirt and the clubfoot steps out of a doorway, smiles apologetically, levels a small black gun at Poke's head, and shoots him square in the face.

2

The Fourth Watcher

From his perspective half a block away, where he appears to be entirely focused on choosing a spray of vaguely reptilian orchids from a sidewalk vendor, the fourth watcher—the one the other three don't know about—tracks the movements of the gun. He stiffens as the little man in the black shirt brings his hand up, takes a useless step forward as Rafferty stumbles back, watches open-mouthed as the trigger is pulled.

Not until he is walking away, his orchids tightly wrapped in news-paper, does he permit himself to laugh.

3

The First One She's Had in Years That Isn't a Street Fake

The first thing Peachy notices is that the man counting her money is perspiring very heavily, almost as heavily as a foreigner. Like many Thais, she finds it perplexing how much *farang* sweat, although Peachy, who has persisted in regarding herself as a lady through a lifelong roller coaster of social ups and downs, would never use a word as common as "sweat." During one of the brief periods of prosperity her family enjoyed when Peachy was growing up, they hired a British governess named Daphne. Almost forty years later, what Peachy remembers most vividly about Daphne is her hatred of the word "sweat." "Horses sweat," Daphne had said, sweating generously in the Bangkok summer. "Men perspire. Women *glow.*"

So the bank teller fumbling with the bills for her payroll is *perspiring*, in defiance of the glacial air-conditioning, which is cold enough to raise little stucco bumps on Peachy's bare arms.

In fact, the teller's shirt is so wet it's transparent. Peachy has seen horses sweat less profusely, even after one of the races to which she used to be . . . well, addicted. If there's a more polite word for "sweat,"

Peachy thinks, counting silently to herself as she watches the stack of thousand-baht bills grow, there should be a more polite word for "addicted" as well. "Habit" is a bit weak, considering that the horses cost Peachy practically everything she owned. She managed to hang on to her business only because a *farang,* an American, had handed her an irresistible, absolutely life-changing wad of money that she couldn't refuse even though it came with a mandatory partner. Together, she and Rose, the partner by command, have rebuilt the business until they have actually begun to show a profit. But the horses had cost her dearly, had cost her much of what she had taken for granted in life, had cost her—

Had cost her, in fact, much more than she is prepared to think about now, especially when she should be watching this very nervous man count out her money.

The teller's hands are shaking, too.

His eyes come up to Peachy's and catch her regarding him. He smiles, or tries to smile. It looks like the smile of a man who wants to prove he can take bad news well. *Cancer? No problem.* The smile is impossible to return. Peachy begins to feel distinctly uneasy.

"Forgive me," she says, leaning forward slightly and politely lowering her voice. "Are you feeling all right?"

The teller straightens as though someone has plugged his stool directly into a wall socket, and his eyes widen into an expanse of white with the irises marooned in the center. Peachy involuntarily thinks about fried eggs. "Me?" the teller asks, swallowing. "Fine, fine. And you?"

Peachy takes a discreet step back. The man smells of something, perhaps illness or even fear. "Fine, thank you."

"It's just . . . you know," the teller says, blinking rapidly. He makes a tremulous gesture at the stack of white-and-brown bills in front of him. "Lot of, um, um, money," he says.

"We pay the girls today," Peachy says, and then replays the sentence in her mind. "They're *housemaids,*" she clarifies. "We run a domestic agency. Bangkok Domestics." Although she's grown fond of Rose, she still can't bring herself to call it Peachy and Rose's Domestics.

The teller tries to square the bills into a neat pile, but his hands aren't steady enough, and he gives up and shoves them under the glass partition like a pile of leaves. "You must be doing well."

"It's getting better," Peachy says. Although the bills all seem to be brand new, they look damp and a little bit sticky, as though they had been absorbing moisture in the perspiring man's pocket. She doesn't, she realizes, actually want to touch them. Below the counter she unsnaps her purse—Gucci, the first one she's had in years that isn't a street fake—and holds it wide. Then, using her expensive new fingernails and hoping she's not being rude, she sweeps the money off the counter and into the purse. "Bye-bye," she says in English, turning away.

THE BANK TELLER'S eyes follow her all the way across the lobby: a woman in her late forties, wearing clothes that could provoke buyer's remorse in a seventeen-year-old. He resolutely refuses to look out through the picture window at the front of the bank, where he knows the man will be. Watching him.

He looks up to face his next customer.

4

Karma Is a Soft Drink

Rose draws the usual quota of stares as she navigates the crowded sidewalk of Bangkok's Pratunam district, threading her way between the stands of the sidewalk vendors. She slows to take a closer look at a T-shirt with a picture of the plump, fuzzy forest spirit Totoro on it. As she looks at the shirt, other people look at her. Almost six feet tall and—as Rafferty insists—hurtfully beautiful, Rose has been conspicuous since she turned fourteen. She has grown used to it.

But she feels the gaze of the extremely pretty girl who is eyeing her from two stalls away. Women look at Rose almost as much as men do, although usually for different reasons, and not for four or five blocks. This girl, Rose is certain, has been tagging along behind her for at least ten minutes.

Someone she knew at the bar, perhaps? No, she'd remember. The girl is probably *hasip-hasip*, literally fifty-fifty, half Asian and half Caucasian. The only *hasip-hasip* girl in the bar where Rose danced, back in the bad old days, was half Thai and half black. Anyway, this girl is too young. It's been a couple of years since Rose last took the stage at the King's Castle in Patpong Road, and this girl can't be more than seventeen.

Still, the face tugs at her. Rose has a remarkable memory for faces, a side benefit of her years in the bar, when a dancer's profits, and occasionally her physical safety, depended on remembering customers' faces. There's *something* familiar about this girl. Something in her bone structure?

For a moment their eyes meet and Rose smiles, but the girl quickly turns away, browsing yet another stall.

Rose offers one-third of the asking price for the Totoro shirt, settles in thirty seconds for half, and bags it. It's her present to herself. Although she's squeezed every baht since she moved in with Rafferty and stepped out from under the waterfall of money that flowed from the pockets of the customers in the bar, today she can buy herself a present. After all, this is *her* day. Then, feeling a little guilty, she buys another—girl's size eight—for Miaow. Unlike virtually all of Miaow's other T-shirts, this one isn't pink, but the child has watched the animated film about Totoro so many times that she goes around the apartment she shares with Rose and Rafferty singing the theme song in phonetic Japanese.

A glance at her oversize plastic wristwatch tells Rose that Peachy will already be in the office, and she has come to expect Rose to be on hand. She dumps the bag with the T-shirts into her purse, a leather tote the size of home base, and edges through the press of shoppers toward the soot-stained four-story office building, an architectural monument to melancholy, where Peachy and Rose's Domestics operates.

As she nears the door, she is reassembling the girl's face in her mind. Just as a tingle of prerecognition begins to build, someone swats her lightly on the shoulder, and the image dissolves.

"Fon," Rose says, feeling the smile break over her face. "Money day."

"Seven months," Fon says proudly. "It's been seven months." In her mid-thirties, dark-skinned, with a plain face made even plainer by a dolefully long upper lip, Fon is still beautiful when she smiles. She barely comes up to Rose's shoulder, so she embraces the taller woman by hugging her arm. "So the money's small, no problem," she says. "They like me, and I like them."

"They should like you," Rose says. "They're lucky to have you."

They start up the stairs, and Rose resolves for the fiftieth time to sweep them sometime soon. They may have been swept to celebrate the millennium, but not very well. Grit scrapes beneath her shoes. It sounds like someone chewing sand.

"It's the kids," Fon says. "I love those kids." With two children of her own, in the care of her mother, up north, Fon has adopted the family who employs her. She stops climbing, and Rose pauses with her. "When I think I was going to go to work at the Love Star, I can't believe how lucky I am."

The Love Star is among the grimmest of the bars that line the red-light street Patpong, a dank little hole where men sit at a bar chugging beer while kneeling girls chug them. Working at the Love Star is the lowest rung on the ladder for aging go-go dancers, last stop before the sidewalk. Fon was only a few days away from spending her working hours on her knees when Rose found her a family who needed a housekeeper and babysitter. While some girls enjoy dancing in the better bars, no one enjoys working at the Love Star.

"You made your own luck," Rose says. "Anyway, that's what Poke says. 'Everybody makes their own luck.'"

"What about karma?" Fon asks, eyebrows raised. They are climbing again.

"Poke's an American. Americans think karma is a soft drink."

Fon gives her a light, corrective pinch on the arm. "How can you explain luck without karma?"

"Americans are crazy," Rose says. "But I'm working on him."

"Any progress?"

They reach the top of the stairs and start down the hall. Three women, wearing the street uniforms of jeans and T-shirts, are lined up outside the open door of the office. They look much more like domestic workers than the go-go dancers they used to be. "Some," Rose says. "He's not living entirely on meat. He's beginning to realize he doesn't know *any*thing."

The women greet Rose and Fon at the door. Fon takes her place at the end of the line, and Rose goes in to see Peachy, looking harried behind her desk. She wears one of her memorable collection of work outfits. This one somehow manages to combine bright-colored stripes and polka dots in a design that looks like the first draft of an optical illusion. Like all of Peachy's dresses, today's is held in place by buttons the size of saucers.

"Everybody was early," Peachy says, lifting a hand to her lacquered hair without actually touching it. Her eyes register Rose's jeans and white men's shirt—one of Rafferty's—with a barely perceptible wince. "There were five of them here when I arrived."

"You look very pretty today," Rose says. The statement is not entirely truthful, but she knows how good it makes Peachy feel. *If you can bring sweetness to somebody's day,* Rose's mother always says, *do it.*

"Really?" Peachy's hand returns to the general territory of her hair. "You like these colors?"

"They're very vivid," Rose says. "Like your personality."

Peachy's smile is so broad her ears wiggle. "I wasn't sure," she says. "I thought it might be a little young for me."

"Poke always says you're as young as you make other people feel."

"And to think," Peachy says, "I didn't like him when I first met him."

"Lots of people don't," Rose says.

Peachy shakes her head. "You're a lucky girl."

"Peachy?" It is the woman at the head of the line. "I'm going to be late for work."

"Sorry, Took," Rose says, stepping aside. "Come in and get rich."

Peachy counts out the week's wages for Took, a gratifying wad of crisp thousand-baht bills and some of the friendly-looking red five hundreds and hands it to her. "Too much," Took says. "I still owe you six thousand from my advance." She gives back fifteen hundred baht. "Only three more paydays," she says happily, "and we'll be even."

Peachy sweeps Took's returned money into the open drawer and pulls out a ledger to enter the repayment.

"Lek," Rose says to the next woman in line, a girl who had danced beside her at the King's Castle. "How is it at the new place?"

"The woman's fine," Lek says, wedging past the departing Took to get to the desk. She is a very short woman whose plump face displays frayed remnants of the baby-chipmunk cuteness that tempted so many men in the bar when she was in her early twenties. Now, ten years later, she has the look of a child's toy that's been through a lot. "The man has something on his mind, but he hasn't done anything stupid yet."

Peachy's eyes come up fast, and Rose mentally kicks herself for raising the topic. When Rafferty first forced the partnership on her, Peachy had been terrified of placing former bar dancers—prostitutes, in her mind—with the firm's clients. "Are you provoking him?" Peachy asks.

"It's hard to dust without bending over," Lek says. "If I could leave my behind at home, there'd be no problem." Peachy blushes, but Lek laughs and says to Rose, "Remember the guys who always looked at the mirror behind us? He's one of them."

"I was always careful of those," Rose says. "No telling what they wanted."

"Oh, yes there was," Lek says. "Anyway, Peachy, don't worry. If he comes on too hard, I'll just ask you to find me someplace else. No way I'm going back to that." She folds her money and slips it into her back pocket. "You know how people talk about money as units? Like this many baht is so many dollars or pounds or whatever? I have my own unit of currency."

"What is it?" Rose asks, against her better judgment.

"The short-time," Lek says. "This money is about six and a half short-times. Six and a half times I don't have to pretend that the guy who's grunting on top of me is the prince I've been waiting for all my life. Six and a half times I'm not lying there reminding myself where I put my shoes in case I have to get out fast."

Rose can't help laughing, but Peachy is scarlet.

"I'm just joking," Lek says to Peachy.

"I should hope so," Peachy says. She looks like she's about to start fanning herself.

"I always knew where I left my shoes," Lek says.

"Next," Peachy says, looking past Lek.

BY TWO O'CLOCK all the women have been paid, and Rose and Peachy face each other over the desk. Peachy takes the remaining money, sadly diminished now, and divides it into four unequal piles: one for the rent, a smaller one for bribes to the cops charged with protecting the business, and one of medium thickness for each of them. Handling the money carefully, out of respect for the portrait of the king on the front of every bill, she politely slides Rose's money into an envelope before handing it across the desk.

"So," Peachy says, leaning back.

"You're doing a good thing, Peachy," Rose says. She stretches her long legs in front of her and crosses her feet. A silver bell dangling from her right ankle jingles. "You're making merit."

"I hope so." Her eyes search the familiar room. "I have to admit, one or two of them worry me."

"They're good girls," Rose says. "Or at least they're trying to be. Some of them probably need more practice."

"At any rate," Peachy says, "it's been an education. I knew about Patpong, of course, everybody does, but I never thought about who the girls actually were. I just thought of them as, well . . ." Her face colors as she searches for a term that won't offend.

"*Dok thong*," Rose suggests, using the name of an herb employed as an aphrodisiac in folk medicine, a word that has come to mean "slut." She adds, "Women who would do anything for a thousand baht."

Peachy makes a tiny fanning gesture beneath her nostrils, Thai physical shorthand for "bad smell," then says, "Such language."

"Well, they were," Rose says, "or rather *we* were." She wiggles a hand side to side. "Although fifteen hundred is more like it."

Peachy leans forward and laces her fingers. She purses her lips for a second as though trying to hold something back that wants to get out and then says, "Please forgive me. How bad was it?"

"Don't take this wrong," Rose says, "but in some ways it was fun. We weren't planting rice or hauling a buffalo around. We were in the big city. We could go to the bathroom indoors. There was food everywhere. Some of the men were nice, and we were just swimming in money. And we had the satisfaction of sending a few hundred baht home every week. That took a bit of the sting out of it."

Peachy is leaning forward on one elbow, her chin in her palm, so absorbed she doesn't notice that her elbow is crumpling a stack of money. "But then there was the other end of it," Rose says. "Going into rooms with men we'd never seen before, not knowing what they wanted. Even when it was just the normal minimum, just the basic guy-on-top, quick-getaway boom-boom, we knew we were damaging ourselves. You know, you can only sleep with so many strangers before making love stops meaning anything. You begin to wonder whether you can still fall in love."

Peachy opens her hand so her fingers cup her cheek. "*You* did," she says.

Rose feels the heat in her face, and Peachy courteously drops her eyes to her desk. This is territory the two women have always avoided until now. Then, abruptly, Rose laughs, and Peachy's eyes swing up to hers. "Poor Poke. I made him prove himself a thousand times. I think part of me wanted to believe he was just another customer."

Peachy's powdered brow furrows. "Why?"

"I knew how to deal with customers," Rose says. "It was love I didn't know anything about."

"Love," Peachy says. "Love is so hard." She glances down and sees that her elbow is on the king's face, and lifts her arm as though the desk were hot. She smooths out the bills. "I mean," she adds, "I mean it can be. Back when . . . when I was married—" She stops. "Well, obviously I'd think it's hard, wouldn't I? Considering that my marriage fell apart, that my husband . . . left me."

As Rose searches for something to say, Peachy straightens the papers on her desk and then straightens them again. Then she lines them up with the edge of the blotter. "Listen to me ramble," she says. "What matters is that you and Poke are happy, and that he brought you to me." She hits the stack of paper with an aggressively decorated fingernail, fanning it across the desk blotter. "Why is this so *difficult*? What I'm trying to say is how happy I am that we're partners, how much I appreciate what you've helped me to do." She looks directly at Rose. "This business is my family. It's my . . . um, my baby. So I wanted to say thank you."

Rose feels the slight prickling that announces that tears are on the way. She blinks. "That's so sweet of you, Peachy."

"I mean it. And today is obviously the right day to tell you."

Rose looks up, surprised. There's no way Peachy could know. "Today?"

"It's eight months today," Peachy says, as though it should be obvious. "This is our anniversary."

"Oh, my gosh. Is it? It doesn't seem possible."

"You forgot," Peachy says bravely, swallowing disappointment. "Oh, well. Your life is so full."

"*My* life?" Rose asks without thinking. "Yes, I guess it is."

"You're lucky," Peachy says.

"I suppose I am. I never thought I was. Maybe I'm not used to it yet."

"*Get* used to it," Peachy says, a bit shortly. "It's a sin not to appreciate a good life. Somebody should hit you with a stick. I wish someone had hit me, fifteen years ago."

Rose lowers her head. "Go ahead."

"No. What I want to do . . ." She hesitates and then plunges in. "I want to invite you to have dinner with me tonight. To celebrate."

Rose sees the hope in Peachy's eyes, sees a different woman from the resentful partner Poke had chained her to all those months ago. She leans across the desk and puts her hand on Peachy's. "I'd love to," she says. "But tonight is something special. Something with Poke, I mean. Can we do it tomorrow?"

Peachy turns her hand palm up and grasps Rose's. She gives it a squeeze. "Tomorrow," she says. "Tomorrow will be fine." She puts the remaining stacks of bills in the desk drawer and pushes her chair back, preparing to rise. "But what's tonight?"

"Nothing much," Rose says. "It's supposed to be for me." She stands, slipping the envelope full of money into her pocket. "But it's really for Poke."

5

How Much It Means to Me That You're There

The little man from the bank steps out into the heat of the evening. He pauses in the shade of the bank's door, pulls out a cell phone, and dials the number he knows best. One ring. Two rings. Three rings, and his stomach dips all the way to his feet.

"Hello?" his wife says.

"*Oh,*" he says without thinking. "Oh, thank you."

"Why? What did I do?" She sounds pleased.

"You're there," he says. "I don't tell you enough how much it means to me that you're there."

They have been married nine years, and he is not a demonstrative man. His wife says, "Are you all right?"

"I'm fine," he says. He waits, eyes closed, listening to his heart pound.

"And that's why you called? To tell me you're glad I'm here?"

"Well," he says, and then a hand lands on his shoulder. Another takes the phone from his hand and snaps it closed. The teller smells cheap cologne. He has to fight the urge to bolt.

"Give it to me," the man says. He is tall for an Asian, with a broad, pale face and very tightly cut eyes on either side of a wide nose that has been broken, perhaps several times. The body beneath the tight jacket is bulky with muscle.

The bank teller reaches into the pocket of his jacket and pulls out a fat envelope. The man takes it, gives it an experimental heft, and doesn't seem to like what he feels. Cologne rolls off him in heavy waves, a scent many flowers died to create. The tight eyes come up to the bank teller's face, flat as burned matches. "How much?"

"One hundred eighty thousand."

"Not enough." His Thai is strongly accented. He slaps the envelope against his hand in disgust.

"Slow day," the bank teller says. His own voice sounds thick and distant.

The man pulls another envelope from beneath his belt and hands it to the teller. Like the first, the new envelope is heavy manila, with the date scrawled across it. "Have a better day Monday," he says. "Or maybe no one will answer the phone next time."

6

A Perfume from About a Thousand Years Ago

t's a perfume from about a thousand years ago," Rafferty says. "It's called White Shoulders, and the man's squirt gun was full of it. I'm lucky he didn't get me in the eyes. Hand me the bowl, okay?"

"It smells *terrible*," Miaow says. She passes him the bowl, wipes pink frosting from her chin with a brown finger, glances at the finger, and puts it in her mouth.

"Terrible like what?" Rafferty says without looking up from what he's doing. "Terrible doesn't tell me anything. If you want to be a writer, Miaow, you need to be specific." The cake won't come out of the pan. He turns the pan upside down over the yellow platter and gives it a discreet whack with his knuckles.

Miaow had startled him two weeks earlier by announcing she was going to be a writer. Like *him*, she said. He'd had to swallow a sudden lump in his throat before he could say anything.

"It's *sweet* terrible," she says. "Terrible like . . ." Concentration plows a tiny furrow across Miaow's flawless eight-year-old nose. "Like if a flower threw up."

Rafferty raises his eyebrows. "Pretty good." He burps the cake pan again. The cake doesn't budge.

Miaow's eyes are on the cake pan. "White Shoulders is a dumb name."

"I didn't name it, Miaow."

She dredges a thumb through the frosting bowl and licks the clot of pink. "Why would they call it White Shoulders?"

"I don't know." He takes the spatula from the bowl and runs it again around the edge of the cake pan, exactly as the magazine recipe directs. He finds the maneuver considerably more difficult than it sounds. "Maybe somebody thought it was sexy."

"And you?" Rose asks from the living room. She is curled like a dark odalisque on Rafferty's white leather hassock, which she has pushed in front of the sliding glass door to catch the light. She is in an indolent race with time, trying to finish painting her toenails before the sun dips below the jagged horizon of the Bangkok skyline. Night comes fast here. Her lustrous black hair has been pinned up, baring a slender neck the color of the gathering dusk, with a throb of pink beneath. Her jeans have been traded for a pair of shorts, baring the legs that literally made Rafferty gasp the first time he saw them, when she stepped onstage in the bar. The white shirt hangs in immaculate folds; in a phenomenon that has mystified Rafferty since he met her, Rose's clothes never wrinkle. She has stuck the ever-present cigarette between her toes to free both hands, and the smoke curls like the ghosts of snakes around her hair. Her eyes slide sideways to his. "You," she repeats. "Poke Rafferty. Do *you* think white shoulders are sexy?"

"Actually," Rafferty says, his gaze sliding easily down the familiar curve of her back, "I'm pretty firmly in the brown-shoulders column."

"Eeeek," Rose says languidly, fanning her toes. "A sex tourist."

At the sound of the word "sex," Miaow's eyes swing to Rose and then up at Rafferty, who is looking straight at her.

"Not in front of the c-h-i-l-d," Rafferty says to Rose, still watching Miaow.

Miaow drops her gaze to the mixing bowl and scoops out more frosting. "W-h-y n-o-t?" she asks.

"Because, Miaow," Rafferty says, "in spite of the fact that you think you know everything in the world, you are approximately eight years old and there are still things adults only talk to adults about." The "approximately" is necessary. None of them actually knows how old she is, but they settled on eight soon after she left the sidewalks and moved into his apartment. For all he knows, she's a tall seven or a short nine.

"Like your dumb book," she says. "You won't talk about that either."

"The word 'dumb' is getting a lot of work," Rafferty says mildly. "Dumb name for a perfume, dumb book. And have you read it, Miaow?"

"You haven't *written* it yet." She turns toward the living room. "He can't get the *cake* out of the *pan*," she sings to Rose in Thai.

"This is just a complete surprise," Rose replies, also in Thai. She is inserting white cotton pads between brown toes and giving her total attention to the task. She takes the cigarette from between her toes, glances at it critically, squeezes that final ghastly puff from the filter, and stubs it into submission in the swimming-pool-size ashtray on the carpet.

Rafferty twists the pan like a Möbius loop. "Of course I can get it out," he says. "Miaow just expects me to behave like a man and put my fist through the pan or jump up and down on it. Instead I'm getting in touch with my feminine side. Look how *patient* I am." He shakes the pan over the platter. "Get *out* of there, you bugger."

"How about this?" Miaow says. "Let's play I'm going to write a story about you. And you have to tell me stuff so I can write it. Why did the man shoot you? And why did he use perfume instead of water?"

"He shot me to make a point," Rafferty says, hearing the irritation in his voice. "And, by the way, we have a name for people who criticize books they haven't read."

"What?" Miaow demands.

"We call them Republicans," Rafferty says, watching his knuckles go white on the rim of the pan.

Miaow shakes her head. "I don't know what that means."

"And they say laughter has no borders." Rafferty tosses a glance across the room at Rose, who is bent lovingly over her foot. He would not be surprised to see her lean down and lick it, and he briefly hopes that she will. A spill of ebony hair has slipped loose, exploded by the failing sun into a riot of dark color, the way a rainbow might shine against the night sky. "Actually, the cake is just a *touch* stuck," he admits.

She does not look up. "Did you remember the butter?"

"The butter?" Rafferty says, and Miaow says, in English, "Oh, brother." He can actually hear her roll her eyes.

"To coat the pan," Rose says to her foot. "You were supposed to rub a stick of butter around inside the—"

"Seemed like a lot of fat," Rafferty says. Rose's head comes up and Miaow's comes around. Their expressions are identical, the reluctant anxiety of someone who is beginning to doubt the intelligence of a new pet. "I used honey," he says.

"*Honey,*" the females say together, and Rose adds, "Why didn't you just use cement?"

"Let me," Miaow says, taking the pan and bumping him with surprising force for a child so small. She puts her thumbs in the center of the pan's bottom and looks from the surface of the cake—slightly burned, Rafferty suddenly notices—up to Rafferty. Her eyes narrow in calculation. "If I can get it out, you have to tell us why you smell so bad. About the man with the squirt gun. And you have to tell Rose, too, as a present for her happybirthday."

"Deal," Rafferty says, watching her handle the pan. "By the way, 'happy' and 'birthday' are two words, not one." The words somehow arrived in Thailand permanently joined, linguistic Siamese twins in Siam.

"That's nice," Miaow says. "What about the man with the gun?"

"Do you want to hear this, Birthday Girl?" Rafferty asks.

"You come home smelling like something hanging from a rearview mirror," Rose says, "and you don't think I want to hear the excuse?"

"Okay," Rafferty says. Miaow puts down the pan and goes to the hassock to join Rose, and Rafferty leans against the kitchen counter. "It was for my book." As little as he wants to talk about this on Rose's birthday, it at least postpones the moment he is dreading, the moment he is certain Rose doesn't expect. He switches to Thai for Rose's benefit. "I'm writing about living . . . um, sort of outside the law. Not really doing anything terrible," he adds as Miaow's eyebrows contract in her Executive Vice President Expression. "Not hurting anyone, but not exactly behaving either. It's called *Living Wrong.*"

"So you got shot because you were being bad," Miaow says in English.

"I was *learning* how to be bad," Rafferty says. "I've found nine people who are . . . well, they're crooks. Each of them will teach me how to do something that's against the law—just a little bit, Miaow, don't get crazy—and then I'm going to do it one time. I'll write about learning how and then about doing it."

"Does somebody want to read about that?" Miaow asks doubtfully.

"I don't know. All I know is that my publishers are paying me to write it. I never ask whether people want to read it until I've cashed the check."

"But what kinds of things *are* you doing?" Miaow demands. "What were you doing when you got shot with the perfume?"

"Learning to be a spy. Arnold Prettyman is teaching me how to be a spy." Prettyman is a former CIA agent who, like hundreds of other spooks orphaned by the thawing of the Cold War, rolled downhill into Bangkok. "Arnold's teaching me to follow people around Bangkok without getting caught, and once in a while he has someone follow *me*. I'm supposed to spot the people who are following me and then get away from them. Today I spotted three. I lost two of them, but the man who caught me shot me with a squirt gun."

"Why perfume?" Rose asks, fanning the fumes away with a tapering hand.

"Better than a bullet," Rafferty says. "Anyhow, it'll help me remember not to make that mistake again. A nice faceful of White Shoulders."

Miaow makes a roof out of her fingers and looks at it as though she is daring it to collapse. It is not a carefree pose.

"So," Rafferty says in what he hopes is a light tone, "that's all there is to it. I was practicing being followed, and I got it wrong, and I got squirted with perfume. Nothing dangerous about it."

"Mmm-hmm," Rose says, a tone so neutral it shimmers with menace.

"But—" Miaow says, and stops. "You didn't want to tell me about this. Why would anybody write a book they can't tell a kid about?"

"I'd like to know that, too," Rose contributes. She has long been of the opinion that Rafferty's books inspire bad behavior in tourists, a conviction he privately shares.

Miaow shakes her head. "I don't know," she says. "Why don't you write about bears? Or fish? Or elephants that can sing? Why don't you write something that makes people happy?"

"Not everybody can write *Fluffy Bunnies in Bubble Land,*" Rafferty says, hearing the defensive edge in his voice. "People write about what they're interested in. This is what I'm interested in." He avoids the strongest argument, which is that he needs the advance his agent has negotiated for *Living Wrong.* His savings, never particularly robust, have become positively tubercular.

"*What's* what you're interested in?" Miaow challenges.

"What I always write about. What goes on at the edges."

"Of what?"

"Of everything." He takes a breath and slows himself. "Look," he says. "You walk down the street, any street, and nine out of ten people are doing the same thing you are: They're shopping, or looking through windows, or going to meet somebody, or just getting from one place to another." He looks across the counter at Miaow. "Right?"

"So what?" Miaow says.

"That's exactly right. So what? Those nine people aren't interesting. But the *other* one, the tenth one, is doing something else. He doesn't want us to know what it is. He's afraid of something. He's waiting for someone he's not supposed to see. He's just broken the law, or he's just about to. He rigged the lottery. There's a tarantula in his pocket. He put broken glass in his shoes that morning as a religious penance. He looks around a little too much. He licks his lips a lot. He's the one I'm interested in."

"I'm not," Miaow says promptly. "That was *me.* When I was begging, or cutting purses, or sneaking behind some restaurant where they threw good food away. Or running away from some man who wanted me to be bad with him. That's not interesting, it's ugly." She looks around the small room. At him, at Rose, at the cake pan on the counter. At the walls keeping them safe and together. "*This* is what's interesting."

"I agree," Rose says.

"Then the two of you can write your own book," Rafferty says. "That's not what I do, okay?"

For a moment nobody speaks. Miaow is looking at him with a puzzled expression. Finally Rose says, "My, my."

"Well," Rafferty says, "you asked."

Rose curves a defensive arm around Miaow. "When you touch a dog and he bites," Rose says, "you're usually touching someplace that hurts."

"What if it wasn't perfume?" Miaow's voice is pitched a half tone higher than usual. "What if it was a real gun?"

"It wasn't," Rafferty says, feeling the whole evening go south. He reaches out and defiantly scoops frosting from the bowl.

"I don't want a fight on my happybirthday," Rose says. "Poke, you promise to stay alive for Miaow and me, and, Miaow, you stop worrying so much. You're going to be an old lady before you're ten."

"I'll be careful, Miaow," Rafferty says. "Honest."

Miaow starts to argue, but Rose lifts a hand. "Miaow," she says, "you said you could get the cake out of the pan. Can you?"

"Sure," Miaow says, her tone making it clear the discussion isn't over. She slides off the hassock and comes around the counter, so she is standing next to Rafferty. She turns the pan over and says, under her breath, "Fluffy bunnies." Rafferty puts a hand on her shoulder, but she steps sideways, out from under it, and says, with the same muted vehemence, "Bubble land," and then she does something fast with her thumbs to the bottom of the pan. The cake falls onto the plate with a surprising *clunk* and immediately breaks in half. Miaow gives it a critical look and says, "I'll fix it with icing."

FROM HIS VANTAGE point on the sidewalk eight stories down, the fourth watcher is bored.

Lights snap on and off in the windows of the apartment he has been gazing at as the people living there move from room to room. He wishes the child had left the apartment empty during the day so he could have installed the little microphones. That would be much more interesting than this.

Anything would be more interesting than this.

He turns into the department-store doorway in which he stands, mannequins frozen fashionably in the dark windows, holding their poses as though they hope he'll take notice. He shields the striking match with his body, worried not about the wind but the brief flare of light, which he knows—from personal experience—lasts long enough for a good shooter to do his work. Normally he wouldn't smoke so much on the job, but this particular assignment is testing the limits of his ability to remain sane. It's his first time in Bangkok, a city that he's been told is the world's largest brothel, and he's never been so bored in his life.

The cigarette, a cheap Korean counterfeit Marlboro he brought into the country with him, burns rewardingly in the back of his throat. It's the burn he's become accustomed to, the burn he looks forward to forty or fifty times a day. When the watcher first arrived in Bangkok, two days earlier, he had bought a pack of real American Marlboros at the airport, lit one eagerly, taken a deep drag, and tossed the pack away. No bite. He likes a cigarette with bite.

So far this evening, he has seen no other watchers, which is something new. The only interesting thing about this job is that the man he's watching seems to be being followed by half the city.

COMING OUT OF the bedroom, Rafferty stops at the sight: the two of them curled together on the couch, snug as puppies. Rose's hair falls over both of them like a lush black shawl, spilling off Miaow's shoulders and over her plump brown knees. Miaow is gazing dreamily down at the three candles burning on the cake, one for each decade of Rose's life. The glow of the candles paints Rose's and Miaow's faces with gold, making them smooth as water-carved stone. Through the sliding glass door beyond them, the lights of Bangkok glitter like bad costume jewelry. A sentence spontaneously assembles itself in Rafferty's mind: *Everything I want is here.*

"You both look beautiful," Rafferty says. His heart is beating so hard it feels like it's taking a hammer to his ribs. Now that the time has come, he is terrified. He slips into his pocket the small box he retrieved from the bureau in his bedroom and comes the rest of the way into the room, trailing a vaporous wake of White Shoulders. Leaning against the cake is a square of white, an envelope with a rose drawn on it in colored pencil, Miaow's medium of choice since she decided that crayons were for babies. Although she showed him half a dozen attempts at the envelope, she has not allowed him to see the card.

"The cake is perfect," Rose says. "I'll remember it my whole life. Look, you can hardly tell it was broken."

"Shall we sing?" Rafferty asks, sitting on the floor, on the other side of the table so he can see them both. His mouth is dry. "You can start, Miaow."

Miaow sits up and crosses her hands in her lap. It makes her look like a miniature lawyer. "Not yet. I have to tell you something first." Then she stops, her eyes on a spot on the table. After a moment she begins to move her lips as though trying out the words she will say. Finally she says, "Ohhhhhhh." She kicks one heel against the couch. "I don't know."

"Don't know what?" Rose leans toward her.

"Don't know if you'll . . ." Miaow's eyes go to Rafferty with an unfamiliar urgency. "Promise you won't get mad."

"Me?" Rafferty asks. "When was the last time I got mad at you?"

"Just a few minutes ago," she says, "but you always forget." And to Rose, "Maybe you . . . maybe you'll be mad."

Rose touches the tip of Miaow's microscopic nose. "Why would we get mad at you?"

Miaow turns her head away from Rose's finger. This time her heel strikes the couch harder, and a puff of dust halos the candle. "I don't know. I don't know. Maybe I shouldn't have . . ."

Rose glances at Rafferty, who raises his shoulders a tenth of an inch and lets them drop. "Shouldn't have what?" Rose asks.

"Ohhh . . ." and suddenly Miaow is blinking fast, a sure sign she's on the verge of tears. "It's . . . it's dumb. I mean, stupid."

"You're never stupid, Miaow."

She reaches across the table and snatches the card she made. "Yes I am. I'm *stupid*. Why would you want—"

"Whatever it is," Rose says, "if you want it, I do, too."

Miaow looks at her hard enough to see through her. "You promise?"

"I promise. From here." Rose touches her heart. "To here." She touches Miaow's. "Tell us."

"I can't," Miaow says. Then she kicks the couch again, jams her eyes closed, and shoves the card at Rose. "Go ahead," she says.

Rose holds the card to the candlelight. "What a beautiful envelope. Did you draw this?"

"Uh-huh." Miaow's voice is barely audible.

"Here goes." Rose slips a nail beneath the flap and opens it. Miaow hears it and grabs her lower lip between her teeth, eyes still closed. Rose removes the card, looks down at it, and her eyes dart to Rafferty's with an amazed appeal Rafferty has never seen in them before. Miaow has opened her eyes and is watching her with all her being, chewing her lower lip.

"Oh," Rose says. It's her turn to blink. "Oh, Miaow."

"Is it—" Miaow fidgets with her entire body. "I mean, are you, are you—"

"No, no, never." She leans down and kisses Miaow on the forehead. "I'm honored."

"You are?" Miaow's arms are still knotted, as if she is cold.

"It makes me very happy," Rose says. She looks down at the card again and then across at Rafferty. "Poke," she says, and then she swallows. "Say happybirthday to Miaow."

"To Miaow?"

Rose turns the card toward him. It depicts a very tall woman with long hair holding hands with a very short girl whose hair is severely parted in the middle. They are surrounded by colored candles, a wreath of flame. Underneath the picture, in English, are the words HAPPY-BIRTHDAY TO US. "Let me read the inside," Rose says. "It says—" Her eyes come back to Rafferty's, and she exhales and starts again. "It says, 'Dear Rose. I don't know my happybirthday. Can I have yours? Because we love each other. Sincerely, Miaow.'"

"It's dumb," Miaow says, close to tears.

"It's beautiful," Rose says. "It's the best present I could have." She puts both arms around Miaow, and Miaow pushes her head fiercely against Rose's chest.

"Hey," Rafferty says, "Let me have some of that." He moves to the couch and wraps his arms around both of them, with Rose in the middle.

"We don't have a present for Miaow," Rafferty says.

"My happybirthday is my present," Miaow says into Rose's shirt.

"We have to do better than that," Rafferty says. He leans across Rose and smooths Miaow's hair. He knows she hates it, but he can't help himself. "Is there something you want?"

"I have everything," she says. A year ago she had been living on the sidewalk.

"There must be something."

"Wait a minute." Miaow sits forward. "Can I be nine?" Her eyes travel from Rafferty to Rose and back again. "If this is my happy-birthday, I should be—"

"Okay," Rafferty says. "You're nine."

"Oh," Rose says, sitting bolt upright. "We have something else." She reaches down and grabs her purse and then roots around in it. When her hand comes out, it has the Totoro T-shirt in it. "And look," she says, bringing up the other one. "One for each of us. We can dress the same on our happybirthday."

Miaow looks from one shirt to the other, and stuns Rafferty by bursting into a wail. Then she grabs the T-shirt and runs from the room. "Help me," Rose says urgently, fumbling with the top button on her shirt. "You start from the bottom."

In less than a minute, the white shirt has been shoved behind the couch and Rose is wearing her Totoro shirt. Miaow comes back into the room wearing hers, scrubbing at her eyes with her forearm. "We're twins," Rose says. "We have the same birthday, so we're twins." Miaow climbs back up on the couch and leans on Rose's shoulder, two furry forest animals in their nest.

"Happybirthday to all of us," Rose says. "It's everybody's happy-birthday." She kisses Miaow on the forehead and turns to kiss Rafferty on the neck. Then, very softly, she licks his ear.

7

Women Are the Only People
Who Look Good Naked

Where are you going?" Rose's smooth thigh lands atop his, warm as fresh bread.

"Just turning on the light."

"I can find what I want in the dark," Rose says in Thai. Her hand wanders down over the sensitive skin of his stomach, heading for the chakra he has come to think of as his own personal theme park, Fun World. She grabs hold. "It's not like it moves around."

"That's not what you said a few minutes ago. You seemed pretty happy with the way it moved around."

"Thai women learn early," she says with an affectionate squeeze, "to seem happy."

He stretches his right arm as far as it will go, and his fingers knock against a small box and just brush the base of the lamp on the bedside table. Rose raises her hand far enough to sink claws lightly into his stomach, and he gives up and relaxes into the pillow. "I *am* happy," he says, surprising himself. He can't remember ever having said that before.

Rose bumps him with her hip and adds emphasis with a little fingernail action around the navel. "I'd be happier with a cigarette."

"So? We're in Bangkok, not Los Angeles. People are allowed to smoke in Bangkok."

"They're in the living room," she says. Then she says, "I think I should stop smoking in front of Miaow."

"If Miaow's in the room at the moment," Rafferty says, "smoking is the least of our worries."

"Listen to yourself. After all those years on the street, do you think there's anything Miaow doesn't know about sex?"

"She's probably theoretically familiar with the grunt mechanics," Rafferty says. "But the secrets of unendurable pleasure indefinitely prolonged, the mystical tantric sexual techniques of the masters—I doubt she knows much about those."

"Was that what you just did? I should have paid attention." Rose runs the tip of her tongue over his shoulder. "The 'grunt mechanics'? Do I grunt?"

"Like a sumo wrestler."

"You're just being sweet." He can hear the smile in her voice.

"We're not getting much done, are we?" he asks.

Rose turns her head so her lips brush his chest when she talks, and the hairs on the back of his neck snap to attention. "Aren't we?"

"Well, I was going to turn on the light. Then you wanted a cigarette. Instead we're just lying here."

"Actually, I was waiting for you to get up and bring it to me. It's my happybirthday, isn't it?"

"It was. Must be three or four in the morning by now."

"Already?" She stretches. "I guess I did have fun."

He jams his eyes shut tight, makes a widemouthed goblin's face in the dark to relieve the tension building in his chest, and lets his features return to normal. "I have something for you," he says, flipping back the covers and getting up.

"Besides the cigarette? Turn on the light, I want to look at you."

"Not a chance. Women are the only people who look good naked."

"Some of us actually do like men," Rose says.

"It's not that we're not *useful*," he says. "It's just a different index. Women are flowers, men are root vegetables. You wouldn't make a bouquet of turnips."

"Sometimes I worry about you," she says.

"Why's that?" He is halfway to the door.

"No one can really be as much like he seems to be as you are."

"I'll think that over," he says. "I'm sure it means something."

After the darkness of the bedroom, its one small window blocked by the air conditioner, the living room is milky with the light that spills through the glass door to the balcony, Bangkok wattage bouncing off the low clouds. The remainder of the lopsided cake sits on the table. The sight of it makes him smile, despite the electric jitter that's broadcasting random bursts of alternating current through his nervous system.

He pulls a pristine pack of Marlboro Lights from the jumble of clutter in the purse, peels the cellophane strip, and worries one out. As he passes through the open doorway into the bedroom, Rose snaps on the light. He slams his eyes shut against the glare. When he opens them again, he sees Rose, sitting up in bed with the sheet pooled around her hips, looking brown and amused. For the thousandth time, he notices how the light bounces off the polished skin of her shoulders, how the smooth muscles announce themselves in shadows on her flat stomach.

"I don't know," she says, giving him an appraising glance. "Maybe you *could* dance go-go." Her eyes drop as he feels himself stir at the sight of her. "Wait, wait," she says. "This would definitely disqualify you."

"Not at the Queen's Corner," he says, crossing the room self-consciously and slipping under the sheets. "Last time I was in there, half the girls weren't."

"Weren't what?" she says, taking the cigarette.

"Weren't girls."

She lights the cigarette, draws deeply, and regards it with comfortable satisfaction. "Did you think they were pretty?"

"Who?" He breathes in the smoke she exhales, seeking to soothe his nerves, wanting one himself.

"The ladyboys." Thai transvestites have an enthusiastic following among the international cognoscenti and have become a standard attraction in many of the go-go bars.

"No. They always look like . . . I don't know, plastic fruit or something. They don't seem to have real faces, or even a real age. They look like they might come in jars."

"Pay them enough and I'm sure they'll come in a jar for you."

"Rose," he says. His heart is beating irregularly.

"Uh-oh," Rose says. She studies his face. "What's happening?"

"I didn't give you your present." He reaches out and takes the cigarette from her and inhales it hard enough to blow a hole in his back. He is immediately sweepingly, reelingly dizzy. "Jesus," he says. "I can't believe I used to do that on purpose."

Rose is bent slightly toward him, watching him closely. She takes the cigarette and looks down at it. "Most people don't try to smoke the whole thing at once."

"So—" Rafferty says, and stops. The silence widens around them like a ripple in the center of a pond.

"Poor baby," Rose says, keeping her eyes on the cigarette as she mashes it in the ashtray. "All those words in your head, and they're not there when you need them."

"It's almost four A.M.," Rafferty says, in full retreat. "Coffee. Coffee is the answer." He grabs the bubble-gum pink robe Miaow made him buy at the weekend market at Chatuchak. Between the color and the cheerful, slightly fey yellow dragon embroidered on the back, it always makes him feel like Bruce Lee's gay stand-in. "Coming?"

She grimaces. "You mean, get up?"

"I know it's drastic."

"Wait," she says, and reaches down to a small zippered bag on the floor. Her hand comes up with a tube of lipstick and a loose Kleenex, and she applies the lipstick quickly and blots it, all in one swift, professional movement. "Ready for anything," she says. She tosses the sheets aside and rises, almost six feet of flawless naked woman. As always, she looks to Rafferty like some ambitious new stage of evolution, an inspired draft of Woman 3.0, a human Car of the Future. She turns her back to pick up the towel she invariably wraps around her, and Rafferty tears his eyes from the long shadowy gully of her spine and the tablespoon-size dimples above her buttocks, and grabs the box on the table. He drops it into his pocket on the way out of the room. Bumping against his hip, it feels as big as a watermelon.

The fluorescent lights reveal a kitchen that looks like it was used for grenade practice. Flour dusts the counters. Virtually every bowl, utensil, and platter Rafferty owns has ambled out of the cupboard, coated itself with something sticky, and assumed its least flattering angle. He pulls a bag of coffee beans from the freezer and drops a couple of fistfuls into the grinder, clearing a space on the counter with his pink silk forearm.

"One cake?" Rose says behind him. "All this for one cake?"

"But what a cake." The whir of the grinder fills the room. Silently counting to twelve, Rafferty reaches up into the cabinet with his free hand and takes down a box of coffee filters. He drops the box to the counter and uncaps the coffee grinder. "Perfect," he says, studying the grind. He opens the box of filters and pulls out a nest of tightly clustered paper cones. As always, the edges are stuck together. He ruffles them ineffectually with his thumb, trying without much hope to separate a single filter from the clump.

"You were going to say something," Rose says, her eyes on his hands. The lowered lids make it hard for him to read her expression. The towel is brilliantly white against the dusk of her skin.

"Yes." He manages to pry free a little clot of four filters, a minor triumph. He lets his hands drop to hide the palsy that seems to have seized control of them. "I was."

"And you had a present for me." She tilts her head to one side, watching his fingers fumble with the filters.

"After coffee," he says, crimping the paper edges to loosen them. They are almost karmically inseparable.

"Is that my present? In your pocket?"

He meets her eyes and feels his face grow hot. "Yes."

She purses her lips. "Not very big."

"Well, it's . . . no, it's not very big." His fingers feel like frozen hams, and the filters are resolutely glued together. His mind is suddenly a large and disordered room with words piled randomly in the corners like children's toys. "I mean, it's not—but you said that already—and it . . . it's . . ."

"Let me." Rose crosses the room, all business, and takes the filters from his hand. She slips a nail under the edge and separates the bundle into two. Then she places the top two filters, still stuck together, between her lips and closes her mouth. When her lips part, the filters come apart neatly, one stuck to each lip, and she removes them and extends them to Rafferty. Each of them has a dark red lip print on its edge. "The answer is yes," she says.

He has the filters in his hands before he hears her. "It is?" is all he can think to say. He stands there, a coffee filter dangling from each hand, the box with the ring in it exerting a supergravitational weight against his right hip. "It really is?" He has to push the words around the soft, formless obstruction in his throat.

"I know what I said when you asked me before," Rose says, and now her eyes are on his. "I remember every word I said. I've remembered it a thousand times. I've walked to work, I've shopped for dinner, I've cleaned apartments, I've cooked *food* remembering what I said, trying to find the place where I should have said something that wasn't about me, about my family, my life, my problems, me, me, me. I was terrible to you. If I'd just stopped talking for one minute, if I'd just stopped being frightened that I'd eventually get hurt, I would have said yes."

"Ahh, Rose," Rafferty says.

"I told you we were a million miles apart."

"We were."

"The only way you could be a million miles from me," Rose says, "would be if I were a million miles from my own heart." Her eyes go to the filters in his hands. "Just show it to me. Put those things down and show it to me."

"Right. Show it to you." He sets the lipsticked filters on the counter, watching his hands from a distance, as through a thick pane of glass. Feels the cool cloth of the robe against the back of his hand as he reaches into his pocket, feels the plush of the box under his fingertips, but all he sees is Rose, although he doesn't even know when he looked over at her, and then his hand comes into the bottom of the picture with the box in it, and she holds his eyes with her own as her long, dark fingers take the box and close around it.

"It's going to be beautiful," she says without looking down.

"It has to be," he says. "It's for you."

She puts her other hand over the box, cupping it between her palms. "Everybody wanted to marry you," she says. "Every girl in the bar. They looked at you and they saw a house and a passport and money for life. And so did I."

"Most of my competition was a hundred pounds overweight."

"Stop it. Just once, let someone say something nice about you."

"Sorry. Thanks." He can barely hear his own voice.

"But those girls didn't love you," Rose says. "I didn't love you either. I didn't even *want* to love you. I didn't want to tell myself I loved you if what I really loved was the house and the passport. I stopped working because of you, did you know that? I told myself I stopped for me, but I didn't. And after I stopped, I talked myself out of you a hundred times. Sometimes my heart hides from me. It took *everything*, Poke. It took a long time, it took months of being with you, it took Miaow, even, seeing the way you are with Miaow, but I love you."

"And I love you," he says helplessly. The words hang in the air with a kind of phantom shimmer, a tossed handful of glitter. Rose looks at him in a way that makes him feel like a developing Polaroid: Out of the infinite potential of nothing comes a specific human face, with all its weaknesses and limitations. When she has his face in focus, or committed to memory, or transformed into what she wanted to see, or whatever she was doing, she looks down at the box and opens it.

The ring has three stones—a topaz, a sapphire, and a ruby, none of them very large. "The sapphire is your birthstone," Rafferty says. "The ruby is mine." It sounds puerile and silly as he says it. "The topaz was my guess at Miaow. Now we can change it, make it a ruby and two sapphires."

"The family," Rose says. "In a ring." She tilts the stones toward him. "Miaow between you and me."

"I guess," Rafferty says, wondering why he never saw that.

"Poor baby," she says for the second time, but her tone is very different. "You want a family so badly."

"I want to put a fence around us," Rafferty says. "Something to hold us together."

Rose says, "We're not going to fall apart. I won't let us." Her face is very grave. She raises the box to him, and he takes it and removes the ring and wraps the warm smoothness of her left hand in his, and slips the ring onto her finger. It sticks at the knuckle, and he pushes at it, and she starts to laugh and chokes it off, and then raises her finger to his mouth so he can wet the knuckle with his tongue. The ring glides over her knuckle. His arms go around her, and she fits herself to him, pressing the length of her body against his. Then she laughs. "Peachy is going to be so happy," she says.

"Peachy can wait," he says. "I want to make love with you when you're wearing the ring." He starts to lead her to the bedroom. "And only the ring."

"Make the coffee first," she says. "I think we're going to need it."

"Right." Back at the counter, he glances down at the filters with her red lip prints on them, then takes the two that are still stuck together and drops them both into the basket. He upends the grinder into them.

"What's wrong with the ones I got for you?" she asks.

"Nothing at all," he says, feeling as though he will rise into the air, lift off, float inches above the floor. "I'll eat them later."

They are halfway across the living room, sipping coffee, hands clasped, when someone begins to hammer on the door.

8

Maybe a Problem

Doesn't anybody have a goddamned wristwatch?" Rafferty stands there in a robe that has never felt pinker, holding the door open a couple of inches and looking at the two uniformed Bangkok policemen standing in the hallway. "Do you have any fucking idea what time it is?"

"We know exactly what time it is," someone says in American English. The cops part to reveal a thin, youngish man in a black suit. He steps between the policemen as though he expects them to leap out of his way, and they almost do. Behind the three of them, Rafferty is startled to see Fon, looking as though she's just learned she has an hour to live.

"Open the door, sir," the man in the suit says. He has short-cropped, receding dark hair with a part as sharp as a scar, a narrow face, and lips thin enough to slice paper. Rimless glasses, clinically clean, perch on a prominent nose.

"Oh, sure," Rafferty says. "Maybe you'd like a piece of cake, too." Rose has fled to the bedroom, clutching the towel.

"Mr. Rafferty," says the man in the suit. "This is not a productive attitude. We need to talk to you and Miss . . . um, Puchan . . . Punchangthong." After mangling the pronunciation of Rose's name, he pushes the door open another few inches before Rafferty gets a bare foot against it. "Now," he says.

"Who the hell are you supposed to be?"

The man reaches into the inside pocket of his suit coat, pulls out a black wallet, flips it open, and then closes it and returns it to the pocket. He takes a step forward and runs into Rafferty's hand, fingers outspread, in the center of his chest.

The man does not look down. "Remove your hand, sir."

"Don't call me 'sir' unless you mean it," Rafferty says. "And do that cute little wallet flip again. You're not on *CSI,* and you didn't get a close-up."

"The hand," the man says. His eyes have not left Rafferty's.

"The wallet," Rafferty says, "or you'll be looking at the outside of the door again. How are you, Fon?"

"Not good," Fon says.

"Sorry to hear it." To the American he says, "What about it? We need a retake on the wallet."

"I can't get to it," the man says through his teeth, "with your hand on my chest."

"Back up," Rafferty says. "So I can close the door if it's a Boy Scout merit badge."

"We're coming in," says one of the cops. He loses some face by looking to the American for approval.

Rafferty doesn't even glance at him. "Maybe, maybe not. Let's see it."

Stiff-faced, the American brings out the wallet again and lets it hang open. A silvery shield with a star in the center reads U.S. SECRET SERVICE.

"I don't know how to break this to you," Rafferty says, "but we're in Thailand."

"That's why these gentlemen are with me," the American says.

"And very terrifying they are, too. This got something to do with you, Fon?"

"It does," says the American.

"I didn't ask you." Rafferty looks past him. "Fon?"

"Yes," she says. It barely registers as a whisper.

Rafferty studies her face: desolate as a razed house. "Then I'll let you in. But hang on a minute," Rafferty says to the American. "And don't let these goons knock the door down unless you want to pay for it." He closes the door in the American's face and goes into the bedroom. Rose is wearing jeans and the Totoro T-shirt, the sight of which makes Rafferty's heart constrict. "Maybe a problem," he says, throwing on a pair of linen slacks and the first T-shirt in the drawer. He has it halfway on before he realizes it says YES I DO. BUT NOT WITH YOU. He stops tugging it down for half a second, says, "The hell with it," and leaves it on. Motioning Rose to stay put, he goes back into the living room and opens the door.

"*Mi casa es su casa,*" he says, moving aside.

"That may be truer than you know," says the American. He steps into the center of the room and looks around. He registers the cake on the table, ignores it, and focuses on the view through the sliding glass door to the balcony. "You've got it nice here."

"*Architectural Digest* is coming in the morning." The cops trail in. One of them has his hand on Fon's upper arm. Rafferty says, "She can walk without help." The cop gives him hard eyes but lets go of her arm. "Do you want to sit down, Fon?" Rafferty asks in Thai.

"English only," says the American.

"Okay," Rafferty says, suddenly blind with fury. "How about '*Fuck you*'?"

There is a moment of silence, and then one of the cops says, "He asked if she wanted to sit down."

"Sure," the American says, his eyes locked on Rafferty's. "Let her sit." Fon collapses onto the couch, eyeing them all uncertainly. She sits bent forward, hands in her lap, as though trying to present the smallest possible target. The American smiles at Rafferty, making his lips disappear completely. "You're forcing me to be unpleasant," he says. "Unfortunately for you, I enjoy being unpleasant."

"A name would be nice," Rafferty says. "Just so I can be sure they bust the right jerk."

"Elson," the American says. "Richard Elson. E-l-s-o-n." He looks around again. "Where's Miss Punchangthong?"

"In the other room. She's choosy about her company."

"That's not what I've heard," Elson says, and the next thing Rafferty knows, one of the cops has hold of his right arm and is pulling him away from Elson.

"Actually," Elson says, "it would be easier if you hit me. We could just take you all in and do this right."

"Don't do anything silly, Poke," Rose says in Thai, and Rafferty turns to see her in the bedroom door. Elson turns at the sound of her voice, and for a moment he's just another man getting his first look at Rose. His eyes widen slightly, his thin lips part, and he inhales sharply.

"Miss Punchangthong?" he says. He pronounces it right this time.

Rose nods without turning to him. It's the non-look she gave to customers in the bar who had no chance of getting any closer to her than across the room.

"Richard Elson, United States Secret Service. You speak English?"

"Small."

Elson flicks a finger at Fon. "Do you know this woman?"

Rose's face is stone. "Yes, know. Her my friend." The crudity of the pidgin surprises Rafferty, and he glances at Rose, who avoids his eyes.

"And an employee," Elson says.

"Where is this going?" Rafferty demands.

"You'll know in a second." Elson doesn't look at him. "An employee?"

"You say so," Rose says. She turns her head to regard Fon. "But her my friend first."

"I want to know what this is about right now," Rafferty says. "Or you can come back here tomorrow with a lawyer."

"It's about this," Elson says, pulling an envelope out of his jacket. He opens it and displays a thin sheaf of currency. He shows it to Rose. "Did you give this to Miss Sribooncha— Jesus, these names. What the hell did you call her? Fon? Did you give this to Fon today?"

"Not give," Rose says.

"That's not what she says."

"Peachy—" Fon begins, but Elson silences her with a glance. "Miss Punchangthong?"

"Fon get money today," Rose says. "But me not give."

"But you own the business."

Rose shakes her head. "Peachy and me own, same-same. *Hasip-*

hasip, you know? You speak Thai?" As angry as he is, Rafferty has to turn to the sliding door to hide his grin.

"No," Elson says, a little grimly. "I don't speak Thai. So, in a sense, you paid her."

"In a sense?" Rose asks. "What mean? What mean, *in a sense*?"

"It means—" Elson begins. He stops. "It means, um . . ."

"English only," Rafferty says happily.

Elson licks his lips and turns to the cops. "One of you explain."

The cops look at each other, and one of them shrugs.

"Want some help?" Rafferty asks.

"What I'm *saying,*" Elson says, "is that it doesn't matter which one of you gave her the money. It came from both of you, since you both own the business."

Rose seems to be reviewing the sentence in her head. Then she shrugs. "Not understand. Fon need money. Her want eat, you know? Pay for room. Same you."

"Right," Elson says. He slides the gleaming glasses down and rubs the bridge of his nose between thumb and forefinger. "Fon needed the money. So let's go over this. Miss . . . um, Fon got the money from you and your partner, right?"

"From Peachy," Rose says stubbornly.

Elson shakes his head. "From your *company.* The company you own part of. And your partner got it where?"

Rose spreads her hands, the bewildered peasant girl "Maybe bank? Bank have money, *na?*"

Elson turns his head and says something like, "Pssshhhh."

"Oh, come on," Rafferty says. "No matter what this is about, how can you even say that's the same money Fon was paid? I mean, is it special-issue, just for her? Does it say 'Fon' on it or something?"

Elson slips the money back into the envelope and closes the flap. "Which bank?"

"Have many bank," Rose says. She scratches her head at the unreasonable nature of the question. "Have bank too much." She points through the window and down toward the street. "Have bank there, and there. . . ." She points farther off. "And there, and—"

"Okay, okay," Elson says. "Banks all over the fucking place. So you don't personally handle the money."

"Me?" Rose asks, giving up on the street and pointing at herself. "I talk you already, me no give money. And 'fuck' talk no good. Not polite."

Elson emits a sound that could be a groan.

"Same question," Rafferty says. "How can anyone be sure this is the actual money Fon got this morning?"

For a moment Rafferty thinks Elson is not going to answer him. He gives Rose one last despairing look and then flicks a finger at Fon. "It's not just old Fon here. Three of the women who work for Miss Punchangthong's company took money to the bank today."

"They probably all did," Rafferty says.

"But I was only at the bank three of them used," Elson says. "And unless all three of them stopped and swapped bills with someone for some reason, every bill they deposited was counterfeit." He smiles at Rafferty, the smile of the smartest kid in class, the only one with the right answer. "And that's a problem."

"Fine," Rafferty says. "So three women walked into a bank with a few thousand baht in counterfeit money. And that's worth a visit at five A.M.? And it's Thai money, so what the hell does it have to do with the United States government?"

"Quite a lot, Mr. Rafferty," Elson says. "As you'll find out." He looks around the room again, as though he is memorizing it. "And now you can go back to your English lesson or whatever you were doing." He gestures for Fon to get up, and the two policemen flank her again. Elson goes to the door.

"Have good night," Rose volunteers from the bedroom doorway. "Maybe you find girl, you boom-boom, you feel better."

Elson ignores her, but his nostrils are white and pinched, and his lips vanish again. "Just so we're clear," he says to Rafferty. "We know where you are if we need you." Holding open the door to the hallway, he motions Fon and the cops through it. He pauses in the doorway as the cops ring for the elevator. "And don't think about going anywhere outside Thailand," he adds, "because as of about ten minutes from now your passport won't even get you into a movie."

9

Carrots Were the Last Straw

He's just a bully." They are in bed again, but the glow they shared an hour earlier is a fading memory. Rafferty's fury, however, is still very much alive.

"He's a *government*," Rose says. The sky has paled during the time it took him to talk her into trying to get some rest. Early light leaks balefully through the gaps in the tape over the space around the window air conditioner. Rose gives the new day the look she reserves for uninvited visitors and follows her train of thought. "Worse, with those policemen along, he's *two* governments. I may not have written a bunch of books, Poke, but I know you don't punch a government."

"I didn't punch him." He can't bring himself to tell her what Elson said to provoke the aborted attack. "And I'm not the one who told him to go get laid."

"He needs it," Rose says.

"I don't think so. He probably jerks off to a spreadsheet."

"What mean 'jerk off'?" Rose asks, reverting to pidgin. "Same-same 'beef jerky'?" She takes another drag on the cigarette and hits the filter. "He has very bad energy," she says in Thai. "He likes power too much. He needs to spend some time in a monastery. And you should have been more careful. You should have kept a cool heart."

"He had it coming. His behavior was, as they say, 'inappropriate.'" He uses the English word because he can't think of a Thai equivalent.

"What does that mean?" Rose lights a new cigarette off her old one, not a good sign. That was the way she smoked when he met her.

"'Inappropriate' is government talk." He slides the ashtray closer to her so she can stub the butt. The stink of burning filter fills the room. "It means someone has fucked up on a planetary scale. When an American congressman is videotaped in bed with a fourteen-year-old male poodle, his behavior is usually described as inappropriate."

"Fourteen is old for a dog," Rose observes.

"Gee, and I thought you weren't listening."

"I'm listening, Poke. I'm even thinking." She shifts her back against the pillow propped behind her. The cloud of smoke she exhales is penetrated in a vaguely religious fashion by the invading fingers of light, *good morning from Cecil B. DeMille.* "This could be very bad for us."

"Oh, relax. It's not like you and Peachy are printing money in the basement. Today they'll go to the bank where she got the bills, and that'll be the end of it."

"Maybe." She pulls the sheet up over her shoulders as though she is cold.

"Sure it will. It was an accident. Bad luck, that's all."

She does not reply. But then she shakes her head and says, "Luck."

He slides his knuckles softly up her arm. "Okay, it's not luck, it's a kink in somebody's karma. Worse comes to worst, you have to replace the counterfeit junk with real bills. Come on, Rose. It's only money."

She does not look impressed by the insight.

It didn't cheer you up either, Rafferty thinks, and then, pop, he's got something he's sure will distract her. "Listen, did I ever tell you that it was money that first made me want to come to Asia?"

"Really." She takes a drag and blows the smoke away from him. "I thought you came here because you were destined to meet me."

"Ah, but destiny moves in strange ways." He laces his fingers together on top of his chest and lets his head sink into the pillow, his eyes on her profile. "In my case it was money. When I was a kid."

Now he gets the full gaze that always makes his spine tingle. "You never talk about when you were little."

"Well, I am now. You want to hear about it?"

"Of course." She gives him the first smile he has seen since Elson drove his snowplow through their evening. "Since it's my job to help you become human."

"My father . . ." he begins. Then he falters. Rose's own father has been dead only two months, and he knows she is still grieving.

"Your father," she says. She is silent for a moment, and he searches her face, ready to wrap his arms around her. But then she says, "Something else you never talk about."

"That's right," he says, trying to sidestep the moment. "When you don't hear me talking, it's probably my father I'm not talking about. Anyway, he spent a long time in Asia before I was born. Ran away when he was fifteen." He thinks about it for a second. "He was sort of a specialist at running away."

"Fifteen? How do you run away to Asia when you're fifteen?"

"Do you want to hear about the money or not?"

"First things first."

In general, Rafferty would rather eat glass than discuss his father, but now that he's opened the box, there doesn't seem to be any graceful way to close it. "He had a fake driver's license, and he used it to get a passport. Things weren't so tight in those days. He'd saved a bunch of money from mowing lawns and . . . I don't know, whatever kids did in those days."

"He told you this?"

"I asked him. He wasn't much on volunteering information."

She puts out the cigarette and doesn't light another, which Rafferty interprets as progress. "Why did he run away?"

"Carrots," Rafferty says. "Or anyway, carrots were the last straw, so to speak. The inciting incident, as a writer would say. My father hated carrots, especially cooked carrots. When my father was thirteen, my grandmother died, and my grandfather married a woman my father didn't like. She was probably okay; she was only in her early twenties, and I'm sure she was doing the best she could, but it wasn't good enough for him. Just like my mother. She wasn't good enough either."

Rose puts her hand on his. "And here you are, trying to build a family."

"Do you want to hear the story or not?"

"I'd be holding my breath if I weren't smoking," Rose says, pulling out a new Marlboro Light.

"Well, he'd been planning to leave since my grandfather remarried, but he had to wait until he looked old enough to get his passport. So he got it, and one day he came in for lunch, and in front of him was a steaming platter of cooked carrots." He looks over at her. "Are you really interested in this?"

She waves the match until it gives up and then blows on it for good measure. "Don't be silly. This is your family you're talking about."

"Okay. The carrots. He shoved the platter away, and his stepmother said something like, 'Eat those carrots. There are children starving in China.'" He can feel Rose's gaze, and he says, "Americans used to say that when their kids wouldn't eat. To make them feel guilty about those poor little Chinese kids, I guess. Anyway, that was the end of the road for my father. He got up, went into the kitchen, got a waxed-paper bag, and brought it back to the table. He shoveled a bunch of the carrots into it and headed for the door. His stepmother said, 'Where are you taking those?' and my father said, 'To the children in China.' Then he went to his room, got his passport and a metal box that had all his money in it and . . . I don't know, a change of socks or something, and went down to the port of San Pedro—they were living in Los Angeles—and took a boat to China."

"Strong kid." Rose picks up the ashtray and balances it on her stomach. She shoves it with a finger to make it wobble. "How long did he stay there?"

"Years. Until the Communists chased everybody out. Then he went back to California and bought a bunch of property. Eventually he married my mother. Then he packed up and ran away again, when I was sixteen. Back to Asia."

Rose gives the ashtray a precise quarter turn. "Are you like him?"

"No," Rafferty says immediately. "For one thing, I don't run away."

"I didn't mean that. I know you're not going to run out on Miaow and me. But, you know, you both went to Asia, you both wound up with Asian women—"

"Half Asian in my mother's case."

"Ah," Rose says. "Well, that's *very* different."

"We both also have two arms and two legs. And that's about all we have in common."

"Mmm-hmmm." She eyes the ashtray as though she expects it to try to escape.

Rafferty gives her a minute to elaborate and then asks, "Do you want to hear about the money or not?"

"Did you ever see him again?"

"No."

"Speak to him?"

"No."

"Did you try?"

"No," he lies. She says nothing, so he repeats the lie. "No."

"Why not?"

"Why would I?"

Slowly she turns to face him. "Because he's your father."

"The way I see it," he says, "he chose not to be."

She picks up the pack of cigarettes and holds it to the light, reading the health warning for the thousandth time, then takes a defiant drag. "He'll be your father as long as he lives," she says. "But we'll talk more about it later. Tell me about the money."

Rafferty grabs the rope she has thrown him. "He had this box in our house. A metal box with a lock on it. Really banged up, like it had fallen off a cliff or something. For all I know, it was the one he took with him to China in the first place. It sat on a table in my parents' room, and I wasn't supposed to open it."

"So you did."

"Well, sure. I mean, most of the time I had nothing at all to do. He bought about five hundred acres of desert outside this little pimple of a town called Lancaster and built a house right in the middle of it, then stuck my mother and me inside. The three of us and a bunch of dirt. You can only spend so many days counting rocks or whatever it is that people who love the desert do when they're wandering around loving it. So I went to school, I read some books, I wrote some stories, and I opened his damn box."

"Don't pause now. It's just getting good."

"I popped the lock with a bobby pin. It took about forty seconds. And inside there were some old yellowed papers, an expired passport, and a bunch of money." He holds his thumb and forefinger about two inches apart. "This thick. But it wasn't American money—it was from all over Asia. And I'd never seen anything like it."

Rose's eyes are focused on her lap, the cigarette forgotten between her fingers. He can actually *feel* her listening; the energy seems to pull the words out of him.

"Where I grew up," he says, "everything was brown. The desert was brown, our house was brown—half the time the sky was brown, courtesy of the smog Los Angeles sent us every day. Buildings were brown and square: flat roofs, small windows to keep the heat out. Nothing was ornamented, nothing was designed a certain way just because somebody thought it would look good. It was like they went out of their way to make it ugly."

"Brown and square," Rose says. "My village was pretty much brown and square, except when the rice was green."

"We didn't even have rice. We had rocks, which were brown, and here and there a plant, and that was brown, too. And then here were these *pictures,* on the money, I mean. I wasn't even old enough to think about what the money could buy. I just saw the bills as pictures."

Her gaze is warm on his cheek. "Of what?"

"Clouds. Trees. Buildings with roofs that tilted up at the corners like a prayer. Lakes with bridges over them, and the bridges looked like . . . I don't know, lace or something. Everything seemed to float. In Lancaster the rocks were heavy and the buildings were like bigger, heavier rocks. And I unfolded that money, and I was looking at a different world, a world where everything was light enough to float. Some of the bills had faces on them, mostly old men, but they had something in their eyes, something that said they knew who they were. There weren't many Asians near us. My mother's family had Filipino blood, and there were a few Chinese and Koreans who ran restaurants, but they all looked like everybody else, like they were waiting for something to happen. The people on the money, though—whatever they had been waiting for, it had happened." He puts his hand over her long fingers, touching the ring. "So there were *two* new worlds, one in the places and the buildings, and one in those guys' eyes. And they both looked a lot better than Lancaster."

"And hiding behind one of those buildings," Rose says, putting her head on his shoulder, "was me."

"If I'd been able to see around that corner," Rafferty says, "I would have come here at fifteen, too."

"Sweet mouth." She yawns. Then she says, "Poke, I love my ring."

"And I love you." He picks up the ashtray and puts it on the table. "We'll work this out, Rose. Don't worry about it."

"I'm all right. But I'd feel better if I knew more about it. Right now the only thing I know is that the money was bad and we're in the middle of it, Peachy and I. Is there someone you can talk to? Someone who could tell you more?"

"I don't even have to think about it," he says. "When the government is causing you trouble, you go to the government."

10

Better Than the Real Thing

Young or old?" Arnold Prettyman asks.

"Youngish," Rafferty says. "He's like what someone said about Richard Nixon: He's an old man's idea of a young man."

"Nixon got a bum rap," Prettyman says, toying with an eighteen-inch-long tube of rolled paper on the table between them. He has eyes the color of faded denim, as remote as the eyes of a stuffed animal. Rafferty always half expects to see dust on them. His features have bunched for company in the center of his square face, below wavy, rapidly receding, light-colored hair he brushes unpersuasively forward. Lately he has cultivated a pointed little goatee apparently inspired by Ming the Merciless. Before he sprouted the chin spinach, people occasionally told him he resembled the singer Phil Collins, but to Rafferty he's always looked like what he is, or was: a spy. He spends way too much time staring people directly in the eyes when he's talking, a trait Rafferty associates with Scientologists and liars, such as spies. He's fairly sure Prettyman isn't a Scientologist.

"As hard as it may be to believe, Arnold," Rafferty says, "I didn't come halfway across Bangkok to reopen the file on Nixon."

"Just taking a stand," Prettyman says. "Anyway, the young ones are the worst. They all think they're Eliot Ness. Probably carries a pearl-handled gun and is dying to put a notch in it."

"But you don't know him."

"Richard Elson," Prettyman says, without much interest. He pulls the tube of paper toward him and raps out a quick three-finger rhythm on one of the rolled edges. "Nope. Never heard the name. Not that I really hung with the Seekies. The Service keeps to itself."

"Just out of curiosity," Rafferty says, "why would a theoretically se-cret organization call itself the *Secret* Service? Kind of lets the cat out of the bag, don't you think? I mean, why not something innocuous? The Adolphe Menjou Fan Club or the Mauritanian Triangle Stamp League or something?"

"If you're looking for logic in Washington, I envy your optimism." Prettyman lifts one end of the roll of paper and lets it drop again. "Don't forget, these guys want to be important. They're like twelve-year-olds. If they had their way, they'd probably call it Heroes Anonymous."

"Okay, so forget Elson personally. What's the Secret Service doing in Bangkok?"

"Under this administration, anything they want. Mostly, though, they come here about counterfeiting. It's a little weird, since you'd ex-pect Treasury to be in charge of counterfeiting, but it's the Seekies' job. That's what I mean about logic in Washington."

"Well, counterfeiting is what he kicked my door in about."

Prettyman's eyes have not left Rafferty's since he looked up from the roll of paper, but now they dart away for a tenth of a second and come right back, and there is real interest in them. He leans forward an eighth of an inch, which for Prettyman is an expansive gesture.

"American currency?"

"No, that's what I can't figure out. Thai."

"Thousand-baht notes," Prettyman says.

Rafferty squares his chair so the sunlight reflecting off the mirrored wall won't hit him in the eyes. "Very impressive, Arnold."

"You don't want to fuck around with this *at all*," Prettyman says. "I know that's hard for you, but resist the impulse."

"Why so ominous, Arnold? And what do you know about counterfeit thousand-baht notes?"

"North Korea," Prettyman says. His lifeless eyes wander the room. He and Rafferty are sitting in a small bar on the second floor of Nana Plaza, a three-story supermarket of sex off Sukhumvit Road. There's not much affection in Prettyman's gaze; few places are more forlorn than a go-go bar in the light of morning. He recently either bought the bar or didn't, depending on which day he's asked. Rafferty waits; Prettyman is a miser with information. He parts with it as though wondering if he's spending it in the right place. Eventually he says, "The American government, and especially the Seekies, is obsessed with North Korea."

Rafferty gives it a beat to see whether anything else is coming. When it's apparent that Prettyman is finished, he says, "I think it's pretty interesting myself, but what's the connection with bad thousand-baht notes?"

Prettyman grimaces as though the prospect of answering the question causes him physical pain. "That's where they come from. The NKs turn them out by the tens of thousands. And they're not *bad*. Aside from the fact that they're not real money, they're better than the real thing. That's one way they spot them: The engraving is actually too good." He glances at himself in the mirror opposite and feathers his hair forward with his fingertips until he looks a little like Caligula. "Do you know anything at all about this?"

"About North Korea? Or counterfeiting?"

"Both."

"Not enough," Rafferty says. "So clue me in."

"Fine." Prettyman gives his head a quarter turn, right and left, to check the tonsorial repair job and then sits forward, crossing his hands. "Are you paying me?"

"Oh, Arnold," Rafferty says. "After all these years."

Prettyman dismisses the appeal without a moment's thought. "You know what Molière said about being a professional writer?"

"No," Rafferty says. "But I'll bet it's fascinating."

"He said, 'First we do it for love. Then we do it for a few friends. Then we do it for money.'"

"Sounds like prostitution."

"I left that out," Prettyman says. "That's what he was comparing writing to."

"I can see why you might have skipped it."

"The operative word was 'professional.' I'm a professional. Twenty thousand baht."

"Ten."

"Fifteen."

"Twelve-five, and that's it. You're not the only spy I know."

"I'm not a spy," Prettyman says automatically. "Okay, North Korea. The Norkies have almost no foreign trade. First, they don't make much of anything, and second, most countries won't do business with them. And why not, you ask?"

"I do," Rafferty says. Prettyman reflectively chews his lip as though wondering whether to renegotiate. Rafferty asks, "Was that enough of a response, or would you like me to actually formulate the question?"

Prettyman does a minimalist head shake, little more than a twitch. "Because they're nuts, that's why. Just completely, totally, off-the-wall nuts. If North Korea were a person, it would be wrapped in an old blanket, muttering to itself on the sidewalk. Relief organizations send them boats full of rice, since half the fucking country is starving to death, and the Norkie navy sinks the boats. They buy stuff from other countries and don't accept the shipment, or they accept it and don't pay for it. This is not a policy that's going to produce large streams of foreign revenue."

"Sort of like opening a store and keeping the doors locked."

"And shooting the guy who delivers your merchandise." Prettyman picks up the tube of paper and holds it to one eye, like a telescope, then lowers it. "But they need money. The Socialist Paradise—that's what the Norkie government calls it—spends every nickel it can generate on the military, which, as you might guess, leaves a hole in the budget when it comes to luxuries like food. So they raise money by counterfeiting stuff."

"You're telling me that a government is producing funny money."

"It's not a government, it's the Sopranos. You want a statistic?"

"Not particularly."

"Well, here comes one." He holds up the roll of paper and says, "Remind me to ask you about this. So . . . the statistic: North Korea makes more foreign revenue from counterfeiting than it does from trade."

Some sort of response seems called for. Rafferty says, "Gadzooks."

"Prescription drugs, cigarettes—your girlfriend smokes, right?"

"Like Pittsburgh."

"Marlboros?"

Rafferty nods.

"Well, your girlfriend's cigarettes come straight from Kim Jong Il. In 1995, agents intercepted a boat on its way from Taiwan to North Korea carrying cigarette papers with the Marlboro logo. Wrap them around some junk tobacco, and there were so many papers they'd have brought one billion dollars on the street. That's billion with a *b*. Nine-tenths of the Marlboros in Southeast Asia are forgeries, courtesy of Office 39, which reports directly to the little guy with the Eraserhead haircut."

"Another reason for her to quit."

"But your Mr. Elson doesn't care about cigarettes, or fake Viagra, or AIDS drugs that don't actually do anything. He cares about money, American money. The same printing plant in Pyongyang that makes the extra-fancy thousand-baht bills makes American fifties and hundreds that are so good they're called 'supernotes.'" Prettyman shakes his head in what might be admiration. His eyes briefly border on expressive. "You have to give them credit. These things are so perfect the Seekies had to blow them up to about twenty feet long and project them on a floor in Washington to find the telltales. They even got the ink right. You heard of color-shifting ink?"

"Is this going to cost me extra?"

"Look at it from different angles, it's different colors. Green and black, mostly. We use it on the new bills now, because it was supposed to be impossible to counterfeit. Well, it isn't. And the paper is the same, with a cloth fiber content of three-quarters cotton and one-quarter linen."

"I thought the paper was a secret, like the formula for Coca-Cola."

"The Norkies were bleaching one-dollar bills for a while but they finally figured the hell with it, that was too expensive, and analyzed the paper six ways from Sunday. Then they started making it on their own. They're printing this stuff like mail from Ed McMahon. Why do you think American money's gotten so fancy all of a sudden? Office 39, that's why. And don't bother getting used to the new bills, because they'll have to change again in a few years."

Rafferty glances at his watch. "So Elson is in Bangkok because the same North Koreans who are making the American play money are also making the Thai stuff."

"And because they pass a lot of the American counterfeits here."

"In Bangkok? Why?"

"About the only thing they haven't figured out is how to get tons of the stuff into the States. About three hundred thousand dollars showed up in Newark on a boat from China a year or so ago, and another seven hundred thousand got snagged in Long Beach. Peanuts, probably just trial runs. So they pass them here, or in the United Kingdom and a bunch of other countries, anywhere they can get them in by the boatload."

"Still," Rafferty says, "how many billion U.S. bucks are in circulation? This has got to be like putting a drop of iodine in a swimming pool."

"People in the Bush administration referred to it as an act of war."

"To the Bush administration, double-parking is an act of war."

"Elson's a Seekie," Prettyman says. "The guys in the Service are the president's men, remember? They tend to take the executive branch's perspective pretty seriously. Also, here's a chance for them to make headlines. I mean, how often does someone take a shot at the president? You can put on those suits and plug in that earpiece and scan the crowd for your whole career without ever feeling like anything except a civil servant whose feet hurt. But lookie here, a chance to put an end to an act of war." He fingers the goatee experimentally. "So I'm telling you, don't get in Elson's way. He's gonna run over you like a cement truck hitting a feather. And the Thais won't lift a finger."

"I think it'll be okay. The bills came from a bank. Elson will talk to Rose's partner, and she'll clear the whole thing up."

"You'd better hope so. Speaking of money." He rolls the tube of paper back and forth beneath his palms.

"Got it," Rafferty says. He pulls out a wad of money with a rubber band around it. "Two consultations, and what you told me you were paying your guys." He reaches into his pocket for more. "And the twelve-five."

"Speaking of my guys," Prettyman says, taking the money, "they pretty much had you for breakfast yesterday."

"You heard about that."

"I didn't need to hear about it. I can smell it." He flips through the bills. "No thousands, right?"

"You're kidding."

"Uh-uh." He peels off two thousand-baht bills and hands them back. "Give me five-hundreds. Last thing I need is the Seekies."

As Rafferty makes the change, Prettyman surveys the room again. It follows the basic scheme: a square bar in the center, surrounding a raised and mirrored stage on which several scantily clad young women sleepwalk each night, more or less rhythmically. The sole distinguishing feature is at the far end of the room: three curtained booths where customers can retire with the sleepwalker of their choice for the house specialty, which requires the sleepwalker to service the seated patron for however long it takes heaven to arrive. This is exactly the kind of bar from which Rose rescued Fon.

"Thinking about an upgrade," Prettyman says.

"Hard to imagine," Rafferty says. "The booths are an interesting touch. Curtains and everything. Very upscale."

"Thanks. But, you know, times change. I think maybe new lights and speakers, maybe a mirror on the stage floor. Old guys get stiff necks trying to look up all the time."

"Next thing you know, you'll be serving fruit shakes."

Prettyman regards the room for another moment, eyes half narrowed to make it look better, then seems to come to a decision. "Tell me what you think of this," he says, unfolding the paper and turning it so it faces Rafferty. It is a chalk drawing that depicts a neon sign, obviously in the design stage, with penciled measurements in meters scribbled here and there. Most of the space is taken up by a large crimson word in balloon type.

"'Gulp'?" Rafferty says, reading.

"Too subtle?" Prettyman asks. He is frowning down at the page.

"It's too a lot of things, Arnold, but subtle is not one of them. What's wrong with 'Charming'? That's been the name of this place for years."

"Fails the basic criteria of business communication," Prettyman says.

It sounds like he's reciting something somebody said to him. "Doesn't tell you anything. Not memorable, not distinctive."

"But *Gulp*? As in, 'Whaddaya say, guys, let's go down to Gulp?' Or, 'No problem, honey, I stopped off at Gulp?' I don't know, Arnold."

Prettyman looks disconcerted. "I was thinking about calling it 'Lewinsky's,'" he says, "but somebody's already using it."

"It's dated," Rafferty says, just to mollify him. "Gulp is . . . um, timeless." He looks down at the paper again. "But what's with the bird?"

Prettyman studies the picture. A blue, somewhat lopsided bird with its wings outstretched hovers above the *G* in "Gulp." "*Nobody* gets it," he says with some bitterness.

"At least I've got company." Rafferty checks his watch once more.

"You in a hurry?" Prettyman rolls up the paper with uncharacteristic vehemence.

"Come on, Arnold. Tell me about the bird. For once in your life, hand out some free information."

"It's a swallow," Prettyman says shortly.

"I take it all back," Rafferty says, rising. "You *are* subtle."

11

The Other End of the Line

T wo cops," the fourth watcher says into the cell phone. The phone is a floater, purchased, along with four others, from the people who stole them from their original owners. Each will be used for one day. By six tonight this one will be at the bottom of the river.

Against his will, the fourth watcher yawns; he had a long night, but a yawn is an admission of weakness. "They were dragging some girl along. But here's the interesting part: There was a guy with them. Dark suit, even a tie."

"Thai government?" says the man on the other end of the line.

"I'm tired," the fourth watcher admits. "I should have told you the guy in the suit was an Anglo."

There is a pause. The fourth watcher yawns again, silently this time, and looks at the traffic. Traffic where he comes from is bad, but nothing like this. Then the man on the other end of the line says, "Shit." He puts a lot into it.

"And since our guy's American, I'm figuring the guy in the suit—"

"Yeah, yeah." The fourth watcher can almost see the other man rubbing his eyes. "Half of Thailand is following him, and now this. Cops and an American at four-thirty in the morning. What the hell is going on, Leung?"

"I just stand around and watch," the man called Leung says. "You're supposed to figure out what's going on."

"They went into the *building*. How do you know they went to his apartment?"

"Lights," says the fourth watcher. "A minute, a minute and a half after they all went in, the lights went on in what I figure is the living room. Opens onto a balcony. Fifteen, twenty minutes later—make it five o'clock—they came out, all of them. Both cops, the Anglo, and the woman. About thirty seconds after that, the lights in the apartment went off again."

"Where are you now?"

"Sex city. Nana Plaza. Our guy just went inside, into a bar."

"At this hour? With a woman like that at home, he's doing a morning quickie?"

"Bar's closed," says Leung. "Some Anglo guy showed up and unlocked it for him."

"Describe him."

"Only saw him for a second. Balding and combing it forward, little-bitty features in a big face. Oh, and a goatee. Got maybe twenty pounds he doesn't want, mostly around his belt."

"Doesn't ring a bell. Any followers on our man?"

"Not unless they're invisible."

"Okay," the man on the other end of the line says. "Wait a few minutes until Ming Li shows up, and then come on in and get some sleep. She'll take him for the rest of the day."

Leung stifles another yawn. "Three or four tails practically riding on his back all the time. Cops in the middle of the night. A guy who couldn't be any more government if he had an eagle on his jacket. What do you think it is?"

"I think it's the same thing you do," says the man on the other end of the phone. "Trouble."

12

A Yellow Heart

The go-go clubs of Nana Plaza, where Prettyman's bar is located, don't light up until 6:00 P.M., but the open-air bars flanking the end of the Plaza that spills into Soi Nana are already packed at 10:30 in the morning and exuding an air of desperate fun. The tables are jammed with drinkers, some of whom can barely sit upright and most of whom look as though they haven't been to bed in days: Bags sag beneath eyes, graying whiskers bristle, hair as lank as raw bacon hangs over foreheads. Trembling hands hoist glasses. Here and there, Rafferty sees a morning-shift girl, her arms draped around one of the drinkers, looking at him as though he's just emerged, naked, gleaming, and perfect, from the sea.

Bad 1980s rock and roll, big-hair metal at its most aggressively ordinary, elbows its way onto the sidewalk. The as-yet-unclaimed women, who will be doing short-times until 7:00 P.M., hug the stools they've staked out, their miniskirts riding up over their thighs as they scan the crowd in the hope of intercepting a speculative glance. Most of them aren't even pretending to be interested. It's too early.

Rafferty knows exactly how they feel. Thanks to the visit from Elson and Rose's nervousness afterward, he got maybe ninety minutes of sleep. His eyes feel like someone poured a handful of sand beneath his lids, and there's something sluggish and heavy at his core. He knows there's only one cure: coffee. The question is whether to go home and drink a pot with Rose or grab some here. He's thickheaded enough that his indecision actually stops him in the middle of the sidewalk. One of the girls in the bar, seeing him pause, calls him in. For a moment he considers it—they've got coffee—but the music and the clientele combine to create a richly textured awfulness that's better avoided at this hour. The light level drops slightly, and he looks up to see some truly alarming clouds.

Can he even make it home before the rain hits?

He is turning to walk to Sukhumvit Road when he sees the girl.

She instantly stops and drops to one knee to fiddle with a shoe, lowering her head so a veil of black hair falls forward and covers her features. In the half second or so that he sees her, however, the face leaps across the darkening day as though a flashbulb has exploded. She is extraordinarily beautiful. Her pale face is angular, sharp-boned, almost unnaturally symmetrical. Eighteen, maybe nineteen. Not Thai. Chinese, perhaps, or even Korean, although something about her features—the high bridge of her nose, the curve of her lower lip—suggests she might be *hasip-hasip*, fifty-fifty Western. But the thing that arrests his gaze is that there is something familiar about her. He knows he has never seen her before. He would remember if he had; she is definitely material for the memory bank. But he recognizes *something* in her face.

He is still staring at her when she glances up from her shoe and catches his eye. She gives him a sliver of a smile, more the thought of a smile than the thing itself, and then stands and walks away, her back to him, heading back up Soi Nana. He is certain she just reversed direction. As she retreats, he sees that she is taller than most Asian women, perhaps five-eight, another reason to think she might be *hasip-hasip*.

Not as tall as Rose, he thinks, and a bolt of guilt pierces him. He should be doing something—anything—about Agent Elson. And Fon, if he can; for all he knows, Fon is still in jail. The first thing that comes to mind is the two cops who were with Elson. He pulls out the phone again, turns it on, and dials the number of his friend Arthit, a colonel in the Bangkok police. As he waits for the ring, he turns back in the direction of Sukhumvit and begins to amble toward it. Arthit's voice mail picks up, and Rafferty leaves a message, asking whether they can meet for lunch in a couple of hours at an outdoor restaurant near Arthit's station.

He snaps the phone shut and asks himself again: home or somewhere here?

His decision arrives in the form of a typical Thai raindrop, perhaps half a pint of warm water, that smacks the top of his forehead much as a Zen master might clobber a meditating student whose attention has wandered. Before he can blink, thunder rumbles and the sky flickers: lights on, off, then on again, and suddenly it's much darker than before. A giant burps high overhead, a noise like someone rolling cannonballs in a huge pan. Rafferty has learned respect for Thai rainstorms, which can empty an Olympic swimming pool on one's head in a matter of minutes, and he hurries toward the intersection, hoping to flag a *tuk-tuk* before the deluge strikes.

Hope, as is so often the case, is disappointed. Poke hasn't gone ten yards before the drain opens in heaven, tons of water falling, the drops so fat and heavy that their splashes reach his knees. A whiplash of light precedes by scant seconds a sound like the sky cracking in half. The rain increases in volume, slapping his shoulders sharply enough to sting. His world shrinks to a circle a few yards wide with himself at its soaked center. It is literally impossible to see across the street.

Rain means the same thing in what the tour books call "exotic Bangkok" that it means in more prosaic cities around the world. It means that there will not be a taxi within miles. It means Rafferty could stand on the curb for hours, stark naked, painted fuchsia, and waving a million-baht note, and no one would hit the brakes. It means he has a chance to find out whether his new jeans are really preshrunk or just *Bangkok* preshrunk, meaning that some seamstress spent several minutes painstakingly sewing on a label that says "preshrunk," which is usually the item that shrinks first.

He's running by now, the phone folded and sheltered in his fist, looking for a restaurant, coffee shop, bar—anyplace he can wait out the rain. As if on cue, golden lights bloom to his right, haloed in the rain. A bell rings as he pushes his way through the door, into a small bakery and coffee shop. He is alone, facing a long glass case full of pastries frosted in an improbable yellow the color of Barbie's hair. The air is thick with coffee, and stools line the window, framing a gray rectangle of rain. He takes a seat and drips contentedly onto the floor, watching the water fall.

As a native of California, where a cloudy day makes the TV news, Rafferty is thrilled by Thailand's enormous weather. Its sheer magnitude seems a kind of wealth, spending itself extravagantly day after day: thunderous rain, blinding heat, clouds as greasy and dark as oil shale. Nothing makes him happier than being in his apartment with Miaow, all the lights on in midafternoon, as monsoon-force winds lash the rain around and rattle the glass door to the balcony.

And now Rose will be there, too. As his wife.

The lie he told Rose in bed that morning nags at him. In fact, he *had* tried to find his father. Within two weeks of his graduation from UCLA, he had returned to Lancaster and ransacked his father's metal box. Two days later he was on a plane to Hong Kong. Once there, he used the decades-old names and addresses he had copied into his notebook to track his father across China, where he ultimately found the woman—fat and blowsy now—for whose decades-old memory Frank Rafferty had left his wife and son behind.

His father had refused to see him.

The only thing Rafferty owes his father is that the search had brought him to Asia, where he has been more or less ever since.

Frank has a yellow heart, his fierce mother had said, the one time she allowed Rafferty to raise the subject of his father's disappearance. At the time he'd thought she meant he was a coward. Only after he realized that he, too, had a yellow heart did he grasp that his father simply loved Asia, could not live anywhere but Asia. Rafferty's mother, half Filipina herself, had understood her husband, although that didn't stop her from hating him later, with that special talent for hatred that Filipinos carry in their blood, mixed in with gaiety and music.

A yellow heart, he thinks.

"*Sawadee, kha,*" someone says behind him. He turns to see a girl, perhaps ten years old. She wears a pair of shorts more or less the same yellow as the pastries behind the glass and a much-laundered T-shirt that says HAPPY TOGETHER above a picture of two fat hippies whom Rafferty recognizes as the singers in an old-time band called the Turtles. She is as brown as a paper bag.

"*Sawadee, khrap,*" Rafferty says. "Caffee *lon,* okay?"

"One hot coffee," Happy Together says. "It will coming up." She looks past him at the rain, and her lips move experimentally. Then she narrows her eyes and takes the plunge. "Have raining, yes?"

"Have raining, yes," Rafferty says. "Have raining *mak-mak.*" The Thai phrase for "a lot."

"Hokay," Happy Together says proudly. "Talking English, *na?*"

"More or less. You speak it well."

"Ho, no," she says. "Only little bit." It sounds like "leeten bit." "Where you come from?"

"U.S.A."

She raises an index finger as though she is going to lecture him, but the message is mathematical. She says, "U.S.A. numbah one."

"No," Rafferty says. "Thailand is number one."

"Hah." Her grin is enormously white. He has passed the national test. "Caffee *lon* now." She disappears behind the counter, only the top of her head visible. She is no taller than Miaow.

Miaow, he thinks. *Miaow* is Rafferty's family now. *Rose* is Rafferty's family now. It has taken him years to assemble a home, and now he has one. *I'm really* hasip-hasip *now,* he thinks. *I have a Thai family.* With his mother's Filipina blood evident in the high bones of his face and his straight black hair, he has often been mistaken for half Thai, although he's only one-quarter Asian. Still, he thinks, he's genetically entitled to his yellow heart.

The coffee, when it is slapped down in front of him, is thick enough to whip. He lifts the heavy china mug and stares at the rain.

"Think too much," Happy Together says, standing beside him. "Think too much, no good."

"Thinking about good things," Rafferty says. "I've got a little girl at home just like you."

"Thai girl?" Happy Together gives the operatic rain a disdainful glance. She's used to it.

"One hundred percent," Rafferty says.

Happy Together glances at his face, looks again. "You, what? *Hasip-hasip?*"

"Part Filipino."

"I know where Pipinenes are," she says, pointing more or less east. "Over there." It comes out "Oweh dah."

"My daughter's smart, too."

She thinks for a second, pushing her lower lip out. "Some *farang* no have baby, right?"

"Right." He has been asked this question before. Most Thais cannot imagine an adult choosing not to have children.

"Why? Why not have baby? No have baby, not happy."

"I don't know. But you're right. Babies are necessary."

Happy Together fills her cheeks with air as she checks the dictionary in her head and then squints at him. "You say what?"

"Necessary," Rafferty repeats, following it with the Thai word.

"Word too big," she says decisively.

"Not for you. You're smart."

She goes up on tiptoes. "You know twelve times twelve?"

"One hundred thirty-eight."

"Ho." She punches him on the leg, hard enough to raise a lump. "You joking me."

"See how smart you are? And look, you've already got your own shop."

She balls her fist to punch him again and thinks better of it. Maybe her hand hurts. "My mama make shop. But I make caffee. Good, *na?*"

"Excellent." Rafferty brings the cup to his lips and watches as someone comes into sight through the window, shrouded in rain. A woman, her clothes pasted to her slender form. She does not keep her head down against the downpour but shields her eyes with a hand, obviously looking for something or someone. He watches idly for a moment, wondering why she hasn't ducked inside to wait out the storm, and then, with a start, realizes who she is.

He pushes back his stool. "How many baht?" he asks Happy Together.

"Twenty. Caffee no good?"

The girl has passed from sight. So he was right; she *had* reversed direction, then turned around and followed him again. "It's excellent," he says. "But I just saw someone I know." He gives Happy Together a bright blue fifty-baht note and hurries out into the rain.

THE MOMENT HE sets foot on the street, a sheet of lightning flattens everything, turning the raindrops ice-white and freezing them in midfall. The boom that follows feels like his own skull crumpling. He starts walking, as fast as he can without breaking into a run, waiting for the girl's form to solidify through the gray curtain in front of him.

He had meant to tell Prettyman to call off the trackers. He decided over his morning coffee to drop the book idea as too risky for someone with a wife and child, kicking off the first day of his new life with a firm resolve that made him feel briefly adult, despite a twinge of resentment; the book's topic had interested him. But now things were different. He had responsibilities. He'd write magazine articles. He'd review books—that sounded safe. Maybe he'd do advertising copy.

The prospect had all the allure of a glass of warm milk, but his wife and daughter would be happier. He and Rose would economize; they'd pay Miaow's tuition, and then worry about everything else. He'd left the apartment with every intention of abandoning the project. Then he had been distracted, thinking about the conversation about Elson, and he'd forgotten to tell Prettyman he was quitting.

Or perhaps, he acknowledges, he likes the excitement. Or maybe he doesn't want to let go of the advance money.

But now he can clear it up.

He passes a drugstore, a restaurant, a small hotel, a hair salon full of women anxiously lining the window, staring at the rain that will ruin their new hairdos, barely paid for. Cars splash by in the street, throwing up sheets of water three feet high. The light increases by several f-stops, and he realizes the rain is lifting. He can see half a block ahead now.

The girl is nowhere in sight.

He breaks into a run, his feet slapping through the water. Then some giant hand turns off the faucet and the rain stops, as suddenly as it began. The boulevard yawns in front of him, gleaming wet, its sidewalk almost deserted.

She must have turned into a side street. He looks back, certain he didn't pass one, and sees nothing. Half a block ahead, though, a *tuk-*

tuk fords a temporary lake across the boulevard and vanishes to the right, obviously heading down a *soi*. Without breaking stride, Rafferty chases it and enters the *soi*.

And sees her, walking briskly, almost a block away. She turns, checking behind her, and spots him. At the same moment, she sees the *tuk-tuk* and raises a hand to flag it. The *tuk-tuk* swerves suicidally to the curb, its driver having obviously seen her face, and she climbs in. As it pulls away, she looks back at Rafferty again. Then, with that same quarter smile, she lifts her hand and waves good-bye.

13

My Sweetness Is Classified

A *magazine article.*

His notebook is pocket-size, awkward for anything but brief reminders, but he scribbles in it anyway, sitting at the outdoor table until the rain drives him inside. "Spytown," he titles it, ten thousand, maybe fifteen thousand words about the oddly matched collection of spies who, like Prettyman, drifted to Bangkok when the world no longer looked like it was heading for a shooting war. He'd met a few of them. His second conversation with Prettyman had taken place in a bar so discreet it didn't even have a sign. Rafferty had needed half an hour, trekking up and down the *soi* on foot, to find it, and when he went inside, it was full of spies.

Well, *retired* spies, or so they said. Now older and fatter, they looked like traveling salesmen whose territories had shrunk out from under them. There was something unanchored about them, something about the way their eyes checked the room without settling on anything, the way they looked at every face twice, and then twice again, that was unnerving. They seemed always to be reassuring themselves that they had an exit, from the room, from the conversation. Rafferty had heard it said that the only people who were at home everywhere were kings and prostitutes. These men were on the other end of the scale. They weren't at home anywhere.

All of them *were* men. They congregated in the booths in groups that assembled and broke up constantly, rehashing operations from twenty years ago, operations on which they'd been on opposing sides. It quickly became apparent that half the men in the bar would have killed the other half on sight in 1985.

Nineteen eighty-five: the year his father had returned to China.

Prettyman had been different in the bar. Rafferty is trying to capture the difference in words when he notices that the rain has stopped again, and he grabs his coffee and his notebook and moves back outside. Arthit will be able to see him better out there, and the air-conditioning on his wet clothing has given him a chill.

A waitress mops the table, but Rafferty, eager to write, sits before she tends to his chair, which has half an inch of water gathered in the low point of the seat. He barely notices, seeing in his mind's eye the loose, confident way Prettyman moved in the bar, as though he were outdoors and in familiar terrain. Until then Prettyman had always struck Rafferty as someone who navigated the world too carefully, the kind of person who checks frequently to make sure the top is screwed tightly on the salt shaker.

Arnold had been in his element in the bar. As Rafferty was when he was writing the kind of material he enjoyed writing.

"Stop that," he says out loud. He starts to write again, thinking he might have to reevaluate Arnold. The man in the spies' bar was more formidable than the vaguely comic ex-spook he thought he knew. Suddenly he realizes he's been patronizing Arnold.

He stops writing, the point of his pen still touching the page.

"Doing a Raymond Chandler?" someone asks, and Rafferty looks up to see Arthit peering down at the notebook.

"What's that mean?"

"Chandler wrote on little pieces of paper," Arthit says, pulling out a chair. "About the size of a paperback book. The trick, he said, was to get a tiny bit of magic on every one of those little pages."

"Is that so?" Rafferty watches Arthit's expression as his bottom hits the miniature pond on the seat. After his friend's eyes have widened rewardingly, Rafferty says, "The seat's wet."

"I know," Arthit says through his teeth. "It's very cooling."

"And how does that piece of information about Raymond Chandler come to be in the possession of a Bangkok policeman?"

"Chandler went to Dulwich, my school in England," Arthit says. "He was the only famous graduate who interested me, so I read about him. He drank too much. Why do writers drink too much?"

"They're alone too much."

"Why don't *you* drink too much?"

"I more or less live in a permanent crowd. How's Noi?"

"She hurts," Arthit says. "It comes and goes. Lately it mostly comes." Arthit's wife, Noi, whom he loves without reservation, is taking a defiant stand against multiple sclerosis. She's two years into the battle now, and despite all the medicine, herbal remedies, prayer, and love, she's losing. Arthit slides back and forth on the seat and then lifts himself a couple of inches and glares down at the wet chair. "She'd love to see you and Rose."

"Is tomorrow night okay?"

"That's what I like about Americans," Arthit says in his best British-inflected English. "They take small talk literally." He resigns himself to being wet and settles in. He's wearing his uniform, natty brown police duds stretched tight over broad shoulders and a hard little bowling ball of a belly. Arthit gives the cop's eye to the other people in the outdoor café, and they either look away or return it with wary curiosity. Bangkok cops have worked hard to earn their reputation for unpredictability.

"So here's the bad news," Arthit continues as a waitress materializes to hover politely above them. Arthit waves her off. "If this Elson is who he says he is, you're not going to get much help from my shop. Counterfeiting is a problem we actually share. The Secret Service gets carte blanche."

"Wow," Rafferty says. "Bilingual."

"I don't want to leave you out of the conversation," Arthit says, "so let me put it another way. As far as my bosses are concerned, these guys shit silver."

"A minute ago, when you were still speaking English, you said that was the bad news. That usually implies that there's also good news."

Arthit starts to put an elbow on the table and thinks better of it. "The good news is that this is a big deal. The Secret Service didn't come to Bangkok to bust maids. They're looking for a source, and we both know that Rose and— What's her name?"

"Peachy."

Arthit's mouth tightens in distaste. "Self-named, no doubt."

"Seems like a safe bet."

"They're probably not passing out millions, are they? Your Mr. Elson will backtrack it to the bank, and that'll be it."

"That's pretty much what I told Rose."

Arthit leans back in his chair and folds his hands over his belly. "Then why are you bothering me?"

"Just an excuse to get together. And I figured, this being a day of rest for ordinary mortals, that you'd be rattling around, bored senseless, and looking for something to do. Instead here you are, all suited up and spit-shined."

"You may have heard that we've had a coup," Arthit says. "When people wake up and see tanks in the streets and then learn they've got a new government—one they didn't elect—the police find themselves putting in a lot of overtime. The official line is that our presence is reassuring, although you and I know that having a whole bunch of cops all over the place all of a sudden is a pretty effective implied threat."

"If they only knew how sweet you actually are."

"My sweetness is classified. And if it were to become public knowledge, it would no doubt be blamed on the former prime minister." Arthit does a quick local survey to make sure no one is listening. "As part of the never-ending effort to find something *else* to blame on the former prime minister."

"I'd have thought the airport would satisfy anyone." In the wake of the coup, the sparkling new Suvarnabhumi International Airport has been found to be quite literally falling apart. "Cracked runways, no bathrooms, leaking roofs. Sagging Jetways. Should be enough corruption there to keep everybody's pointing finger busy for a couple of years."

"As a loyal servant of the Thai government," Arthit says, "I prefer to think of the problem as one of misplaced optimism. We Thais have a sunny turn of mind. Who but optimists would build an airport on a piece of land called Cobra Swamp? Even if one ignores the cobras, the word 'swamp' should have given someone pause."

"They probably paused long enough to buy it," Rafferty says. "*Somebody* sold that land to the government. Of course, it'll probably turn out to have been the former prime minister."

Arthit glances at his watch. "As much as I'm enjoying sitting here in this nice, wet chair and chatting with you about the state of the nation, I've got things to do. But before I go, I want to make sure that you took my larger meaning, which I implied with all the Asian subtlety at my command. Do *not* do anything to anger Agent Elson."

"That's pretty much what Arnold Prettyman said."

"Arnold's good at survival," Arthit says.

"How's Fon? Is there anything I can do for her?"

"She's fine," Arthit says. "Nothing severe, just sitting in a cell with the two other girls who deposited Peachy's money, talking up a storm. How do women *do* that? They've known each other for years, and sometimes two of them are talking at once. Don't women ever run out of things to say?"

"My guess is that they're sort of furnishing the cell," Rafferty says. "They're in an uncongenial environment, probably feeling threatened, so they fill it up with words and feelings until it's more comfortable."

"Aren't you Mr. Sensitivity?" Arthit says. "Anyway, they'll probably get out on Monday, when the banks open."

"Not until then?"

"Probably not. Your Mr. Elson seems to be a bit of a hardnose."

"That's what worries me. Rose says he enjoys power too much."

"Rose is a good Buddhist." Arthit checks his watch again.

"Arthit," Rafferty says. He pauses, looking for a way to frame it, and then plunges straight in. "Rose said yes."

Arthit looks at him blankly. "In a vacuum? When she was by herself? Was there a question involved?"

"I asked her to marry me." Even now he can feel his pulse accelerate.

Arthit's smile seems to reach all the way to his hairline. "And she said yes?"

"Believe it or not."

Arthit reaches over and pats Rafferty's hand. "Noi will be so happy." He gets up and pushes his chair back. "See what I mean? We Thais are optimists."

RAFFERTY HAS BEEN writing for fifteen minutes, working on his magazine story with a certain amount of guilty enjoyment, when the first one hits. It strikes him in the temple, hard enough to brighten the day for a heartbeat. For one absurd, soul-shriveling tenth of a second, he thinks he is dead, and in that transparent slice of time he forms two complete thoughts. The first is a question—*Will I hear the shot before I die?*—and the second is a statement—*I will never marry Rose.* And then the world does not end, and he glances down to see the small black ball that is rolling back and forth at his feet, smooth and gleaming, about the size of a large marble.

A chill at his temple brings his fingers up, and they come away wet. Whatever the fluid is, it is clear. So at least he's not bleeding. He touches the tip of his tongue to his finger. Sweet.

The restaurant has filled now that the rain is gone, but no one seems to have noticed anything. Since the world has not ended, time continues to flow. Traffic creeps by on the boulevard uninterrupted.

Rafferty looks for the source of the missile. No eyes are turned his way, so he bends and picks up the little ball. He is holding the pit of a fresh lychee nut, from which someone has just gnawed the sugary pulp. Hard as a marble, although not exactly a lethal weapon. But what produces that kind of accuracy—some sort of blowgun?

Yeah, he is thinking, *a fruit-hurling blowgun,* when the second one catches him square between the eyes. He sees a burst of stars, something out of a cartoon, and then he's blinking away tears. He looks in the direction from which the seed was blown, shot, thrown, catapulted, *projected.* There are no likely suspects, so he gets up and surveys the outdoor portion of the restaurant, which is now crowded almost to capacity: round white plastic tables jammed together in a space about forty feet wide and eight feet deep, from the building's glass wall to the quaint white picket fence that borders the sidewalk. People glance over at him, but they're all occupied, eating, talking. The sidewalk is crowded, but every sidewalk in Bangkok is crowded when the rain stops.

He sits down again, and instantly a wasp stings his cheek. This time he sees her, finishing up a follow-through that would impress Randy Johnson. The girl from the *tuk-tuk*. He shoves his chair back, drops some money on the table, and begins to push his way between the tables.

14

It's Not Coming from the Direction You Expect

S he is taking her time.

She can afford to dawdle. She has a half-block head start. Rafferty had to negotiate his way between the tables of the restaurant, had to explain to the woman at the front that he'd left the money on the table. He's walking fast but not running.

She makes a turn into an elbow-shaped *soi* that Rafferty knows is a dead end. As she rounds the corner, she glances back at him. The smile is a little fuller this time.

When he enters the *soi*, she has vanished.

Nothing. An empty sidewalk, some parked vehicles. A few shops, closed early for Saturday. Rafferty picks up the pace, trying to avoid looking at any one thing, taking in as much of the picture as possible. Prettyman's Third Law: It's not coming from the direction you expect.

Studying the street, he feels another pang of regret for his abandoned book. This is exactly the kind of episode he enjoys writing. Except, in the final draft, he wouldn't have lost her.

And then, halfway down the short block, he sees it.

A van, sitting at the curb. With the passenger door wide open. He steps off the curb and approaches it from the traffic side, only to find the girl gazing at him through the open window.

"You're not very good at this," she says. She is sitting sideways on the backseat, looking over her shoulder, legs curled comfortably under her. On her lap is a purse large enough to satisfy Rose.

"You speak English," Rafferty says.

Her eyes widen. "I do?" She reaches up and scratches her head in mock amazement. "How about that?"

"Listen," he says, "you can leave me alone now."

"I'm just getting started," she says. "If you want to talk, come around to the other side. I'm getting a stiff neck." Her English is pure American.

"No, I mean it's off," Rafferty says through the window. "Wait a minute." He goes around to the other side of the van. He can see her better this way, and he is struck once again by her beauty. "I meant to tell Arnold, but I forgot. I'm not going to write the book."

She shakes her head. "I have no idea what you're talking about."

"Just tell Arnold," Rafferty says. "And you've got quite an arm."

"Years of practice. The old inner-tube-hanging-from-the-tree technique."

"Very impressive. Anyway, good-bye. Go back to Little League or whatever it is."

"Stop," she says, and her hand comes out of the big purse with a gun in it. "Don't take a step. And put your hands about chest-high. Nothing obvious, just away from your belt." If she's nervous about holding a gun on him, it doesn't show. Her hand is as steady as a photograph, and her eyes are calm.

"This is silly," Rafferty says. "Arnold never—"

"I don't know who Arnold is," the girl says. "And I don't want to use this." She produces an apologetic smile. "But I will." She slides further across the seat, away from him. "Slowly, now. Get in."

Rafferty's cell phone rings. He reaches automatically toward his shirt pocket, but she says, "Uh-uh."

Rafferty says, "So shoot me." He pulls out the phone and looks at it. Sees ROSE AND PEACHY, opens it, and puts it to his ear. "Hello?"

"Poke," someone wails. "Poke, it's Peachy. I need— I need to talk to you. Now. *Now,* can you come?"

The girl extends the hand with the gun in it and lifts her eyebrows. There is no way she can miss at this distance.

"I'm a little tied up at the moment."

The girl says, "You certainly are."

"You *have* to," Peachy says, and then she starts to sob. "It's—it's the end of the world."

"Hang on, hang on," Rafferty says. "Just get hold of yourself and tell me—" He sees the girl's eyes go past him, sees the shadow of the man behind him, actually feels the warmth of the man's body, and then his head explodes.

SOMEWHERE IN THE fog, his mother and father are arguing.

This is unusual. They rarely speak enough to argue.

Poke has grown up with his father's silence. It fills the house they share, the small stone house Poke's father built with his own hands. No other house is visible, and the unpaved driveway washes out in the infrequent winter rains to make their isolation complete. The desert is silent, the house is silent. His mother communicates mostly by banging pots and pans. Most of the time, the only conversations are the ones in Poke's mind. But now his mother and father are arguing.

". . . fucking idiotic thing to do," his father is saying.

"There was no other choice," his mother says. Then there is silence again.

". . . a thug's grab," his father says. "Leung should have known better."

Leung, Poke knows, is a Chinese name. Knowing this, *knowing* that he knows it, brings him back to himself.

His head hurts.

Sandals slap a hard floor.

He is cold. It seems to him it has been a long time since he was cold. His clothes are still damp from the rain, and he is lying on a cold floor, probably cement. Something is beating at the back of his head, even though the back of his head seems to be resting on the floor. He wants to touch his head, but he cannot move his hands.

There had been a cement floor in the old Shanghai apartment house where he'd finally found the woman his father had run to. She was short and almost spherically fat. She held her arm at an oblique angle where it had been broken in some Chinese upheaval or other, and her cheeks were painted with spots of bright red, round and hard-edged as coins. Her lipstick shrank her mouth by half, turning it into the flower of some poisonous fruit. She had been distantly kind to him but had said nothing about his father, redirecting his questions into paths of her own. She had neither denied nor admitted that Frank was there, but Poke knew. The air in the apartment had been sweet with the aroma of his father's pipe.

"Give him the blanket," says the woman's voice, and something soft settles over him. Poke opens his eyes.

A large room: maybe a garage or a warehouse. The ceiling is high enough to be dark beyond the two bare bulbs that dangle from wires above him. He has a vague impression of metal beams, more the shadows than the beams themselves, and then a head comes into his field of vision. He cannot see the face against the bright lights above it, but it is surrounded by straight dark hair.

"How are you?" It is the female voice he has been hearing.

"Nice of you to ask." He wants to reach behind him and lift himself up, even though his head is swimming, but his hands are fastened together in front of him.

"Oh, great," says the young woman from the van, giving the irony back to him. "Now *everybody's* mad at me."

"'When all men are arrayed against you,'" Rafferty misquotes, "'maybe you're the problem.' What's with my hands?"

"They're cuffed," she says. "Just to make sure you'll sit still long enough to realize we have to talk."

"We could have talked in the street."

"We thought you had watchers. You've been quite extravagantly tailed the last few days. Did you know that?"

Poke does not reply.

"Who are they? Who's Arnold? Who was the guy with the police last night?"

"None of your fucking business." He shifts his back on the floor to see her better. Still beautiful. "Okay, we're talking. Do something about my hands."

"Let me give you some information first, and then some rules. The information is that nobody wants to hurt you. Not any more than we already have, I mean, and that was sort of an accident. We're actually here to try to help you."

"Maybe a greeting card," Poke suggests. "With a perfume strip. Or a phone call. Something casual, something that doesn't involve brain injury."

She continues as though he has not spoken. "The *rules* are that you're not going to do anything stupid, at least not while we're talking You're going to listen to us until we're finished, and then it's up to you. You can do anything you want. If you decide to ignore what we tell you, it'll be your own fault. You can walk right out of here. We felt obliged to warn you, but we're not your guardians."

"I don't need guardians."

"You have no idea." She holds up her right index finger. "Humor me for a second. Can you see this?"

"Of course."

"Only one? No ghosting, no double vision?"

"No."

"Follow it with your eyes." She moves it slowly from side to side, and Poke tracks it. Then she moves it toward the bridge of his nose until his eyes cross, and she laughs. The merriness of the laugh makes him even angrier. "You'll live. If we take off the cuffs, will you behave?"

"I'll listen. After that, it's anybody's call." The word "call" brings back Peachy's anguished voice. "But I need my phone. Now."

"Afterward," she says. "And we're not concerned with what you do after we talk." She looks over her shoulder. "Or at least I'm not. Leung."

A man peers into the circle of light above Poke's head. A cigarette dangles from one corner of his mouth. "Feeling better?" His English is heavily accented.

"Who the hell are *you*?"

"Say hi to Leung," the young woman says. "He's been following you. Actually, we've all been following you. If you didn't spot us, it's because we were lost in the crowd of *other* people who were following you. You want to tell us what that's about?"

"Just get the cuffs, okay?"

The blanket is whisked back, and the man called Leung bends down and busies himself with Poke's hands. Needles drill them as the circulation rushes back in. Poke gets both hands on the floor behind him and pushes himself to a sitting position.

It seems to be a garage, the floor irregularly spotted with pools of dark oil. The light is cast entirely by the two bulbs overhead, leaving the rest of the space in darkness. Either there are no windows or the sun has gone down. The van lurks in the gloom at the near end, ticking as the engine cools.

The back of his head hurts badly enough to be dented.

"Here's a chair," the girl says, pushing one forward. It's a cheap folding chair, made of battered gray metal. "Get off that cold floor."

His damp clothes feel heavy as he works himself up—first to his hands and knees and then, grasping the back of the chair, to a posture that makes him feel like Rumpelstiltskin. His head begins to spin a warning, and he eases himself sideways onto the chair without rising further.

"Better?" she asks.

"What about an aspirin?"

"Aspirin's bad for you." She gives him the almost-smile he had seen in the street.

"Aspirin is an anti-inflammatory," Rafferty says. "Getting hit on the head is bad for you."

"I'm no nurse. My job was to see whether you were still being followed and then to get you here. I'm essentially finished."

"I thought you wanted to talk."

"Not me," she says. "*He* wants to talk."

"He."

"Him." She steps aside, and Poke sees an old man shuffle around the end of the van, his feet in cheap carpet slippers. The edge of the light hits his knees, and then, as he moves forward, his waist, and then his shoulders, and then his face, and Poke looks at the face twice before he launches himself from the chair, shaking off Leung's hand, and does his level best to break his father's nose.

PART II

FOLDING MONEY

15

The End of the World

Miaow's ice cream is melting. For the past minute or two, she's been remorselessly stirring it into a soup, following the movement of the spoon with her eyes as though she expects some spectacular chemical reaction. The silence between her and Rose stretches uncomfortably, measured by the circular movement of the spoon.

The brown of the chocolate and the chemical pink of the strawberry make a particularly unpleasant-looking swirl. Rose raises her eyes from the bowl, telling herself she's not really rolling them, and waits.

"Why him not talk me?" Miaow says at last, in the defensive pidgin she has been using since the conversation began.

Privately Rose thinks this is an excellent question. As happy as she has been with Rafferty since his proposal the previous evening, if he were here right now, she'd haul off and kick him in the shins. "He should have talked to you," she says in Thai. "He made a mistake. Maybe he was nervous or something."

Tired of making circles, Miaow scrabbles the spoon back and forth through the thinning slop in a hard, straight zigzag. Rose finds herself counting silently to ten.

The Häagen-Dazs on Silom, where they went to dodge the rain, is empty. The downpour had stopped practically the moment the door closed behind them, but Rose knew there was no escape, so she bought both of them a post-happybirthday ice cream. They had settled at a table, and the moment Rose picked up her spoon, Miaow had seen the ring.

For the past twenty minutes, Rose has been trying to explain to a girl of eight—no, make that nine—that the upcoming marriage is nothing for her to worry about.

"Everything will be the same, but better," she says for the third time.

Miaow continues to slash through the spirals, giving Rose a first-class view of the knife-straight part she imposes on her hair.

Rose fights an impulse to grab the spoon. "It's like when Poke told you he wanted to adopt you. You didn't want that at first either."

"Did too," Miaow says in English.

Rose briefly toys with saying, *Did not,* but rejects it. There are conversations Miaow literally cannot lose, and that's the opening gambit to one of them. "Miaow," she says. "Poke and I love each other. We're grown-ups. We *should* be married."

"Not married before," Miaow says. She is sticking with English because she knows it gives her an edge.

Rose sticks with Thai for the same reason. "Poke adopted you because he wanted you to *really* be his daughter. He's marrying me so I can really be your mama."

Miaow's spoon stops. She regards the mess in her bowl as though she hopes an answer will float to the top. When she speaks, directly to her ice cream, Rose has to lean forward to hear her. What she says is, "You already my mama."

In the eighteen months Rose has known her, Miaow has never said this before. Even as a mist springs directly from Rose's heart to her eyes, her mind recognizes a master manipulator at work. Rose honed serious manipulative skills working in the bar, and she automatically awards Miaow a B-plus, even as she blinks away a tear. "But not *really*," she says. "Not *one hundred percent*."

The words fail to make a dent. Rose reaches over and takes the spoon from Miaow's hand. The child's eyes follow the spoon, and Rose realizes she might just have committed a tactical error, so she licks the spoon and hands it back, trying not to make a face at the mixture of flavors. She dips her own spoon into her scoop of coconut sherbet and holds it out. Miaow examines it as though it might contain tiny frogs, then opens her mouth. Rose feeds her, and as she tilts the spoon up, the thought breaks over her: *My baby.* "Miaow," she says without thinking. "Do you know how much I love you?"

Miaow looks up at her, her mouth a perfect O. She has chocolate on her upper lip. "You . . ." she says. Then she looks away, staring at the Silom sidewalk through the window. A very fat woman, weighed down further with half a dozen plastic shopping bags, hauls herself past the window, and Miaow's eyes follow her as though someone has told her she is seeing her own future. Then, without turning back to Rose, she says, "I know."

Having finally managed to insert the thin edge of the wedge, Rose leans down on it. "And Poke. You know that Poke loves you more than anyone in the world."

"Love you number one," Miaow says, still in English. "But that's okay."

"Look at this," Rose says, holding up the hand with the ring on it. "This is Poke," she says, touching the ruby. Her fingernail moves to the tiny sapphire. "This is me." She taps the surface of the topaz. "This one, in the middle. Who do you think this is? Who do you think this is, right next to Poke?"

Miaow says, "Oh." Her chin develops a sudden pattern of tiny dimples, but she masters it. She puts down the spoon. When she looks from the ring to Rose again, she is back in control. "Why am I yellow?"

"Tomorrow you'll be a sapphire, same as me, because we have the same happybirthday. But you'll still be in the middle."

Miaow processes this for a long moment. Then she asks, "Why?"

"Because you're the center of our lives." Rose passes her finger along the three stones. "This is us, Miaow. Do you know how old jewels are? Jewels last forever. This is Poke's way of saying he wants us to be together forever."

Miaow stares at the ring. Rose sees her mouth silently form the words: *One, two, three.* Then Miaow says, "Okay." She picks up the bowl, lifts it to her lips, and drains it. The moment she puts the bowl down, she says, "Can I have a cell phone?"

NINETY MINUTES AND three cell-phone shops later, Rose has heard approximately ten thousand words from Miaow on cell phones in general, how they can play music, how great the games are, how much safer she'll be with one, and—above all—an encyclopedic disquisition on text messages: They're cool, they're cheap, and *all her friends* send them *all the time.* Rose's comment that she thought Miaow's friends spent at least some of their time at school didn't create a pause long enough to slip a comma into. Now, as Miaow works her thumbs on the touch pad of her new phone, so fast that Rose can't see them move, Rose fishes through her bag and realizes she left her own phone at home. She borrows Miaow's, after waiting until the child finishes keying in the third act of *Macbeth* or whatever it is, and dials Rafferty's number. His phone, Rose learns, is not in service, which means he has turned it off. She hands the phone back to Miaow, who immediately polishes it on her T-shirt.

"I'll send this one to you," Miaow says, doing the thumbs thing again. "It'll be on your phone when we get home."

"Which is where we should go," Rose says. "Poke will be there soon. When he's all alone, he breaks things."

Miaow finishes punching at the keys and then checks the shine on the phone. She uses the front of her T-shirt to rub at a stubborn spot. "Let's go to Foodland," she says. "Let's buy him a steak." She flips the phone open again. "I can call Foodland and see if they have steak."

"They have steak," Rose says. "I was going to make noodles with duck and green onions."

"Poke's American," Miaow says. "He *eats* anything, but he always *wants* steak."

"Poor baby. He tries so hard. Do you remember the night I gave him a thousand-year egg?" Thousand-year eggs, which found their way to Thailand via China, are not really a thousand years old, but they might as well be. They're black, hard, and as sulfurous as a high-school chemistry experiment. Rose starts to laugh. "Did you see his face?"

Miaow is laughing, too. "And how many times he swallowed?" She mimes someone trying desperately to get something down.

"Like it was trying to climb back up again," Rose says, and the two of them stand in the middle of the sidewalk laughing, with Miaow hanging on to Rose's hand as though without it she'd dissolve into a pool on the sidewalk.

"You're right," Rose says, wiping her eyes. "If I'm going to be his wife, I should feed him a steak once in a while."

"He wants to be Thai," Miaow says, and Rose, startled, meets her eyes. Then the two of them start laughing again.

IT IS ALMOST SEVEN by the time they step off the elevator, dragging the bags that contain at least one of practically everything Foodland had on discount: shampoo, bleach, detergent, toothpaste, toilet paper, four place mats, two stuffed penguins, five pairs of underpants for Poke (who doesn't wear underpants), a baby blanket because it was pink, a flower vase, some flowers to put in it, and five porterhouse steaks. As the elevator doors open, Rose says, "We saved a fortune," and then the two of them stop dead at what looks at first like a pile of wrinkled clothes someone has thrown against the door to the apartment.

But then the pile of clothes stirs, and Peachy looks up at them.

This is a Peachy whom Rose has never seen before. Her lacquered hair is snarled and tangled, her face blotchy where the powder has been wiped away. Two long tracks of mascara trail down her cheeks.

"That man," she begins, and then starts to sob. "That—that American—"

Rose drops the bags and hurries to her, takes both of her hands, and brings her to her feet. As Peachy straightens, a crinkled brown paper shopping bag, crimped closed at the top, tumbles from her lap to the floor, and Peachy jumps back from it as though it were a cobra.

"It's okay," Rose says. "Poke says it'll be okay."

"It's not okay," Peachy says. "It's the end of the world." She points a trembling finger at the paper bag, and Rose squats down and opens it.

And stares down into it, still as stone.

Then she says, in English, "Oh, my God."

16

I Don't Know What "Usual" Means to You

S he's your sister," Frank says. "Say hello, Ming Li."
From beside Frank, Ming Li says, deadpan, "Hello, Ming Li." She sounds as if she finds nothing out of the ordinary, as if meeting her half brother for the first time in an abandoned garage, after she's had someone cave his head in and he's tried to assault their father, is nothing to get ruffled about.

Rafferty is pinned to the chair again, his hands cuffed behind him. His launch toward his father had been aborted by Leung's hand grabbing his shirt. He'd belly flopped on the cement floor, gasping for breath with the chair flat on its back behind him, as the Chinese man snapped the cuffs back on, set the chair upright, and plopped Rafferty into it as though he were no heavier than a puppy. Leung is a *lot* faster than Rafferty.

"I should have known," Rafferty says. He's so angry at himself he feels like spitting in his own lap. "She looks as much like you as it's possible for a beautiful Asian woman to look."

"Looks like you, too," Frank says. "It's the bone structure." He is sitting in a chair about a yard away from Rafferty, his face haloed by a fringe of white hair. Ming Li stands beside him, a pale hand resting on his shoulder.

Rafferty regards Ming Li, who gives him a cool downward gaze. "You and I don't look alike," he says to Frank.

Frank shrugs. "You may not *want* my bone structure," he says, "but you've got it."

"I hope that's all we've got in common."

Frank pushes his chair back a couple of inches. "Why don't we postpone all that for now? Recriminations and hurt feelings and so forth. It's not very appealing under the best of circumstances, and these aren't them. I've kept up with you, Poke—from a distance, obviously. I've read your books, checked into what you're up to here in Bangkok. You're making a nice life for yourself, aren't you?"

"Checked how?"

Frank shrugs again. "Usual channels." Except for a slight stoop, a lot of missing hair, and that shuffling walk, he looks surprisingly like the man Rafferty remembers from all those years ago. He has to be in his seventies, but time has barely laid a glove on him. It strikes Rafferty for the hundredth time that serenity and selfishness aren't that dissimilar. They both keep people young. His mother, even with her Filipina blood, has aged much more than his father has.

Rafferty says, "I don't know what 'usual' means to you. I don't know anything about you at all. And I didn't get much help from that woman in Shanghai—"

"Ming Li's mother," Frank says evenly.

"—from Ming Li's mother. And of course you couldn't be bothered, could you? You were *busy* or something."

"I was impressed you'd found us."

"Well, that makes me feel warm all over. Imagine what a home run it would have been if you'd said it in person." He shifts in the chair. "You can take the cuffs off."

"You're sure?" Frank seems amused, and Rafferty realizes he has seen precisely the same expression on Ming Li's face.

"It was an impulse. It's passed. I'd still like to bust you one, but you're safe in front of your daughter."

Ming Li laughs, and after a long moment Frank joins her. "Go ahead," she says. "Hit him. Frank gets hit a lot."

"I'd imagine."

"Get the cuffs off, Leung. He's going to be nice." Frank watches as Leung emerges from the shadows to move behind Rafferty and free his wrists.

"Another of yours?" Poke rubs his hands together to restore circulation.

"No. He has the misfortune to be a friend."

"No problem," Leung says. He twirls the cuffs around his index finger. He has high Tibetan cheekbones, narrow eyes of a startlingly pale brown, and a wide mouth that smiles easily, although the smile does not make him look any more cheerful. For all the effect it has on his eyes, it might as well be on someone else's face.

Rafferty looks at Leung's smiling, cheerless expression and recognizes one of the people who don't like other humans because they've seen too much of them. This is the group from which professional killers are recruited. "Aside from all the obvious reasons," Rafferty asks, "why is it a misfortune to be your friend?"

"Well," Frank says, shifting on his seat. It is a hedge, and for a moment Rafferty feels satisfaction at his father's discomfort. "That's what we have to talk about."

"YOU LIVE RATHER publicly," Frank says. There is a damped disapproval in his tone.

Even at six-thirty on this Saturday evening, the restaurant is crowded with Thais in large groups, wet and noisily merry as though the warm rain, which has begun again, is a personal joke. When they entered, Frank had said something into the ear of the woman who greeted them, and she'd shown them to a small booth against the back wall, where they can see the entire room and hear each other without shouting. They had made the trip in two *tuk-tuks*—Frank, Ming Li, and Rafferty riding silently in the first and Leung solo in the second. Covering their backs, Rafferty figures.

"I've got no reason to sneak around," Rafferty says.

Frank turns over a reasonable palm. "Just an observation, Poke. In

Bangkok—hell, in Asia—information is money. No need to make it so accessible."

"For me, *money* is money. Information is just information." The booth is a tight fit. Rafferty is jammed next to Leung, who had come in a few minutes after them and then scanned the room, as objective as a metal detector, before joining them. Rafferty can smell Leung's wet clothes, cigarettes, and a hair oil that owes a distant debt to bay rum. Pressing up against Rafferty's hip is a hard object in Leung's pocket that Rafferty assumes is a gun, which means that at least two of the three in Frank's party are packing. Ming Li sits beside Frank, surveying Poke with a curiosity she had not displayed in the garage. Even dripping water she is beautiful.

"You never know what the local currency is," Frank is saying. "The first time I saw the little girl I thought, *whoops,* the boy's a twist, where did I go wrong? But you were so public with her. The real twists don't like daylight. And then, of course, I saw the woman. What's her name again?"

Rafferty does not reply.

"Rose, right? Amazingly beautiful, isn't she? Very reassuring, knowing you've got taste like that."

"I assume there's more to this miraculous reappearance than a sudden need to express approval of my life."

Frank lifts a cup of coffee and puts it down untouched. Poke is startled to see the age spots on the back of his hand. "At your age, Poke, you shouldn't still be harping on all that. I know it's fashionable in America for adults to blame their parents for everything they did or didn't do, but the general feeling here is, *get over it.* One more example of the wisdom of the East."

"Gee, I don't know." Rafferty turns his eyes to Ming Li. "Give me some of the wisdom of the East. You're half qualified. Let's suppose one day—two days after Christmas, as it turns out—old Frank here just took a walk. Went out to buy a pound of rice and some dried shrimp and never came back. Left you and your mother flat, hopped a plane across the Pacific. Didn't even bother to say, 'Hey, good-bye, see you later, take care of your mom, kid.'"

"My mother can take care of herself," Ming Li says. "If she couldn't, she'd be dead."

"Oh, that's right, I forgot. He left her, too, didn't he? Sort of a leit-motif, isn't it? Like background music. 'Frank's Theme.'"

Something flickers in Ming Li's eyes. "He came back."

"And you're . . . what? Nineteen, twenty?"

"Twenty-two," she says. "Frank looks young for his age, and so do I. You, too, actually." Her long fingers are curled around a cup of tea.

"You work fast," Rafferty says to Frank.

"It would have been faster, but China's a big place," Frank says. "I had to find my wife first."

The babble of conversation in the restaurant stumbles up against one of those mysterious group pauses, and Poke says, into the silence, "Your wife was in fucking Lancaster, California."

"My first wife," Frank says placidly.

The words seem to shrink the booth and squeeze them all closer to one another, and Rafferty pushes himself back against the padding to find some distance, keeping his face empty. "Ah. Gosh, I guess we're finally having that father-son chat."

"I met her when she was twelve years old." Frank ignores Poke's tone. "She was washing sheets in a brothel in Shanghai."

"I don't really want to know," Rafferty says, thinking, *Twelve?*

"And I don't really give a good goddamn whether you want to know. I'm telling you because I have to." He has leaned forward sharply, his hands curved stiffly around the perimeter of his saucer, and the coffee slops onto his left hand as the cup slides forward. If it burns, he ignores it. "You need to understand what's going on, because it involves you now."

"And you need to understand something, too. If you've done any-thing that's going to fuck with my life here, especially at this point, I'm going to grind you to paste." He wills his spine to relax and adds, "Dad."

Frank wipes the liquid from the back of his hand and lifts the coffee to sip at it, raising one finger—*wait*—as though Rafferty has politely expressed interest. "She'd been there—in the brothel, I mean—since she was ten. Just tidying up and stuff, not working yet. Sold by her fam-ily, of course, but I suppose you know all about that, considering what you write about. I had business with the guys who ran the place—I had given myself a crash course in accounting, and I did their books—and she took care of me when I was there, brought me tea. A couple of times, she massaged my feet. A really sweet, exquisitely beautiful kid."

Rafferty tries, and fails, to match this description to the woman he had met in Shanghai.

"She learned my name," Frank says, "although she couldn't pronounce it for shit. But it meant something to me to hear her say it." He catches his upper lip between his teeth and then blows out, so hard it ripples the surface of his coffee. "Anyway, the time came for her to make her debut. So to speak. At the age of twelve." Leung is turned away from Rafferty, watching the room. Ming Li listens impassively, as though they are talking about someone she does not know. She runs the tip of her right index finger over the blunt-cut nails of her left hand as though thinking about pulling out an emery board.

"So I bought her," Frank says. "I bought her for her first week, before some asshole could jerk off into her and then forget her. *She'd* never forget it, of course. It would have been the beginning of her life as a whore." He dips his head as though in apology. "One of those moments when someone else's life changes forever, and I was just standing there with my hands in my pockets. So I bought her for a week. I gave her a place to sleep. I fed her. I got her some nice clothes. I left her alone at night, obviously. She was a child. It was a typically stupid Westerner's gesture, Don Quixote to the rescue, putting a Band-Aid on an amputation. Great, she had a week before the machine took its first bite out of her, and she'd be different forever."

"It was a good thing to do," Ming Li says.

He lifts a hand and rests it briefly on her shoulder. Ming Li leans against it and produces her fractional smile. "But it was pointless. I thought about it every night she was in my house. Kept me awake all night long. You know, I'd seen hundreds of whores in Asia—everybody from the top-level courtesans to the saltwater sisters who accommodated sailors against the walls of the alleys around the harbor. And of course lots of kids—twelve, thirteen, fourteen years old. Shanghai was the commercial sex capital of the world then. I was surrounded by prostitutes, and not just in my professional capacity. But I hadn't seen one at *that moment,* the moment when her real life ended, when she became something else. So I made a commitment. When it was time to take her back, I didn't. I stole her."

Rafferty has no idea what to say, so he doesn't.

"Well, that created a fuss." Frank is watching Leung watch the room. "As I said, I'd been doing the books for the brothel, one in a chain. All short-time stuff, just in and out, so to speak. Today they'd probably call it McSex. The firm I was working for, very proper and British in public, was really Chinese-owned, and it was on retainer for every triad in Shanghai. So I had some insight into how the system worked. I bought her for a second week, just to get a head start, and then we took off."

"You should write a book," Rafferty says, but he is interested in spite of himself.

"I'm in enough trouble already." His eyes flick away. "Anything happening, Leung?"

"Only cops," Leung says.

"Where?" Rafferty doesn't see any uniforms.

"Table near the door. Three of them. Plainclothes. You can tell by the phones."

Sure enough, black boxy things with short antennae. "I'm impressed."

"Leung earns his keep," Frank says.

"I work cheap," Leung says, and laughs. Then he says to Frank, "Back door?"

"Through the kitchen," Frank says, lifting his chin half an inch in the direction of a swinging door behind Leung. It is a very Chinese gesture.

Leung nods and lets his back touch the upholstery behind him. His version of relaxed.

"We got out of Shanghai and headed south, with Wang—that's Ming Li's mother's name, by the way, Wang—dressed as a boy, a servant. Sorry not to be more original, but there you are. She was my valet."

"She's still your valet," Ming Li says with a smile.

"I need a lot of looking after," Frank says.

Poke is watching the way Ming Li looks at her father. "You didn't used to."

"Well, it wasn't like your mother lived to take care of me." He raises his hand before Poke can speak. "I'm not saying anything against her. Angela is a wonderful person."

"She'd be thrilled to hear you say that."

"Angela is well taken care of," Frank says. "I left her a rich woman."

"Yeah, but you left her."

"For twenty years I was a good husband." Frank finally allows his irritation to show, a sudden bunching of the muscles at the corners of his eyes. "I stayed home, I raised a family. I built a house for her."

"She burned it down," Poke says with some pleasure.

Frank's cup stops halfway back to the saucer. "She what?"

"The day you left. She read the letter you wrote her—real personal, by the way, a bunch of bank-account numbers and some safe-deposit keys—and then she toted all the stuff she cared about outside and set fire to the Christmas tree. Oh, I forgot, she called a cab first. Then she sat there, and we watched it burn until the cab came."

"That was a nice house," Frank says. "I put a lot of work into that house."

"It made a lovely light." He leans forward, driven by an impulse to cause pain. "Oh, and you'll like this. Seven years later she had you declared dead."

"I'm dead?" Frank says. He seems more interested than surprised.

"She ran an obituary and everything."

Frank and Leung exchange a glance Rafferty can't read. Frank says, "That could be useful." Leung raises his eyebrows and draws down the corners of his mouth.

Frank blinks and leaves his eyes closed a little too long. When he opens them, he is looking at a spot above Poke's head. "I lived with Wang down south, out of sight in Yunnan, for a year, until I had to leave China. We lived like brother and sister. You have to remember, Poke, I was really only a kid myself then. We were happy. If things had gone on, eventually, we'd have found our way to bed. But come 1950 it was obvious that I was going to have to leave. I put it off for as long as I could—too long, actually. So we went out to a stone where we sat every day—have you ever been to Yunnan?"

"No."

"It's exquisite, at least where the rice is grown. Whole mountains carved into terraces that are flooded with water that reflects the sky. We sat each evening on a stone that looked down on a giant stairway of rice paddies, and waited for the stars to come out. The night before I had to leave, after I'd spent days packing and trying to prepare her, we went up to the stone and married each other. We took each other's hands when the sun went down and waited until the stars appeared in the paddies below us, and then we said we were married. She needed that. She needed to know I was coming back."

"Why didn't she go with you?"

"She wouldn't. She was afraid to leave China. And you forget, she was one of the oppressed masses. Remember them? She was one of the ones who were supposed to benefit. People's paradise and all that shit. Who was more downtrodden than a peasant girl who'd been sold into prostitution? What she didn't know was that Mao was a puritan. Officially, I mean. He had his fifteen-year-old Girl Guides—whole squadrons of them, if his doctor's memoir is to be believed—but everybody else was supposed to sleep one to a bed. Prostitutes were contrary to the common good. It's been said that the thing about Communists is that they have nothing and they want to share it with you. The problem with prostitutes was that they still had what they'd been sharing. So they were all shipped off to be 'reeducated.' They got Wang's attention by breaking her arm."

"You know," Poke says, "it's an interesting story, and it probably would have held my attention about twenty years ago, but now? It doesn't have anything to do with me."

"Just shut up," Ming Li says. "He's obviously got a point."

Rafferty continues over her. "I've got a family now—I won't bother telling you who they are, since you've spent all that time paddling around in the usual channels—but they're going to get worried if I don't get back to them. So cut to it, okay? What's happening that's so important you had to kidnap me? You want to tell me about the past, write a letter."

"We're *going* to get to it," Frank says. "In a second." He reaches into his pocket and pulls out a cell phone, then holds out his other hand to Leung, who reaches into his own pocket and brings out Rafferty's. Frank turns on Rafferty's phone, dials a number on his own, and waits until Rafferty's rings. Then he turns off Rafferty's phone again and hands it back to Leung. "In case you need my number," he says.

Rafferty says, "I'll give you a call on Father's Day."

"Fine. Until then Ming Li's right. Shut up. There's a point here. We grabbed you the way we grabbed you because you were being followed

all the time, and we didn't know by whom. Did you know you were
being followed?"

"Yes," Poke says.

"Who is it?"

"Nothing to do with you."

"I'd like to be the judge of that."

"We'd all like something," Rafferty says. "But what we get is each
other."

"Poke." Frank leans back, and the light catches the puffiness beneath
his eyes and a new heaviness under the chin. Suddenly, Rafferty sees
that time and gravity have gotten to his father after all. "I can't apolo-
gize to you. I can only explain. Okay, so I'm not Father of the Year.
But I owed something to Wang. I made her a promise. You can't just
walk away from something like that. Still, I waited. I waited until you
were almost grown and away from home, and I waited until there was
enough money for Angela. Then I took what I needed, and no more
than I needed, and I went back."

"And when I came after you—"

Frank's head is still resting against the wall behind him, his chin
raised, but his eyes drop to Poke's. "Did it ever occur to you," he says,
"that I was ashamed to face you? That I left it to Wang because I was a
coward?" He reaches over and takes Ming Li's hand, and she turns to
face him. "Also, I have to tell you, I saw no reason to bring my families
together."

"Until now," Rafferty says.

Frank rubs the top of his head as though it aches, and he closes his
eyes. "Well, yes," he says. "Until now."

"But you forgot something, didn't you?"

"What?" Frank asks, his eyes still closed.

"You forgot to ask us." He pushes Leung aside and keeps pushing
until the man is all the way out of the booth. Then he stands. "Go
back," he says. "Wherever you came from, go back."

Frank's eyes open. "They're after me, Poke. The ones I stole Wang
from. They're after me."

"All these years later? Boy, some people really hold a grudge."

"It's a triad. It's not about Wang anymore. I have something they
want."

"Then you'd better give it to them, hadn't you? Or keep running. I hear Malaysia's nice."

"This is why we needed to talk, why I had to tell you that story." He puts both hands on the table, one on top of the other. Takes a deep breath. "Trying to find me," Frank says, "they could come for you."

Rafferty steps forward so fast he hits the edge of the table. Ming Li's tea slops out of the cup. Leung steps toward him but stops at a glance from Frank.

"You listen to me, old man," Rafferty says. "If anything happens to my family because of you, I will personally beat you to death." He reaches down with both hands and lifts the edge of the table, sending Frank's coffee cup into his lap. "Are we clear on that?"

Despite the coffee spreading across his lap, Frank does not take his eyes off Poke. Rafferty can feel them on him all the way out of the restaurant.

17

The Leading Sphincter on the Planet

Rafferty?" Prettyman says, knitting his brow in a way that would make most people look thoughtful. "The same last name as you?"

"He's my *father*, Arnold," Rafferty says, trying not to grind his teeth. "As I told you a minute ago. Maybe you should speak English more often."

Prettyman tears his eyes away from the front door of the bar. He's been watching it the same way Leung watched the door of the restaurant, and probably for the same reason. Eighteen years' worth of CIA training dies hard.

Ignored by both of them, three lightly clad girls dance listlessly on the stage. Except for their shoes, which are high-heeled, calf-hugging boots, they are saving a fortune on clothes. They shuffle their feet and hang on to the vertical chrome poles as they endure "Walk of Life" for the three-thousandth time. Their exposed skin, and there is quite a lot of it, is goose-bumped; the bar is aggressively air-conditioned. Rose once told Rafferty the bar owners kept the places cold so the girls' nipples would stand out.

One of the girls wears a large triangular plastic watch, and the others glance at it from time to time. Two of the bar's other main attractions sit in the laps of overweight customers, and another has been sufficiently lucky, or unlucky, to be taken behind the curtain in one of the booths.

"So you're asking me to check up on your father?" Prettyman asks, having apparently reviewed the conversation in his mind. His eyes flick to Rafferty's for confirmation. "Not a very close family, is it?"

"I barely remember the man," Rafferty says, wishing it were true. "He disappeared into China more than twenty years ago. Not a lot of cards and letters. But here's the thing, Arnold. He's got—how should I put this?—he's got *skills*."

"Living in China for those particular years would take some skills," Prettyman says listlessly. A Steely Dan riff punches its way through the speakers, and he turns to eye the girls onstage as though he is wondering about their Blue Book value. "Where in China?"

"Shanghai and Shenzhen. Yunnan, Fujian. Also, apparently, a little time in Pailin. In Cambodia." Frank had mentioned Pailin in the *tuk-tuk* on the way to the restaurant.

Prettyman looks remotely interested for the first time. "Pailin is old Khmer Rouge and rubies. Fujian is people smuggling. Shanghai and Shenzhen are everything we can both think of, and lots we can't. You think it's any of that?"

"For all I know he makes Garfield the Cat in a plush-toy factory. That's what I'm asking you to find out, Arnold." He decides, on the fly, that the word "triad" might dampen Prettyman's enthusiasm. Such as it is.

Prettyman's lifeless eyes go back to the door. Then he says, "Money, of course."

"Of course. Twenty thousand now and twenty more when you come through."

"Thirty. When I come through, thirty."

"I'm a little squeezed at the moment, Arnold." Nothing like understatement.

Prettyman nods. "Then you'll owe me."

One of the girls onstage stumbles, grabs the arm of the one next to her, and they both go down, laughing, in a tangle of elbows, thighs, and buttocks. Rafferty turns at the sound.

"You want one?" Prettyman is following Poke's gaze. "Add it to your tab."

"Thanks anyway, Arnold. I'm sort of booked up."

"Suit yourself." Prettyman regards the girls another moment, looking like a man counting his change, then seems to come to a decision. "China," Prettyman says. "I'm still connected in China. I don't know about that money, though. Seems pretty short."

Rafferty touches Prettyman's arm, and Prettyman yanks it back, all the way off the table. "Arnold. I'm not in a mood to be fucked around with. It'll cost exactly what I said it would cost."

Prettyman says, "Or?"

"Or," Rafferty says. "This is a nice bar. Mirrors, sound system, lots of liquor, those fancy booths, everything. Lot of cash sunk into this room. Cops would line up to bend you over a barrel for a higher cut. I know a lot of cops, Arnold." It's not exactly true, but it's enough to make Prettyman purse his lips. Then he shakes his head slowly, a man who has grown used to disappointment.

"No bargaining, no give-and-take," Prettyman says, and sighs. "None of the old back-and-forth. It's not the same world, is it, Poke?"

"I doubt it ever was."

"Maybe not." Prettyman looks depressed.

"One more thing, Arnold." Rafferty taps the table for emphasis. "What you find out, whatever it is. It belongs to me. It is not capital. It's not for sale, loan, or affectionate sharing. The man may be one of the world's premium assholes, he may be the leading sphincter on the planet, but he's still my father. This is bought and paid for by me, not merchandise for additional profit."

Prettyman turns to him, gives him the full blue-eyed treatment. "Poke," he says, "don't you trust me?"

Rafferty looks at him.

Prettyman shrugs and turns back to the door. "Just asking," he says.

18

Green and White and Brown and White

Rafferty's first indication that something *else* is wrong is the sight of a police uniform in his living room. His spirits rise briefly when he realizes that the person wearing the uniform is Arthit, then plummet again at the sight of his friend's face, which is several stops beyond grim. They plunge further when he spots the bundle of misery on his couch, which turns out to be Peachy, reclining in a position as close to fetal as a tight skirt with large buttons will allow. Rose is nowhere in sight.

"You have a problem," Arthit says.

Rafferty pulls the door closed. "You're telling me."

Something happens to Arthit's face. Rafferty couldn't describe it precisely, but if Arthit were a dog, his ears would have gone up.

"Are you saying you know about this already?"

A surge of irritation begins at Rafferty's toes and rises all the way to the roots of his hair. "I'm not saying anything."

The knobs at the corners of Arthit's jaw pulse. "That's not wise."

"For Christ's sake, Arthit, it's not a declaration of policy. It's a statement of fact. I wasn't saying anything, and I told you so. Let's review, okay? You told me I had a problem—"

"You do."

"And I said, as I recall, 'You're telling me.'" Arthit's hard gaze doesn't waver. "Maybe someone should be recording this conversation. That way we'll only have to have it once."

"In an hour or two, somebody probably *will* be recording it."

Rafferty grabs a breath and lifts both hands. "Okay, okay. Let's admit I came in here with a bad attitude. So let's pretend I didn't, and that I've just this second come through that door with a big smile on my face and offered you a beer. 'Hi, Arthit,' I said. 'What a nice surprise to see you again so soon.' Something like that. Would that make anything better?"

"No," Arthit says.

Rose comes in from the bedroom and stops at the sight of him. "Poke," she says. "We have a problem."

Rafferty is struck by a bolt of pure panic. "Miaow? Is it Miaow?"

"No," Arthit says, his face softening slightly. "It's not Miaow."

"Okay," Rafferty says. His spine loosens a bit. "Rose is here, Miaow is all right. How bad could it be?"

"Bad," Arthit says. Peachy contributes a stifled sob. Arthit looks at her as though he's just realized she's in the room and says, "I shouldn't be here."

"He came because I called him," Rose says. She is speaking Thai. "I didn't know who else I could—"

"He's a great guy," Rafferty says. "We don't even need to vote on it. What the hell is wrong?"

"I really should leave," Arthit says. "This is completely inappropriate."

"Poke taught me that word last night," Rose says. "It means you slept with a poodle, isn't that right, Poke?"

"Yes, although I wasn't applying it to Arthit. What do you mean, you should leave? And why the hell isn't there anywhere for me to sit? I have no intention of taking bad news standing up." He moves toward the couch, and Peachy shrivels in a manner so abject that Rafferty is instantly ashamed of himself. "Did we sell the hassock?" he asks Rose.

"It's in the bedroom. I was standing on it. To hide something."

"I *really* shouldn't be here," Arthit says, making no move to leave.

"I'll get it," Rose says, leaving the room.

"While you're at it," Rafferty calls after her, "bring whatever you were hiding."

"For the record," Arthit says, "I did not suggest that she hide it." He sounds like he's on television.

"Well, gee, I hope that gets you off the hook, whatever the hook is. *Do* you want a beer?"

"I guess," Arthit says. "This is as good a time to be drunk as any."

When Rafferty comes out of the kitchen, a bottle of Singha in each hand, Rose is standing by the white leather hassock, clutching a wrinkled brown paper supermarket bag. Peachy is staring at the bag as though it has a red digital countdown on its side, signaling the number of seconds before the world ends.

Rafferty hands Arthit one of the beers and takes a long pull off the other one. Then, as insurance, he takes another long pull and sits down on the hassock. Rose gives him the bag, and he opens it.

He sees rectangles, green and white and brown and white, a loose, disordered pile of them. Closes his eyes, squeezes them tight, opens them wide, and looks again. Nothing has changed.

"Thirty-two thousand dollars," Arthit says. "Six hundred thousand baht, all in thousand-baht notes, and one hundred fifty American hundred-dollar bills. All brand new. And, since it's almost certainly counterfeit, it's exactly what Agent Elson is looking for."

"IN THE DESK," Peachy is saying. She claws her fingers through her hair again, snags them on the same clot of hairspray, and lets her hand drop. "The middle drawer. Rose knows. It's the drawer I keep the account books in."

"That's right," Rose says. "We advance money to the girls when they're short, and that's where Peachy puts the book we track it in."

"Is the desk kept locked?" Rafferty asks. He is on the floor now, leaning against the wall. Rose shares the couch with Peachy, who is finally sitting upright.

"No." Peachy starts toward the hair again and stops herself. "There's no reason to lock it. Nobody would go into it."

"Someone obviously did."

"Why were you in the office?" Arthit asks. He has replaced Rafferty on the hassock, which he sees as a position of greater authority, and is working on his second beer. His face is beginning to turn red. Two more and he'll look like a stop sign.

"*Why?* It's my office." Peachy sounds bewildered by the question.

"On Saturday," Rafferty says. "He means, why were you in the office on Saturday?"

Peachy starts to answer, then shakes her head as though this is leading somewhere she doesn't want to go. "I'm always in the office. I go in every day."

"Why?" Arthit says.

"Because . . . because . . ." She blinks heavily, and then her face seems to crumple, and Rafferty knows she is moments away from tears. "Where else would I go? What else would I do?"

"Family?" Arthit asks.

"Oh," Peachy says. "That." Her lower lip does a watery little ripple. "We, I mean, I— Well, not really, you know, I mean . . ." She undoes a button with shaky fingers and does it up again. "I spend a lot of time in the office."

"Okay," Arthit says uncomfortably. "Sorry. So when you left on Friday—"

"Last night," Peachy says, and Rafferty suddenly sits up. All this started only last night? The proposal to Rose, Agent Elson, his father, the money? All since *last night*?

"When you left the office last night," Arthit says. "Was everything normal? I mean, was the place the way you usually leave it?"

"Sure," Peachy says.

"And did you lock the door?"

"I always lock the door." The questions seem to be calming her.

"This morning, when you went in— Wait, what time did you arrive?"

"About eleven." The hand goes up again, but this time it pats the hair instead of ravaging it.

"At eleven, then. Was the door still locked?"

"Yes. I had to use both keys to get in."

"And you double-locked it when you left."

Rafferty sits there, admiring Arthit at work.

Peachy's eyes go unfocused, as though she is doing addition in her head. "I think so. I usually do. But sometimes I forget."

Arthit has been sneaking a hit of beer while Peachy thinks, and now he lowers the bottle. "Who else has a key?"

"Um . . ." Peachy says. A blush mounts her cheeks. Her eyes rove the room like someone looking for an exit. She passes her index finger over her front teeth and inspects it, scanning for lipstick. Then she says, "Who *else* has . . ."

"I do," Rose says.

"Yes," Peachy says, looking relieved. "Rose. Rose does."

"Nobody else."

"The landlord," Rose says.

"Who's the landlord?" Arthit asks.

"Somkid Paramet," Peachy says, naming one of the richest men in Bangkok. "He owns the whole block."

"Scratch the landlord," Rafferty says.

Arthit tugs at the crease in his trousers and stares longingly at the bottle of beer in his hand. "When does the cleaning crew come in?"

"Never," Rose says. "Peachy and I clean the place on Mondays. We go in early."

"Rose does most of the cleaning," Peachy says apologetically. "When I was growing up, I never learned how to clean properly. And my husband, my *former* husband's family, they . . ."

Arthit's eyes flick to Rafferty, who finds something interesting to study on the carpet. Rose admires the ceiling. Peachy's genteel upbringing has been a frequent topic of conversation among them. "And when you went in this morning, everything was still in place?"

"Except for *that.*" Peachy indicates the paper bag without looking at it.

"Right, right. Except for that." Arthit sits back and stares out through the sliding glass door at the lights of Bangkok. The bottle of beer dangles from his hand, forgotten for the moment. "Well," he says to Rafferty, without turning, "isn't this interesting?"

"It's fucking riveting." Even in her distraught state, Peachy stiffens at the word. "Here's the thing, Arthit," Rafferty says. "It's Saturday."

"Thank you," Arthit says, inclining his head. "I always like to be reminded what day it is."

"They didn't know she'd go in."

"Ah," Arthit says. He shifts himself around and stares at the wall above Rafferty's head. "That's right, isn't it?"

"What's right?" Rose asks.

"Whoever put that money there," Arthit says, "doesn't know it's been found."

"Monday," Rafferty says. "They think it'll be found on Monday."

"It's not much, is it?" Arthit says.

"*What's* not much?" Rose asks with an edge in her voice.

"One day," Rafferty says. "Before whatever is supposed to happen actually happens. We have one day to try to screw it up."

"It's a little better than that," Arthit says. He hoists the beer and swallows. "We also have tonight."

19

Simoleons

The bar is fashionably dim. The same authority that decrees that casinos should be bright apparently mandates that bars should be dim. This one is dim enough that the street outside, visible through the open door, is a source of light even at a few minutes before midnight.

"Walk back the cat," Arthit says. He seems to be talking to his reflection, partially visible behind the row of bottles, most of which, in defiance of their fancy labels, contain cheap generic whiskey.

Rafferty has switched to club soda, much to the amusement of the female bartender. "That's a striking image," he says. "What the hell does it mean?"

Arthit puts down his second glass of so-called Johnnie Walker Black on the rocks. Like many Asians, he lacks an enzyme that metabolizes alcohol, and his face is a shade of crimson that would fascinate a cardiologist. "You obviously don't read much espionage fiction."

"I don't read much of anything that was written after 1900. If you want to be dazzled, ask me about Anthony Trollope."

"I always loved that name." Arthit raps his wedding ring on the edge of his glass. Rafferty wonders if he is checking to make sure he can still hear. "'Walking back the cat' is a technique for unraveling an operation." He lifts the glass and drinks. "First, of course, you have to assume it's an operation."

Rafferty glances around. As far as he can determine through the gloom, the other six customers seem to be absorbed in their own conversations. "It's certainly something," he says. "Even in counterfeit money, thirty thousand bucks is a lot of simoleons."

"'Simoleons'? Anthony Trollope used the term 'simoleons'?"

"Not often," Rafferty concedes.

"Here's how many simoleons it actually is," Arthit says. "Let's say you're a customer of whoever is making these things—"

"The North Koreans, Arnold Prettyman says."

"Arnold? You're talking to Arnold again? It's a good thing you're not on parole."

"One takes information where one can get it."

"Well, Arnold's right. So. Let's say you want to get your hands on some of these things. You can buy a North Korean hundred-dollar bill—in bulk, of course—for anywhere from sixty to seventy-five dollars, depending on market forces."

"For example."

Arthit tilts his head to the left. "How badly the North Koreans need cash. How much trouble they're having getting the things into circulation. Fluctuations in the price of plutonium. How low Kim Jong Il's cognac reserves are." He raps the glass again, and this time the bartender looks over at him. Arthit raises a finger and points it, pistol style, at Rafferty's soda glass, which contains nothing but a straw and a slice of lime. "So figure it out. Take a middle value, say seventy dollars to the hundred. Seven hundred to the thousand."

"Jiminy," Rafferty says. "Twenty-two thousand dollars."

"Very impressive. Somebody spent twenty-two thousand dollars, or passed up on the opportunity to *make* twenty-two thousand dollars, to put that bag in Peachy's drawer."

"I see the distinction."

"That's a substantial investment. So to walk back the cat, you ask yourself a few questions. Who would be willing to make that investment?

Why? Why now? Why Peachy? Why an obscure domestic-service agency in a crappy corner of Pratunam?"

"Not so crappy." Rafferty's new glass of soda arrives, floating in on a big smile from the bartender, and he sips it and feels his tongue try to roll itself up. It's tonic water. He starts to send it back and thinks, *What the hell. Try something new.* He returns the smile and takes another swallow. It tastes like malaria medicine.

"You know what I mean," Arthit says. "If you're going to set off a bomb, why do it there?"

"You're smart when you're drunk."

"This isn't drunk. This is mellow. *Drunk* is when I fall sideways off the stool."

"Let's arrange a signal, so I can get out of the way."

"Who and why," Arthit says. "Work from what we know and focus on who and why."

"If we're going to walk back the cat," Rafferty says, "we have to start with yesterday, when those maids took the bad bills to the bank. Actually, we have to go back further, to when Peachy got the stuff in the first place."

Arthit says, "Bingo."

"Right," Rafferty says. His mind is working so fast he doesn't even taste the tonic as he swallows it. "We've said from the beginning that this would be all over as soon as Elson goes to the bank where Peachy got the money."

"And that would be?" Arthit asks.

"On Monday."

"Coincidence?" Arthit asks, and then lowers his voice and says dramatically, *"I don't think so."*

"So the *why*," Rafferty says, "is to keep Elson from backtracking to the bank."

"Sure. All this fake money, right there in the desk. Even if she did go to the bank, so what? The bills she gave to the maids came out of the bag."

"That leaves the who," Rafferty says. "Or, maybe more important, it leaves the how."

"What how? Some master keys or a good set of picks, a paper bag full of money, an open desk drawer."

"How the *who* knew to put it there."

Arthit swivels his stool back and forth for a moment. "*That* how," he says. He picks up his glass and puts it down again. "This line of speculation leads to some very uncomfortable territory."

"The wood of the wolves," Rafferty says. Then he says, "But still. Wherever the cat goes."

Arthit has discovered that his stool squeaks when he turns more than six or seven inches to the left, and he plays with it for a moment, to Rafferty's annoyance. Satisfied with the amount of noise he has made, he comes back to face the bar. "There were four people in your apartment. Elson, my two colleagues, and the girl— What's her name?"

"Fon."

"Right, Fon. And Fon's been in jail ever since, so I suppose we can cross her off the list." He takes an ambitious pull off the amber whatever-it-is in his glass and says, "And it doesn't matter whether the someone put the money there himself or had someone else do it."

"Not in the least."

"Of course," Arthit says carefully, "there's always the possibility that Peachy put it there herself."

"No," Rafferty says. "There isn't."

"Let's just follow it for a second. She hands out the bad bills, right?"

"Right. So?"

"And the girls get caught. She's stuck with the story about the bank, and she knows it won't hold up, so she grabs her bag of pretty paper from home or wherever she keeps it and shows up at your place, all distraught. 'Look what I found,' she says. And here we are, thinking about other people."

"Never in a million years."

Arthit wipes condensation from his glass with his index finger and dries it on his pants. "She's had some problems, did you know that?"

"They're hard to miss. She's got pretensions to gentility, a bad marriage, a business that was going on the rocks."

"She's a gambler, Poke. She lost a small fortune playing the horses. It almost cost her—and her husband—everything. She was into the loan sharks for more than I make in a year." He looks down at the wet smear on his trousers. "In fact, it cost her Prem, her husband."

"He left her," Rafferty says. "She told Rose about it."

"Whatever she told Rose," Arthit says, "it wasn't true. Prem killed himself."

Rafferty buries his face in his hands. "Oh, Jesus. Poor Peachy."

"I could have kicked myself when I asked about her family. I wasn't thinking straight."

"And you know about her husband how?"

"I checked," Arthit says. "When Rose went into business with her, I did a little background research."

"I see." Rafferty looks down at his tonic water, focusing on the lonely little slice of lime, and Peachy's face, hidden beneath its mask of makeup, floats into view. He flags the bartender. "This is tonic," he says. "Could you please dump some gin into it?"

"IF YOU REALLY thought it was Peachy," Rafferty says, "you wouldn't be here."

They have moved to a booth, mostly because Rafferty couldn't stand hearing Arthit's stool squeak one more time.

"I wouldn't?" Arthit is drunk enough to be leaning forward on both elbows. Rafferty has forcibly switched him to soda, then tasted it to make sure nothing has been slipped into it while he wasn't looking.

"What you kept saying at the apartment. 'I shouldn't be here.' You must have said it half a dozen times."

Arthit tastes his soda and gives it an Easter Island grimace. "I never claimed to be interesting."

"You're here because you don't trust those cops." He watches his friend's face. "Or Elson."

Arthit looks around the bar as if he hopes there will be somebody else there to talk to. Then he says, "Peachy's too hapless. Too distracted by her life. She wouldn't have the faintest idea where to get that paper. Also, the business is finally beginning to pay off. This would not be a good time for her to embark on a life of crime."

"Then what was all that stuff—"

"It's a *case*," Arthit says, baring his upper teeth. "It's a pretty convincing case, if you don't know Peachy. It's the case I think they're going to try to make on Monday."

"Ah," Rafferty says.

"And there's no way it's not going to splash onto Rose."

A little chill of pure dread runs through Rafferty's chest and is immediately replaced by fury. "I'm going to see that it doesn't."

"So," Arthit says, rubbing his eyes. "It's Elson or the two cops, or someone they talked to."

"Too many. We've only got until Monday." Rafferty looks over at Arthit, red-faced and sweating opposite him. "Thanks for not leaving."

"There, there," Arthit says. "Let's not get emotional."

"But if this backfires, it could be serious for you."

"No. If this backfires, it'll be fatal." He slides the glass of soda toward the center of the table. "Could I replace this with something that contains an active ingredient?"

"It's your hangover." Rafferty flags the bartender. "Black Label?"

"Black seems appropriate," Arthit says.

"One more Black for my unwise friend," Rafferty says. Then, to Arthit, he says, "Go away. Finish your drink and distance yourself. You weren't at my apartment, we didn't go to any bars. I haven't seen you since this afternoon."

Arthit is watching the bartender make his drink. Spotting him in the mirror, she adds an extra slug. "And walk away from all this fun?"

"You have to decide," Rafferty says, "whether you want to hear what I'm about to say."

"If I wanted to go deaf, I would have done it earlier."

"Okay. We can't figure out the who by Monday, but whoever they are, I think I can fuck up their plan pretty thoroughly."

"Do tell." The drink arrives, and Arthit looks like he wants to kiss it.

Rafferty tells him.

"My, my," Arthit says. "That's genuinely devious. And you think you can do it by Sunday night?"

Rafferty shrugs with an indifference he doesn't feel. "I have to."

"Is all this running around tomorrow going to give you time to go on an errand with me?"

"Oh, sure. My time is your time. What did you have in mind?"

"I thought we might crack open Agent Elson's shell. Just a little. Sort of give us an idea of what's inside it."

"How?" Rafferty's cell phone rings, and he says, "Hold that thought," and answers it.

"Poke?" It is Prettyman's voice, and it sounds strained to the point of strangulation. "Get your ass over here. *Right now.*"

20

Moby-Dick

W hat the *fuck* have you gotten me into?" Prettyman demands, leaning so close that Rafferty can see the gray in his
Ming the Merciless goatee. Prettyman's well-established
distaste for personal proximity is no match for the urgency he feels.
Rafferty has seen the man under pressure before—in fact, Prettyman's
approach to life seems to be to create pressure and then cave in to it—but
this is something new. The intensity even reaches his eyes.

And that makes Rafferty very uncomfortable. During their acquain-
tance Prettyman has revealed few admirable qualities, but he doesn't
frighten easily. At the moment he is scared half to death. They are in
the back room of the Nana Plaza bar, and the bass from the sound
system thumps in two-four time through the wall, synchronized approximately with Rafferty's heartbeat. The room is empty except for
the table at which they sit, the four chairs that have gathered around
it for company, a wall full of framed photographs, and a Plexiglas box
padlocked on a black stand. Beneath the box, displayed like an Acad-
emy Award, is a SIG-Sauer nine-millimeter automatic.

"I gather you had a nibble," Rafferty says.

"A *nibble*? It was like sinking a hook in fucking Moby-Dick." Prettyman shows a lot of teeth. It is not a smile. "First person I called, *wham*. All I did was mention the name, and I thought the guy was going to come through the line and grab my tongue. So I think, Whoa, slow down, and I get off the line. And three other guys call me within fifteen minutes." Prettyman hears the pitch of his own voice and sits back, eyeing the room as though he wishes it were much larger and, perhaps, made of steel. "A number I didn't think anybody had," he says, more quietly if not more calmly. Despite the coolness of the room, his shirt is patchy with sweat, and not just in the obvious places.

Rafferty gives him a minute in the name of tact and then says, "What kind of guys?"

"Not your problem." Prettyman seems to be regretting his volatility. He makes a show of straightening his cuffs. A cup of coffee toted in from the bar is cooling in front of him untouched, and a paint-thinner smell announces the brandy it's been laced with.

"It certainly *is* my problem, Arnold. Look, I'm not asking for names and addresses. Americans, Chinese, Thais, military, diplomats, spooks, cops, gangsters—what?"

"All of the above," Prettyman says in the satisfied tone of someone who predicted disaster and turned out to be right. "And with a lot of weight—very high-density guys." He drums the table with his fingernails. "What are those little stars called? The ones that are so dense?"

"Little dense stars?" Rafferty guesses. His heart isn't in it.

"*Dwarf* stars," Prettyman says. "A cubic inch of a dwarf star weighs as much as the earth. Think dwarf star. That kind of density."

"And what did these very heavy guys tell you?" Rafferty lifts his own coffee, pretends to sip. His hand is not completely steady, so he puts it on the table again.

Prettyman is still buying time by adjusting his clothes. "From one perspective they didn't tell me shit. No answers, not even rude ones. What they wanted was to know what *I* knew. From another perspective, of course, they told me quite a bit."

"For example."

"The whole world wants to get its teeth into Frank Rafferty. Way it sounded, they'd chew your father up and fight over the scraps."

Rafferty's initial doubts about involving Prettyman suddenly intensify. He pushes his chair back and gets up, feeling the other man's eyes
follow him. Three or four steps carry him to the wall with the photos
on it. A younger Prettyman stares out from each of them: in a jungle,
wearing fatigues; centered and fuzzy in an obvious telephoto shot,
talking to a woman on some Middle European street; posed dramatically in front of the Kremlin in a trench coat that might as well have SPY
stenciled on the back. The others are all variations on the theme: spook
at work.

"I didn't know you guys liked to have your picture taken so much,"
Rafferty says. "This looks like the wall at a local chamber of com-
merce."

"Fuck the pictures," Prettyman says.

"So they're eager," Rafferty says, still studying the photos. "So
they've got a lot of weight. Puts you in an interesting position."

"Puts me right up the fecal creek," Prettyman says. Then he hears
the implication. "You don't actually think I'd shop you, Poke?" Rafferty turns to see him widen his eyes, which succeeds only in making
them bigger. They're still the eyes of someone who could spot an opportunity through a sheet of lead.

"Please, Arnold," Poke says.

"And even if I would," Prettyman says immediately, "I don't actually know anything, do I? I'm the guy in the middle, the one all these
wide-track trucks think has the marbles, and I don't even know if the
guy is really your father."

"Of course you do. There's no way you haven't learned that much."

"This does not make me happy, Poke," Prettyman says. He turns
his coffee cup ninety degrees and then back again, and wipes sweat
from the side of his neck. "It's not the kind of attention I want to at-
tract. I'm a settled man here, retired from the Company, whatever you
may think. The world has passed me by, and that's fine. A man at my
time of life doesn't need the adrenaline jolts I liked twenty years ago. A
little money, the occasional girl, regular habits. The same pillow every
evening. A house I can leave in the morning knowing I'll be coming
back to it at the end of the day. No more night crawls, no more tracking
boring people across boring cities and then discovering that they're not
so boring after all, that in fact they'd like to kill you."

Infected by Prettyman's anxiety, Rafferty does his own scan of the room, wondering whether there's a microphone somewhere. He lifts the pictures, crosses the room and looks under the table, comes up, catches Prettyman studying him, and says, "Have you left the bar tonight, Arnold?"

Prettyman hesitates, just his normal disinclination to part with information. "I went home for dinner."

"After you made the calls?"

"Some of them. I made more from home."

"And when you left here, or when you came back, were you followed?"

The question makes Prettyman shift in his chair, sliding from side to side as though smoothing down a lump in the cushion. He licks his lips. "That book you were going to write," he says. "How good did you get at spotting a tail?"

"Obviously not too good." He sits again. "I still smell like an issue of *Vanity Fair*."

"Then you know," Prettyman says. "It's not easy. Give me half a dozen good people and I could follow Santa all the way around the world without tipping him off." He blinks a couple of times and blots his upper lip with the side of his index finger. "But I don't think so. For one thing, no one knows where I live."

"They didn't know the phone number either."

"No," Prettyman says grimly. "And don't think I'm not keeping that in mind."

"Because of course you *do* know something, don't you? You know that Frank's in Bangkok and that I'm in contact with him. You know where I live. Not exactly a Chinese wall. You've probably operated on less."

Prettyman lays both hands flat on the table, as though to rise. "Are you back to that? Suggesting that I'd sell you?"

Rafferty shoves the table a few inches toward him, trapping Prettyman's knees beneath it. "You're on the wet spot, aren't you? If they tried the stick, which it sounds like they did, there's also the carrot. Probably a whole bunch of carrots if, as you say, they want him so much. Especially if there's some sort of contest to take the first bite."

"The discussion didn't get that far." Prettyman settles, and finally drinks some of the coffee, his eyes on the room again. "Anyway, I don't sell people."

It would be silly to argue. "What time did you make the first call?"

A moment of elaborate consideration that Rafferty automatically discounts as a dodge. Prettyman has a chronograph implanted in his cerebellum, running several time zones simultaneously. Finally he says, "What time did you and I talk?"

"I don't know. Nine, nine-thirty. And why are you stalling, Arnold?"

"Right after that." Prettyman lowers his voice, imparting a confidence even though they are alone in the room. "You wanted answers, Poke. I got right on it."

"Answers from China," Rafferty says.

Prettyman starts to answer, hesitates, and says, "I didn't start in China."

Rafferty waits for more and then asks, "Bangkok?"

Prettyman nods so slightly that Rafferty can barely see it.

"So let's say ten. Sound about right?"

He gets an equivocal shake of the hand, side to side. *"Más o menos."*

"And then the phone started to ring."

"The people in China didn't seem to care what time it was. They were too interested."

"And did you mention me? They must have put some pressure on you."

An upraised palm. *"Poke.* I wouldn't—"

"So you say, Arnold, and naturally I believe you. I'm just giving you a chance to convince me."

"Think about it, Poke. Even if I were willing to sell your father, which of course I'm not, would I lead them to you? Let's suppose, just for discussion's sake, that I'd entertain the idea. I mean, it's preposterous—" He waits for Rafferty to agree and then plunges ahead. "But just to move the talk along, let's say I would. If I give you to them, they don't need me."

"That has a certain logic. Then again, if that's all you have—me, I mean—there might be a price for that. Was there?"

After a pause almost too short to measure, Prettyman says, "You think too much, Poke." He sounds like Rose. "As long as you've lived here, I'm surprised. Everything isn't logic, you know. Sooner or later you have to trust your feelings, your instincts."

Rafferty does not explain that his instincts are what inspired the question.

Prettyman lets the silence stretch out before speaking. "I can understand why you'd be concerned. With your family and all."

"I'm sure you can."

"Maybe I can help," Prettyman says, his eyes floating toward the ceiling. "I've got more experience than you do."

"That's swell of you Arnold, but I think I've got it covered."

Prettyman nods. "Fine, fine," he says. "Good to hear it."

"When you call them back—"

"Hold it," Prettyman says with some urgency. "Let's not operate under a misunderstanding. I'm going right back into my little hole. This kind of weight I don't need."

"And you think they're just going to forget you called? Say, 'Oh, that Arnold, what a tease.' You duck out of sight and they're going to send a regiment after you."

Prettyman does something with his mouth that, on a child, would be a pout. "I know what I'm doing, Poke."

"They want Frank, and it's obviously not just a whim. You make one call in Bangkok, middle of the night, and the long-distance lines start humming all the way to China. Heavyweights, as you say. Working late, just for you. Dialing a secret number, one they shouldn't have. These are not people you can wave off, Arnold: 'Sorry, it's some other Frank Rafferty.' Either they're going to come after you now or they're going to come after you later. They've probably already bought their tickets. Not to mention the ones you talked to in Bangkok. *They're* already here."

Across the table Prettyman blinks away perspiration that has run down his forehead and into his eyes. Rafferty finds that he feels sorry for the man. He should have mentioned the triads.

But he hadn't. "We both need the same thing," he continues. "Information. You pretend to play with them, keep them busy for a few days, and get whatever you can. That way you won't be picking up that nice pillow you go home to every night to see whether somebody put a scorpion under it, and when we get back together, we'll have a better idea what we're up against." He waits, and Prettyman's eyes slide left, toward the door. Rafferty knocks sharply on the table. "And if you don't play, Arnold, or if you sell me and my family out, I'll get through it somehow, and when I do, I'll come after you and kill you myself. Just, as you say, so we're not operating under a misunderstanding."

Prettyman's eyes go very small, and he puts his hands in his lap. Rafferty knows he is wishing he had a gun there. The one in the plastic box is too far away.

"So, Arnold," Rafferty says, shoving his chair back. "Looks like we've both got a problem."

21

He's More Like Arnold Than He Is Like Me

After returning her nod, he silently shares the elevator with Mrs. Pongsiri, the apartment house's central gossip conduit, whose opinion of Poke has improved with Arthit's frequent visits. Uniforms, Rafferty supposes, inspire confidence. Given the hours Mrs. Pongsiri keeps—going to work at 6:00 P.M. and returning home around 3:00 in the morning—her occupation is a topic of continuing speculation among the residents. She looks tired tonight, her figure sheathed in a too-tight cocktail dress that is so saturated with stale cigarette smoke that the elevator smells like an ashtray by the time they reach the eighth floor. Once the doors open, they exchange minimal smiles and go in their separate directions. As she walks away, Rafferty sees she has already unzipped the top four inches of her gown.

The digital clock on his desk blinks a green hello when he finishes double-locking the door and turns to face the living room. The clock reads 2:17 A.M., so Mrs. Pongsiri has come home early. Rafferty has managed only a couple of hours' sleep in the past two days, and he feels it all the way down to the cellular level.

He smells smoke, and it isn't Mrs. Pongsiri. Then he sees the light beneath the bedroom door.

Rose is sitting up in bed, wrapped in the mandatory towel, a cigarette between her fingers. From the pile of butts in the ashtray, she's been at it for quite a while.

"I was worried about you," she says in Thai.

"Everything's under control," he replies, also in Thai. He kicks off his shoes and climbs up beside her. "I gather Peachy actually went home."

"Not happily. I think she's very lonely since her husband left her."

"It's worse than that. Arthit told me tonight that he killed himself over the debts she ran up."

Rose's fingertips fly to her mouth. "Ohhh, *Peachy.* How terrible for her."

"Another reason for us to be grateful for what we've got." He spreads his arms and stretches. He feels like he's been shut up in a small box for days. "Every day we're together is a blessing. You, Miaow, and me. And there's no promise that it'll go on forever, so we need to be thankful one day at a time. There was probably a time when things were fine between Peachy and her husband, and they took it for granted. And then things weren't fine anymore." He strokes her arm, the skin he loves. "I'm never going to take you for granted." Then, at what he hoped would be the romantic high spot, he yawns.

"Poor baby, you're tired."

He shakes his head, half expecting to feel his brain slosh around inside. "This has been the longest day of my life."

"I'm so sorry about all that."

"It's not you. Oh, I mean, sure, it's partly the thing with the bag of money. But I think I can put that on hold for a little while."

She runs a finger down the side of his face, and his right side erupts in goose bumps. "If you say so, I'm sure you can. What's the rest of it?"

"Give me a minute. Let me figure out what order to tell it in." He closes his eyes for a moment, lets some of the day's images pass before his eyes, and the next thing he knows, there's a tug on his arm.

"You were snoring," Rose says.

"Not a chance."

"Like a helicopter." She leans over and kisses him on the cheek. "Go to sleep. You can tell me in the morning."

"No. You need to know what's going on." He focuses on what he needs to say for a moment, making sure he has the Thai words at his command. "Okay, okay, let's start with the relatively easy stuff." And he tells her about his talk with Arthit, about how happy Arthit was to hear that Rose had accepted Rafferty's proposal.

"I *finally* accepted it," Rose says. "Before one of us died of old age." She slides a hand over his shoulder and says, "You're so tight you're practically in a spasm. Turn around so I can work on your neck."

"It's carrying this head around," he says. "Just too many ideas inside."

"Not to mention all that bone." Her fingers probe, stretch, and isolate his muscles.

"And then," Rafferty says, and hesitates. "I had a little surprise today. My father is in Bangkok."

Her hands stop moving. He feels their warmth against his skin, and he starts to drift off again. "Is this a joke?" she asks.

"I wish it were. He's here, and he's brought along my half-Chinese half sister and a Southern Chinese guy who seems to be a hired gun."

"A sister, too? But this is wonderful for you," she says. "It's your chance."

"For what?"

"To make it up with him." She makes a *tsk-tsk* noise, a reaction that Rafferty has learned is a lot less mild than it sounds. "We're talking about your *father*, Poke. He's here, in Bangkok. With your sister. He came looking for you."

"Yeah? That makes us even or something?"

She lifts a hand and slaps his back. "This is one of the things that's wrong with you."

"*One* of them? And, by the way, ow."

"One of many. You're in your head too much. You're so busy making a judgment that you close yourself off to understanding anything. You talk about being 'even' with your father, like you're making some sort of business deal, like you don't have any feelings about it. For years it's been like your father was dead, and now he's here. You can make things right again. You have a second chance. Do you know what I'd give for a second chance with my own father? Do you know what I'd give to be able to talk to him for five minutes? Two minutes ago you were talking about how it's a blessing for us to be together. Every day is a blessing, you said. Well, here's your father, back from the dead. And you don't think that's a blessing?"

"Actually, no," he says, still in Thai. "I was just fine. From one day to the next, I never gave him a thought. I haven't seen him since I was sixteen, remember? It's not like he's earned a lifetime of love and loyalty."

"Your parents don't need to *earn* your love," Rose says. "They gave you life. That's enough. What did Miaow do to earn your love? You make love sound like money."

"At least you get change from money if you give too much of it."

She rolls over so her back is to him and lights a cigarette. "You don't even mean what you're saying. You're just stubborn. You've gotten used to the idea that your father is no good, and it's too much work to learn that it might not be true. You've been living in your side of the story since you were sixteen. Now you don't want to hear his side."

"I already heard it. That's what I'm trying to tell you. Whether I like it or not, he's barged back into my life, without an invitation—"

Rose raises an arm and lets it drop. "Oh, Poke."

"—and he's toting a bag of threats."

Rose turns her head enough to give him her profile. "Against who?"

"The whole hemisphere, is what it sounded like." He hesitates, then takes the plunge. "I asked Arnold to find out what he could."

"This is impossible," Rose says. "Your father comes all the way to Bangkok, bringing your sister, and instead of welcoming them, instead of bringing them home so I could meet them, you . . . you assign *Arnold* to him. Do you know what I think?"

"I already do. I'm stubborn, I don't know anything about love—"

"I think you're afraid of what it might mean to you. Here you are, with this opportunity. So what do you do? You go looking for facts. More facts. Like facts can tell you how to feel or what you should do. He's your *father*, but you don't want to know what that might really mean."

"Well, how do I know what he's up to? What's his agenda? He's not exactly aces in the trust department. Anyway," he adds in English, "it takes one to know one."

"What does that mean?" Her voice is several degrees chillier.

"It's just the way he *is*. He may be my father, but he's more like Arnold than he is like me."

He turns to her, puts a hand on her arm. "I'm just being careful. *This*," he says, "this room, you, me, Miaow—nothing can threaten this. I can't let anything threaten this. Not my father, not Elson, not anything."

"We'll talk tomorrow. For now go to sleep." She puts out her cigarette and lies down again with her back to him. Then she says, "This is silly," and turns and puts both arms around him. He feels her breath on his cheek.

He is asleep in seconds.

He is back in the Lancaster house, in the living room, which has developed windows that look out on a Southeast Asian landscape, all palms and heat shimmer, when the phone rings.

He sits up, says "Shit" in his wake-up frog voice, and flips the phone open.

"Who'd call at this hour?" Rose asks.

Before Rafferty can say a word, he hears his father's voice.

"Get out of there," Frank Rafferty says. "All of you, get out of there *this minute*."

22

The Color of Ancient Ice

Get dressed and wake up Miaow." Rafferty slips the cell phone into his hip pocket and goes to the safe hidden in the headboard of the bed. "Don't turn on any lights."

Rose is throwing on a T-shirt. "Who was it?"

"Dear old Dad. We have to get out of here right now."

"But where can we go?" Her jeans are halfway up her thighs.

"Grab your purse." He waves a hand in a useless effort to dispel Rose's cigarette smoke. "I want this place to look empty."

As Rose heads for Miaow's room, Rafferty pulls over his head the heavy chain he wears around his neck. Dangling from it is a small key, which he uses to open the safe. From it he removes a thick stack of thousand-baht notes from the money he keeps in reserve, folds the bills once, and stuffs them into his pocket. Then he withdraws a shapeless package wrapped in oilcloth. He drops it heavily onto the bed and pulls out a couple of loaded nine-millimeter magazines, grabs a corner of the cloth and lifts, and when the Glock rolls free, he slips one of the magazines into the grip. As always, the click of it snapping into place both reassures and frightens him.

The gun feels like dry ice against the skin of his stomach.

He barrels through the door to the living room, and in the haze of light through the glass door he sees Rose with Miaow in her arms, wearing her pink bunny pajamas. She is half awake, eyeing the room groggily. The sight fills him with fury. These people, except for his mother, are the only people in the world he loves, and now they're in danger. Thanks, Pop.

No, he thinks. *Arnold.*

Rafferty surveys the room and then opens the door to the hallway. "Out."

Cold blue fluorescent light, the color of ancient ice, the old embedded smell of cooking oil. "Go down to Mrs. Pongsiri's," he says.

He turns to his own door and slips the key into the lock that controls the dead bolt. He clicks the lock home and then thinks better of it and turns the key back, leaving only the flimsy Indonesian lock that he can literally pick with a bobby pin: no point inviting them to kick the door in. He hears Rose and Miaow moving down the hallway, and then the elevator, directly opposite Rafferty's front door, groans into motion.

Heading down to the lobby. Someone coming up.

"Hurry," he calls. "Bang on the door." He twists the key, tries to pull it out.

It sticks in the lock.

"She'll be asleep," Rose says.

"*Now.*" He yanks at the key again. The lock won't let it go.

It's been giving him trouble for weeks, but not like this. The lock has been reluctant to let the key slip out, but he's always been able to wiggle it free. He tries a wiggle or two and then puts a foot against the door and uses all his body weight. The key won't budge. His shirt is suddenly wet beneath the arms.

He can hear Rose knocking politely on Mrs. Pongsiri's door, halfway along the hall on the other side, and he swears aloud, lets go of the key, runs down the hallway, and slams his fist against the thin metal door, heavily enough to buckle it. The elevator is louder now, coming up, probably only three or four floors away. He raises his fist again, and the door opens to reveal Mrs. Pongsiri in a silk bathrobe, her face smeared with some kind of white cream.

"Mr. Rafferty," she says.

"In," Rafferty says to Rose. Miaow's eyes are wide now. To Mrs. Pongsiri he says, "Sorry, sorry. I'll explain later."

Mrs. Pongsiri blinks at him as though he's out of focus, and then something hard happens to her face beneath its mask of cream, something that tells Rafferty she knows what it is to be on the run in the middle of the night. "Of course," she says, stepping aside. "Come in."

Rafferty pulls the door closed behind them and sprints back to his own door. He twists the key and yanks all the way from the knees, practically wrenching his back. Nothing. Grabbing a deep breath, he forces himself to be still for a moment, then gently turns the key all the way in the other direction, brings it vertical again, and tugs.

The elevator bell rings.

The key glides free.

No time to get to Mrs. Pongsiri's. He runs to the end of the hall, hearing the elevator doors begin to slide apart, and slips through the door to the fire stairs. At the last moment, he sticks the tongue of his belt between the latch and the doorframe to keep it from clicking shut.

Voices in the hall, speaking Thai.

Rafferty eases the door open half an inch and puts an eye to the crack.

Three of them, gathered at his door. They look like farmers, burned dark by the Thai sun, wearing loose clothes and flap sandals, but they don't move like farmers. The one in the center motions the others away and puts his ear to the door. In a fluid movement, he lifts his shirttail and pulls out a gun.

The man nearest Rafferty also has a gun in his hand, a tiny popgun just big enough to die from. The third holds a knife, nicked and rusty in spots, but with a honed, shiny edge, an edge that has had a lot of care lavished on it. It is maybe ten inches long, a little smaller than a machete. The man in the center makes an abrupt gesture, hand toward the floor, and the one with the knife drops to his hands and knees and looks for light seeping through the crack under Rafferty's door. He gets up again, shaking his head.

The man in the center, clearly the one in charge, waves the others to either side of the door and tries the knob. Then he leans down to examine the lock. The gun disappears beneath his shirt, and his hand comes back out with a small piece of metal in it. It takes him only a few seconds to spring the lock. When he tries to pull the pick free, it sticks.

He tries again, but the pick is frozen in the lock. The three of them consult in whispers, apparently arguing about whether to leave it in the lock, and then the man in the middle gives it a dismissive wave and pushes the door open very slowly, standing back as it swings inward. He motions the one to his left, the one with the knife, against the wall—*Stay here* is the message—and the other two go in, moving quickly and silently. Their guns are extended in front of them, gripped in both hands.

They've had practice at this.

The man with his back to the wall purses his lips as though to whistle and looks at his watch. He is plump and almost merry-looking, except for the knife. He leans back and closes his eyes, letting the knife dangle from his hand. For a very brief moment, Rafferty considers taking it away from him and wrapping it around his head, but the man's eyes open and he glances down the hall in Rafferty's direction.

Rafferty freezes, feeling his heartbeat all the way down to his wrists. If he closes the door, the man will spot the motion. If he leaves it ajar, the man may see it and come to investigate. As slowly as he can ever remember moving, Rafferty eases the gun out of his pants and waits, holding his breath, and the man's eyes travel past the door and back up the hall. He actually *is* whistling, very quietly, and this fact ping-pongs around in Rafferty's mind, stirring up a substantial amount of new discomfort. He would be happier if the man were nervous.

The whistling stops, and Rafferty shifts his feet so he can see what's caught the man's eye. He finds himself looking at the dent he left in Mrs. Pongsiri's door.

The fat man frowns, pushes himself away from the wall, and begins to move down the hall. He walks like a bear, heavy on his feet, his knees slightly bent and bowed out. The knife swishes once against the leg of his trousers, and Rafferty's mind amplifies it into a slap.

Rafferty slips out of his shoes and puts his shoulder to the door.

A brusque interrogative whisper: The other two have come out of Rafferty's apartment. The one who picked the lock looks down the hall and snaps his fingers once, a sound as sharp as a breaking bone, and the fat one turns back and then points at Mrs. Pongsiri's door, eyebrows raised in question. The leader shakes his head and turns back to Rafferty's door, pulling it closed and applying himself again to extricating the pick from the lock. The third man crosses the hall and pushes the button for the elevator.

The fat man whispers urgently, but the pick wins the battle for the leader's attention, and he waves the fat man away. The fat man takes the leader's shoulder and turns him up the hall, pointing down at the floor, at the strip of light beneath Mrs. Pongsiri's door. The leader stops, one hand on the stuck pick, his eyes following the direction of the fat man's finger. All three of them stand motionless.

The elevator bell rings, but nobody moves. Rafferty watches the light from the elevator car brighten and strike the three men as the doors slide open, then diminish as they begin to close again. At the last moment, the leader gives up on freeing the pick and lunges for the elevator, extending a hand to force the doors open again. The others start to follow.

Rafferty's cell phone rings.

All three heads swivel toward the end of the hall, and Rafferty lets the door slip closed, already halfway up the first flight of stairs, the shoes in his hand hampering him as he punches at the phone to turn it off—it's his father calling, he sees. He takes the steps three at a time, as lightly as possible, hearing the door on his landing open and the sharp whisper of commands ricocheting up the stairwell. They don't know whether he's gone up or down; they'll have to split up, so the only question is whether one or two of them will be coming after him. The one thing he's halfway sure of is that they won't send the man with the knife on his own; the man in charge will want a gun in both directions.

Rafferty lives on the eighth floor of twelve. The door to the roof is kept bolted from inside as a burglary precaution, but there's no way to know whether the padlock on the bolt will be hanging open, as it often is, or whether Mrs. Song, his landlady, will have secured it on her rounds. That gives him four floors to maneuver in, and he doesn't know a soul on any of them.

He hears shoes echoing on the stairs, but there's no way to sort them out, to see how many are going up or down. A grunt from below, something clattering, metal on metal: a ring on the handrail or a gun in someone's hand. He can hear labored breathing—the fat man coming up? Then there's a burst of argument from below: Something's wrong.

He doesn't remember having passed the tenth floor, but he tries the door to the eleventh, hoping to distract them by slipping out and calling for the elevator, and realizes what they were arguing about. The door is locked. It can be opened only from the inside.

That almost certainly means they're *all* locked, including the door to the roof. The only open door will be the one leading into the lobby. He's in a vertical dead end.

The feet below him have slowed, their owner probably listening to the discussion farther down the stairs: two voices, which means they decided that Rafferty was trying to get down to the street, and sent the weight in that direction. Only one coming after him, then. One with a gun.

On the other hand, Rafferty thinks, *maybe not,* registering the heft of his own gun in his hand. He sights the Glock down the stairs, aiming for the concrete wall at a thirty-degree angle, hoping for a nice, lethal series of caroms, and pulls the trigger.

A shout of surprise from the man just below him, then a sharp command from farther down. The shot is ringing in his ears, but he can hear the voices over it.

He fires again, twice, aiming obliquely at the wall. The bullets *spang* off it and hit several other walls before one of them bangs into the metal stairs with a sound like the Bell at the Center of the World.

The man below him gives a panicky grunt, then calls a question, but Rafferty can't make out the words. Then there is silence.

He leans back against the wall, waiting, watching the stairs. If it was the fat man he heard panting, his pursuer is armed only with a knife. He has no doubt he can gut-shoot the man; it's a big gut, and its owner will have a whole flight of stairs to climb between the time he comes into shooting range and the point at which he'll be able to do Rafferty any harm. That'll leave two, both carrying automatics.

Not the best odds.

He edges his way across the landing, tasting salt in his mouth. He's bitten through his lower lip. When he can see the corner of the stairs, the few inches that will give him the most time to aim, he raises the Glock in both hands and waits.

Nothing.

Then a scuffle of movement, fast, and he feels the muscles in his legs loosen in panic, and he jams his back against the wall for support, but no one appears on the stairs below him, no fat man with a knife, no one ducking into view for a quick look. Just feet on the stairs.

Going down.

23

It Starts Ugly and Gets Worse

Months later, when Rafferty looks back on the three days that followed their abandonment of the apartment, what he will remember is the blur of movement, the weight of exhaustion, and the smell of rain. Bits and pieces of what happened will stay with him, hard and flashbulb bright, sharp-edged and fragmentary as reflections in bits of a broken mirror.

Snapshots in a loose pile, random and unsequenced.

Maybe, he will think, it is better that he remembers it that way. Better he doesn't have to carry with him the fear and the fury, the desperation and the moments of soul-sinking hopelessness when he knew for a certainty that everything he cared about in the world was about to be destroyed, scattered, irretrievably lost.

He doesn't remember the call he placed to Arthit after his shots chased the three intruders away, but he retains a vivid mental image of the blinking cherry lights on the police cars, four of them, that Arthit dispatched to the basement parking area beneath his building. Cars that took him in one direction and Rose, with Miaow bundled in her arms, in another, the two cars without passengers screeching up the driveway and vanishing aimlessly into the night. He wasn't there to see it, but he knows that the car carrying Miaow and Rose disappeared into the parking lot of Arthit's police station. Five minutes later three cars came out again, each taking a different direction. When the driver of the car with Rose and Miaow in it had done enough figure eights to be satisfied that any possible watchers were following the other cars, he took them to Arthit's house, where Noi let them in, and she and Rose put Miaow to bed.

Rose said it took more than an hour, with both her and Noi sitting at Miaow's bedside, for the child to fall asleep.

Rafferty remembers very clearly how he felt when Rose told him that. He wanted, slowly and creatively, to kill Arnold Prettyman.

Another detail: the pouches of weariness beneath Arthit's eyes, shaded a poisonous green by the fluorescent lights bouncing off the walls in the interrogation room where he and Rafferty talked after Rose and Miaow had been safely tucked away. The room is painted that peculiar shade of spoiled pea soup that's been sold by the millions of gallons to government institutions around the world. Rafferty, whose mind is searching desperately for something neutral to focus on for a moment, finds himself wondering what the salesman's pitch might possibly be: "It starts ugly and gets worse"?

"He was terrified," Rafferty says.

Arthit slides a big cop shoe over the scuffed linoleum, producing a gritty sound that makes Rafferty's teeth itch. "You don't actually know that, do you? He was a medium-level spook, Poke, delusions of grandeur aside. They're good actors. Their critics kill them if they're not convincing."

"No," Rafferty says. "He was sweating like a pig."

"Do pigs sweat?" This is the kind of thing that interests Arthit.

Rafferty makes a show of pulling out his notebook. "That's a fascinating question, Arthit, one I plan to look into as soon as I have the time." He writes it down in large letters.

"Curiosity is an essential part of the good policeman's armament," Arthit says sententiously, and Rafferty realizes that his friend is trying to calm him. "Almost as important as a strong bladder."

"So yes, I believe him. I think he was frightened enough to sell me."

Arthit closes his eyes. He is clearly exhausted. "Before we go shoot him through the head, run it past me again. Just the high points."

Rafferty begins to check off his fingers, starting with his thumb. "My sainted father emerges from the mists of time—"

"A coelacanth dredged from the depths," Arthit suggests through a yawn. "The alluvial ancestor of the pangolin."

Rafferty waves him off and goes to finger number two. "I ask Arnold to employ his skills. Many people who terrify Arnold express interest. He perspires extravagantly and keeps making eyes at his gun." He raises finger number three, which happens to be the middle one. Arthit eyes it expressionlessly. "The Three Musketeers appear."

"Well, if you put it like *that* . . ." Arthit says.

Rafferty rests his chin on his hand, realizes it is a mistake, and sits upright. That way, if he goes to sleep, the fall will wake him. "What are those things scientists look for? Starts with a *v*."

"Variables," Arthit says, stressing the patience. "As you know perfectly well."

"Well, there haven't been any other variables in my life."

Arthit sits forward. "You don't call a U.S. Secret Service agent and thirty thousand in counterfeit money a variable? Your life must be much more interesting than mine."

"Those people have a plan in place. It has nothing to do with busting into my apartment in the middle of the night with guns in their hands."

Arthit's hands are flat on the table. "About your father," he says. "How much of this do you intend to share with us?"

"With the cops in general, not bloody much. With you personally, everything."

"And the reason?"

"I still don't know about those two cops with Elson."

Arthit is still for a moment, and then he gives Rafferty a minimal nod. "So. We've done the A-plus-B thing and come up with C. What about your intuition?"

"What is this, Down with Reason Week? First Arnold, then Rose, now you. Is this some sort of plot to accelerate the decline of the West? Replace the scientific method with *feelings*?"

"The question stands," Arthit says.

"All right. In deference to your cultural orientation, I'll play. My intuition tells me that my father got himself into some very deep shit in China and it's chased him to Bangkok. And that Arnold got leaned on by the chasers and decided it was easier to sell me than to get his bones broken one at a time."

"That's a fair summary," Arthit says. He cups his hands on the table as though he's trapped a grasshopper under them. "A little thin on feelings, but fair."

"Boy. And to think I've been selling feelings short."

"My own personal feeling," Arthit says, "is that the enemy of my enemy is my friend. The Arabs say that."

"I'm sure they do, but I have no idea what it means in this case. I mean, who's the enemy?"

"Your enemy," Arthit says.

"Who's the other enemy?"

Arthit's gaze flickers. "You, I suppose."

"I thought we were friends."

"No. You're *their* enemy." He sketches an invisible diagram on the table with his fingers and stares at it. "The . . . um, enemy's enemy," he adds.

"The *other* enemy," Rafferty says by way of clarification. "I mean, if I'm an enemy and they're an enemy, who's the friend?"

Arthit pulls in the corners of his mouth. "I am?"

Rafferty nods. "Do you know any other Arab sayings that burn to be spoken at the moment?"

"A good friend is like water in your camel," Arthit says at once.

"I've heard that one a million times."

"Wise people, the Arabs," Arthit says, nodding sagely.

"They discovered zero," Rafferty replies, "although I've never been sure why that's anything to write home about."

"Back to my feelings," Arthit says, erasing the invisible diagram with his palm. "I feel that this is a good time to go take a tire iron to Arnold."

"Jesus," Rafferty says. "I thought you'd never feel that."

ARNOLD PRETTYMAN'S TOP-SECRET hideaway, which it had taken Arthit fifteen seconds to locate on a computer, is situated in a drab, two-story squat of poured cement. The street-level floor has a slide-down metal door, which is open six inches at the bottom, allowing a splash of light to paint the sidewalk. American screech rock, all guitars and tight-jeans falsetto, is playing loudly inside.

Arthit closes the car door quietly and motions for Rafferty to do the same. He pulls his gun.

Rafferty puts his hand on the grip of his own gun, but Arthit stops him.

"Don't even think about it," he says. "If anybody's going to get shot tonight, he's going to get shot by a cop."

Rafferty shakes his head, and Arthit leans in. "Use some sense here," he hisses. "There's only so much I can do, Poke. I can't protect you if you kill someone."

He holds Poke's eyes for a moment and then shifts the gun to his left hand, slips his right under the edge of the door, and slams it upward.

Two teenage boys jump to their feet, register Arthit and the gun, and put their hands on top of their heads as if they know the drill. They are covered in grease.

Rafferty scans the shop and sees six or seven motorcycles in various stages of dismemberment. The reason for the boys' fear is obvious. This is a chop shop, where stolen motorcycles are broken up and combined into new ones.

Arthit wiggles his gun, pointing the barrel at the floor. "Sit," he says. The boys sit at once, hugging their knees, hands in plain sight. Arthit and Poke zigzag between fragments of motorcycle until they are standing directly over the boys. Arthit studies them for a second and points his gun at the more obviously terrified of the two.

"You. Anyone upstairs?"

"Don't know," the boy says. The smears of black grease surrounding his eyes make them a brilliant porcelain white. "People come and go."

Arthit glances at Rafferty, who shrugs.

"Both of you," Arthit says. "Give me your wallets."

The boys shift awkwardly to get their wallets out of their hip pockets and hand them over. Arthit passes them to Rafferty, who pulls out the identity cards and compares them to the faces staring up at him. Allowing for the grease, the boys' faces match the ones on the cards.

"You'll get these back when we come down," Arthit says. "If

you're not here, I promise you a nice long time in the monkey house. Clear?"

"Clear," says the tougher of the boys.

Arthit lifts his chin toward the back of the shop, where there is a narrow flight of very steep concrete stairs. Poke follows him, and the music chases them up, echoing in the passageway.

Six feet from the top, Arthit stops and says, "Oh, no."

By the time Poke smells it, a sharp char of flesh, Arthit is already through the door, his gun extended. He stops there as though he has run into a wall of glass, and Poke stops behind him and looks over his friend's shoulder, looks at one of those snapshots that will stay with him forever. A single glance brands it on his brain, and he turns away, very quickly, trying to look at anything else in the world. Then he forces himself to face it again.

Arnold Prettyman is wired to a chromium-backed chair, the wire cutting deeply into his arms and shoulders. His hands, wired tightly together, rest in his lap, if "rest" is a word that can be used to describe fists. His head lists to one side at a contortionist's angle, and the left side of his face is black. His faded blue eyes look at Poke as though Poke were a window. The stench of burned flesh is overpowering. Poke gags.

Arthit automatically looks at his watch and says, "Four-twenty-three." Then his shoulders sag and his head droops forward. "You," he says to Poke without turning. "Get out of here."

24

Major-League Heat

I *killed him,* Poke thinks. *I didn't mention the triad, and I killed him.* With Prettyman's death reverberating in his mind, the day he originally planned, a day he meant to spend dealing with the counterfeiting situation, suddenly seems irrelevant. The threat seems almost quaint. The new day's first light is tinting the sky as he uses the key Arthit gave him to open the front door of the house. He locks it behind him and trudges into the living room, weighing several thousand pounds.

Rose is asleep on the couch. A yellow cotton blanket covers her to the shoulders. Her knees are drawn up—the couch is too short for her—and one arm is outthrown, the hand dangling at the wrist, palm up. There is something terribly vulnerable in that loose hand, with its pale palm and curled fingers.

Rose is not a light sleeper, and she doesn't stir as he approaches her.

He kneels to examine the face he has come to love: the mouth, its upper lip high in the middle and the lower full and generous. The delicate seashell whorl of her nostrils, perhaps the most beautiful curve he has ever seen. The smooth swelling of her cheekbones. He studies her face, every detail, for at least five minutes.

She and Miaow are his life now. Nothing that concerns them is irrelevant.

Then he turns around and goes out into the paling day to hail a *tuk-tuk*.

Just to be on the safe side, he takes the *tuk-tuk* for a few blocks and gets out, waiting to see whether anyone seems to be paying attention to him. At this hour, though, there is virtually no one on the streets. He hails a cab, makes the driver circle his building three times as he looks for watchers, and then has the man drop him in the basement garage.

To avoid the noise of the elevator in case someone is waiting on his floor, he takes the stairs. He gets all the way to the fifth floor, each step a yard high, before he remembers that the doors are locked on each floor. Muttering unflattering self-appraisal, he goes back down to the lobby, crosses his fingers, and pushes the "up" button.

Not much he can do when the elevator doors open except stand as far as possible to one side with the gun out. The hallway is empty.

It takes him a couple of minutes to work the pick out of the lock and insert his own key. When he pulls the key back, it slips out as though it has been greased. He thinks briefly of kicking the door into small pieces but decides that the satisfaction isn't worth the noise and enters the apartment with his gun in both hands.

He needn't have bothered. The place is deserted.

It takes only a few minutes to get what he needs, a change of clothes for all of them and—as an afterthought—Miaow's new cell phone, which she had left on top of her desk, surrounded by a circlet of browning ginger flowers like a small metallic shrine. The bag of counterfeit money, much to his relief, is still in its hiding place on the top shelf of the closet. The men last night had been looking for people, not loot. From the safe concealed in the headboard above his bed, he removes his third ammunition clip and the rest of his own reserve of money. He will need every baht of it. On the way out, he makes one more stop in the kitchen to get a jar of Nescafé for Rose, who lives on it, since he's not sure Noi will have any in her kitchen. He throws it all into a canvas tote bag, takes a last, regretful look around, and heads for the stairs.

As he reaches the seventh floor, his cell phone rings.

"Where the hell are you?" Arthit demands.

"How nice to hear your voice."

"Why aren't you at my house? You're not supposed to be out wandering around." He can hear Noi's voice in the background, questioning and concerned. "Tell me you haven't gone someplace really stupid," Arthit says. "Your apartment, for example."

"Okay, I won't tell you I went to my apartment."

"There are moments, long moments, when I doubt your sanity. You're contaminated now. There's no way you can come back here until I can arrange something so complicated it would take a small army to track it."

"I've got things to do. I won't come back without calling you."

"You certainly won't."

"Are we still on to creep Elson?"

"We are. I need some sleep first."

"So why aren't you getting it?"

"The chopper choppers," Arthit says. "The boys downstairs from the apartment we visited a few hours ago."

"Yes, Arthit? Are you going to make me ask you about them?"

"Aren't we touchy this morning? Four guys, they said. Three of them you've already met, by the descriptions. The fourth was a very tall, very thin Chinese man in his seventies. Military-looking, they said."

"Anything more? A tonsure, a third eye, or anything? Something that would distinguish him from any other very tall, very thin Chinese man in his seventies?"

"One of those moles the Chinese seem to admire. About the size of a ten-baht coin—or, to translate it into American for you, a quarter—with hairs growing out of it. Three or four inches long."

"How'd they know he was Chinese? As opposed, say, to Korean."

"One of the boys has a Chinese mother. He heard the thin man swear at one of the others in what is apparently a timelessly popular Chinese oath."

"They hear any names?"

"If they had heard any names," Arthit says, more than a bit briskly, "do you think that information would be so far down on this list?"

"Sorry. Guess we're both a little cranky."

"Well," Arthit says, "when you want some sleep, call me and I'll arrange some way for you to get to my place." He yawns. "I'll phone you later. And, Poke?"

"Yeah?"

"Try to keep today's to-do list of stupid things really short. You might limit it to the one you've already done."

"My phone's breaking up," Rafferty says. He punches it off and slips it into his pocket. Then, for the second time in less than six hours, he walks away from the place he has grown to think of as home.

IN THE SILOM BRANCH of Coffee World, he fools around on Google for thirty minutes or so as he drinks a quart of black coffee with half a dozen shots of espresso thrown in to raise the octane level. The words "Chinese triads" bring up 1,180,000 hits. He narrows it to "Chinese triads Shanghai," and the number is still something on the magnitude of science's best guess about the age of the earth, so he gives it up and concentrates on the act of jangling his central nervous system into some persuasive imitation of consciousness.

When he realizes he has reached the point of diminishing returns, he takes out the phone and punches in the number he had thought he would never dial.

"Poke." It is Ming Li, sounding cool and unsurprised as always.

"Is he there?"

"He's asleep."

"Wake him up."

"You're on your cell," she says. "Nothing worth waking him up for should be said on a cell. What time is it?"

"Eight-twenty. And it's important to you and important to me."

"Tell me where you are."

Why not? It's a little late to worry about any threat from Frank. He tells her.

"Twenty minutes," Ming Li says. Then she hangs up.

It's too early for his first planned stop of the day. The man he is going to see, whom he interviewed when he was in the first stages of researching his abandoned book, works seven days a week, but he won't be open for business until eleven or so. Since Rafferty's in front of a keyboard, he decides he'll take the most optimistic outlook: Everything will work out, and he still has to earn a living. He pulls his notebook from his pocket, opens Word, and begins to key in his notes about the spies.

He's surprised at how easily it comes. He transcribes a few words from the notebook, and then new impressions and new observations crowd in on him, and he weaves them into his notes. What had been the outline of a story begins to become the story itself, complete with the details that bring a place, a person, to life. Tired as he is, the words slip out with little resistance, and gradually the picture assembles itself, sentence by sentence, before his eyes. The trails these men took to come here, the peculiar mixture of openness and secrecy that characterizes their conversations, the eyes, different colors and different shapes, but always in motion.

Arnold Prettyman's eyes, open and unseeing.

His burned hands wired to the chair.

"Not very vigilant," Ming Li says, and he jumps two inches straight up from his seat. Ming Li steps back and says, "My, my. Maybe you shouldn't have any more coffee, older brother."

"I haven't slept in forty-eight hours," Rafferty says. "If it weren't for coffee, I'd be speaking to you from the floor."

She pulls up the stool next to him. She is immaculate in a free-hanging white T-shirt and loose-fitting black slacks. Every man in the coffeehouse stares at her. "What's that?" she says, leaning forward to read the screen.

"It's money," he says. He highlights the text, hits "copy," drops it into an e-mail to himself, and sends it off. Then he gets up and says, "Let's go."

"I want some coffee."

He looks through the window at the developing day. "Get it to go."

IN THE NEXT twenty minutes, Ming Li leads him through a tangle of turnarounds, drop-backs, blind alleys, stop-and-watch points, and random reversals that would disorient a homing pigeon. Even Rafferty doesn't know where they are, and he says so.

"Six weeks with city maps before we came," Ming Li says. "I must have spent a hundred hours on Google Earth." She turns into a clothing store and positions herself at the window, behind the mannequins.

"Frank's drill," she says, watching the street. She finishes the coffee, slurping it a bit.

"Frank's drill," he repeats, looking over her shoulder. Nothing catches his eye. "Did Frank's drill include teaching you to throw major-league heat?"

Her eyes continue to search the sidewalks. "Major *what*?"

"Pitching. Like you did with the lychee seeds."

"Ahh," Ming Li says. "Day in and day out." Without a glance back at him, she leaves the shop. Rafferty follows like a good little puppy.

"Why?"

"Why what?" They are side by side in the morning sun, and Ming Li leads them across the street. To most people it would look like a simple maneuver to get into the shade, but Rafferty knows that it pulls followers out of position, if there aren't many of them.

"Why did he teach you to pitch?"

She looks at him and then past him. Satisfied that no one is there who shouldn't be, she says, "He wanted me to be good at it."

Rafferty experiences a pang of something so much like jealousy that it would be silly to call it anything else. "He never taught me squat."

"Poor baby," Ming Li says without a hint of sympathy.

"Unless you count sitting silently around the house. He taught me all there is to know about that. My father the end table."

"Maybe when you were a kid, he wasn't homesick," she says.

Rafferty burps some of his newly acquired coffee. "He may not have been homesick, but he read every fucking word about China he could get his hands on."

"China wasn't *home*, older brother. China was my mother. She's pretty much a nightmare in some ways, but he loves her. He loves yours, too. But he couldn't bring her with him, could he? Had to leave her back there, with the rest of America. But *baseball*, baseball we could get. He picked it up on the shortwave at first, and then on satellite TV. Everything in our lives stopped for the World Series. Soon as I was big enough to get my fingers on the seams of the ball, he started to teach me. Hung an old tire in the courtyard of the house we shared with nine other families and had me throw through it, and I mean for hours. Every couple of weeks, I'd move a step back. I'm good to about fifty feet, but I haven't got the lift for longer."

"Huh," Rafferty says from the middle of a cloud of feelings. They swarm around him like mosquitoes, except he can't swat them away.

"When I was pitching, I was America," she says. "And I was you."

The words distract him so much he stumbles off the curb. "How did you feel about that?"

"I liked it. It made me feel important. It was getting the ball through the tire that was hard."

Rafferty realizes he can see it all: the dusty courtyard, the perspiring girl, the inner tube in the tree. And, behind her, his father. *Her* father. A life he never imagined. "Where is Frank?"

"He's where we're going. He did talk about you, you know. He was—he *is*—proud of you." The two of them turn into a small street that Rafferty, after a moment, recognizes as Soi Convent, now known more for its restaurants and coffeehouses than for the religious retreat responsible for its name. "He's got all your books."

Rafferty says, "I don't want to talk about this."

"Too bad. And he's kept up with you in Bangkok."

This strikes a nerve. "Just exactly how?"

"Frank knows everybody." She steps off the curb into the morning traffic and raises a hand. "Too many people, in fact. That's part of the problem." A *tuk-tuk* swerves to the curb, its driver gaping at Ming Li as though he's never seen a woman before, and Rafferty thinks she must get a lot of that. "Mah Boon Krong," she says, naming a neighborhood Rafferty rarely frequents. She slides over on the seat. "Get in."

He does, and she gathers her loose black trousers around her.

"What about Leung?" Rafferty asks.

"One thing I've learned," she says, "is never to worry about Leung."

The driver lurches into traffic, both eyes on Ming Li in the rearview mirror.

"And does Leung worry about you?" He catches the driver's eyes in the mirror and says, in Thai, "Look at the road."

"More than he needs to. Frank's a good teacher."

The courtyard, the dust, the girl, the woman upstairs. All real, moment to moment, day after day, as real as his life in Lancaster. He forces his mind to the present. "It's not all baseball, huh?"

"Baseball and other games. Frank thinks four, five moves out."

"So where is he?"

"I'm not sure thinking ahead like that is something you can learn," Ming Li says, ignoring the question. "You have to keep all the pieces in your head all the time, be able to see the whole board in six or eight possible configurations. Either you have it or you don't. Do you play chess?"

Rafferty's turn to ignore the question. "I suppose he taught you."

"You know," she says with a hint of impatience, "all this started long before you were born, before Frank went home and met your mother. He had a *life* in China, he wasn't just a tourist. If anything was an afterthought, it was you."

"That's not exactly the point, is it? You don't start a family when you've already got one. In America it's called bigamy."

"In China it's called common sense. He had no way of knowing he'd ever be back. The Communists took the whole *country,* older brother. A lot of lives were changed. It looked permanent, and not just to Frank. What was he supposed to do, go into a monastery? Although," she adds, "I've always thought Frank would make a good monk. He's got the discipline and the patience for it. And the focus."

"A Jesuit, maybe."

"Exactly, although I'm sure you don't mean it the same way I do."

"What's he running away from?"

"You'd know already if you hadn't ridden your stupid horse out of that restaurant."

"Whatever it was," Rafferty says, "it followed him."

"No it didn't," she says with considerable force. "Nothing follows Frank unless he lets it." She turns and pokes him square in the chest. "*You* brought it here."

25

Ugliest Mole in China

Colonel Chu," Frank says. He looks at Leung, who does something economical with his shoulders that might be a shrug. "Ugliest mole in China."

"He and three others," Rafferty says. "Thai."

"Local help," Frank says. "Nobodies," He sits on the edge of the bed in a backpackers' hotel on Khao San Road. Ming Li had changed *tuk-tuks* in Mah Boon Krong and redirected them to Bangkok's budget travelers' district, her eyes on the road behind them every yard of the way. Now Rafferty sits on the opposite bed, beside Ming Li. Leung squats peasant style, smoking a cigarette in a corner near the door.

Frank wears a rumpled shirt that he obviously slept in, and his thin hair has a bad case of bed head. "Arnold Prettyman," he says disgustedly. "Why didn't you just hire a skywriter?"

"You knew Arnold?"

"Knew about him. Arnold was a stumblebum. Now he's a dead stumblebum." He looks older and frailer in the morning light. When he glances up at Poke, Poke sees the little burst of gold in the brown iris of his left eye, something that had fascinated him as a kid and that he had forgotten completely. "Christ," Frank grumbles, "even when he was working, Arnold was usually the flare."

"The flare?" Rafferty glances at Ming Li, who has her eyes fastened disapprovingly on the wrinkles in Frank's shirt.

"The distress signal, the guy you give the wrong info to, so he can leak it to make people look somewhere else while you do whatever you have to do. Of course, the flare can't be smart enough to figure out the dope is wrong, because if the other guys decide to come after him and get persuasive, he has to believe it. That's what Arnold was really good at, believing nonsense. For that, he was highly qualified. He was un-evolved, one foot in the Mesozoic and the other in his mouth. You were probably okay until you called him. We came here to warn you just in case, because you're my kid, but now you've really screwed yourself. And worse than that. Not just yourself."

"You, for example," Rafferty says.

Frank pulverizes a peanut he has been holding and lets the whole thing drop. "Don't worry about me."

"I don't." The sharpness in Rafferty's voice surprises even him.

"No, of course not. You're the aggrieved party, the blameless victim."

"Actually," Rafferty says, "that's my mother. I'm just fine."

Frank reaches out to the small table between the bed and picks up the bowl of unshelled peanuts he has been dipping into. Beside it is a saucer with several shelled nuts on it. "Fine? You're an open wound."

"Like a lot of egotists, you overestimate your impact."

"I wish that were true," Frank says. "But it's not." He drops a shell to the floor and adds a nut to the pile on the saucer, then holds the saucer out with exaggerated politeness. "Peanut?"

Poke gives him the politeness right back. "No, thanks, but it's *so* kind of you to offer."

"You're being a horse's ass." Frank's eyes wander away from Poke and gradually settle on Leung. "Colonel Chu. Well, that's not a sur-prise."

"I assume he's got some weight," Rafferty says.

"Oh, yes," Frank says. "The colonel has some weight."

"If he's here," Leung says, "there are others."

Frank makes the face of someone who's just realized he put salt in his coffee. "Not a chance. He can't let anyone know about the box. That's why he's using locals."

"Who went after my family," Rafferty says, and suddenly he is furious. "Picking my lock in the middle of the night. Going into my apartment with their guns drawn. Where my wife is. Where my child is."

"I called you," Frank says. "If I hadn't been watching . . ."

Rafferty feels his face grow hot. "Gee, and I forgot to bring your fucking medal. Just once, just for practice, why don't you try seeing something from somebody else's perspective? Just for the sake of your tiny, mummified little soul. You pop up, materialize out of whatever dimension you normally hang around in, and barge into my life—which is finally on the verge of being the life I want, the life I've worked for—dragging a bunch of unwholesome shit, like Marley's chains. You were *dead,* remember? And you've been gone longer than I knew you. How do I know who you are by now? So I tried to find out. Poor old Arnold was the litmus paper, and guess what? He turned blue." Poke gets up, just to move. "Whoever you are, you failed the acid test. You said you were on the run. I didn't want to know why, I didn't want to spend a few chatty hours catching up with you. I just wish to Christ you'd run in a different direction."

"I knew this was going to be difficult," Frank says.

Ming Li says, "Poke. You have to know."

He stops pacing. He feels light, empty, as though there is a vacuum at his center.

"For God's sake, sit down," Frank says. "Trust me for three minutes. Stretch yourself. It's good for your character. Have a fucking peanut." He holds out the dish.

Rafferty takes a seat on the other bed. Ming Li sighs. The bed is hard and narrow, the room furnished with nothing small enough to steal. The guesthouse in which Frank has gone to ground is a recessed, nondescript building announced by a sign that originally said HOME AWAY FROM HOME GUEST HOUSE before someone changed one letter with Magic Marker to make it read HOMO AWAY FROM HOME. A statistically improbable number of teenage boys had been lounging on the couches in the lobby when Rafferty and Ming Li came in. A couple of them had been wearing lipstick.

"I already know some of it," Rafferty says. "Courtesy of my chat with that woman—I mean, Wang, Ming Li's mother—all those years ago."

"Back further." Frank makes a waving gesture, paddling time toward the past. "I told you I stole her. What I didn't tell you, because you walked out, was that I stole more than that." He reaches behind him and plumps a pillow, settles it against his lower back, and leans against the wall. "This is ancient history, but it's pertinent." He sighs and glances up at Ming Li.

"I was young," Frank says. "Hell, I was just a kid. You ever do anything stupid, Poke? And of course I was in love, which, for all the nice songs about it, doesn't really raise the old IQ. You have no idea how beautiful Wang was. Or maybe you do. Look at Ming Li—that's where she gets it. She was so beautiful it made me ache, and she was lost. More lost than I ever thought anyone could be. Just a kid, and about to be punctured by some fat toad, and then she'd have eight, ten years of getting screwed front, back, and sideways seven or eight times a day before they tossed her into the street to fight dogs for garbage."

Ming Li gets up and moves to the other bed to sit beside her father. She puts her right hand on the back of his left. He uses his other hand to pat his shirt pocket.

"You don't smoke anymore," Ming Li says.

"And if I did," Frank says to Rafferty, "she'd tell Wang."

"She'd know," Ming Li says, "without me telling her."

"But obviously," Frank says, resuming the thread, "my employers weren't going to give me any bonuses for stealing Wang. She was capital to them, they'd invested money in her—all those bowls of rice, all those nights sharing the bed with twelve other girls. They'd paid her mother for her, probably twenty dollars. And the problem was, they were as real as she was. They really did kill people once in a while, sometimes even for cause. So I used the skills they'd taught me, and I took a little something along when Wang and I decided Shanghai wasn't home anymore."

"How little?" Rafferty asks.

"Twenty-seven thousand dollars, American. A fortune in those days."

"It's not scratch paper now."

"And to these particular guys, it was also a loss of face. They couldn't allow it. It would have been like taking out a full-page ad: 'Free Money.'

The trouble with being a crook is that you have to work with crooks. Give them an inch and they'll take your foot."

"Worse still," Ming Li says, "you were a foreigner."

"So it was a racial slap, too," Frank says. "There were still signs in Shanghai then, 'No Dogs or Chinese Allowed.' The men I worked for took that personally, and why wouldn't they? They'd been shit on often enough."

"All this," Rafferty says. "It's a long time ago."

Frank gives him an assessing glance. "That's what I thought, too. When I went back."

AS FRANK TELLS IT, it had taken him almost a year to find Wang. It took his former employers less than a week to find the two of them.

At the time Frank thought they'd been watching Wang. It wasn't until later that he realized that the People's Republic was a nation of spies, a tightly woven fabric of betrayal. All the way from the top down, from cities to neighborhoods to blocks to individual apartment houses, there was always someone whose job it was to keep an eye open, to report anything out of the ordinary. A white man in China, living with a Chinese woman, in the 1980s—that was out of the ordinary. Word was passed along. And, unfortunately for Frank and Wang, word reached the wrong ears.

They'd been shopping that day, buying a space heater. Shanghai was cold in December, and Wang's room had no heat. They'd been huddling beneath blankets for days, watching their breath drift upward as they talked. When they returned to the room and opened the door, two men were waiting for them.

They wore the same gray, shapeless uniforms that Frank saw everywhere, had the same nicotine-stained fingers, the same winter-city pallor. They could have been anyone: fry cooks, night-soil collectors, gardeners. Their rank showed only in their eyes and in the heavy jade rings they wore. The man in charge, the taller of the two, had sharply incised Mongolian eyes, the lids sloping heavily downward to frame pupils as hard and dry as marbles. A large nut-brown mole, bristling with coarse hairs, decorated his left cheek. The shorter one trained a gun on Wang, but it was the tall one Frank feared. The tall one didn't need a gun.

The man without the gun smiled, a perfunctory rearrangement of the facial muscles that could have signaled either enjoyment or gas pains, and said, "Welcome back."

Suddenly Frank needed badly to visit the bathroom. "Mr. Chu," he said.

Mr. Chu snapped the smile off, quick as a binary switch, and let his eyes flick from Frank to Wang and back again. "*Colonel* Chu," he said, and slid the hard eyes back to Wang. He made a sympathetic clucking sound. "She's changed more than you have," he said. "Do you like her this way?"

"I like her fine," Frank said. His mouth was so dry his lips stuck to his teeth.

"Time is so cruel to women. How much do you weigh now, darling?" Chu asked Wang.

"Seventy-three kilos," Wang said in a whisper.

"And how much did you weigh when he left?"

"About forty kilos."

Chu nodded. "Seventy-three kilos. What does that come to in pounds, Mr. Accountant?"

"About one-sixty," Frank said.

"If I could sell her for two hundred dollars a pound," Chu said, "I could recoup what you stole. Unfortunately, she wasn't worth that much when she was beautiful. Now she's not worth anything. Enough fat to make a few dozen candles. Would you like some candles, Mr. Accountant? The nights are long now. You could read by her light."

"I can pay you back," Frank said.

The man holding the gun laughed, a sound rough enough to have bark on it.

"I don't believe you can," Chu said. He turned to face Wang, his whole body, not just his eyes. "Undress," he said.

Frank took a step forward, feeling heavy as iron, and the gun swiveled around to him. "Leave her alone," he said to Chu. He barely recognized his own voice. It sounded like something from the bottom of a well.

Wang was already taking off her coat.

"Don't do it," Frank said to her.

"She's smarter than you are," Chu said. "If I'd known how stupid you were, I'd never have hired you. I was paying for brains, discretion, and honesty. I didn't get any of them. The pants now," he said to Wang, and Wang untied the drawstring on her pants and let them drop to the floor. She hooked her thumbs under the elastic of her frayed underpants. "Come on, come on," he said sharply. "Are you out of practice? They used to come off quickly enough."

He had been speaking English, but now he switched to Mandarin for Wang's benefit. "You thought she was a virgin, didn't you? You whore-loving son of a pig. She'd been taking it in the ass for years, from me, from my partners, from anyone with a dollar and some grease. You could have bought her from me, you stupid Anglo, I'd have sold her to you for a hundred dollars, employee's discount. Tell him, Wang. Tell him about all your butt-pluggers."

"It's true," Wang said. She was naked, her arms at her sides, making no effort to hide her heavy breasts, her sagging belly. She was covered in gooseflesh. The sight of the broken arm brought the sting of tears to Frank's eyes, but the hopelessness in her face filled him with a heat so intense he thought it would blow the top of his head off, and he stepped toward Chu, barely seeing him through the sudden darkness in the room.

"Look at her," Chu said, his eyes locked on Frank's. "Old and fat, gorging at the people's trough. She's obviously expensive to feed now, and for what? What's she good for? I know a man not far from here who makes films of women with dogs and horses. He might use her, if no one else was available. I don't know about the dogs and horses, though. They're used to better."

Frank took another step. Each leg weighed a hundred pounds.

"Would you like those candles?" Chu asked pleasantly. "Or would you prefer the film? For me the candles would be easier." He shrugs. "But of course you'd use up the candles eventually, and you could keep the film forever. The mind's eye," he said. "It fades as we get older."

"I have the money," Frank said without hope.

"And the interest? Must be a couple of hundred thousand by now. For *that*? It must be true," he said to the other man, eyebrows lifted as though he'd just discovered something interesting. "Love *is* blind."

"I can get it. All of it. I can pay it back."

"*And you will,*" Chu said with enough venom to stun a snake. "But not that way. You'll do it our way, or she's a present to the dogs." He cleared his throat roughly and spit at Wang, hitting her midchest. Wang didn't even flinch. "Get dressed. Your ugliness offends me. And you," he snapped at the other man, "put the gun away. It's rude."

Chu watched the gun being holstered and then sank cross-legged to a sitting position. "Get those clothes on, whore, and make us some tea. And, Frank," he said, "sit." The smile returned, and for an instant he looked like someone's happy, benevolent grandfather. "We have so much to talk about. You've only just come back to us. I'm not sure you know how much the world has changed."

26

The Secret Map

Y ou became their white man," Rafferty says. It has dimmed outside, and Leung has gone out twice to make the circuit and come back in, wet enough to tell Rafferty it is raining again. The room is uncomfortably hot. Ming Li is stretched out on the opposite bed, an arm over her eyes, either asleep or pretending to be. Leung drips silently in the corner.

"Chu was right," Frank says. "The world *had* changed. Assholes were still on top. But now they were *Chinese* assholes, vindicated after all those years, finally fulfilling their destiny as the only true humans in a world of apes. They had power at last. The problem was that white people still had most of the money.

"China was Opening Up," he says, framing the last two words with his hands, as though they were on a marquee. "I always loved that phrase. It sounded like part of some master agenda, another damn five-year plan, when what really happened was one day they woke up and looked around and realized they'd built a new Great Wall, and all the money was on the other side. The *government* woke up, I mean. Colonel Chu and all the other Colonel Chus had always known where the money was, and they'd erected some amazing financial structures, cash siphons of staggering complexity, mostly through Hong Kong and a few million overseas Chinese who had thoughtlessly left their loved ones behind as collateral. Every time your mother bought dim sum at Choy's Café in Lancaster, Colonel Chu, or someone like Colonel Chu, pocketed a dime."

"Was that why you never ate there?"

"You know," Frank says wearily, "one of the three or four million things I regret is that I never got all dressed up and took your mother there. Not that it was the kind of place you dressed up for, but . . ." His voice trails off, his gaze on Poke.

"I know what you mean," Rafferty says.

Frank lets his eyes roam the room. "I didn't understand anything then, not how anything worked, or . . . I just knew that it hurt to eat Chinese food. It might as well have been glass. Even the smell of it made me hate myself. I read the papers every day. I knew what was happening there. You have to understand, Poke, that none of it made me love your mother any less. I loved her every day I was with her. I still love her."

After a moment Poke says, "Fine."

Frank lowers his head, looking down at his lap. "Thanks," he says.

"China was opening up," Poke prompts, more at ease with the past.

"They needed me. Well, they needed somebody, and I was there, and they knew I'd do anything to protect Wang. They could have told me to walk on coals, and I would have asked which shoe to take off first. But they didn't want me to walk on coals. It was my face they needed. They knew that white people were more comfortable dealing with white people. I was the front."

"And this involved what?"

"A lot of things. *Business,* you know? If a business deal wasn't forthcoming, we pushed it along. 'Facilitated it,' Colonel Chu would say. Drugs, girls, boys, espionage frames, if that's what was needed. Take some rough-and-tumble tire executive from . . . oh, I don't know . . . Akron, Ohio, some bush leaguer with a crew cut and a calculator who's holding out for a deal breaker, and put him in a room with a willing girl or boy. Let the tape roll. Get his hotel to put the movie on next time he turns on the TV. Or give him a bunch of papers in Chinese that turn out to be specs for some outdated missile system and point the cops, whom you own, at him. Akron's a long way off, and the contracts are in the next room. The deal breakers turn out to be not so serious after all, and suddenly you own part of a tire factory."

"In the meantime, though," Rafferty says, "Mr. Akron blames you. Word's got to get around, got to damage your usefulness."

"Me?" Frank grabs a handful of peanuts and drops a couple into his mouth. "I had no idea. I do Claude Rains: I'm shocked—*shocked*—to learn about it. Tell me everything, I say, and I'll see what I can do. Give me the details, and we'll go to court and break the contract. Well, of course, he's not about to give me the details, just like he's not about to go back to the office and say, 'Hey, you know that factory we just built? If I'd kept my pants on, it'd be in Malaysia.'"

Rafferty relaxes slightly. It's not as bad as he'd feared. Corruption is old news in Asia, reflexive as breathing. "But come on, the factory delivers, right? These guys are smart enough to make sure the bottom line's okay, no matter how it got built."

"Sure," Frank says listlessly. "Lots of money left over even after the skim."

"And nobody got killed."

A pause. "No." Frank dumps the peanuts back into the saucer. "Not in a case like that."

Rafferty gets up—maybe too quickly, feeling a little light-headed—and goes to the window, looks down on a wet and shining street, courtesy of yet another instant rainstorm. A car plows past, its headlights bright cones of rain against the cloud-seeded gloom of the day. *The world going on,* he thinks. To Frank he says, "I'm not sure I want to know any more."

"That's most of it." Poke's father sounds drained. "Just bear with me for a minute more."

"Why not?" Poke says. "It's raining anyway."

"Over the next few years, I learned a lot." Frank folds his hands, leans back against the wall, and closes his eyes. He swallows noisily and clears his throat. Rafferty realizes he has clenched his own fists, and he relaxes them, one shoulder pressed against the cool glass of the window, wishing he could melt through it, out of the room and back into his life.

"After ten or twelve years, I had a set of skills that I hadn't known anyone possessed and a map of China in my head that didn't look like anything on paper. Take any country, Poke, and on top of the paper map you can put another map, a map of how the authority flows and where the obligations are, a map of hidden paths and corners. Blind alleys. The feng shui of power. The secret map, under the radar. One that nobody else has.

"So I began my own map. Each project I took on, I added to that map. I built it up a province, a city at a time. Other countries, every once in a while. A relationship, a promise, a pressure point. A betrayal here, a broken heart there. Somebody's in love, somebody owes somebody money, somebody's got a secret, somebody wants revenge. Revenge is always a good one—you can open a lot of doors when somebody wants revenge. The Chinese are superlative haters. They honed the skill during hundreds of years of being treated like shit. I found fulcrums and figured out how much pressure it would take to use them."

Frank nods, apparently satisfied with the way the story is unfolding. "By then they had some fulcrums of their own. Ming Li had been born, which relaxed Colonel Chu considerably. He was having trouble believing that I still cared about Wang. But with a baby, he knew he had me. Like a lot of Chinese, he believes that the bond of fatherhood is sacred, unbreakable. What he didn't know was that I had plans for Ming Li."

"Major-league baseball?" Rafferty asks.

"Do you mind if we discuss you in the third person, Ming Li?" Frank asks.

"Why not?" She doesn't stir.

Rafferty has thought she was asleep. "What kind of plans?"

Frank doesn't open his eyes. "How many windows in this room, Ming Li?"

"Three." She still has her arm over her face.

"How many light fixtures, and where?"

"Ceiling, console, bathroom. Number four is just outside the door in the hallway."

"Door open out or in?"

"In. Hinges on the left, if you're facing it from inside the room. The top hinge pin is high in the bracket, easy to get a knife under."

"What color are the bathroom towels?"

"The color of piss, but they used to be bright yellow. They say 'His' and 'His.'"

Rafferty asks, "How many boys were in the lobby when we came in?"

"Six. Two of them wore lipstick. One of the pretty boys and one of the butches were talking on cell phones. One of the butches had a bleached buzz cut and a port-wine birthmark on his cheek." She rolls over onto her side, facing him, her head resting on her arm. "Left cheek," she adds. She pokes her tongue into her cheek to show where it was.

"We started when she was two," Frank says. "She was drawing maps by the time she was six. At seven she followed me across town without my knowing it."

"Not easy," Leung says.

"Not that hard," Ming Li says, grinning.

"And the point was . . . ?" Rafferty asks.

"Anything that was on my map that wasn't on theirs was leverage. Ming Li was on my map. Leung was on my map."

Frank absently checks his watch. "So Ming Li was a double-edged sword, although Chu didn't know it. He didn't know he'd given me Leung either. Chu assigned Leung to keep an eye on me for an operation in Pailin, in Cambodia. Industrial rubies, smuggled as costume jewelry, the biggest, ugliest stuff you ever saw. Millions of dollars' worth, set into crud too vulgar for Imelda Marcos. No customs officer in his right mind would think it was real. Like me, Leung was under a certain amount of pressure."

"Sister," Leung says. "Chu never threatened her, just sent her chocolates on her birthday every year. So I'd know that he could get to her whenever he wanted to."

"And Leung was better than I was," Frank says. "So I learned from him, and then I turned it around, and when he called Chu to report in, I was there."

"With a gun," Leung adds. "We had a candid exchange of views."

"And came to an understanding. That was two years ago. We took our time, because you don't hurry with these boys. Five days ago Leung's sister fell off the map, went down the rabbit hole. Caused no end of consternation on Colonel Chu's end of the phone. I helped out as best I could, sent his guys to three or four plausible places, and while the hounds were hunting, I made Wang disappear."

"This isn't about that," Rafferty says. He is so tired he can barely stand upright. "This isn't just an escape. It's bigger than that."

"He's not slow after all," Ming Li says.

Frank's eyes are on Poke, the fleck of gold in the left one catching the light. "You're right, Poke. It is. I did something before I closed up shop in China. I stole the rest of Colonel Chu's life."

"THIS IS GREAT," Rafferty says. He is still at the window and feels as though he has been there for hours. "You took something that could have been business—nasty, dirty business, but *business*—and you turned it personal."

"Afraid so." Frank shells another peanut, and Rafferty suddenly feels beneath his bare feet the sharp edges of peanut shells, perpetually scattered over the living-room carpet in Lancaster. Remembers his mother grumbling behind the vacuum.

"Essentially, that makes me fair game. My family and me."

"You were always fair game. Chu isn't someone who plays by rules. This is a guy who would shoot a hotel telephone operator who got his wake-up call wrong."

"In case you think Frank is just being vivid," Ming Li says, "he's not."

"So you . . . what? You tried to kill him? Obviously, you missed. But this means no negotiation, doesn't it? One of you is going to have to die."

Frank smooths his long, thinning strands of hair. "I didn't say I tried to kill him, Poke. I said I took the rest of his life."

Rafferty brings up his hand and massages his eyes. His chest feels uncomfortably dense, as though his lungs are full of water. "The rest of . . ." The phrase means nothing, but a word pops into his mind, and he looks at his father. "What box?"

"Ah," Frank says. He looks at Ming Li.

"You said Chu wouldn't want anyone to know about the box. What box?"

"Good for you," Frank says. "Actually, there is probably some room for negotiation, enough at least to get him within range."

"Of what?"

"A really good gun." Frank leans down and reaches beneath the bed, and when he comes back up, there is a leather box in his hand, about the size of three hardcover books in a stack. It has a small clasp on the front, and Frank twists it open and lifts the lid. "Pailin," he says.

Rafferty crosses to the bed, leans forward, and sees rubies, maybe three or four hundred of them, anywhere from half a carat to two or three carats. They shine under the fluorescents like frozen blood.

"They're flawless," Frank says. "Most rubies are occluded, did you know that? They've got clouds of opaque mineral material in them. Very few are clear enough to cut into big stones. That's why they're so expensive. Chu's been sifting through the Pailin take for decades to fill this box. It was part of his getaway stash, just in case."

"Worth how much?" Rafferty asks. He can't take his eyes off them.

Frank looks down at them regretfully. "Well, if you have the luxury of selling them one at a time, through legitimate channels, maybe three million. The way I'll have to do it, I figure I'll get one."

"Is this about three million dollars, or is it about face?"

"Both. And something else. Dig down through the rubies. All the way to the bottom."

Rafferty sits and does as he's told, the rubies cold and smooth on his skin. At the bottom of the box, he feels paper. A large envelope. He works it out carefully, not wanting to spill any of the rubies from the box.

"Open it."

The envelope is half an inch thick. He opens the flap and pours the contents onto the bed. He sees papers, folded in thirds, and an American passport. When he opens the passport, he sees a photo of an old man with a large mole on his cheek and the name IRWIN LEE. Slipped into the passport are a Virginia driver's license in the same name, and a Social Security card.

"What the hell?"

"Look at the other papers."

The deed to a house in Richmond, Virginia, also in the name of Irwin Lee. Credit-card statements, some of them showing activity less than a month old. Irwin Lee is a vigorous consumer. Rafferty says, "This is a whole life."

"It's Chu's future," Frank says. "He's had someone being Irwin Lee for almost fifteen years. Creating a space for Chu to slip into, like a piece in a jigsaw puzzle."

"It's his retirement plan?" Rafferty asks.

"He's more than seventy," Frank says. "There's a generation behind him that's getting impatient. They're entrepreneurs, Poke, like so many people in China today. They're tired of the old ways and the old men who won't let go of them. If Chu doesn't make a move of some kind, he's going to get the ax, and that's probably not a figure of speech."

"Jesus," Rafferty said. "Why didn't you just kill him?"

Frank is silent, but Ming Li says, "Because we wanted him to suffer first."

"You have to understand, Poke," Frank says. "We never thought he'd come here. We were only going to be in Bangkok long enough to sell the rubies, and then we were going to disappear off the face of the earth."

Poke says, "But I talked to Arnold."

"Yeah," Frank says. "And Arnold was a stumblebum."

"Let's assume you can still get out of here. Do you actually know somebody who has a million on hand to pay for a box of rocks?"

"Sure," Frank says. "The North Koreans. Anything that's discounted right now, anything they can turn around—"

Rafferty slices the air with the edge of his hand, and Frank stops in mid-word. "How do you know the North Koreans?"

"My shop, so to speak," Frank says, as though it were obvious. "And shops like my shop. They're among the very few people in the world who'll do business with the North Koreans."

Rafferty reaches out, grabs a handful of his father's peanuts, and gets settled. He smiles at Ming Li, who gives him a puzzled smile in return. "Do tell," he says.

27

The Snoop

R ubies, he thinks.

Even the word has a shimmer around it. Just behind the shimmer, he can see something, something that looks a little bit like daylight. He has no idea how to get to it yet. But he *does* know what he has to do: He has to leave it alone for a while, close the door on it, and let it grow unobserved. He either will or won't have it—whatever it is—when he needs it.

Half an hour after Frank opened the box that contains the rest of Chu's life, Ming Li and Leung led Rafferty out into the rain and through a dizzyingly complicated route that eventually took them, unobserved as far as any of them could tell, to Sukhumvit. If there was a single back alley that they missed, Rafferty doesn't know about it.

It is now almost three o'clock. Since leaving the Home Away from Home, Rafferty has made the stop he planned the previous day and has broken at least three laws in at least two countries. The tote bag he filled at the apartment is marginally lighter. He has reached a new and previously unimaginable level of exhaustion and is considering calling

Arthit to ask for help getting to a bed when his phone rings. He pulls it out, checks the caller ID, and opens it.

"Time to go snoop on your Agent Elson," Arthit says. "He's just gone to eat something. The Erawan Hotel, and make it quick."

"On the way." Rafferty hails a cab, thinking, *It's a sign. The rain stopped.*

"THE ROOMS ON either side?" Arthit demands.

The assistant manager who has been delegated to let them in says, "What about them?"

"Both occupied?"

"Room 134 is," the assistant manager says. A little finger brushes his lower lip. He's tall, slender, and too handsome for his own spiritual good, and he knows it. He has a habit of touching his face as though he wants to make sure it's still there. The fingers of his other hand are curled elegantly around a slender cell phone, which he checks between trips to his face.

The phone makes Rafferty nervous.

Arthit wiggles his fingers for attention. "And 138? On the other side?"

The assistant manager massages the tip of his chin with a fingernail that's been coated in clear polish. Both the finger and the chin make Rafferty want to hit him, or maybe he's just tired. "It's empty."

"Adjoining door?" Arthit asks.

"Yes, of course. So we can open it into a suite."

"We'll take the suite," Arthit says. "Unlock the door to 138. Then let us into 136 through the adjoining door."

If he touches his face again, Rafferty thinks, *I'll belt him.* Now, though, the man's fingers stop at the knot in his tie, which he adjusts. He takes his time, weighing the demand. He's been told to open one room, not two. On the other hand, Arthit has his cop face on. "Fine," he says at last. He floats down the hall to 138 and opens the door, politely stepping aside.

"You first," Arthit says. "You've got another door to open for us."

Rafferty says, "And we wouldn't want to get between you and the mirror." Arthit looks down at his shoes.

Inside, the man unlocks the connecting door to 136 and waits.

"You can go," Arthit says. "We'll let you know when we're done."

A reluctant nod, and the man leaves. Rafferty watches to make sure his shoes actually touch the carpet. Arthit goes into Elson's room.

"What was all that with the phone?" Rafferty asks, following Arthit.

"Probably waiting for a call from MTV," Arthit says. "Or the Miss Universe Pageant."

Elson's room is immaculate and dim, the curtains drawn against the sun. Rafferty opens them a few inches. The room still seems clean. "What are we searching for?"

"An edge," Arthit says. "Doesn't have to be a sharp one." He goes to the laptop on the desk and powers it on. "You check the suitcase."

The suitcase is open, centered on the bed nearest the window. Elson has not bothered to unpack, and Rafferty immediately sees why.

"Jesus," he says to Arthit, "this guy safety-pins his socks together." He pulls out a pair. "What do you think, he's afraid they'll have a fight and separate or something?" There are six pairs of socks, each pair pinned, identical black calf huggers so new that the writing hasn't been laundered off the bottom. Below the socks are two narrow black ties, folded precisely into thirds. Then several sheets of dry-cleaning film, each enclosing an immaculate white shirt.

"Shit," Arthit says from the desk. "He's got a password program."

"Figures." Rafferty lifts the shirts to check beneath them. "This goes beyond neat. This is diseased." He runs his hands over the lining of the suitcase, not expecting anything fancy: Elson will have been walked through Thai customs as though he were radioactive. The Secret Service, he's pretty sure, doesn't get searched much. At the bottom of the suitcase is an envelope and a pair of shoes, black lace-ups similar to the ones the agent wore the night he barged into Rafferty's apartment. Rafferty removes the envelope and the shoes. He puts the envelope aside and experimentally inserts his fingers into a shoe. He hits something hard and cold and oddly slick. He slides it out, makes a face, and then looks in the other shoe.

"What do you think?" he says to Arthit. "An edge?"

Arthit closes the laptop and comes to take a look. Rafferty is holding a deck of condoms, at least twenty of them, and an economy-size tube of lube.

"If he went to the trouble of hiding them," Arthit says, "it's an edge. What's in the envelope?"

The envelope isn't sealed. The flap has just been tucked, very neatly, into the opening. Rafferty worries it open, intentionally wrinkling it a little. "Credit-card receipts," he says. "Mr. Organized, tracking his expenses." He picks one at random and opens it. "The Lilac," he says. "On the back he's written *'Dinner with Thai police liaisons.'*"

"Read me another," Arthit says. He looks like he's on the verge of a grin.

"Wattana Enterprises," Rafferty reads. "The note is *'Souvenirs.'*"

"Come on, Poke," Arthit says. "I know you haven't slept, but still. The Lilac. *Wattana.*"

"Wattana," Rafferty says. "Isn't he that guy who ran for the senate a year back? The . . . the— Oh, good Lord, I *must* be tired. The massage-parlor king."

"And the Lilac," Arthit says, "is a no-hands restaurant. You know the drill: You're seated between two girls and you're not allowed to use your hands to eat anything while they feed you, but you can do anything else with your hands that might occur to you."

"They're on his government-issued credit card," Rafferty says.

Arthit says, "There's your edge."

Rafferty puts everything back into the suitcase except the condoms, the credit-card receipts, and the lube, then goes to the desk. He takes a hotel pen and writes a single word, all caps in large print, on a sheet of stationery, then drops it dead center on top of the stuff in the suitcase. He places the condoms on one side, the lube on the other, and the envelope beneath, so they frame the word.

The word is *"HI!"*

28

As Though He's Been Invited

About the same time Rafferty is searching Elson's suitcase, Arthit's wife, Noi, is awakened, as she is so often these days, by the pain of her nerves burning away as multiple sclerosis licks at the sheathing tissue that covers them. She has come to think of the disease as a fire in her body, sometimes banked and sometimes burning out of control, whipped up by something she does not understand. When the disease is raging, especially late at night, it seems there is a third person in the room with her and Arthit, someone who knows how to fan the flames just by staring at her. She feels his emotionless, clinical gaze through the darkness at times when Arthit is sleeping beside her, and on those nights she chews on the corner of her pillowcase to keep from moaning. Noi does not want Arthit to know how fierce the pain has become.

The room is full of light. Of course, it is afternoon. Arthit is off with Poke, making the world—as he likes to say—a more boring place. Her guests will probably be asleep, Rose on the couch and Miaow in the spare bedroom, the one she and Arthit thought would be the nursery until the disease chose their door from all the doors on the block and knocked.

There is a child in the house, she thinks.

She stretches experimentally, feeling the coals burning in her elbows and fingers—not too bad, a thin layer of ash on them—and explores the weakness in her legs. She has learned in the past few months to test her legs one at a time while she is still in bed, putting one foot atop the other and pushing down, before she tries to stand. On the days when she knows she will be too unsteady to stay upright, she pretends to sleep until Arthit has left the house and then reaches under the mattress on her side of the bed for the aluminum cane he has never seen.

She *hopes* he has never seen it.

Lately it seems to her that they are playing two different games with similar rules. Noi does not tell Arthit about the progress of the disease because she does not want to burden him. Arthit pretends not to see it because he does not want to injure her pride. So the two of them, each with the other in mind, ignore the thing that has come to occupy the central place in their lives, filling that place with silence.

The place they thought a child would fill.

As she pushes back the covers, she realizes she awoke earlier, dragged up from sleep briefly and then allowed to sink again. It seems to her that the figure who fans the fire was standing at the foot of the bed, looking down at her. The image creates a cold ball of dread in her belly.

Her legs tremble beneath her, but hold, as she bends over the foot of the bed to pick up the robe Arthit bought her for no reason, not even her birthday. She hates the color, a sort of faded, pickled, unripe-banana green, but loves the idea of Arthit shopping for her. She can see those thick fingers picking up one flimsy garment after another as he stands stiff and conspicuously uncomfortable in his uniform in some department store, surrounded by women but unwilling to flee until he finds the one he likes, the one that makes her look as yellow as a wax candle. She slides her arms into the sleeves, pausing as she realizes she is standing exactly where the figure stood the first time she opened her eyes. The dread in her belly solidifies into a gelatinous mass.

Pushing it aside with an enormous effort, Noi limps into the hall. No cane today, not in front of her guests. The thought of the child, Miaow, carries her along.

The door to the spare room is ajar. Noi pushes it open a few inches to find Rose sitting on the bed looking at her, with Miaow asleep at her side, the child's head pillowed on Rose's arm. Even in sleep Miaow looks as if she's in motion; her knees are drawn up like someone doing a cannonball into a swimming pool, and her mouth is half open. Rose smiles and lifts a finger to her lips, then eases her arm out from beneath Miaow. Miaow shifts and emits a syllable of complaint. Rose holds perfectly still until the child seems to be asleep again.

The kitchen is as warm as a hive, rich with the honey-colored afternoon light that slants through the windows and fragrant from the small pots of basil and rosemary Noi grows on the sill. Rose's hair is a glorious tangle that Noi briefly envies and then forgets, concentrating on moving smoothly. "Coffee or tea?"

Rose gives her a sleepy smile. "Do you have Nescafé?"

"Of course." Noi slides to the cabinet above the counter, lifting her feet as little as possible—it is the moment when they come back into contact with the floor that gives her the most trouble. She tries to make it look like a preference, perhaps a joke, but she can feel Rose's eyes on her.

"Poke hates Nescafé," Rose says. "It's enough to drive me away."

"Arthit drinks it by the quart. Hot, cold, lukewarm. He sprinkles it on ice cream." She unscrews the lid of the jar, smaller and lighter than the ones she used to buy, more expensive but easier to handle. "Arthit's not happy unless he's nervous."

"Poke truly loves Arthit," Rose says, stretching long arms. "It's a good thing I'm not jealous. Or very jealous anyway."

"Life blesses you when you least expect it." Noi puts the kettle on the burner and listens for the little *poof* as it ignites; she has a deep-seated dread of the kitchen filling with gas. "Arthit was certain he was through making friends. One thing I don't understand is why it gets more difficult to make friends as you get older. Remember how many friends you used to have?"

"Thousands," Rose says. "You said hi to somebody and they were glued to you. And it was impossible to be nosy then. Everybody *wanted* you to know everything. Nobody had a subconscious. And then one day everybody turned into a box of secrets."

"It's not that they got worse," Noi says. She leans against the stove, feeling the comfortable warmth at her back. "Good people get better, I think, and bad people were already bad. It's just that people close themselves up. I think of young people as standing like this"—she opens her arms—"and older people like *this*"—she crosses her arms protectively across her chest.

"Or this," Rose says, shielding her privates. Noi laughs.

"It's one reason I'm grateful for this illness," Noi says. "It brought Poke and Arthit together." Arthit had originally requested an interview with Rafferty when he learned Poke was writing the book that eventually became *Looking for Trouble in Thailand.* He went out and bought one of the earlier books in the series, *Looking for Trouble in the Philippines,* to satisfy himself that the new book wouldn't fall into the genre of self-improvement for pedophiles, and the two of them had met for the first time over an unreasonable number of Singha beers. During the course of their mutual decline into inebriation, Arthit had told Poke about Noi's disease, then in its earliest stages, and Rafferty had put him into contact with a doctor in Japan who was working on a promising new treatment. The treatment hadn't worked, but the friendship had.

"He talked about Arthit for days," Rose says. He had talked about Noi, too, but Rose does not say this. Poke had pitied Noi then, something that became unthinkable to Rose after the two women met. Noi is too strong to pity.

Noi feels a draft on the back of her neck, something that happens with increasing frequency these days. Some trick of the nerves, yet another way they've found to call attention to themselves, the pigs. She turns back to the kettle, but the water is not boiling yet.

"You said *one* of the things you were grateful for," Rose says. "What are the others?"

"It gave me notice," Noi says, facing her again. "If it had been faster, I never would have been able to have told Arthit, to have *shown* Arthit, the way I feel about him. It would have been terrible to be . . . I don't know, snatched away without the time I've been given to make things right."

"You're tough," Rose observes.

"I've had practice." She starts to maneuver herself back around to the stove and stops, staring over at Rose. "What's that?"

"What?" Rose looks down at herself, and then back up at Noi. "Oh," she says, putting her hands below the table.

"Ho, *ho*," Noi says. "Is this something a friend would tell a friend about?"

Rose brings her hands back up, turning the ring self-consciously. It still feels thick on her finger. "There hasn't been time. It only happened two nights ago."

"And you said . . . ?"

"Oh, well. This time I didn't have the heart to say no. He was *terrified*. He'd had it in his pocket for hours, patting it every fifteen seconds like he was hoping it had disappeared. I had to take pity on him. As Miaow says, he tries so hard."

"They don't deserve us," Noi says. "Except when they do."

"The first time I knew he was going to ask, I did everything I could to chase him away, short of shooting him," Rose says. "I was awful. I talked for *hours*. I trotted out my mother and my father, their money problems, my infinite number of younger sisters, my past, other men—anything I could think of to scare him off. It's no wonder he looked so frightened."

"Has it changed the way you feel?"

Without thinking about it, Rose runs her fingers over the three stones. "The ring is us," she says. "It's a picture of us, Poke's way of trying to make the three of us permanent. It makes me feel—I guess the word is 'fierce.' It makes me believe I'd do anything to protect him and Miaow." She does not add what she thinks, which is, *The way you protect Arthit.*

"We all know that children need protection," Noi says, "but we're supposed to keep it a secret that men do." She feels the draft again and rubs her neck. "Well," she says, "come here."

Noi opens her arms, and Rose gets up and embraces her. Noi's nose barely comes to her breastbone, but the heat flows from her in waves, and Rose's breath catches, and she suddenly realizes she is crying.

"It's not so terrible," Noi says, patting her. And then she starts to laugh, and the laugh turns into a sob, and the two women stand there hugging each other and weeping until Noi says, "This is silly," and dries her eyes on the lapel of the awful green robe. "What a pair," she says, turning back to the stove. "Do you like it strong?"

"Strong enough to dissolve the cup," Rose says. "Has Poke said anything to Arthit?"

"If Arthit knows, he hasn't said a word to me. I've barely seen him since this morning," Noi adds, pouring.

"I thought maybe he just told you." Rose feels a vague disappointment and realizes she should know better.

"*Just* told me? When?" Noi stirs the cup, which contains a liquid black enough to be a petroleum derivative.

"Fifteen, twenty minutes ago. When he came home."

Noi turns to her and hands her the cup, which Rose half drains. "Arthit came home?"

"I didn't see him, but I heard him as I was waking up. He was walking in the hall."

Noi feels a prickling low in her back and then, again, the draft on her neck, and she turns to look across the kitchen at the back door. It is ajar.

Suddenly the heat inside her is gone, and she is freezing. She goes to the door and tries to pull it closed.

Instead it is pulled outward.

The man standing there—tall, thin, with an enormous mole on his cheek—gives her a grandfatherly smile and comes in as though he's been invited.

MIAOW HAS BEEN curled up in bed, listening to the women talking. Their voices give her a warm, comfortable feeling, softer than the quilt Rose threw over her. Then, abruptly, the talk stops. She turns her head to the open door and hears something new: quick movement, a gasp, a man's voice.

It takes her a moment to get off the bed, slowly enough for it not to creak, and to throw the quilt over it. She slips through the door and tiptoes down the hall. The hallway is dim, but the kitchen is a warm, buttery yellow, and she can see them.

Four men. Two of them holding Noi. And then Rose comes into sight, at a run, and grabs a teapot from the stove and hurls it at the nearest man. Hot water—Miaow can see it steam—arcs from the pot and splashes on the man as the teapot hits him in the chest, and the man cries out. Suddenly there are guns, and Rose is backing away.

Miaow steps back. No one has looked toward her. Moving slowly, afraid to take her eyes off them, she reaches the room where she slept, where she thinks her cell phone might be.

But when she looks, it's not there.

She hears a burst of protest from Rose, followed by a slap and then silence. Miaow is looking everywhere in the room for something, anything, she can use as a weapon, and then she hears voices again. The men are moving through the house now, talking in low voices. The house is not big; it's only a matter of moments before they find her. The fear she feels is a familiar companion from her years on the street, the same fear she felt in back alleys when she was hiding from one of the men who liked to hurt children.

The important thing, she knows, is to think clearly.

They are in the living room now. One man is giving orders. He mentions a place that Miaow knows, because Rafferty took her there, and Miaow makes herself memorize the name, afraid the fear will chase it out of her mind. If they are in the living room, how much time does she have? Her mental map of the house is vague. She was very drowsy when they carried her in. She is sure, though, there are only one or two rooms to go. She forces herself to continue to survey the room without rushing, looking for anything that might be useful. On the bookshelf, she sees it. It's not a weapon, but she can use it.

A children's book, full of bright animals and easy words in big print, the kind of thing Rafferty used to buy her. She grabs it, snatches a pen from the desk, and creeps into the closet. The closet will give her an extra minute.

She has to leave something for Poke. It can't be anything the men can read.

If only she had her phone.

The idea sweeps over her. She closes her eyes for a moment, trying to visualize. As she hears them coming nearer, she rips a page out of the book and begins to write, just numbers. She writes them fast, almost without thinking.

By the time they open the closet door and she looks up at them, she has shoved the book and the pen into the far corner of the closet and folded the note into a tight square in her palm. There are two of them.

Miaow keeps her face calm. At least she can deny them the satisfaction of her fear.

The tall man with the mole says something to the fat man behind him, and the fat man bends down and picks her up as though she were a bagful of happybirthday presents, slinging her over his shoulder with her arms trailing down his back.

The man with the mole is walking ahead of them, so he can't see. Miaow holds her breath and drops the square of paper.

29

Asterisks Would Take Too Long

S ounds to me like you've got a partner," Arthit is saying. He is a terrible driver even when he's paying attention. When he drives and talks at the same time, Rafferty would generally prefer to be running alongside the car.

The wheels stray blithely over the centerline in the road.

"Forget it," Rafferty says, looking for the inevitable oncoming truck. "You've got to trust a partner."

"You're rigid," Arthit says. "I think it's an American trait."

"Would you like it if I suddenly started to list Thai traits?"

"But listen to yourself." Arthit launches into a left turn from the right-hand lane, and Rafferty hears a peeved little "Hallelujah Chorus" of brakes and horns behind them. "You haven't seen the man in more than twenty years. He could be completely different by now, all the way to his core. And you're behaving like he's been gone fifteen minutes, like he just got back from a trip to the store. Like he hasn't even changed his shirt."

"What he's told me about how he spent that twenty years isn't very reassuring."

"That's exactly why he can help you," Arthit says. He accelerates out of sheer enthusiasm. "He's right. The triads and the North Koreans do business. When they're not trying to kill each other. Who knows? Maybe this is a chance for you to put your relationship back together."

"I can't tell you how tired I am of all this family counseling. I've gotten along without him for more than half of my life. I'm used to it. It's not like there's a gaping hole with 'Pop' written on it. Anyway, he's a crook."

"A crook," Arthit says, "is just what you need. Maybe it's fate."

"I'm not passive enough to have a fate. And I think we've got the counterfeiting thing under control."

"The best-laid plans," Arthit says.

Rafferty settles back in his seat and closes his eyes. "Thanks for the vote of confidence."

"You'll be more fun when you've slept." Arthit makes a second left, onto his street this time, scraping the curb as he always does.

"Did I used to be fun?" Rafferty asks.

"Within reason," Arthit says. "Considering that you're not Thai. But I guess the Filipinos know how to enjoy—" He breaks off and slows the car.

"What?" Rafferty asks, and then follows his friend's eyes.

The front door to Arthit's house is standing wide open.

RAFFERTY'S FIRST PASS through the house is taken at a dead run, slamming into furniture and bursting into and out of rooms in the hope that somebody will be in them, a panicked circuit that brings him back to the living room and onto the couch, although he has no memory of having sat down. He draws four or five deep breaths to center himself, focuses on his heartbeat until it drops into double digits per minute, and decides to begin again. No one he loves, no one Arthit loves, is here, but there must be *something*.

He hears Arthit somewhere, banging doors open and closed.

The living room reflects Noi's knack for graceful order. Nothing is out of place other than the canvas director's chair he knocked over when he ran through the first time. If there was a struggle, resistance of any kind, it didn't take place here.

Pushing himself to his feet, he moves down the hallway, his sneakers squeaking on the gleaming hardwood, and into the kitchen. Arthit stands in the doorway, looking at the table. Rafferty can't meet his eyes. A cup of coffee, Nescafé from the thick dregs of pitch in the bottom of one of them, sits on one edge of the table, off center in its saucer. A spill of sugar surrounding the cup marks the spot as Rose's. She has a leaden hand with the sugar, adding it in heaps and scattering it like confetti. Another cup, as yet unfilled with water, is on the stove. Coffee measured, water not poured. And then he sees the teapot on the floor, surrounded by water. An unwelcome interruption of some sort.

He can't make himself focus on what that could have been.

The kitchen door—open, as the front had been—leads to the back garden, Noi's pride before the disease began to make movement painful. Rafferty stands in the doorframe, his shadow stretching in front of him all the way to the stone-defined border, where dead begonias and zinnias silently signal neglect. Few things are sadder to Rafferty than a dying garden, and this one prompts a surge of the purest grief. He can still see it as a wash of bloom. Noi harvested flowers by the armload whenever he and Rose had dinner with them; he vividly remembers craning at the three of them over the explosion of color in the middle of the table.

Arthit comes up behind him and, after a moment, puts a hand on his shoulder.

Rafferty reaches up and pats the hand and then steps back inside, and Arthit closes the door and locks it automatically. Then he stops moving, looking down at what he has just done. When his face comes up to Rafferty's, the expression on it is almost unbearable.

"The rest of the house," Rafferty says. It is the first time either of them has spoken. "Let's do it together."

"Right," Arthit says. "Together."

The kitchen and breakfast area run the width of the house. The door on the right leads to the dining room, and the corridor on the left will take them back down the hallway to the bedrooms before it ends in the living room. They check the dining room from the doorway, Arthit snapping on the light. Rafferty can smell the lemon polish Noi uses on the table even now, when she and Arthit eat most of their meals in the kitchen to save her steps.

The chairs are pulled neatly up to the table as though awaiting tardy guests. An overly formal bouquet of silk flowers, a melancholy replacement for the loose arrangements of bloom and scent of a year ago, sits dead center on the table's mirror-smooth surface. A spill of mail is the only spontaneous thing in the room. Everything else seems to be in place, as it was in the living room, and Rafferty feels his spirits lift slightly. He can't imagine Rose allowing anyone to take her—and especially Miaow—out of the house without a mammoth struggle. There should be damage everywhere. He has an adrenaline-imprinted memory of the evening in the King's Castle Bar when she poleaxed a six-foot Aussie. Beer-blitzed, the Aussie had yanked the buttons off the blouse of an excruciatingly shy new barmaid, a tiny, wide-eyed girl just arrived from the northeast. The Aussie had taken a table and two stools down with him on his way to the floor and landed flat on his back with his eyes rolling back like fruit salad in a slot machine.

"They would have put up more of a fight," Rafferty says.

"If they could," Arthit says.

The two of them stand there, listening to what they've just said. Rafferty says, "Arthit. I'm so sorry."

Arthit doesn't even glance at him. "We haven't got time for that. Let's go." They take another look at the living room, Rafferty pausing to put the director's chair upright, and then the master bedroom. Noi and Arthit's bed is rumpled on one side: Noi's afternoon nap, Rafferty guesses. The covers have been folded back neatly. The sheets have the sharp, topographical creases that come with sweat, although the room is cool. To Rafferty the sheets are a map of pain. He sees it in the sheets, he has seen it in the halting rhythm of Noi's walk, he has seen it in Arthit's face. He has never seen it in Noi's.

But still: The room is neat. Against his better judgment, his hopes continue to rise.

He follows Arthit into the bathroom, spotless except for one long black hair in the tub, one of the dozens Rose sheds every day without any apparent effect. Her toothbrush stands in a glass next to Miaow's bright pink one. Just for the hell of it, Rafferty runs his thumb over the bristles. "Damp," he says. Arthit nods.

And then Arthit pushes open the door to the guest room, pushes it farther than Rafferty had, and they both see it: a small, tightly folded square of paper. Rafferty starts to bend down, but Arthit grunts and shoulders him out of the way, pulls a handkerchief from his pocket. Using the handkerchief, he picks up the square of paper, and the two of them go into the living room, where Arthit carefully opens it.

Rafferty could have told from six feet away that Miaow wrote it. The compulsively neat hand, the ruler-straight lines: She brings to writing the same obsessive control she puts into the part in her hair and the corners of the sheets when she makes a bed. For years she could control nothing in her life. Now she controls the things she can.

"What the hell?" Arthit says. Rafferty looks at it more closely.

It says:

4.61.32.62.41.82.62.74.61.63.53.32.52.53

"They're pairs," Arthit says. "Figure the periods are just separators." He slides the note, still protected by the handkerchief, a few inches in Rafferty's direction.

"Not the first number," Rafferty says. "It's alone."

The two of them sit close together, studying it, looking for patterns, trying—Rafferty realizes—not to think about anything else. Avoiding the beast in the room: the memory of Arnold Prettyman wired to a chair with half his face burned away.

"This *is* Miaow, right?" Arthit demands.

"No question."

Arthit holds the paper up to the light. A bright yellow illustration of a cheerful duck bleeds through from the other side. "Why periods?"

"They're fast," Rafferty says. "Anything else, like asterisks, would take too long."

"The numbers," Arthit says. He screws up his face. "Nothing higher than the eighties, nothing lower than the thirties."

"The second digits in the pairs," Rafferty says. "One, two, three, four."

"Nothing above four." The two of them sit, shoulders touching, heads bent over the note.

"She took the time," Arthit says. "She hid somewhere and took the time to do this." He looks up at Rafferty. "She was sleeping in the guest room. Maybe they came in through the kitchen. Noi and Rose are there, about to share a cup of coffee. Miaow is awake, down the hall. She hears something, sees something. She hides—" He blinks. "The front door," he says, his face suddenly soft. "If they came in through the kitchen, she could have gotten out through the front door. Maybe even gotten away. Instead she hid and wrote this."

"My girl," Rafferty says. The words, heavy and rough-edged, scrape the inside of his throat. "Brave as a fucking lion."

Arthit makes a sound that might be a sob. He makes it once. Then he wipes his face with a fist like a ham and says, "Next steps."

Poke takes another look at Miaow's note. "Arnold introduced me to a guy," he says. He pushes the picture of Prettyman from his mind. "He does codes."

"Get him." Arthit stands and crosses the room. Looks out the window at the front yard as though he half expects to see them there, laughing and waving at him. Pleased with their joke.

Rafferty pulls the phone from his pocket, and it rings. He snaps it open and pushes the "answer" key so hard the phone flips out of his hand, and he has to scrabble beneath the table to recover it. He picks it up and puts it to his ear.

"Mr. Rafferty," a man's voice says. "My name is Colonel Chu."

30

You Guys Are So Old

Y ou," Rafferty says. "He wants you."

Frank's eyes are lowered slightly. He sits, once again, on the edge of the bed, seemingly unaware of Arthit's glare. Given its intensity, Rafferty wouldn't be surprised to see two smoking holes appear in the center of his father's chest.

"Only me?" Frank says without even glancing up. He looks like a man listening to music from a distant room. "Not Leung? Not Ming Li?"

"Only you. Mr. One and Only."

"He doesn't know about Ming Li," Frank says. He turns his head slightly, but his eyes remain fixed on a point in the middle of the floor. "He knows she exists, but he doesn't know who she is, who I've trained her to be. He probably thinks she's with her mother. I'm surprised about Leung, though."

"I've been thinking about that myself," Rafferty says. Leung, sitting on a rickety wooden chair, gives him a startled glance and looks away.

"You can't give Frank to him," Ming Li says.

"And why not, exactly?" This is Arthit.

"He'll kill them all," Ming Li says as though it's the most obvious thing in the world. "Your wife and daughter." She looks over at Arthit. "*His* wife. Anything else would be too much work."

"I don't know," Frank says. "If you give me to him, I mean. He might not."

"He'll kill *you*," Ming Li says.

"Of course he will. But he might not kill the others."

Rafferty stares at his father. Ming Li follows his lead. A silence stretches around them.

"He's not stupid," Frank continues. He still has not looked at anyone in the room. "He just needs a reason to let them live."

"What kind of reason?" Arthit asks.

"Something to his benefit."

"Like what?" Ming Li says. "If he gets you, if he gets the box, he's got everything he wants."

"No," Frank says. "Not quite. He hasn't gotten out alive." He leans back against the wall. "Give me a minute."

Arthit pushes himself away from the wall, the shoulders of his uniform dark with the rain that has begun to fall again. He and Rafferty had gotten wet changing vehicles four times on their way to Khao San Road.

While Frank thinks, Ming Li asks, "You're supposed to call him?"

"Yeah. Let it ring a couple of times and hang up. Then, within thirty minutes, he'll call me back."

"He's on a cell, and we've got the number," Arthit says. "Wherever he is, he doesn't want to get triangulated. So he'll get as far as he can from his base and then call back."

Ming Li says, with an edge in her voice, "So, older brother, why didn't you just tell him where we are? If you don't care about Frank, what kept you from handing us to him?"

Rafferty and Arthit share a glance. "Because I agree with you. We deliver Frank and he kills them all."

"And that's the only reason?" Ming Li asks.

Rafferty shakes his head, deflecting the question. "So I told him I'd talked with Frank once but had no idea where he was and no reason in the world to want to find out. He thought that was funny."

"He has a keen sense of humor," Ming Li says. "People die laughing."

"Wrong word," Rafferty says. "He thought it was peculiar."

"Just to go on record," Arthit says, "I'm not certain he'll kill them. I'm only about sixty percent sure he would. If I could get that down to, say, forty percent, I'd hand Frank over like an old pair of gloves."

"*Guanxi,*" Frank finally says.

Arthit says, "What?"

"Connections. It's the thing he understands most in the world. For Chu, life is just *guanxi*. That's his map: who's got the power, who doesn't. He already knows you're a cop. What he doesn't know is that you're a massively connected cop, a cop with so much *guanxi* in Thailand that he has no chance of getting out of this country in one piece if anything happens to your wife."

"I'm not," Arthit says.

"Yes you are," Frank says. "You're connected with the other police forces—all of them—and with the military. With the administration. He set a twenty-four-hour deadline. He can't possibly learn otherwise in that amount of time. And, Poke, you tell him that the cops will turn this whole country upside down if anything happens to the hostages before the exchange."

They all listen to the implication in what Frank has said.

It is Ming Li who voices it. "So then what? We scare him into not killing them, and then we give you to him?"

"Maybe," Frank says. "One thing at a time."

"I wish to shit," Arthit says, looking like he'd enjoy kicking a hole in the wall, "that we could read Miaow's note."

Frank looks up at Arthit. "What note?"

Arthit hesitates, and Rafferty says, "Why not?" Arthit reaches into the breast pocket of his uniform and pulls out a photocopy of the note. Frank and Ming Li bend over it. For what seems like a long time, no one speaks. Ming Li is tracing the line of numbers with a graceful finger. Finally she says, "This is infuriating. It's *familiar,* somehow. Like an alphabet I used to be able to read." She squeezes her eyes closed. Rafferty can see them moving, left to right, behind her lids. "I don't know," she says, opening her eyes and flicking a corner of the note. "It feels so close. It feels like it's perfectly clear but there's a layer of dust over it, and I should just be able to blow it away and read it."

"It doesn't make any sense to me at all," Frank says. "What's in your frame of reference that's not in mine?"

"Hip-hop? MTV?" Ming Li looks at her father and shakes her head. "The Internet? Can't be Internet addresses, can't be chess moves."

"I'd recognize chess moves," Frank says. "If you're right, if you're close to being able to read this and I'm not, then it's something generational. Something you do, something you know, that I don't."

"I've been trying to reach a guy who works with codes," Rafferty says. "I could try to phone him again."

Ming Li looks up. Her eyes are slightly glassy. "Phone?" she says.

"Yeah," Rafferty says. "You know, small object, you push a bunch of buttons and put it to your ear. Then somebody says—"

"Oh, for heaven's sake," Ming Li says. She extends a hand. "Give it to me."

Rafferty passes her his phone. For a moment her eyes go back and forth between the phone and the note, and then her face splits into a wide grin.

"Your little girl is really smart," she says. "And you guys are so *old*." She looks at the phone again, her lips moving. "It's a text message," she says. "Somebody get me a pencil."

"ONCE YOU SEE the pairs, it's obvious," Ming Li says. "There are no three-digit numbers, there's no second number higher than four. I should have recognized it the minute I looked at it. Look. The first number in each pair is the number on the button. The second one is the number of times you push to get to the letter you want. So '6' is the six button, and if you push it one time, you get *M*. Push it twice, you get *N*. Three times is *O*." She points at the paper, isolating the one pair of numbers. "Here, the first time she writes it, it's '61,' so that's *M*."

They are all gathered around her. "And the '4,' the one that's not in a pair?" Rafferty asks.

"It's just what it looks like, silly," Ming Li says. "It's a four." She finishes writing, puts dashes between the words, and pushes the pad away so they can all see it.

It says:

4-men-guns-mole-kl

Tears spring to Rafferty's eyes. He turns his head to blink them away, but he can't do anything about the sudden catch in his throat. *Miaow.*

"You should be proud of yourself," Ming Li says. "That's some kid."

He swallows, hard. "I can't take the credit," he says.

"She was interrupted," Arthit says, bent over the pad.

Rafferty grabs a ragged breath. "She needed time to fold it, time to put it someplace, probably hide it in her hand, so she could drop it."

"KL," Ming Li says. Her eyebrows are contracted so tightly they almost meet.

"Look what she gives us," Arthit says. "Everything is important. A count, a description. She tells us there are guns. She's got *no time.* What else is that important?"

Rafferty says, "Destination."

Leung speaks for the first time. "Kuala Lumpur?"

Rafferty and Ming Li say, in unison, "No." Then Rafferty says, "He's here, obviously. And he'll stay here for this swap or whatever it's going to be."

"It *has* to be a destination," Frank says. "Maybe . . ." His voice trails off.

"I'm not even sure Miaow knows Kuala Lumpur is two words," Rafferty says. "I think she probably would have started with *Ku* or something."

"I know where it is," Frank says. "I know what she was writing."

"So do I," Arthit says. "Klong Toey."

"Where their ships come in," Frank says. "Where they offload everything. Illegal immigrants, illegal pharmaceuticals, endangered animals, aphrodisiacs made from endangered animals, weapons, truck parts, hijacked American cars, Korean counterfeit money. They've got three warehouses down there, prime position near the docks."

"Three," Ming Li says. "Two too many. We could watch all week."

"No," Rafferty says. "All we have to do is get some eyes on them and then pull him out."

"Pull him out?" Frank says. "How?"

"He's set it up himself." Rafferty holds up his phone. "I call him."

31

Aurora Borealis

Whoever is in charge of the rain has turned it up and provided an enhancement in the form of random bursts of wind that send people running for cover. The rain falls through a pinpoint mist that diffuses the light from the neon signs above them and scatters it through the night like a fine, colored powder.

"So what do you think of Dad?"

"I think he could be useful," Arthit says, lighting up and blowing smoke through his nostrils like a cartoon bull. The smoke fills the car, and Rafferty takes a surreptitious secondhand hit. "I'll suspend further judgment until we see just *how* useful he is." The rain spatters the top of Arthit's car and sends rivulets racing each other down the windshield. The sidewalk where they are parked is deserted except for one beggar huddled under a bright blue plastic sheet, and the car smells of wet cloth.

"If I'd had any idea Noi would be in danger—" Rafferty begins.

Arthit holds up the hand with the cigarette in it. His face is hard enough to deflect a bullet. "Stop it. It was my decision, not yours. We can either sit here and comfort each other or we can do something.

That means focus on the data. Despite what I said to you last night, one thing cops learn is to ignore leaps of intuition and look at the data."

"And one thing writers learn is to ignore the data until a leap of intuition tells you what it means."

"So somewhere between us, we ought to be able to figure out what to do next. I just wish I shared your father's conviction that Chu doesn't have time to learn how connected I'm not."

"I suppose it depends on who *he's* connected to. On the force, I mean."

Arthit puts two fingers on the wheel and wiggles it left and right. Cigarette ash tumbles into his lap. "These guys get a lot of protection. That's not something you can get from a sergeant. And the cash flow is tremendous. Enough to buy a lot of weight."

"The three at my apartment," Rafferty says. He has wanted to say this before but has been reluctant to do so. "They were dressed like farmers, but they moved like cops."

"Probably were. Probably street cops." Arthit makes a fist and slams it against his own thigh. "In case you had any doubt about how good his connections might be, ask yourself where he got my address and the information that Rose and Miaow were there."

Rafferty says, "Here's something that might matter: My father thinks Chu will have kept this whole thing a secret. Nobody's supposed to know that he's arranged an escape route. His colleagues would see it as a betrayal."

Arthit thinks about it, takes a drag, and then nods. "I guess that's interesting."

"So Frank thinks Chu's traveling solo, with no Chinese foot soldiers along. And he won't want word to get back that he's chasing some *laowai* who ripped off his retirement plan."

Arthit takes the two fingers from the wheel and holds them up. "Two assumptions."

"Here's another one: He might not kill Noi anyway. The main reason kidnappers kill their victims is to keep from being identified. We already know who he is."

"Unfortunately," Arthit says, "the other reason is revenge."

"Right," Rafferty says. The cramps that have been at work in his belly since he saw Arthit's open door pay another visit.

"So we have to get them back." Arthit checks the sidewalk, just a cop's reflex. "By the way, you're fortunate in your women."

"Meaning?"

"Rose and Miaow, of course. And your sister is, as they used to say in England, crackerjack."

Rafferty watches Bangkok ripple through the windshield like a ghost city. "I guess so."

"We'll get them," Arthit says. "Your father is right: One thing at a time."

"Set up the watchers."

"Two cops and Ming Li," Arthit says.

"I still think he might recognize her."

"He hasn't seen her since she was ten," Arthit says. "And even then, your father says he didn't pay any attention to her." He cracks the window, gets a faceful of rain, and rolls it up again. He takes another puff in self-defense. "Anyway, half the cops I could pull aren't as good as she is."

"She's a kid."

"A very smart kid. And there's one more thing to recommend her: Unlike some cops, we know she's not on Chu's payroll."

"I wish I were certain Leung isn't."

Arthit shakes his head. "Doesn't make sense. If Leung were working with Chu, none of this would be necessary. Your father would be ten feet underwater and halfway to the gulf by now." He starts the car and slides the lever to kick up the air-conditioning. Then he stares out through the windshield and sighs deeply. "You don't know this," he says, "but my father was a cop."

Rafferty looks over at him. Arthit fiddles with the temperature controls.

"On the take, of course." Arthit still does not turn to face Poke. The air conditioner seems to require all his attention, and the cigarette burns forgotten in his free hand. "All Thai cops were on the take in those days. He took from everybody. He took money to keep people out of jail. The old one-two-three: Get the case, crack the case, take a bribe. Pimps, thieves, hired muscle. Twice, or at least twice that I know of, a murderer." The rain kicks up, shaped by a sudden gust of wind into a curtain of faintly colored mist that ripples and curls in front of

Rafferty's eyes like the aurora borealis. "Of course, usually that meant other people went to jail. See, when a cop takes a payoff, the crime doesn't go away. Somebody's got to take a fall."

Poke wants to put an arm around Arthit's shoulders but is sure it wouldn't be appreciated. "I know."

"So the guilty got off and the innocent got screwed," Arthit says. "That's what my father did for a living. He did it practically every day. But you know what, Poke? There was always food on the table. My brother and I went to school. I wound up in England, getting a very expensive education paid for by crooks and, I suppose, by the people who were stuck in those cells for things they didn't do." He puts his face near the window and exhales a cloud of smoke onto the glass, then wipes it clear with his sleeve. "Because of where my father was, who he was. That was what he had to do to live, to take care of the people he loved. And he did. He took care of all of us."

Poke says, "I know why Noi married you."

"Really?" Arthit says. He stubs out the cigarette in the ashtray, so hard that sparks fly. "I wish I did."

IT SEEMS SILLY at this point not to go home, now that the only things worth protecting have already been taken. So when Arthit heads for the station to line up his two cops, Poke goes back to the apartment.

The place feels immensely empty. When he first rented it, almost three years ago, it seemed like the perfect size for a man on his own. He filled it completely. He had a bedroom, a kitchen, a living room, and an office. He rattled happily from one room to another, doing his work, making his mess, and cleaning it up. He ate at the kitchen counter and drank his morning coffee on the balcony overlooking the Chinese cemetery his landlady had proudly pointed out as the source of the building's dubiously good feng shui. Never once had it felt too big for him.

Now it seems enormous.

There's nothing in it anymore that is his alone. His office is Miaow's room. The bedroom is the secret space he shares with Rose. The living room, the kitchen, all the objects in them—they belong to his family. The pencils have Rose's tooth marks on them. Miaow's sneakers have left ghost marks on the carpet. The surface of the sliding glass door has reflected all of them.

Living on that barren acreage in Lancaster, enveloped in his father's silences, Rafferty grew used to being alone. His mother was affectionate one moment and distant the next. Frank's attention was thousands of miles away. The solitary child who lived in the space between these adults developed into a solitary man. In many ways he had enjoyed it. Being alone gave him freedom. He did what he wanted, when he wanted. After he discovered Asia, he *went* where he wanted. A passport and an airline ticket were the only traveling companions he needed. Rafferty persuaded himself gradually that he had chosen to be alone, that this was the life he had created for himself, a life he filled completely. Now, standing in the center of his empty living room, he asks himself whether he could survive being alone again.

He has things to do to prepare for the next day—one thing at a time, as the world keeps reminding him—but first he goes down the hall into Miaow's room. The cardboard smiley face she drew to mean "Come right in" is hanging on the doorknob, its companion, the frowny face temporarily banished to one of her drawers.

Except for the mussed bed, abandoned in the middle of the night, her room is, as always, immaculate. Her shoes are in a regimentally straight line. There are still times when Miaow sits in the center of the floor, carefully lining up her shoes so she can scatter them and line them up again. For most of her life, she went barefoot.

Drawings in colored pencil are taped to the walls, along with a few older ones in crayon. Here and there he sees a version of the cheerful house below a blue sky and a fat primary-yellow sun that children everywhere draw, but most of the pictures are of the three of them: Rose, preternaturally tall and slender; Rafferty in an ugly T-shirt; and between them—always between them—Miaow, her skin darker than theirs, the part in her hair drawn with a ruler. The wall above the dresser is filled with pictures, but lower and to the left Rafferty spots a brand-new one. He leans down to take a closer look. It shows a lopsided birthday cake, candles gleaming, with three people barely visible in the darkness behind it. In the center of the cake, written in the inevitable pink, is the number 9.

Rafferty lets out more air than he knew he had in him. The cake.

It feels to Rafferty, at that moment, like they had baked that cake and lit those candles months ago. But they had celebrated Rose's birthday on Friday night, and this is Sunday night. It had been only forty-eight hours.

"I'll bring you back," he says to the room. "Both of you. I promise."

He closes the door behind him gently and goes into the living room to call Peachy.

32

In the Bag

Peachy and Rafferty are watching from a stall four doors away when the two uniformed cops and Elson, looking sharp and mordantly businesslike in his black suit, enter the building at 8:10 on Monday morning. Peachy is perspiring as anxiously as someone waiting for a firing squad, and Poke carries a wrinkled brown supermarket shopping bag. When she sees Elson, Peachy takes a step back, and Rafferty grabs the sleeve of her blouse to make sure she won't keep going.

She has already been upstairs once, at 6:15, to open the more daunting of the two locks, so they wait only three minutes—enough, Rafferty is sure, for the cops to pop the easy lock—and then he more or less hauls her through the street door and up the stairs. Rafferty stands to one side and puts an encouraging hand in the small of her back. When Peachy tries to slip her key into the lock, the door swings open.

Men's startled voices, Peachy expressing surprise. Rafferty counts to ten and gives the door a shove.

Peachy is up against the wall to the left of the door. One of the cops has the top filing drawer open, and the other is going through the papers on Peachy's desk. Elson stands beside the cop at the desk, one hand extended to Peachy, palm out, meaning *Stay there*. The door hinge squeals as Rafferty pushes in, and all of them look up.

"What the *hell* are you doing?" Rafferty says, bringing the paper bag protectively in front of him. And then he watches their eyes.

Elson glances down at the bag and opens his suit coat. Rafferty can practically see the word "weapon" form in his mind. One of the two cops—the one at the filing cabinet—looks at Rafferty and goes back to work. The cop sitting behind Peachy's desk sees the bag, and his jaw drops. His hand starts to go for the middle drawer and stops.

His nameplate, pinned on the left side of his chest, says PETCHARA.

"We're conducting a legal search, under authority of the Bangkok police," Elson says. "Stand over there, next to your friend, and stay there. Where's Miss, um . . . ?"

"She's up north," Rafferty says, going to stand next to Peachy. "The buffalo is in the hospital."

"Excuse me?"

"The family buffalo," Rafferty explains. "Fallen arches, very painful. It's something of a crisis for a farming family. She's gone up to offer moral support."

"Moral?" Elson asks.

"That's twice," Rafferty says. "One more remark like that and I'll break your glasses in half and show you how to use them as a suppository."

"It's too bad for the rest of us," Elson says, "that someone once told you that you were amusing." His voice is level, but there are pinched little white lines on either side of his nose. "Get back to it," he says to the cops, and they return to work, although Officer Petchara has to tear his eyes from the paper bag first.

"Why are you here, Mr. Rafferty?" Elson asks. "I didn't think you were in the domestics business."

"Sloppy research," Rafferty says. "I own twenty percent of the company."

Elson smiles. His front teeth are uneven and pushed in slightly, a characteristic Rafferty has always associated with thumb suckers. "Your name's not on the license."

"Gee," Rafferty says, "am I in trouble?"

"You're willing to admit you're part owner?"

"I just did."

"In writing," Elson says.

"Sure," Rafferty says. "Though I doubt anyone will ever read it."

"What's in the bag?"

"My supplies." Rafferty starts to open it. Elson puts his hand inside his coat, and Petchara looks like he will slide off Peachy's chair.

"Very slowly," Elson says. His hand comes out with an automatic in it. "Open it very slowly, and don't put your hand inside. Tilt it and show it to me."

"I'm afraid you're going to feel a little silly," Rafferty says. "Of course, you're probably used to that." He holds the bag wide open and tips it toward Elson. It contains what looks like the back half of a rooster.

"What in the world is that?" Elson says.

Rafferty tilts the bag back and looks down into it. "My feather duster," he says. "Monday is cleaning day." He takes one of the feathers between two fingers and pulls, and the duster comes out. "You want to be careful," he says. "Might get dust on that nice budget suit."

"Let the bag drop," Elson says. Rafferty does, and it drifts to the floor and lands with a hollow little popping sound. "So. You clean, too. Maybe the agency should find you a job."

"Golly, Dick. Was that a joke? Is that Secret Service humor?"

"You're just making my job easier," Elson says.

"Glad to hear it. If it were any harder, they'd have to give it to someone else. And then I'd have to start creating rapport all over again."

"Just stand there and shut up. Keep your hands in sight. Come *on*," he says to the cops. "This isn't worth the whole day."

"Take your time," Rafferty says. "It isn't often I get to watch my tax dollars at work."

The cop at the filing cabinet pulls out folder after folder and flips through them. Papers float free and drop to the floor. The cop at the desk—Petchara—picks up one piece of paper after another, glances at it, and throws it aside. Within two minutes there are papers all over the floor, and Peachy has begun to tremble.

"You guys going to clean this up?" Rafferty asks.

Elson is watching the cop at the filing cabinet. "I told you to shut up."

"I forgot."

"Would you like to be handcuffed?"

"It might be more effective to gag me."

"Mr. Rafferty. One more word out of you and you'll be gagged, cuffed, and sitting on the floor."

Rafferty nods and mimes zipping his mouth shut.

Officer Petchara opens the middle drawer.

"What's this?" he says to Rafferty, pulling out the paper bag. His hands are shaking slightly as he opens it.

"I don't know. What's that, Peachy?" Rafferty asks.

"I can explain," Peachy says.

"Of course you can," Elson says, elbowing Petchara aside and sitting behind the desk. He reaches into the bag and pulls out a pile of crisp new bills. Since both his hands are full, he clears a space on the desk with his elbows and drops the money there.

"A big withdrawal," he says to Peachy. "I'm sure the people at the bank will remember it clearly."

"I didn't—" Peachy begins, and then she grabs a new breath and says, "I didn't get it at the bank."

Rafferty says, "Peachy. What the hell?"

"Still so eager to sign a statement that you own part of this business?" Elson is messing the bills around on the desk with both hands. He looks almost happy.

"As you said, Dick, it's not on the license. I must have remembered incorrectly."

"Doesn't matter," Elson says. He dips back into the bag and comes up with more money. "My colleagues heard your admission."

"I guess you've got me, then," Rafferty says, watching Officer Petchara, whose head has snapped forward on his neck at an angle that looks painful. He is staring at the money as though it has spontaneously burst into flame.

Elson feels the attention and glances at Petchara, then looks down at the money in his hand. Some of it is old and soft, crumpled from use. He drops it onto the desk and reaches into the bag again, bringing up more well-worn money. He looks from the money to Petchara and down at the money again. Then his eyes swing up to Rafferty's.

"I didn't know about any of this," Rafferty says.

Elson says, "Goddamn it, shut the fuck up," and picks up some of the bills. He examines them, one at a time, and then drops them and picks up some more. And then he is scrabbling through the older bills to get to the new ones, smoothing them out, turning them over, holding them to the light. After what seems like ten minutes, his hands drop to the desk.

"You lucky son of a bitch," he says to Rafferty.

"I've always been lucky. Some are, some—"

"The horses," Peachy interrupts faintly. "I play the horses."

"You." Elson is blinking fast. "You play the horses." He sounds like someone who has learned a language by rote.

"I thought she had it under control," Rafferty says. "But, golly, I guess . . ."

Elson doesn't even glance at him. He paws listlessly through the money, nodding to himself, picking up bills at random and holding them up, then letting them drop again. "I don't suppose," he says to Peachy, "that you paid the girls out of this money."

"No," Peachy says. "I told you that I went to the bank."

"Rose told you that, too," Rafferty contributes.

"The bank," Elson repeats. He looks up at Officer Petchara in a way that makes Rafferty happy the man isn't even standing near him. "The bank," Elson says again. "Where we could be *right now*."

Petchara has dark half-moons of sweat beneath his arms. His eyes flick to Rafferty's and away again. "Right. The bank."

Elson begins mechanically to shovel the money back into the bag. To Peachy he says, "You have backup for this?"

Peachy winces. "Backup?"

"You know—winning tickets, disbursement slips, anything to show you really won it."

"No," Peachy says as though she barely understands the question.

"Peachy doesn't go to the track," Rafferty says. "This is street betting. As an industry it's really meticulous about not keeping written records."

"Of course," Elson says lifelessly. To Petchara he says, "Can you arrest her for this?"

Even Petchara looks surprised. "For betting?"

"They'd have to arrest half of Bangkok," Rafferty says.

"Maybe that would be a good idea." Elson lets the rest of the money drop to the desk and stands up. He looks at Rafferty for several seconds, his mouth pulled in at the corners, and then says, "We're not going to find anything here, are we?"

"Not unless Peachy had a really terrific week."

"That wouldn't surprise me at all," Elson says. He kicks idly at the nearest leg of the desk. Then he buttons his jacket, lifts the bag a couple of inches, and lets it drop again. "You know," he says, shaking his head, "you shouldn't keep this much money in a paper bag." He slides his palm down his tie, straightening it.

"Why?" Rafferty asks. "Will it spoil?"

"A safe," Elson says absently. "A strongbox."

Rafferty says, "Haven't got one."

"A briefcase, then. At the very least. With a lock."

"People leave paper bags alone," Rafferty says. "I mean, not people like you, of course. Real people. But they open briefcases. There's something about a briefcase that just begs to be opened."

"Whatever you say." Elson steps around the desk.

"They're like suitcases," Rafferty says, and Elson stops dead, so abruptly he looks like someone caught by a strobe. "It's amazing," Rafferty continues. "The things people put in suitcases."

Elson slowly swings his head toward Rafferty, and Rafferty gives him the Groucho Marx eyebrows, up and down twice, very fast. Elson's eyes narrow so tightly they almost disappear, and a dark flush of red climbs his cheeks.

Rafferty steps up to him. "Anybody ever do this to you in high school?" he asks, and then he puts his index and middle finger into his mouth, pulls them out again, and draws a line of spit down the center of the lenses of Elson's glasses. Elson inhales in a slow hiss. Then Rafferty leans in and whispers, "If I were you, I'd keep an eye on Officer Petchara."

PART III

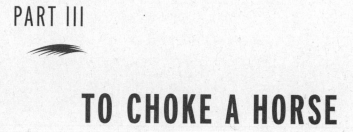

TO CHOKE A HORSE

33

That Makes Me the Fool

The sky over Bangkok is as gray as Arthit's disguise. The weather front has decided to acquire an address and stay.

"It cost seven thousand, and it was worth it," Rafferty says.

"Seven thousand? You mean U.S.?" Arthit is dressed in shapeless, style-free clothing that's supposed to make him look like a maintenance man, and it might, from across the street. Up close, Arthit is cop all the way through; he has the look of a man who sleeps in his uniform. He picks up his coffee, gives it a sniff, and puts it down again.

"That's what it cost to trade the Korean money for the real thing," Rafferty says. "Thirty-one thousand in counterfeit for twenty-three thousand in genuine baht and bucks. I got a special rate, but I had to put in my rainy-day money to get the total up." Rafferty is on the hassock, giving Arthit the place of honor on the couch. "Something wrong with the coffee?"

"The coffee's not the problem. Did you have to do that thing with his glasses?"

"Yes," Rafferty says. "I did."

"You've made an enemy."

"We weren't on the same tag team to begin with. And he's such a hypocrite. He's carrying enough lube to service a Buick, eating at a no-hands restaurant, and making bar-girl cracks about Rose. And he hasn't got any lips."

Arthit smooths the unfamiliar shirt, which sports a patch over the pocket that says PAUL. "It's bad policy to make people lose face unnecessarily."

"It was the best moment of my week."

"You may need him later."

Rafferty waves it off, more brusquely than he intends. He's been having second thoughts, too. "If I need him, I'll get him. Petchara is the one I'm worried about."

The light in the apartment thins, and the buildings on the other side of the sliding glass door begin to fade as a falling mist dims the day. "Petchara is spotless," Arthit says. "No blots at all. Eighteen years on the force and not a complaint from anyone. They're not going to give the Secret Service some hack."

"Well, they did. And a crooked hack, at that."

"I don't doubt you." Arthit picks up the coffee and blows on it, although it can't be much above room temperature by now. He's been toying with this one cup while Rafferty drank three. "I'm just telling you he's not an easy target." He puts the cup down again and glances at his watch, a shiny hunk of shrapnel on a band so loose that the watch continually slips around to the inside of his wrist. That's where it is at the moment, so Arthit gives it a practiced flip to bring it into position. "Our guys should be on the scene by now."

"And Ming Li," Rafferty says, the doubt finding its way into his tone.

"She'll be fine. The question is where Chu's local help is at the moment."

"You want a guess?"

"No," Arthit says tightly. "But I wouldn't mind some informed speculation."

"At least two of them are keeping an eye on this building."

Arthit gives him a *That's obvious* shrug. "I'd hate to think I'm wearing this outfit if nobody's watching."

"Chu's got to have someone on me. He can't really believe I don't know where Frank is."

"That would be the easy way, wouldn't it? Follow you to Frank and kill everybody, including you, right on the spot and then disappear."

"Yeah." Rafferty thinks about it for a second. "Shame I don't have somebody else behind me."

"One of ours?"

"Sure. Maybe we could take them."

Arthit sticks his index finger into the coffee, licks it, and makes a vinegar face. "And the point would be . . . ? Other than getting Chu pissed off?"

"Corroboration. Suppose Chu's not staying in the warehouse where they're keeping Noi and Rose and Miaow. Maybe he's too smart for that. Maybe he's in the warehouse next door, or the one two over. I draw him out, he gets spotted, and a few hours later we hit the wrong warehouse. We might as well send in a truck with a loudspeaker: 'Look, we're coming!' I doubt Chu has stayed alive this long by being stupid."

Arthit picks up the cup, glares at it, and puts it down with a clatter. "I wish you hadn't said that."

"Sorry."

"*Damn* it. I'm not thinking clearly." Arthit gets up and goes to the glass door. He opens it, shoving it hard enough to bang it against the frame. "Great following weather," he says nastily. "Can't see across the street."

"Arthit. It's the weather we've got."

"I don't even know who I'd call." Arthit's hands are jammed into his pockets. From the bulges they make, they're curled into fists.

Rafferty joins him at the door, and the two of them gaze into the gray. "There are times when I hate this city," Arthit says. "I don't know why we stay here. Noi would be happier in some three-buffalo village where I could be the big whistle, chief of police. Get to know everybody's face, break up the occasional fight, nab the occasional motorcycle rustler, get fat and sloppy, and enjoy the time we have left."

"I guess that sounds good."

"I'd be bored senseless, of course. But Noi and I would have more time together."

"One thing at a time," Rafferty says. "That seems to be the theme. First, let's get them back."

The mist is heavier now, the air is the soft gray of goose down. "Make the call," Arthit says.

RAFFERTY SPOTS THEM through the glass doors of the lobby the moment he gets off the elevator. Two of the three probable cops who showed up at his apartment the night he, Rose, and Miaow ran: the fat one who had the knife and one of the two gunmen, not the leader. They are huddled in a doorway across the street and a few doors down. He turns up his collar, pushes the door open, and goes in the opposite direction without a backward glance.

Colonel Chu should call back in ten or twelve minutes.

Rafferty walks fast, trying to look like a man who knows where he's going. The mist has intensified to a drizzle. He crosses Silom, dodging cars until he is beneath the elevated track of the Sky Train, hearing brakes behind him as drivers slow for his followers. Prettyman's laws swarm in his mind, and one floats to the top: Stay out of blind alleys unless you want one.

He wants one.

A left takes him up Patpong, its neon dark, the sidewalks deserted now except for the occasional wet, resentful tout waiting to lure some hapless newcomer into a second-story rip-off bar where he'll be charged ten dollars for a Coke and a nonexistent floor show. Rafferty waves them off and picks up the pace.

Minus the obstacle course of the night market and the distracted throng of bar customers, Patpong is a surprisingly short street. He reaches Suriwong in about a minute and turns right. Maybe nine minutes now. He reflexively checks his watch, and on the way back down, his hand brushes the Glock jammed into the front of his pants. When he put it there, he made sure the safety was on. Now he's having some doubts. He can feel the tension gathering beneath his heart, coiling like a living thing in a space too small for it.

The drizzle is shouldered aside by a light rain.

It's not even noon. Normally the sidewalks would be jammed, but now they gleam almost empty except for the food vendors, busily putting up the plastic tarps that will keep their charcoal burning despite the damp. Smoke and steam mingle into a single, needle-sharp smell.

The tarps are bad for visibility, so Rafferty slows slightly, fighting the urge to make it as difficult for them as possible. The few pedestrians are not taking the rain cheerfully: They glance at the sky, shield their eyes with an open hand, and mutter to themselves. One fat and extremely drunk *farang*, his shirt half tucked in, his eyes as unfocused as poached eggs, bumps heavily into Rafferty and mumbles an apology that seems to be all consonants. A moment later Rafferty hears it again as the fat man lurches into the pursuers.

Just to get them wetter, Rafferty stops at an ATM. Sheltered by the overhang, he fumbles slowly with his wallet, takes out the wrong card, puts it into the wrong slot, pulls it out, puts it into the right slot backward, tries to force it, then withdraws it, a man defeated by technology. He turns around, watching out of the corner of his eye as the fat cop scrambles back between two parked cars. Wallet in hand, Rafferty stands there, looking irresolute. Then he spends a minute arranging his credit cards in alphabetical order before deciding it's more harmonious to organize them by color. Then he does it in ascending order of the balance due. The chore done, he slips the wallet back into his pocket and loiters comfortably beneath the overhang, safely out of the rain. He checks the sky and then his watch, then the sky again. With a little surge of malicious pleasure, he sees the rain intensify. He slips his hands into his pockets and leans back against the ATM to wait it out, and his cell phone rings.

The display says CHU. Rafferty takes two fast, deep breaths, flips the phone open, and says, "I still don't know where he is."

"You brought me out in this weather to tell me that?"

"This is nothing," Rafferty says. "By Bangkok standards this is sunny."

"According to my watch, you have a little less than nine hours left."

"It might as well be nine days. I'll never find him."

"This is your problem, not mine."

"Really? I thought you wanted him."

"You're his son," Chu says. "He came to Bangkok because you're here. He'll get in touch with you again."

"I doubt it. I pretty much told him to go fuck himself."

"You said that to your *father*? I'm glad you're not my son."

"That's two of us."

Chu clucks in disapproval. "No one should speak to his father like that."

"Yeah, well, you don't know him like I do."

"I think I know him much better than you do. Until recently, I actually liked him."

"I didn't."

"I'm sorry you have problems with your father," Chu says slowly. "That's a terrible thing. But believe me, he'll try to overcome it. Put yourself in his shoes. You're a father now—"

"Don't," Rafferty says. "You, of all people. Don't say another word."

"Time is passing, Mr. Rafferty."

"He didn't come here to see me," Rafferty says.

"Of course he did." Chu actually sounds surprised. "Why else would—"

"I was an afterthought. As usual. He came here to sell something."

There is a silence on the line. Rafferty scans the street and sees the fat cop still huddled behind the parked car. Then Chu says, "He told you that?"

"That was one of his topics."

"Did he tell you what it was?"

"I didn't care enough to ask."

"It will be extremely unfortunate for you if he succeeds."

"If it's any comfort to you, I didn't get the impression he was in a hurry."

"Oh, he's in a hurry," Chu says. "And you should be, too. Don't call me again unless you have something to tell me."

"Got it."

"And if I don't hear from you, I'll make sure you know where to find them. What's left of them." Chu hangs up.

Rafferty's heart is pounding in his ears like a battering ram, and his lips feel thinner than Elson's. He jams his finger at the button to return the call, and the phone rings for a long time before Chu picks it up and says, "What?"

"You don't get the last line," Rafferty says. "Listen to me. If you kill the cop's wife, you're dead. This is a guy who knows everybody. He's assigned to help the United States government on terrorist issues, the Muslim unrest in the south, and all that. He's connected like a fucking octopus. And I personally guarantee you that if anything happens to my wife and daughter, I will devote my life to finding you and killing you. And don't think I can't find you. You were the other thing my father talked about."

"I'm terrified. Are you finished? I'm getting wet."

"No, I'm not finished. You hurt them and you'll spend the rest of your life looking over your shoulder."

"I already spend my life looking over my shoulder. But thanks for the tip about the cop. And don't call back until you're ready to tell me where Frank is." Lightning freezes the day for a second, and there is a burst of static on the line. When Chu comes back, he is saying, "Tick, tick, tick." Then he hangs up again.

Rafferty slams the phone closed with such force he cracks the display screen on the outside of it. Black paramecia swarm through the rain in front of his eyes. He grabs his wallet, turns back to the ATM, pushes in a card, and then reaches down and flicks off the safety on the Glock. He keys in his PIN, waits, snatches the ten thousand baht from the machine's jaws, and pockets it, along with his card. Then he walks straight across the sidewalk and into the street. A truck is lumbering past, and Rafferty slants past it as it roars by, then darts behind it and runs alongside for a quarter of a block before peeling off and crossing the rest of the way to the sidewalk. He slows to a quick walk without looking back.

Half a block past Patpong, the sidewalk borders a construction site for a building that has been going up for years. Hiding it from the sidewalk is an ugly fence of rippled metal. It has an opening in it just wide enough for one person to slip through, and Rafferty snags his shirt as he squeezes through it. He finds himself in an expanse of mud, liberally pockmarked by puddles too wide to jump: red-brown mud and the slate gray sky framed on the surface of the standing water. The skeleton of the building stretches skyward to disappear into the rain and mist. The floors and the elevator shafts are in place. Rafferty thinks briefly about the elevator and then dismisses it. All they'll have to do is wait at the bottom.

He needs them closer.

He hears the corrugated fence creak as the two of them force their way through the opening.

Work on the site has been called on account of the rain, but in a small trailer all the way across the site a light gleams through the falling water. The door is on the far side, and he heads for it, his feet slipping in the mud. It seems to take much longer to reach it than it should, and his back feels like it's six feet wide and painted bright orange, but eventually he is there, and he circles around, climbs the first two of the four steps leading to the trailer, and tries the door.

It opens. The light inside is a leathery yellow, an incandescent bulb in a lampshade the color of parchment. No one home.

Moving quickly, he climbs the last two steps, leaving muddy footprints on them, and plants his boots on the floor. The trailer sags slightly beneath him. He moves left, all the way to a door, which he opens. It's a bathroom. He leaves the door ajar and then pulls off his shoes and backtracks, avoiding his footprints. At the top of the stairs, he jumps. The mud underfoot is amazingly cold.

He figures they will split up and come around both sides of the trailer, so he drops to his belly and slithers beneath its center, pulling himself along on his elbows until he is facing back the way he came. In a moment he sees their boots approaching.

They pause in front of the trailer and hold a whispered conversation. The one on the right—the thinner one, Rafferty guesses—is in charge. He has the last word. They do as Rafferty expected, one going left and the other right. Silently, Rafferty pulls himself around 180 degrees so he is looking at the side of the trailer where the door is.

The two pairs of boots trudge through the mud, pausing cautiously at the trailer's corners, approach the steps, and stop. They are probably listening. Then one of them disappears behind the steps, followed by the other. Rafferty can no longer see their feet.

But he can hear them. More whispering, followed by the sound of one pair of boots climbing the steps. The door opens, hard and fast. An instant later the other follows.

Rafferty is out from under the trailer in two seconds flat, clawing at the gun. It is in his hand as he steps through the door and realizes immediately that he has made a mistake.

The fat one is to his left, in front of the bathroom door. He turns in surprise as the trailer dips beneath Rafferty's weight, glances at the gun, and brings his hands up, but he's not the one Rafferty is thinking about as the door creaks behind him. A point of ice touches the back of his neck.

"Put the gun on the desk," the man behind him says in Thai. The fat one smiles. He has a merry smile.

"Or what?" Rafferty says, not moving.

"Or I'll shoot you. It's not what I'm supposed to do, but right now your gun is all I'm thinking about."

"How about this? How about you give me *your* gun, or I shoot your friend."

"That's his problem," says the man behind him. The fat one's smile slips a notch.

"Shoot me and Chu will kill you."

"Chu's not here," says the fat one. "You are."

Moving slowly, Rafferty puts his gun on the work desk to his right. "Now what?"

"*Now* is a little awkward," says the man behind him. "Why didn't you just let us follow you? Why did you have to make fools of us?"

"With all due respect," Rafferty says, "I just put my gun down, and you didn't. I think that makes me the fool."

"It's a problem," says the fat one, not entirely unsympathetically. "You spotted us, you pulled us into this place. Our superiors won't be happy."

"Why don't we just keep it to ourselves?" Rafferty says. "Go somewhere, get dry, maybe have a cup of coffee."

"You're joking," says the one behind him. He prods Rafferty's neck with the gun. "Take three steps forward."

"I'll buy," Rafferty says. Once he has moved, there will be no way he can reach the gun.

"You shouldn't have embarrassed us," says the fat one.

Another prod. "I said move."

"Oh, come on. There's got to be a way—"

"*Now.*"

Rafferty steps forward, and as he does so, he sees the fat one reach behind himself, sees his hand come back with the long knife in it.

The fat one shrugs an apology and starts to move in, and Rafferty balances on the balls of his feet, ready to leap forward. Then the man behind Rafferty gasps, and the cold spot of the gun barrel disappears. The fat one backs up hastily, fast enough to bang his back on the bathroom door.

Rafferty turns, sees the arm around the thin one's throat, the gun at his temple, and behind him the cold, calm eyes of Leung.

34

You Have Thirty-One Left

S he needs her medicine," Rose says.

"She should have told us that at the house," says the man with the gun.

Noi moans again, this time at a higher pitch. Her eyes are clamped closed, her face sheened with sweat that glues her bangs to her forehead. Her arms are drawn in as though she is chilled, and bent at acute angles, bringing the knotted hands to the level of her heart. Fine vertical lines edge her mouth. Rose had piled up ten or twelve empty burlap sacks to make a bed for her, but Noi has twisted herself halfway off them, so that her legs are bare against the cold concrete floor.

"Are you human?" Rose says. "Look at her. She's in pain you can't even imagine."

"Probably not," the man says. "Although that hot water hurt." He looks at an irregular red patch on his forearm.

"I can go get it," Miaow says. "I can take a taxi."

"Listen to you," the man says. The rain rattles on the tin roof like a handful of tacks. In places water has seeped in beneath the walls. The man is sitting on a wooden packing crate, the gun dangling lazily between spread knees. A dozen cigarette butts lie at his feet, folded over and smashed flat in a light snowfall of ash.

"I can go now," Miaow says. She stands up, and the gun comes to life, the barrel lifting six inches, a snake poising to strike.

"No you can't," the man says. "Sit down or I'll shoot you."

"You will not," Miaow says. "I'm a little girl."

"And I've got one at home," the man says. He hitches up his left trouser leg to preserve the crease and gives it a critical glance. "But I'll shoot you anyway. Sit." Miaow steps back, so she is flat against the wall, but she remains standing.

"That means you have a wife," Rose says. "Suppose Noi was your wife. Suppose your wife was in this kind of pain."

"Suppose I shoot you all now," the man says. "I'm going to have to do it sooner or later."

Miaow says, "You won't."

The man inserts two fingers into his shirt pocket and comes up with a cigarette. He checks the position of the filter, puts it between his lips, and picks up the lighter that's beside him on the packing case, next to the empty ashtray. "I don't particularly want to," he says, lighting up. "But I will."

"Will not," Miaow says.

Rose says, "*Miaow.*"

Miaow says, "Give my mother a cigarette."

The man's eyes widen, and then he chokes on smoke, and the choke becomes a laugh. "Give your mother . . ." he says, and then he laughs again.

"She needs one," Miaow says. "She smokes all the time. Even more than you."

"She burned me," the man says. Miaow just stands there, one hand extended. He laughs again. "Okay, come here. You take it to her."

Miaow, still in her pink bunny pajamas, pushes herself away from the wall and goes to the man. He takes out a second cigarette and gives it to her, and Miaow puts it between her lips. The man lights it. Miaow blows the smoke out of her mouth, uses her sleeve to wipe the taste off her tongue, and eyes the coal professionally to make sure it's alive. Then she looks up at the man.

"You won't, you know," she says.

"HE CAME OUT of Warehouse Two," Arthit says into the phone.

"Are Ming Li and your guys still there?" Rafferty says. "Make sure they see which one he goes back into."

"Thank you," Arthit says. "Are there any other routine procedures you'd like to suggest?"

"That's the only one that occurs to me. Listen, we've got kind of a problem at this end."

"*Kind* of a problem? And who's 'we'?"

"Leung and me."

"Leung's at your apartment?"

"Well, no."

Something slams down on Arthit's desk. "Poke—"

"I know, I know. I couldn't stay there. So I went out, and two of Chu's goons picked me up. Anyway, Leung and I have them now."

"Leung and you have them now," Arthit parrots.

"Yeah. Both of them."

"And you think this is *kind of* a problem?" Arthit's voice has risen into an unfamiliar tenor range. "What's Chu going to do when they don't come back? For all you know, they're supposed to be checking in every half hour."

"Okay, but in the meantime we've got them."

"What a cock-up." The British schoolboy inside Arthit occasionally surfaces in times of stress.

"That's not really constructive," Rafferty says.

"Fine. Constructive. Let's think positively here. Give me your 'ideal scenario,' as they say in those books."

Rafferty eyes the two men, now sitting on the floor with their fingers interlaced over their heads while Leung leans against the desk, staring at them as though they were already dead. Their police badges are on the desk. The fat one doesn't look so merry anymore. Neither of them meets Rafferty's eyes. He says, "Just a minute," and goes out onto the steps and closes the door behind him. "Okay. We get them to tell us which warehouse, and then we let them go, and they hurry back to Chu and keep their mouths shut."

"That certainly qualifies as ideal," Arthit says.

"You asked."

"I was hoping for something in the realm of the possible."

"It's possible," Rafferty says.

"Would you like to— Wait, hang on. Call you back. My other phone's ringing."

Rafferty folds his own phone, goes back into the trailer, and tries to emulate Leung's stare. He might as well be intimidating furniture, for all the reaction he gets.

"Hey," he says. They look up at him. "It's a funny thing," he says. "I look at you guys and I don't see killers."

"We're not," says the fat one.

"Tell you what, then. Let's sit here until Arnold Prettyman walks through this door."

"That was Chu," the fat one says. "We wired Prettyman to the chair and knocked him around some, and then Chu sent us out of the room."

"He didn't want us to hear anything Prettyman said," the fat one says. "He never wants anyone to hear anything."

Rafferty looks at the badges on the desk, which say SRIYAT and PRADYA. "Which one of you is Pradya?"

"I am," says the fat one.

"Well, Pradya, it's too bad nobody got that on video, because right now it looks like the nail in your coffin."

"We didn't know Chu was going to kill him," says the thin one, Sriyat.

"Right."

"He said he had questions, said it might get rough. But he never said that—"

"Fine. I'm sure it came as a total surprise." Without looking away from the prisoners, Rafferty goes to Leung, the trailer creaking beneath him, and whispers into Leung's ear. Leung nods and pockets the gun he took off the thinner cop. Then he straightens and gestures to Pradya, the fat cop, to go into the bathroom.

Rafferty pulls his own gun and points it at Sriyat.

Both men look confused, but Pradya gets up and reluctantly opens the bathroom door. Leung lazily trails him in.

Rafferty gazes down at the seated cop for a moment and then waves him to his feet and backs up to the far side of the trailer. Sriyat follows. Rafferty puts a finger to his lips, raises his eyebrows, and waits. Fifteen or twenty seconds creep past.

From the other side of the bathroom door, a shot. Then another.

Sriyat goes white, and his head involuntarily jerks around so he can look at the door. It remains closed.

"Sriyat," Rafferty says. "I'm over here." The man turns to face him. His mouth is working as though he's trying to dry-swallow a handful of pills.

"Your friend just gave the wrong answer," Rafferty says. "This is the question. Which warehouse are the women and the girl in?"

"Three," the man says at once.

Rafferty raises the gun so it points directly at the man's right eye. "*Which* one? And louder."

"*Three!*" Sriyat shouts.

The door opens, and Leung pushes Pradya through it. Pradya looks wetter than he did when they came in from the rain, and he walks as though the trailer floor were pitching beneath his feet.

"Same answer," Leung says.

Rafferty's phone rings, and he flips it open.

"He went into three," Arthit says.

"It's three," Rafferty says. "We've got confirmation here."

"Of course," Arthit says, "Chu will probably move them when those guys don't come back. If he doesn't just kill the girls and leave them there."

"They're *going* back," Rafferty says. "That's where you come in. Hold on. I can't talk here."

He goes out again through the trailer door and into the rain. "Offer them a ticket," he says. "They're cops, right? Badges and everything. We've got them dead to rights. Murder, kidnapping, practically anything you can think of. You could come here and arrest them right now, and their lives would be over. Or you can promise to let them walk if they'll go back to Chu and keep their mouths shut."

"I don't know whether I can keep that promise."

"Arthit. Who cares?"

"How do we know that they won't—"

"We don't."

After a moment of silence, Arthit says, "That's what I was looking for. Certainty."

"If you were in their shoes, whose side would you come down on?"

"I wouldn't be in their shoes. But I take your point. If they stick with Chu, they're going to take a big one the minute he's gone. If they go with us, they've got my promise. It doesn't mean much, and they'll probably suspect that, but . . . If the boat is sinking, you're going to grab anything that looks like a life vest."

"I couldn't put it better myself."

"Still, it all depends on how much faith they put in my promise and how scared they are of Chu, and there's no way for us to know any of that."

"So we're back where we started."

"Let me think about it."

"When Chu called, I gave him a line about you, one that might be tough for him to check." He tells Arthit the story he sold Chu.

"It's not bad at all," Arthit says. "That counterterrorism stuff, they keep all that pretty close. I doubt that Chu could get a line to anyone who could contradict that." He pauses. "But it only works for Noi. The goal has to be to get all three of them."

"Look, Arthit, you can put these guys away forever. They've probably got families to worry about. And cops in prison have a short life expectancy. When they finally get out, if they ever do, they'll still have to worry about Chu. We have to persuade them that if they play with us, the whole thing goes away."

"We could make them promise to try to protect Rose and Miaow."

"We could try." Poke hopes Arthit can't hear the doubt in his voice. He looks out over the mud-smeared desolation of the building site. All it lacks to mirror his emotional state is a dead dog. "So will you talk to them?"

"Oh, well," Arthit says. "Let's give it a go."

Rafferty climbs back up the stairs, feeling like he's done it a hundred times, and opens the door. The two men on the floor follow him with their eyes, trying to read his face. He puts the cell phone on the desk and presses the "speaker" button. Into the phone he says, "Arthit, meet Pradya and Sriyat." He points at the two cops. "You're going to talk to someone. He's a police colonel, and he's the only guy in the world who can get you out of this."

"YOUR SHIRT IS yellow," Miaow says.

Noi, her head in Rose's lap, opens her eyes and looks, startled, at Miaow.

The man with the gun glances down at himself, as though checking. "And?"

"That means you love the king."

The man squints at her, puzzled. "Everybody loves the king."

"And you have a bracelet," Miaow says. "Can I look at it?"

"Why not?" The man transfers the gun to his left hand and extends his right. Miaow comes up to him and slips a finger under the yellow rubber bracelet. "'Long live the king,'" she reads aloud. Like yellow clothing, the bracelets are everywhere in Thailand since King Bhumibol entered the fiftieth year of his reign.

"The king is everyone's father," the man says.

Miaow tugs the bracelet and lets go, so it snaps lightly against the man's arm, and brings her eyes up to his. "Would the king be proud of you now?"

The man straightens as though he has been struck, and the muscles in his face go rigid as plaster. He brings his right hand up, across his chest and all the way to his left shoulder, and he backhands Miaow across the face.

The blow knocks Miaow sideways. She lands on her right arm, her elbow making a cracking sound as it strikes the cement. A line of blood threads down from one nostril, but she ignores it and raises herself on the injured elbow to look the man in the eyes.

Rose has started to rise, but Noi's weight holds her down. "*You,*" Rose spits. "You would make the king weep."

The man gets up very quickly and holds the gun out, his arm shaking and his face tight enough to crack. He racks a shell into the chamber.

The rain grows louder as the door to the warehouse opens, and Colonel Chu comes in, peeling off a raincoat. He stops at the tableau in front of him and hisses like a snake. The man with the gun snaps his head around to see Chu's eyes blowing holes in him.

"Lower the gun," Chu says quietly, almost a whisper.

The man does so, looking down at the floor. He is suddenly perspiring.

Chu crosses the floor and extends a hand. After a one-heartbeat pause, the man holds out the gun. Without looking at it, Chu pushes the magazine release. The magazine snicks out into his waiting hand. He ejects the shell in the chamber and flips the gun so he's holding it by the barrel. He says, "Show me your teeth."

The man glances around the room as though he hopes there is help there somewhere, and says, "My teeth?"

"Now," Chu says. "Show them to me now."

The man peels back his lips to reveal two crooked lines of teeth, and Chu lifts the automatic and snaps it forward precisely, using a corner of the grip to break one of the man's incisors. The man chokes off a scream and drops to one knee, a hand clapped over his bleeding mouth.

"You have thirty-one left," Chu says, "and I'll break every one of them." His face is as calm as that of someone who is reading an uninteresting book. "These people are my currency," he says. "Shoot them and you're stealing from me. People who steal from me have short, unhappy lives, although I'm sure that many of them would like to die long before they're allowed to." His eyes slide over to Miaow, still on the floor, and he says, "You. If you want to grow up, wipe your face and get back over there, where you belong."

35

Not Really the Go-To Guy on Hip-Hop

One thing at a time.

He can only think about one thing at a time. If he doesn't focus, he'll be paralyzed. He won't know which direction to pursue.

Can't think about Miaow, Rose, and Noi. Can't think about his father. Can't worry about Colonel Chu.

What he can do right now is sit next to Peachy, in what must be the worst restaurant in Bangkok, and look through the window at the bank.

"It's the wrong man," Peachy says for the second time. This time she yanks at his sleeve to drive the point home. "They're talking to the wrong man."

"What a surprise," Rafferty says. "Since it's Petchara who pointed him out."

The only thing in the restaurant's plus column is a tinted front window, covered with a reflective film on the outside, installed to keep the afternoon sun from roasting the diners before they die of food poisoning.

Rafferty is thankful to be unobserved, although no one on the other side of the street is exercising much vigilance. He and Peachy might as well be standing on the sidewalk in Ronald McDonald costumes and waving. Elson hasn't looked up in a quarter of an hour. After ten minutes of bullying the teller through the glass divider, he did his *CSI* wallet flip and was led to the other side of the partition, where he shooed the teller off his stool and took control of the man's computer. He attacked it like a finalist in the Geek Olympics, occasionally shaking his head in impatience. The teller hovers anxiously, literally wringing his hands, while Petchara and the other cop stand around on the lobby side of the glass in the loose-jointed stance of people with nothing to do.

The most attentive person in the bank is the teller Peachy identified as the one who passed her the bad bills. He sits bolt upright at his station, three windows down, his eyes darting everywhere, a man following the flight of an invisible hummingbird. His pallor is evident even under the bank's fluorescent lights.

Elson stands, shoving the stool back, his finger jammed accusingly against the computer screen. He snaps a question. From behind him a man in a wrinkled suit, who seems to be the branch manager, ducks his head several times. If he had a cap, Rafferty thinks, he'd doff it and tug his forelock. Without turning away from the computer, Elson says something, and the manager scurries off.

"I don't understand," Peachy says.

"Sure you do." Rafferty sips his coffee, made from some instant left over from World War II and three times the suggested amount of water. "They did everything they could to keep Elson away from the bank. We screwed that up, so now they're keeping him away from the man who knows where the money came from."

Peachy says, "Oh."

Outside, a young woman wearing the blue skirt and white blouse of a Thai high-school girl, a stack of books clasped to her chest, dawdles indolently up to the window, exuding the flat rejection of the entire planet that characterizes teens everywhere. There's nowhere in the world, her stance says, that she wants to go, and she isn't even eager not to get there. She stops and leans wearily against the window with her back to Rafferty, giving him an excellent view of her shoulders and her long, straight black hair. If she were transparent, he could see Elson, but as it is, he can't.

"That's funny," Peachy says.

"Not very," Rafferty says, craning to see around the girl.

"She shouldn't be standing there. She's very pale. Why would she stand in the sun like that?" Thais are keenly aware of skin color, with the pale end of the spectrum being the most desirable.

"Pale, is she?" Rafferty asks, being polite. He still can't see Elson, but the bank manager comes into view from some office somewhere, carrying a cardboard box full of small pieces of papers—deposit slips, Rafferty would guess.

"Pale as a Chinese," Peachy says, and makes a *tsk-tsk* sound. She puts her fingers to her cheek. "She's going to *ruin* her skin. Prem always says—"

Rafferty says, "Chinese?" He leans forward and raps the glass twice, sharply, with his ring.

The girl turns and smiles. It is Ming Li. She gives him a snotty little schoolgirl wave, just the tips of her fingers, and heads for the door.

In the bank across the street, Elson is also waving, waving a piece of paper beneath the nose of the unfortunate teller. The teller takes it, and his face falls. He looks at Elson, and his shoulders rise and drop down again, the universal gesture for *Huh?* Then Elson does a *Come here* gesture to the cops and holds out his hand for the slip.

"Food any good?" Ming Li slips into the booth.

"Depends," Rafferty says, watching the bank. "When was the last time you ate?"

"Last night. We had to be at the warehouses pretty early."

"Not long enough," Rafferty says. "Give it a week and come back."

Ming Li studies Rafferty's plate. "What have you got?"

He ignores her, intent on the scene across the street, but she bangs the edge of the plate with a fork as a prompt, and he says, "Gristle, fat, elderly tomatoes, and some sort of roots with dirt on them."

"Yum," Ming Li says. She picks up his chopsticks, dips them in his water glass, and wipes them on a napkin. He turns to watch her tweeze some shreds of meat and put them into her mouth. She chews experimentally and swallows. "Awful," she says, taking more.

Peachy jams a finger into his arm and says, "Look."

Elson has brought the teller out of the enclosure and into the lobby area. The two cops pat the man down, then take him by the elbows and steer him toward the doors to the sidewalk. Elson follows, being trailed by the bank manager, who's obviously protesting. Something he says stops Elson, and the Secret Service man turns to him. The two of them have a somewhat heated exchange.

"Do you know about the other guy?" Ming Li asks with her mouth full.

"The other guy," Rafferty says.

"I knew you hadn't spotted him. I passed him a couple of times, just leaning against a building a couple of shops up and looking through that same window. Big, broad in the shoulders, maybe some kind of weight lifter. Looks like a steroids poster. Scarred face, broken nose. Maybe Chinese, maybe Korean."

"You passed him twice? And he didn't see you?"

"Actually," Ming Li says, using her fingers to scrub dirt from the roots of whatever she's eating, "I passed him three times. And no, he didn't see me. Why would he? You didn't."

"You didn't pass me three times."

"If you say so." She wipes her fingers on the napkin and looks at the smear of dirt. "Can I have some of your coffee?"

"It's not actually coffee," Rafferty says. "It's a cup that might have held coffee in 1973, and hot water has been poured into it."

Ming Li picks it up and drinks anyway. Then she looks down at the cup and says, "That's *nasty*." She reviews the word for a moment and says, "Nasty? Is that what they say?"

Looking out the window, Rafferty says, "Is that what who says?" Elson, his argument over, makes an impatient wave at Petchara and the other cop, and they hustle the teller through the doors.

Ming Li gives Rafferty a little whuffing sound to indicate how obvious it is. "Those hip-hop singers on MTV."

As the doors close behind him, Elson calls for the others to wait, pulls out a cell phone, and punches a number.

Rafferty says, "I'm not really the go-to guy on hip-hop. If you want to know anything about OFR, though, I'm your man."

"What's OFR?"

"Old Fart Rock."

"No, thanks. Except, how long do you think until the Rolling Stones are doing ads for Viagra? Maybe use that song—what's it called?—'Start Me Up.'"

"The young are so cruel."

Ming Li is watching Elson and his crew approach the corner, the teller arguing at every step. "So we're not going to follow those guys?"

"They're not going anyplace interesting. See the guy three seats away from the empty window?"

Ming Li counts chairs. "The one with the wet shirt?"

"Him," Rafferty says. "I think *he's* going someplace interesting. And my guess is that your steroids guy is going there, too." He glances at his watch. "About forty-five minutes left. Can you get Leung here?"

Ming Li picks up some more of the greens between her chopsticks, touches the roots, and rubs her fingers together. "I know they grow vegetables in dirt, but this is silly."

"Leung," Rafferty repeats. "Can you get Leung here?"

"He's here already," she says. She chews, and he can hear the grit between her teeth. "If you can't see Leung, it means he's here."

FORTY MINUTES LATER, Rafferty says, "This is it." He is watching the bank. "You straight with it?"

"Sure," Ming Li says. "Leung's half a block from here, on the other side of the big guy. I dawdle my way up there, looking demure and harmless. Just chillin'."

"Jesus," Rafferty says.

"So the big guy's between us, in the tweezers," Ming Li says. "That's what Frank calls it, the tweezers. You and Peachy pick up the teller. Then we see what happens."

"Okay, good," Rafferty says. "Are you armed?"

Ming Li lifts the cover of the book on top of her stack to reveal a recessed square cut into the pages. Nestled into it is a small automatic, maybe a twenty-five-millimeter. It's been blued, but the bluing has worn off around the grip and trigger guard to reveal the shine of steel. It's seen some use. "School's fierce. Got to watch out for the homeys."

"And you can shoot that thing?"

"Better than I can pitch."

The lights in the bank lobby flicker and dim, and the manager opens the door for the last couple of customers.

"Here we go," Rafferty says, but Ming Li is already out the door. He throws some bills on the table. A moment later the bank door opens again, and two men and a woman exit. The last one out is the man they want. Peachy says, "I'm not sure I can do this."

"I'm not sure you can either," Rafferty says. "But I haven't got anybody else."

36

Death Threats and a Strawberry Shake

"T he little wet man's coming toward us," Ming Li says on the phone. "Don't turn the corner. He looks over his shoulder all the time."

"What are you doing?"

"We're standing here. I'm a rich schoolgirl on the phone, and Leung is my faithful servant. He just took the books so I could make a call, and now he's standing a respectful distance away, appropriate to our class difference. *Ouch.*"

"What happened?" Rafferty and Peachy are stopped in the middle of the sidewalk, people parting left and right to get around them.

"Leung pinched me."

"You had it coming. What I mean is, why are you with Leung? You're supposed to be on either side of the big guy. What happened to the old tweezers?"

"He noticed me. Looked at me a couple of times. Probably got a thing for schoolgirls. So I had to pass him. Don't worry, he's written me off. He's watching your little wet man, and the little wet man keeps looking behind him."

"I need to know everything they do."

"Gosh," Ming Li says. "Everything? I'm just a girl."

"This is the big leagues."

"Okay, here he comes. The big one. I think you can come around the corner now."

Rafferty grabs Peachy's sleeve and hauls her behind him, with Peachy apologizing to everyone they bump into. They round the corner, and Rafferty sees the big man take the arm of the teller and drag him to the curb. There is a quick verbal exchange, the big man bending down to get his face close to the teller's, and the teller nods eight or nine times, very fast, and then attempts some sort of argument, which is broken off when the big man shakes him like a rag mop. The teller looks like he is going to burst into tears. Then the big man reaches into his suit coat, and the teller mirrors the movement. Each comes up with a manila envelope.

Ten or twelve yards beyond them, Ming Li chatters brightly into her phone, right foot lifted and hooked behind the white sock on the left ankle. With her free hand, she toys with her hair, rolling a wisp of it between her fingers as though nothing in the world were more urgent than split ends.

The men exchange envelopes.

"Ming Li. You and Leung stay with the big guy. I don't care what it takes, don't lose him."

"Big brother," Ming Li says. "I've been training for this all my life."

"Good. Keep your phone on."

The big man gives the teller a shove, just enough to make him stagger back a step, and heads off down the sidewalk. He passes Ming Li and Leung without a glance but then sneaks a look back at Ming Li. The teller exhales heavily, wipes his face, and pulls out a cell phone.

"Go, Peachy," Rafferty says.

Reluctantly Peachy covers the distance to the teller, as slowly as someone navigating a forest of thorns. She has lifted a hand to touch him politely on the shoulder when he looks up and sees her. The cell phone drops from his hand and hits the pavement, and the battery pops out. He takes a quick step back, mouth open, as though Peachy has fangs, claws, and a snake's forked tongue. A second backward step brings him up against Rafferty. Rafferty has already pulled his wallet out, and when the man whirls to face him, Rafferty lets it drop open and then flips it closed again before the man can register that the shiny object inside it is a large silver cuff link.

"Give me the envelope," Rafferty says in Thai.

Half a dozen emotions chase each other across the teller's face, but the one that stakes it out and claims it is despair. He slowly closes his eyes and reaches into his jacket. Eyes still shut, he holds it out. Rafferty takes it, opens it, looks inside, sees the bright new money, and says into the phone, "You still with the big guy?"

"He's waiting outside another bank, half a block down," Ming Li says. "I'm putting my hair up."

"Gee, that's interesting."

"Well, who knew he liked schoolgirls? Probably hangs around playgrounds. Leung has a different jacket for me, too. And some glasses. I'll look like an office lady."

"Good," Rafferty says. "If he meets someone, let Leung take the one he meets, and you stay with the big guy. When Leung's got whoever he talks to, I want him to call me. You just follow the Chinese guy—"

"I think he's Korean."

"I don't care if he's a Tibetan Sherpa. You stay with him. I mean this, Ming Li, you can't lose him. He could be your father's emergency exit."

"Poke?" Ming Li says.

He brings the phone back to his ear. "What?"

"He's your father, too." She hangs up.

Rafferty stares down at the phone and then dials Arthit's number.

HEADLIGHTS ARE BLOSSOMING on the oncoming cars. Arthit reaches down and flips on his own.

"There has to be more than one teller at each bank," Arthit says. He is balancing two fat manila envelopes in his lap as he drives. "No single teller could pass a quarter of a million in one day."

The two envelopes, one taken from the little wet teller and the other from the teller the Korean grabbed outside the second bank, contain a total of five hundred thousand baht in brand-new counterfeit bills, plus thirty-eight thousand dollars in bogus American hundreds.

"I was wondering about that," Rafferty says. He has his cell phone against one ear, with Ming Li on the other end, but he is talking to Arthit. "Elson found something at the other teller's station. Probably the distributor—the Korean weight lifter—contacts only one teller directly, and that teller gives it to the others. So Petchara handed Elson someone who has no idea where the junk money comes from. As much as that might interest Elson, I don't give a shit. I personally don't care about the mechanics. What I care about is what we're going to do with the money."

"Which is what?" Arthit asks.

"I'm thinking about that."

"Americans are so collaborative." Arthit makes a turn against an oncoming stream of traffic, and Rafferty closes his eyes. Leung, alone in the backseat, laughs. On Rafferty's cell phone, Ming Li says, "I'm pretty sure he's finished."

"Why?"

"He's home, I think. A guesthouse, two stories. A light just went on, second floor right."

"You're extremely good."

"Tell that to Frank. He'd like to hear it."

"I will. Where are you?"

"Soi 38, half a block off Sukhumvit."

"We'll be there in—" He looks out the window. Neon signs glow above the sidewalks now, beacons in the premature dusk. Arthit hits the switch for the wipers, and for what seems like the thousandth time since Rose and Miaow were taken, Rafferty inhales the sharp smell of newly wet dust. He locates a landmark. "Make it ten, twelve minutes."

"It's a shame we couldn't get the third teller," Ming Li says.

"We got two," Rafferty says. "That's two more than we had an hour ago."

"We should have had Frank with us."

"No. Frank needs to stay where he is. He's out of sight, and he needs to stay out of sight."

"He must be going crazy."

"Call him," Rafferty says. "Let him know what's happening."

"I don't know what's happening."

Rafferty says, "Why should you be different?" He hangs up.

"Where?" Arthit says.

"Soi 38. Can you get us some help there?"

"Cops?" Arthit's reluctance is both visible and audible.

"Unless you have connections with the army."

Arthit brakes behind a bus and drums his fingers impatiently against the wheel. "Do we think he's alone?"

"We don't have the faintest idea."

"It's hard to believe," Arthit says, cutting around the bus, "but I'm slowly becoming comfortable with that condition." He picks up his own cell phone. "I can get three I'd trust to keep things to themselves."

As Arthit dials, Leung leans forward in the backseat. "What's in the other envelopes? The ones the big guy kept."

Rafferty turns to him, feeling the stiffness of exhaustion in his neck and shoulders. "My guess is that it's real money. The tellers pass the bad stuff and pocket good bills to balance it out. Say you withdraw five thousand baht. They give you five thousand in counterfeit and then pull the same amount out of the cash drawer and put it into the envelope. They've got the withdrawal slip, the drawer is minus the right amount of money, and they've passed the counterfeit. Everything adds up at the end of the day, and Mr. Korea's envelope is full of real money."

"*Yes, now,*" Arthit says into his cell phone. "Soi 38, stay out of sight."

"And they keep the tellers quiet by threatening their families," Rafferty says. "Poor schmucks."

"Schmucks?" Arthit says, dropping the phone onto the seat. "Is 'schmucks' English?"

"English is a polyglot tongue," Rafferty says. "A linguistic hybrid enriched by grafts from many branches of the world's verbal tree."

Arthit nods gravely. "Thank you, Doctor."

"Anything I can do," Rafferty says, closing his eyes and leaning back, "to illuminate the path of the ignorant with the torch of knowledge."

"He talk like this a lot?" Leung asks.

"Inexhaustibly," Arthit says. "If bullshit were oil, Poke would be OPEC."

Rafferty, eyes still closed, says, "I think this is going to work, Arthit."

"What's going to work?"

"I don't know yet." He feels himself start to drift sideways, like a boat on a tide, and forces his eyes open. He turns to Arthit. "But look what we've got. Half a million bad baht plus almost forty thousand counterfeit U.S., and probably more where that came from. We know where the women and Miaow are, where Chu is. We've got—maybe—a couple of people inside, unless those two cops get really stupid. We didn't have any of that eight hours ago. I've got a door opener for Elson, if I can figure out how to use it."

Arthit says, "Why would you want to?"

"Weight. Just plain old weight."

"A bullet weighs a lot if you put it in the right place," Leung says. "Why not just kick the door in? Get your women. Kill Chu."

"We might," Rafferty says. "But if we do, I want to make sure one more time that they're where we think they are. And I want to know who's holding the gun on them."

"There's one thing we don't have," Arthit says. "Time."

"Yeah," Rafferty says. His watch says they have less than three hours left. "Right now I'd trade rubies for time."

HALF AN HOUR LATER, Rafferty, Ming Li, Leung, and Arthit sit in Arthit's car, around the corner from the Korean's guesthouse. Water from Ming Li's long hair is dripping onto the upholstery, sounding like a leak in the car's roof. Arthit has a window cracked open so he can smoke.

"My hair is going to stink," Ming Li says, waving the smoke away.

"Be glad it's not a pipe," Arthit says.

"You should really quit." She is haloed by the headlights of the police car that has pulled up to the curb behind them. The wet skin on her neck gleams. Two of Arthit's most trusted cops sit in the second car while a third, wearing a T-shirt and jeans, sits behind the wheel of a *tuk-tuk* and waits in the rain outside the guesthouse, keeping an eye on the door.

"You know, quitting is at the very top of my to-do list," Arthit says. "Right after I get my wife back and ice Colonel Chu. Oh, and figure out what to do about this counterfeiting thing." He looks at his wrist, flips the watch around so he can see it, and says, "He'll call any minute now."

"Why don't you buy a shorter band?" Rafferty asks.

"It gives me character, makes me memorable," Arthit says. "The same way some men wear bow ties."

"That's kind of sad," Ming Li says, wringing out her hair. "Why don't you get some cowboy boots or something? Or let your eyebrows grow together above your nose?"

"This is a carefully calculated affectation," Arthit says. "It calls attention to the weight of my very masculine watch. It shows that I care what time it is but I'm not obsessed with it. It has a certain enviable flair."

"What it does," Ming Li says, "is make you look like a kid who borrowed his father's watch."

"Speak right up," Arthit says. "No need to be deferential."

"It is *so* not the bomb," Ming Li says. To Rafferty she says, "Did I get that right?"

"It's about as dated as Crosby, Stills and Nash."

Ming Li says, "Well, how am I supposed to know? I'm from *China*, for heaven's sake."

Rafferty's phone rings, and when he opens it, Chu says, "Where is he?"

"No idea."

"That's very sad. My watch says—"

"The nice thing about watches," Rafferty says over him, "is that you can reset them. They've got that little stem you can turn, right next to the three."

Chu's voice is cold enough to lower the temperature in the car. "And why would I do that?"

"Because you have to. Frank just called me. He'll meet me at five-thirty in the morning."

"Where?"

"He didn't say."

"When *will* he say?"

"He'll call me at five."

Rafferty can almost hear Chu thinking. "It sounds like he doesn't trust you."

"Probably afraid I take after him."

"Why so early?"

"My guess would be he thinks it'll be easier to tell whether anyone's with me."

"I don't like it."

"I'm not crazy about it either."

"Get him to change it."

"You think I didn't try that already?"

Chu says, "This feels wrong." Rafferty can hear people in the background and the clatter of dishes and silverware. Chu is in a restaurant.

"Where are you eating?"

"McDonald's," Chu says.

"You're a regular Yank."

"They're all over China. I got used to the food."

"Quarter Pounder or what?"

"Big Mac and fries. Is this an attempt at friendly conversation?"

"We're stuck with each other," Rafferty says. "No sense in wasting testosterone. At least not until it's time for us to kill each other."

"I suppose not," Chu says. Then he says, "Actually, since we're being candid, I hate McDonald's. Everything tastes like it's fried in whale fat."

"Then why are you there?"

"Takeout. Your little girl was hungry."

Rafferty's heart seems to have leaped intact into his throat, where it's hanging on for dear life. He attempts to clear it away. When he's sure of his voice, he asks, "What did she want?"

"Chicken McNuggets and a large order of fries. And one of those chemical milk shakes."

"What flavor?"

"Is this a quiz? Strawberry."

"Pink," Rafferty says. He hears the word as though from a great distance, and Arthit turns at the rasp in his voice.

Chu says, "Excuse me?"

"My girl," Rafferty says. "She likes pink."

"She's braver than she should be," Chu says. "They both are. Don't take this as a threat, please. I would hate to have to hurt them."

"We've covered this before."

"Just reminding you. It's in your hands. I'll expect to hear from you at five." The line goes dead. Rafferty lets the phone fall into his lap. He exhales so hard that the entire windshield fogs.

"Anything new?" Arthit says.

"Same old stuff. Death threats and a strawberry shake." He picks up the cracked phone and closes it, opens it, and closes it again. "I can't actually *see* anything. This is like putting together a puzzle without a picture on it. All we can do is grab as many pieces as we can get our mitts on."

Arthit puts a hand on the handle of his door. "So shall we grab another piece?"

"We shall," Rafferty says. He pops his own door and slides out into warm rain. Arthit is already halfway to the second car, taking long strides and waving the two cops out. At the edge of his vision, Rafferty sees Ming Li and Leung fall into step with him. The two cops meet them beside their car. The plainclothes officer from the *tuk-tuk* comes up behind them.

"Front and back," Arthit says, raising his voice over the sound of the rain. "Fast. In and straight up the stairs. Exactly"—he flips the watch around—"one minute from now. Nobody stays in sight of that window for more than a second or two." To the plainclothes cop from the *tuk-tuk,* he says, "You get the door for us and stay there. Everybody got it?"

The cops nod. One of the two from the car is young enough to give Rafferty a twinge of paternal worry—wide, anxious eyes and not a line on his face. The other has skin like an old saddle and a burning cigarette cupped against the rain. His nameplate says KOSIT. He looks as anxious as someone waiting for a bus.

"Don't take him down unless your life depends on it," Arthit says. He checks the watch again. "Forty seconds. *Go.*"

Kosit and the young cop take off at a run and slant to the right of the building; they're going to hit the rear entrance and remain on the first floor in case the Korean makes it down the stairs. Arthit slips his gun free, looks from Ming Li to Leung, and slaps Rafferty lightly on the shoulder, saying, "Now."

The four of them round the corner, running full out, and the plainclothes cop angles across the street in front of them to get the door open. Arthit pauses midstreet for a second, the others stumbling to a halt behind him as a car slashes through the standing water on the road, and then he's running again, up the steps and through the door, with the others a step behind.

The hallway is dirty and short. A single, cobwebbed forty-watt bulb dangles by a frayed wire at the foot of the stairs, swaying back and forth in the wind coming through the door. The stairs aren't carpeted, and Rafferty thinks, *Noise.* Arthit waves them to a halt as the back door opens and the other two cops come in, dripping. The swinging light makes their shadows ripple as though they're underwater. Arthit gestures for the older one to take a position at the front door, beside the cop who let them in. His eyes meet Rafferty's, and he jerks his head in the direction of the back door.

Rafferty shakes his head.

Arthit studies him for a moment, reading his resolve, and then points his index finger at Ming Li and flicks it toward the door. Ming Li does something that might be the first stage of a pout but cancels it and goes dutifully down the hall, the little gun dainty in her hand. The young cop looks at her, looks again, and gives her a nervous smile.

Arthit holds up three fingers, twice for emphasis, then folds them again. He raises his hand to show one, then two, and on *three,* he, Rafferty, and Leung charge up the stairs. At the top they turn right and sprint to the last door on the right. In unison, Arthit and Leung lift their right legs, and Arthit whispers, "Look away." Then the two of them snap their legs forward and kick the door in. Arthit throws something inside and leaps back.

There is a blinding flash of light and a *whump,* and Rafferty sees a blur of movement inside, the big man throwing himself toward the window. The flash from the concussion grenade reveals nothing but the size of the room and the presence of the man, frozen by the flash in front of a cheap blue couch. Rafferty has no time to register anything else, other than the sweet, strident smell of cheap cologne, before Leung launches himself through the air and hits the man at the back of his knees. The Korean goes down so heavily the floor shakes, kicks back at Leung, and rolls away, coming partway up with something shiny in his hand, and time seems to slow as Rafferty sees the man—probably half blind from the flash of the grenade—bring the hand around toward

Arthit, silhouetted clearly in the doorway, and then the world erupts in a roar that should have blown the windows out.

But Leung has lashed out with a leg, knocking the big man's gun up, and the lighting fixture in the center of the ceiling explodes, throwing the room into darkness except for the rectangle of gray that defines the window and a yellowish fall of light through the door. A chair or something slams to the floor, and Rafferty sees movement as someone rises from the tangled knot that was Leung and the Korean, and the standing man—too big to be Leung—bends at the waist and charges, taking Rafferty up and into the air with a low shoulder to the gut. Rafferty has just enough time to slam his gun against the side of the man's head before he's tossed to the floor, thrown as easily as a feather pillow, and the man is most of the way to the open door when Arthit blocks it with his body, lowers the barrel of his gun, and fires twice at the man's legs. The Korean stumbles and lists to the left, but he keeps coming, and another shot bursts against Rafferty's eardrums, and suddenly Arthit is no longer standing in the doorway, and the man is almost through it, one hand clasping his left thigh. He grabs the doorframe and starts to pull himself through, and then there is something small and white in front of him. He does a surprised stutter-step, and Ming Li brings up the little gun and shoots him from a distance of three feet.

The Korean drops to one knee. Instantly Leung is on him, raking his eyes with clawed fingers, and as the man reflexively lifts his hands, Leung gets his own hand around the center of the gun above the trigger guard and twists violently. Even over the ringing in his ears, Rafferty can hear fingers break. The gun comes free. Leung puts both barrels—his and the Korean's—against the man's head, and everything goes still.

Except for Ming Li, slowly sinking to her knees in the hallway. Behind her the older cop, Kosit, is staring down, his gun dangling forgotten in his hand. Leung says, "Cuffs here, *now*," and Kosit tears his eyes away, comes into the room, and secures the Korean's hands with flexible plastic cuffs, yanking them so tight that the Korean feels it even through the pain of his wounds, and grunts.

Rafferty crawls on all fours to the doorway. Ming Li throws him a single terrified glance and then begins again to pump with all her weight, her hands cupped and centered over Arthit's heart.

37

He Doesn't Deserve You

I t's melted," Miaow says accusingly.

"So what?" Chu has three pistols partly disassembled on the crate beside him, and metallic fumes of machine oil compete with the deep-fried smell of the chicken and fries. The cleaning rod in his right hand slides through the barrel of the gun in his left. The cop who'd been on guard sits sulking on another crate, halfway across the warehouse. His upper lip is split and so swollen it has lifted to reveal his teeth. Every few minutes he probes the broken one with his tongue and inhales sharply at the pain.

Chu pulls out the rod and studies the cloth it is wrapped in. Satisfied, he puts the gun down and picks up another. To Miaow he says, "Your father said you wanted strawberry because it's pink. It's still pink."

"You talked to Poke?" Rose asks.

"We never stop talking," Chu says, eyes on his work. "We should get a special rate from the cell-phone company."

"How is he?"

"How would he be? He's worried."

Miaow says, "He'll get you."

Chu shakes his head but doesn't look up from the gun. "I doubt that. Compared to some of the people who have tried to get me, he's thin porridge."

Rose takes one of the chicken nuggets and feeds it to Noi, who chews it slowly, her eyes closed. She has refused to look at Chu since the moment he broke the guard's tooth.

"Poke's not afraid of you," Miaow says.

"Neither are you." Chu sights down the barrel of the gun. "But being brave isn't the same thing as being smart."

Miaow regards him for a moment and then dredges a piece of chicken through her milk shake and eats it. She slides her eyes to Rose, waiting for a reproof.

Giving the task all his attention, Chu serenely slides the rod into the barrel. His concentration is complete. He might be a doctor sterilizing his surgical instruments or a violinist tending to his strings. The door to the warehouse bangs open, and Pradya, the fat policeman, comes in. He's soaked to the skin, and his wet hair has been blown stiffly to the left. It looks like something has been dropped, at an acute angle, on his head. He has to put his back to the door and push to close it against the wind.

"Where have you been?" Chu says, irritated at the distraction. He pulls out the rod, glances at the cloth, and starts on the third gun.

Pradya wipes his face. "All over the place. We picked him up a few blocks from the apartment, and then he sat with some woman in a restaurant. After a while a girl went in and sat with them."

"A girl?" Chu says. He is scraping at something on the trigger guard with the yellow fingernail on his right little finger, a nail so long it has begun to curve under.

"A Thai schoolgirl. Young, maybe seventeen. They were watching a bank across the street."

Rose inhales sharply enough for Chu to hear her. He stops working on the gun.

"A schoolgirl?" Chu asks her. "What's he doing with a schoolgirl?"

"How would I know?" Rose says. "I'm here."

Chu weighs the gun in his hand, but he is not thinking about the gun. "Is Sriyat still following them?"

"Yes," Pradya says, "but it's hard. We had to do most of it with binoculars, from at least a block away. They're all keeping their eyes open."

Chu turns his head an inch or two. He seems to be listening for something, perhaps in a corner of the warehouse. He says, "All?"

Pradya shifts his weight uncomfortably. "Rafferty, the girl, and a guy they hooked up with later."

"Hooked up with where?" Chu glares at the cop and snaps his fingers. "This isn't a television serial. Tell me the fucking story. What are they *doing*?"

Pradya goes through it: the man from the bank, the Korean, the envelopes, the followers splitting up. He and Sriyat had split up, too. "I stayed with Rafferty, but Sriyat says the Korean guy met another guy from another bank. Same thing. They swapped envelopes, and after the Korean left, the girl followed him. The man with her grabbed the guy from the bank and took away the envelope. Then he got into a police car, with her husband"—he indicates Noi—"driving. Rafferty was in the car, too."

Chu thinks for a moment. The gun comes to rest flat on his leg. "Banks," he says. His eyes close and reopen, focused on something that isn't there. "Nothing to do with me." Without looking down, he slides the automatic back and forth along his thigh, polishing it, as he studies the gloom in the corner. "But maybe Rafferty doesn't know that."

After a moment Pradya says, "Whatever you say."

Chu stops the polishing and sits still. He pushes his lower lip forward. "I don't like it. It must be important or he wouldn't be wasting time on it."

Rose says, "I know what he's doing. It's not about you."

Chu looks at her, the sharp-cut eyes hooded. Daring her to tell him a lie. "Go on."

Rose tells him about the counterfeit money and the visit from Elson. "He's trying to help Peachy and me," she says.

Chu leans back, tilts his head up, and studies the ceiling. When the words come, they are slow and dreamy, a thought spoken to the air. "And where did he get his help?"

Rose sits a bit straighter. "I don't know."

Chu's gaze, when it strikes her, is as fast as a lash. "*Where did he get his help?*"

"I told you, I don't—"

"Describe them," Chu says to Pradya, his voice garrote tight. "The girl and the man. Describe them."

Pradya closes his eyes for a better look. "The girl, like I said, about seventeen, Thai school uniform, Chinese-looking but got something about her."

"That suggests she might be a *mix*," Chu says. His voice could grate stone. He clears his throat violently and spits. "And the man is wiry, medium height, and very fast."

Pradya nods, licks his lips, and nods again, more vigorously.

"Your husband has a snake for a mother," Chu says. "He's *playing* with me." In a single fluid motion, he gets to his feet, snatches up a magazine, and slaps it into the gun in his hand. The barrel of the gun is pointed at Rose's head. "I should kill you right now," Chu says.

Miaow deliberately puts down her milk shake, stands, and takes two steps, placing herself between him and Rose.

"Good idea," Chu says. "Save me a bullet."

Rose puts a hand on Miaow's arm and pushes her aside. Miaow twists away and steps in front of her again. Rose steers her away again and says, "Not the child."

Chu lets the gun go back and forth between them, and then he spits onto the floor. He turns and kicks the crate he's been sitting on. "Ahhhhhh," he says. "He doesn't deserve you. Either of you." His eyes drop to the gun in his hand, and he puts it on the crate, beside the others. "And what good would it do?" For a moment his body goes loose, his face slack. "The girl," he says, as though to himself. He turns to Pradya. "Get back there. Do whatever you have to do. I don't care if you have to shoot people. Bring me that girl. And you," he says to the one with the broken tooth. "Move these people. I want them out of here in an hour."

PART IV

MILLION-DOLLAR MINUTE

38

We've Got People to Kill

The mask is clear plastic, more terrible because it hides nothing. It cups Arthit's nose, his slack mouth, and his chin. A transparent tube runs into it, supplying oxygen; one of the medical technicians had carefully stubbed out his cigarette before turning the valve on the tank he had wheeled up behind him. The banging of the tank against the stairs is the first sound Rafferty can remember since the shot from Ming Li's gun that put the Korean down. The ten or twelve minutes between the time he saw Arthit sprawled on the hallway floor and the bumpy progress of the tank up the stairs seem to have passed in complete silence.

Rafferty, collapsed heavily on the couch, can't look at Arthit's paper-white face, can't look at the mask. A pink froth of blood speckles the inner surface. It looks like Arthit chewed a pencil eraser and spit it out.

"The lung," says the medical tech who is holding the mask in place. He lifts one of Arthit's eyelids, peers under it, and lets it drop. "The bullet hit the lung. Probably took a bounce off a rib. No exit wound, so it's still in there somewhere. Maybe a .22, not enough velocity for a pass-through."

To Rafferty it seems that the tech is speaking very slowly. Everything that is happening in the tight knot of people gathered around Arthit seems to take an excruciatingly long time. He lowers his eyes again until he is looking at the suitcase between his knees. The suitcase is safe to look at.

From Rafferty's left, the older cop, Kosit, says, "It's a .22." Kosit has the Korean's gun wrapped in a handkerchief.

Rafferty knows he has to get up, knows he and Ming Li and Leung have to get out of there, but he can't make himself move. Arthit going down; Arthit hitting the floor; the blood on Arthit's shirt . . .

"What about him?" asks the other tech, thumbing the Korean, trussed and bleeding on the floor in front of the couch.

"Fuck him," says the first tech. "Let the second team—"

"Blood pressure dropping," says the second tech. His voice is tight.

"Up and out," the first tech says. "Now." The two techs and their helpers lift the stretcher and carry it down the hall, moving fast. Rafferty hears their feet on the stairs, synchronized with the flashes of red on the ceiling, thrown by the lights on the ambulance below.

He feels the young cop's eyes on him. "I saw what you did," the young cop says. "I saw you take the money."

"I did . . . I did what Arthit would have done," Rafferty says. In fact, he can barely remember his frenzied rush through the apartment, fueled by sheer terror at the thought of Arthit's dying. He couldn't help Arthit, but he had to do *something*. What he recalls is a blur of motion, punctuated by full-stop images: a closet filled waist-high with neatly stacked brand-new counterfeit bills, a canvas bag stuffed with loose money, dirty and well handled, a big hard-sided suitcase under the bed. He and Leung jamming money into the suitcase, Leung grabbing the canvas bag. But now that energy is gone. Now there's nothing except the apartment, the sound of the men rushing downstairs, and the weight of his own body. He can't lift his head to meet the cop's stare. He remains focused on the suitcase and, beyond it, the bare feet of the wounded Korean. If he raises his eyes, he'll see the broad smears of blood on the front of Ming Li's white blouse, as though someone had wiped a paintbrush across it.

Arthit's blood.

"You can't just steal—" the young cop begins.

Kosit says, "Stop it. Just shut up."

"You saw us together," Rafferty says to the younger cop. He can barely form the words. "We're friends. We did this together. I did what he would have wanted me to do."

"It's true," Kosit says. "Arthit talked about him all the time. They were friends."

"We *are* friends," Rafferty says sharply. "He's not dead."

No one replies. Kosit studies the floor.

"Oh, dear sweet God," Rafferty hears himself say.

"We have to go," Leung says from the window. "More cops will be coming."

"*Coming?*" Kosit says. "They should be here by now."

Rafferty says, to no one in particular, "I'm not sure I can stand up."

"Yes you can." Ming Li is standing in front of him, although he isn't aware of her having crossed the room. "You have to."

"What you have to do is get out of here," Kosit says. "You're just going to make things more complicated. Arthit is the only one who can explain why you were here in the first place. Not to mention why you're with a couple of Chinese." He goes to the doorway and looks down the hall. "If my colleagues find you here, they'll take you all in. I'm not sure even Arthit could get you out of it. Even if Arthit . . ." The words hang unfinished.

"Listen to him, Poke," Ming Li says. "If they arrest you, if you're not there to meet Chu at five-thirty, your wife and daughter will die. I promise you. He'll kill them."

Kosit turns back to the room. "Whatever this is about, get moving. And use the back door. We called in more than ten minutes ago. They'll be here any second." He fumbles in his pocket and comes out with a card, which he extends to Leung. "Give this to him. It's got my name and number. You," he says to Rafferty. "Wake up. Do what you're supposed to do. You can call me later about Arthit, about how he's doing."

"Poke," Ming Li says. She bends down, bringing her face to his. He feels the warmth of her breath. "One thing at a time, remember? Right now we need to go. The only thing that matters is getting out of here.

You can't help Arthit now." He feels her hands on his arm, feels the strength flowing from them, and somehow he finds himself on his feet. Leung has come from nowhere to grasp his other arm, and Rafferty hears a grunt as Leung lifts the suitcase with his free hand. Ming Li has picked up the canvas bag. Propelled between them, Rafferty sees the straight lines of the door grow nearer, as though the wall were coming toward him in some amusement-park mystery house, and then the hallway slides past and he is on the stairs, the world tilting downward. Leung moves in front of him to catch him if he falls.

Outside, car doors closing, men's voices.

"Faster," Ming Li says, and then they're through the back door.

Rain slaps Rafferty in the face. His eyes sting.

Two steps lead down to a small garden: broad-leaved palms whipping around in the wind, tall ferns blown almost flat against the ground, black water standing a few inches deep. In one corner the spirit house, made of rough wood, has toppled over. The garden ends in a low, unpainted wooden gate, and beyond and above it there's a streetlight, a yellow flame in a halo of rain.

"Don't move," Leung says. He drops the suitcase in front of them and goes through the gate without a backward glance. The gate squeals open into a narrow alley and then is blown shut. In seconds, Leung is invisible, a shadow wrapped in rain.

"Are you here, Poke?" Ming Li asks. Her hair clings to her face in long tendrils. "We need you to be here."

He lifts his face to the rain, lets it needle his eyelids and cheeks. "I'm here."

"*Hate*," Ming Li says. She pinches his arm and gives the pinch a twist. "What you need is hate. Hate will keep you moving."

"I've got enough hate for that," Rafferty says.

"Good. Hang on to it. Feed it. Hate got us out of China. It'll get your wife and little girl back."

"And Arthit's wife," Rafferty says raggedly. "*Noi*. He'll want . . . he'll want her near him."

"He'll have her," Ming Li says. She lets go of his arm and steps back, searching his face. "By the time he opens his eyes, he'll have her."

Rafferty wraps his arms around her and hauls her so close that he can feel her spine pop. She stiffens, and then her arms go around him and they stand there, hugging each other, as the rain pours down on them. Ming Li says, "It's all right, older brother," and something dark blooms in Rafferty's chest, spreads long, soft wings, and then seems to vaporize and disappear, escaping into the night on an endless breath.

"Okay," he says, releasing her. Her gaze locks with his, and the muscles beneath her eyes tighten in recognition. She takes a step away, turns her head to look at him again.

"Let's move," he says. "We've got people to kill."

THE PLAINCLOTHES COP'S *tuk-tuk*, which Leung has borrowed without asking, makes an uneven popping sound, one of its cylinders misfiring occasionally, as it threads through the rain-slowed traffic on Silom. The water falls in sheets, the windshield wipers sluggish with the sheer weight of it. Rafferty and Ming Li sit side by side in the back. Ming Li holds on her lap the canvas bag full of older, well-used money, and Rafferty squeezes the big suitcase between his knees.

Rafferty has no way of knowing how long they've been traveling: It could have been ten minutes or ten hours. He seems to have been journeying through some internal space, the space between thoughts. The space between gunshots. He feels vast and icily empty inside, but he is intensely aware of the mass of his body as it presses against the seat, of the touch of Ming Li's thigh against his, of the cold wetness on his skin. The hardness of the suitcase, the contents of which Arthit may have died for.

"We're almost there," Ming Li says.

Rafferty shakes himself, the way he sometimes does when he wakes from a dream gone wrong. A dream Rose would want to hear every detail of, looking for the scraps of meaning that might help them avert disaster. The movement brings him back to himself, in a *tuk-tuk,* on a wet night, next to his new sister, in a world where disaster has already struck. He leans down to peer beneath the *tuk-tuk*'s sloping roof. "Twice around," he says. "I need to see if we've got watchers."

"No one following!" Leung shouts over his shoulder.

"That's not going to help if they're already here. Do the block twice, like I said."

"What now?" Ming Li says as Leung makes the turn.

"What now? Damned if I know." His eyes are on the sidewalks. "But I think you should drop me and then get back to Frank. Talk it over with him, see what you come up with. What I've got barely qualifies as an idea."

"Fine," Ming Li says. "We'll call you in a couple of hours."

"Chu's not going to give me any more time. Whatever the hell we're doing, we need to be ready."

"We've been ready for years," Ming Li says. "Now we're down to details."

Rafferty says, "Frank did a good job with you."

"He did some of it," Ming Li says, watching the other sidewalk. "Some of it is talent."

THE MONEY HE grabbed from the closet and packed into the suitcase is stiff as starch, the greens and browns too green and brown, the whites too white, the paper too clean. It stacks in perfect rectangular towers, each bill flat enough to have been ironed.

In a quantity this large, it wouldn't fool a blind man.

On the other hand, the money jammed into the canvas bag is soft, worn, dog-eared, soiled from use. The oil and grime from a thousand hands have given it a smudged patina like a layer of dirt on an old painting. It's seen wallets, purses, bar spills, hot coffee, knife fights, crowded cash drawers. It smells of sweat and dirt and face powder. It has notes written on it: phone numbers, prayers, aimless chains of obscenity. It's been exchanged for drinks, drugs, food, a dry room, a doctor's care, sex, a lover's gift, perhaps a murder or two. Hearts have been drawn here and there, stick figures, arrows, candles, teardrops, interlinking squares, the marginalia of idle minds.

In short, Rafferty thinks, it's *money.* The stuff in the suitcase is printing.

The new bills in the suitcase are what the Korean was circulating. The bills in the canvas bag were taken from the banks by the tellers and then passed on in those manila envelopes.

Rafferty keeps seeing Arthit's face, the colorlessness of Arthit's face.

Halfway through a distracted count, he heaves a stack of bills across the room. They separate and flutter to the floor, covering the carpet and the coffee table. A wad with a rubber band around it lands on the hassock. He stares at it. It's real money, taken from the envelopes the Korean grabbed from the tellers, and the rubber band compresses it in the center, leaving the ends loose and soft. It looks almost . . . fluffy.

The paper-banded stacks of counterfeit look like bricks.

He thinks, *Fluffy*.

The word galvanizes him. This is something he believes he knows how to do. And then, in an instant, he sees the rest of it, or at least a possible sequence, as though, during the hour or more of paralysis, it's been quietly assembling itself, waiting for him to notice. For a moment he sits perfectly still, staring at the money and seeing none of it, trying to sequence the stepping-stones that might lead them out of this cataclysm. Looking for the surprise, the wrong turn, the ankle breaker, the gate that won't open, the twig that will snap in the night, the stone that's poised over a hole a hundred feet deep.

He knows he can't see it all. So small steps first. Things he knows how to do.

He goes to the kitchen and checks the cabinet beneath the sink, where they keep the laundry supplies. Straightening up, he realizes that the sound he just heard was his own laughter. He leaves the cabinet yawning open and goes to the living-room desk, where he takes Rose's phone book out of the drawer she uses. He finds the numbers he wants and makes four short calls.

When he leaves the apartment, he leaves the door ajar. His helpers may arrive before he returns.

39

He Wasn't Much, but He Had a Name

Rafferty covers the peephole with his thumb and then knocks again.

The door opens only two or three inches, and the chain is secured, but Rafferty's kick yanks the entire assembly out of the wooden doorframe, and the door snaps back, cracking Elson on the forehead. Rafferty catches it on the rebound and pushes it open, and Elson retreats automatically, one hand pressed to his head. Rafferty follows him in and closes the door with his foot.

"My turn to visit," he says. "Nice pj's."

Elson's face is naked, defenseless, and even narrower without the rimless glasses. He hasn't shaved since morning, and he is a man who should shave twice a day. The stubble holds shadows, accentuating the high, nervous bone structure of his face. He wears loose white pajamas in what appears to be light cotton, patterned with little blue clocks, a theme that is repeated on the buttons. He rubs his forehead and checks his fingers for blood. With the hand still in front of him, he says, "You're looking at jail."

"I'm looking at you," Rafferty says. "I'm looking at someone who hasn't done one thing right since he arrived in Bangkok. You've stumbled around like someone using a map that was printed on April Fools' Day. You'll be lucky if you don't wind up on library patrol."

Elson glances toward the low dresser, where his holstered gun sits next to his computer, and says, "Get out of here." His lips have vanished completely, baring the thumb sucker's dent in his front teeth.

Rafferty comes farther into the room, pushing into the man's space and shifting to his right, toward the dresser. "Don't like it much, do you? I didn't either. There's a difference, though. You came to cause me trouble. I came to save your ass."

Elson seems to realize how he looks and gives the shirt of his pajamas a downward tug, straightening it as though that could turn it into something else. "I'm not going to engage in a dialogue with you, Rafferty. I came in the discharge of my lawful duty."

"And you wrong-footed it, didn't you? Chasing a couple of women who haven't got fifty thousand baht in the bank. Grabbing the wrong teller out of the bank. Letting Petchara lead you around like a pony in a ring. Petchara's crooked. I own inanimate objects that could have seen that. My fucking *toaster* could have seen it."

"I'm calling security," Elson says, taking a step toward the phone on the table between the beds.

"Wrong," Rafferty says, and Elson glances back and stops, off balance, in midstride at the sight of the gun Rafferty has pulled from the tote bag hanging from his shoulder. It takes a quick little shuffle for Elson to remain upright, and he looks furious that it was necessary. "Here's what you're doing," Rafferty says. "You're sitting on the end of that bed. I'm sitting on this one. We're going to talk, just a couple of Americans in a confusing foreign country. And I'm going to be generous, by way of an apology for what a jerk I've been. I'm going to show you mine first, and then you can decide whether you want to continue the conversation."

Elson sits slowly, as though he thinks the bed might be wet. The bed is low and his legs are long, forcing his knees to fold in acute, storklike angles. He shifts his legs to the left for balance and starts to lean right, toward the table, then stops. He says, "I need my glasses."

"Get them. Just leave the phone alone."

"I heard you." Once the glasses are in place, Elson sits a little straighter. He puts his hands on his knees, fingers spread. He has a pianist's hands.

Rafferty sits and puts the gun down beside him on the bed, lifting his own hands to show that they're empty. Elson doesn't even register it, just watches and waits. "First," Rafferty says, "I'm sorry. I'm not consumed with guilt, it's not keeping me up nights, but I'm sorry for the way I treated you. You came on wrong, and you threatened someone I love, but I shouldn't have been such a smart-ass. You can accept the apology or see it as weakness or do whatever you want, but I'm making it anyway."

Elson offers a stiff-necked nod, more a punctuation mark than anything else. His left hand fingers one of the little clocks on his pajamas as though he's curious about the time printed there.

"Second. Here's a present. Late last night the government you work for lost an asset here, or at least a former asset—God knows which. Have you heard about this?"

Elson tilts his head an inch to the right. "Prettyman. The CIA guy." He shrugs. "I know about it, but so what? Not my business."

"It's your business if you clear it up."

For a moment Elson's eyes lose focus and slide down to Rafferty's chest, and then they come most of the way back, with quite a lot going on behind them. "Marginally, I suppose." He is talking to Rafferty's neck.

"If you're going to lie, at least choose a lie I might believe. A former CIA guy gets killed in Bangkok, the American government loses face, and in Asia that's important. Even *this* administration is smart enough to know that. The man who comes up with the killers is going to get a little gold happy face on his lapel."

"Maybe." Elson shifts his weight uncomfortably. His eyes are making tiny motions, as though he is counting gnats. "You're saying you know who did it."

"I know exactly who did it, and I can give him to you."

He puts a hand on the bed behind him, leans back slightly, and eases one foot forward with a small grimace of relief. "How?"

"I'll tell you, if this chat gets that far. But I can promise you he's somebody you want anyway. Somebody who *is* your business."

Elson straightens his glasses, which already look like they were positioned by someone using a carpenter's level. "I need to know who it is and why he's my business."

"A thousand baht is worth a million words," Rafferty says. "Catch." He dips into the canvas tote. Elson brings his hands up far too slowly, and the six-inch brick of money hits him in the middle of the clocks on his pajama top and bounces to the floor. He stares down at it, his mouth open.

"Take a look," Rafferty says. "That's your second present."

Elson bends forward and comes up with the packet of thousand-baht notes. His eyes flick up to Rafferty, and then he flips through the stack, pulls a few out from the middle, and looks at them closely. He blinks twice, heavily enough to make Rafferty wonder if it's a tic. "I need to get up," he says.

"It's your room."

Tucking the brick of money beneath his left arm and clutching the loose bills in his right hand like a little bouquet, Elson goes to the desk near the window and snaps on the lamp. He holds the bills in the pool of light one at a time, inspects them front and back, and then he removes the shade from the lamp. He chooses a bill at random and positions it in front of the naked bulb, as though trying to see the bulb through it. Dropping it onto the desk, he picks up another and then another, examining each of them for several seconds. He runs a thumbnail over the front of two bills, feeling for texture. Then he shapes the loose bills into a stack and yanks a few more from the brick, repeating the routine with each of them.

"There are some American hundreds at the bottom," Rafferty says.

Elson gives him a sharp glance and then finds the bills and gives them a moment of scrutiny. When he has finished, he turns to Rafferty and says, "You have my attention."

"Good. There's another sixty million baht where that came from."

"*Sixty?*"

"Give or take. That's about a million seven in U.S. All brand new and uncirculated. And two hundred thousand in American hundreds, fresh as milk. The North Korean who was passing them out is getting stitched up right now, but he'll be good enough to travel."

Elson squints as he replays the end of the sentence. "Getting stitched up?"

"He got shot."

"Did you shoot him?"

"He was shot by a schoolgirl. Listen, none of this matters. What matters is that you can have him."

"I can't have him if I don't know where he is."

"You'll know in a few hours. By then it'll all be available: the money, the North Korean who's been passing it, and the guy who murdered Prettyman." He studies Elson's face. "He's in the same business as the North Korean, but on a much bigger scale."

Elson's eyes drop to the spill of money on the surface of the desk. He stands there, studying it, and then he picks up the bundle and riffles through it, making a sound like a deck of cards being shuffled. Without turning to Rafferty, he says, "I'm pretty much by the book. I don't go outside the lines much."

"I guess it'll depend on how badly you want what's on the other side."

"I want it. I'm just telling you, my comfort level is low when it comes to playing cowboy. And I don't like surprises."

"Then you're in the wrong city."

Elson slaps the money against his thigh, then brings it up and looks at Rafferty over it. "How far outside the lines am I going to have to go?"

"Some unpleasant things may happen, but I don't think you'll have to do any of them. You won't even be on the scene when they go down, if they do. You'll have—what's the phrase?—plausible deniability. Your end should be pretty much inside the lines."

Elson nods. He has the distracted expression of a man evaluating a position on a chessboard: if *this*, then *what*? Finally he says, "Even assuming this is something I can do, I need a cop. I can't do anything here without a Thai cop. That's a rule I can't screw with."

"I can get you a cop."

"Why doesn't that surprise me?" With a quick movement, he folds the money in half, one-handed, and his thumb pages idly through it. Elson has obviously counted a lot of money in his time. He lifts the bundle and fans it expertly, as though preparing for a card trick. "Should be a cop who's been assigned to me."

"It won't be."

Another nod, confirmation rather than agreement. "If this is big enough, I can probably get the Thais to say they assigned me whoever it is. Especially if we can prove that Petchara is dirty. They'll be embarrassed about that."

"Petchara put the bag in Peachy's desk. You saw his reaction when you pulled out the old money."

A gust of wind makes the window shiver, but Elson doesn't seem to hear it. When he speaks, his voice has been hammered flat. "The bag. You mean the *paper* bag. The bag you didn't know anything about."

"It was originally full of counterfeit, thirty-two thousand worth. Peachy found it on Saturday, and I changed it for the real stuff."

"She found it on Saturday?"

"She goes into the office a lot."

He shakes his head. "But then . . . why bother to exchange it? Why not just move it? Put it someplace we wouldn't find it?"

"I needed reactions. I needed to know who was setting us up."

Surprise widens Elson's eyes. "You thought it was *me?*"

Rafferty passes a hand over his hair, and a chilly rivulet of rainwater runs down the center of his back. "Could have been anybody."

"I'm an agent of the federal government." He sounds like his feelings are hurt.

"Look at it, would you? You practically kick my door in, you make slurs about my fiancée, you embargo my passport, and then all this junk money shows up, just materializes in a desk drawer. And I'm supposed to think, Oh, no, not him, because you've got that thing in your wallet."

Elson fills his cheeks with air and blows it out. "Okay," he says. He glances at the storm's special effects through the window and shakes his head in disapproval. Finally he says, "Now I'll show you mine. We're under a lot of pressure. The Service, I mean. Personally, I think the administration is overreacting, but I'm not paid to have personal opinions. Look at it mathematically, though, and the level of concern is way over the top. There's about seven hundred and fifty billion bucks in our currency—I mean cash, actual paper—circulating at any given moment, around sixty percent of it outside the country. These jokers are turning out somewhere between seventy-five million to five hundred million a year. Sounds like a lot of money, but put it all together and it wouldn't make a dimple in this year's deficit."

"Somewhere between seventy-five million and five hundred million?

Is that supposed to be some sort of scientific estimate, or did somebody draw a number out of a hat?"

"It's a punch line," Elson says. "The work is too fucking good. We have no idea how much of this stuff is actually out there. And we're being boneheads about getting banks to work with us." He holds up the loose bills. "Say you run a Thai bank, okay? Or a Singaporean bank, or one in Macau, where these guys are *really* active. And one day you get nine or ten of these things across the counter." He passes the bills from one hand to another, giving them to himself. "So you're holding junk. You've essentially got two choices. You can call us up, wait around until we can be bothered to clear a space on our desk calendar, and we take the bills and maybe say thanks, but we don't give you a penny. Or you can skip the call and just hand them to the next customer who wants hundreds."

"That's a tough one," Rafferty says.

"I'm sure they agonize over it. So they don't cooperate. And multiply it: These guys, the North Koreans, are operating in something like a hundred and thirty countries. They're the first government to counterfeit another country's currency since the Nazis, and they seem to be able to drop it practically anywhere, while we sit around looking like the only reason our thumbs evolved was so we could stick them up our butts. We're a relatively small outfit, you know? And we're, like, sitting at the president's feet, and the president has a huge hard-on for Kim Jong Il, so we get a lot of heat." He waves a hand in front of his face once, as though to clear away smoke. "And there's the other piece, the *really* big piece. We want the North Koreans at the negotiating table. We're not thrilled about their nuclear program. The idea is, if we can put a big enough crimp into their counterfeiting income, they'll pull up a chair and listen to how much money they could make by not screwing around with plutonium. Whether they'd really sit down or not—and they might not, because these guys are certifiably nuts—there's a lot of motivation to give it a try, so the president can declare a foreign-policy triumph and say, 'America is safer today.' He likes to say that." His eyes when they come back to Rafferty's have a kind of appeal in them. "So what I'm saying is, yeah, sometimes we act like assholes."

"Some people probably respond to it better than I do."

Elson says, "Pretty much everybody responds to it better than you do." He drops the money on the desk. "In that office, when I said I'd told you to shut up and you said you forgot, I damn near laughed."

"Shame you didn't. Things might have gone a little better."

"We're where we are," Elson says. He comes back to the bed and sits, facing Rafferty. "I've got a million questions," he says. "This all seems very sweet, but not if my ass is going to be hanging out there, getting rained on."

On cue, a gust of wind slams against the window, rain hitting the glass like bullets. Elson bares his teeth at it and says, "How can you live here?"

"I like it."

"This is my first monsoon," he says. "One is enough." Behind him, through the window, the wind is lashing palm trees around as though they were peacock feathers. "Such a great word, 'monsoon.' I expected something—oh, I don't know—something more romantic. Girls in sarongs hanging on to palm trees or something."

"You're in Bangkok. You want girls in sarongs hanging on to palm trees, I can probably give you a phone number."

Elson actually grins. "Bullshit."

"Monsoons grow on you. And this one's going to be a dilly."

Elson regards the storm with a little more interest. A huge palm frond whips past the window, and he turns back to Rafferty. "So. I get the money, the North Korean and his connections—"

"You'll have to get those out of him yourself."

"Fine. And the big guy who's also in the game and who torched the CIA man."

"*Prettyman,*" Rafferty says, surprised at his own vehemence. "Arnold Prettyman. He wasn't much, but he had a name."

Elson lifts a palm, fingers pointing up, and wipes it back and forth, erasing the words. "Okay, okay, he had a name. I'm going to tell you something else I shouldn't. There's a folder in that desk over there. You're in it. You're not the cleanest guy in the world, but you're not the dirtiest either. Some people say nice things about you. I should have read it before I busted in on you."

"You've read it now," Rafferty says.

"Yeah, and it's enough to make me wonder what you're getting out of this."

"Something that was taken from me."

Elson lowers his head and regards Rafferty over the top of his glasses. "Yours legally?"

"To the extent that anybody belongs legally to anybody else."

The agent's lips purse as though he is going to whistle. "People?"

Rafferty nods.

"People you care about."

"Are you married?"

Elson hesitates and then says, "Yes."

"Got kids?"

"Two."

"What would you do to get them back if someone took them?"

Elson's face empties while he thinks about it. "Anything."

"What about the lines?"

"If my family's involved? Fuck the lines."

"Pretty much the way I feel."

"I'm sorry to hear it. And not to be a prick, but that's your issue and I'm sure you're going to take care of it. On my end of things, what do I do?"

"You wait for me to call you around five this morning and tell you where it's going down. And I'll tell you then how it works, and you can pull out if you want to."

"Why not now?"

"I'm waiting to put a few more stepping-stones in place."

"Great," Elson says. "You're working on the fly."

"My turn to ask a question."

Elson closes his eyes, drops his head, and puts his fingers wearily to his forehead, where the door hit it. "Why not?"

"I've seen you flash that gun around. Are you any good with it?"

For a moment Rafferty thinks Elson will smile again. Instead he says, "Better than you can imagine."

40

I'll Never Sleep on It Again Anyway

H e's getting the rubies," Frank says on Rafferty's cell phone. "The papers."

"He's not going to settle for the rubies and the papers." Rafferty is on his way home from Elson's hotel, in the backseat of a cab. He chose a cab instead of a *tuk-tuk* in deference to the rain, which has achieved epic scale. In four blocks they have passed half a dozen stalled cars and two accidents. The sidewalk neons are shapeless smears of diluted color, echoed on the wet pavement.

"What about the money?" Ming Li's voice comes from the bottom of a cave, and Rafferty has to press the phone harder against his ear to hear her. Frank has his cell phone on speaker.

"The money's an extra. He's not expecting it, so that could help. But let's face it, what he wants is Frank."

Ming Li says, "We've talked about this before. The answer is still no."

Frank says, "Ming Li. Don't talk, listen." Then he says to Rafferty, "Where?"

"I'll let you know in an hour or two."

"You *can't* give him Frank," Ming Li says.

"Maybe you can think of something else." A car speeds by in the opposite direction, throwing up a five-foot wave that shatters against the windows of Rafferty's cab. His driver says the Thai equivalent of "fuckhead" and hits the horn in retaliation.

"At the very least, we need to know where it's going to happen," Ming Li says.

"You're not going to know, until the last minute, and neither will I. I'm letting Chu pick the place."

"Are you crazy? If he picks the place, we can't set anything up."

"That's exactly right. He's not stupid. One sniff of anything screwy and he's gone. He'll kill everyone and disappear. And he'll still be after you. He'll be after you until either he or Frank is dead. We have to end it here, and that means he thinks he's in control and that he's going to get everything he wants."

"Poke's right," Frank says. "I know Chu. He's not going to walk into anything that could be a setup."

"So we're going to let him set *us* up?" Ming Li says.

"He won't get a chance," Rafferty says. "I'm going to give him fifteen, twenty minutes between the time he sets the place and the time we walk into it. And I'm ninety percent sure I know where it'll be."

"How?" Ming Li asks.

"I'm going to force it," Rafferty says. "Send Leung with the box. I'll talk to you in an hour."

He closes the cell phone, looks out the window, and resigns himself to the fact that he's not going to be able to see where he is until he's home. He digs a business card out of his shirt pocket and dials the number on it.

"Kosit," says the leather-faced cop.

"This is Rafferty. How's Arthit?"

"No word yet. The doctors are still in there."

"I need to see you."

"Um," Kosit says, "I'm not sure I should leave here."

"This is for Arthit. Believe me, he'd want you to do it."

"What do you mean, it's for Arthit?"

"It's between you and me. Are you okay with that?"

"I might be. What is it?"

"Fine. You be the judge." He tells Kosit about Noi, about Rose and Miaow, and about the meeting with Chu.

"Worse and worse." Kosit sounds as drained as Rafferty feels. "What do you want me to do?"

"I'll tell you at my place."

Kosit says, "Somebody's got to be coming out of Arthit's room soon. Give me half an hour. If we don't hear anything by then, I'll leave. And listen, for Arthit I can get you a hundred cops, if you need them."

"Thanks," Rafferty says. "But I think Arthit would say we don't need them."

ONLY ONE JAR of Nescafé this time. The color should vary. Rafferty stirs it in, examines the tint of the water in the washer's tub, and rummages through the cabinets until he finds a tin of powdered green tea. He can hear the hair dryers whirring in the other room, broken occasionally by the sound of women laughing. Fon comes into the kitchen, lugging two very heavy-looking plastic bags from Foodland, conveniently open twenty-four hours.

"They've only got two left," she says. "We've practically bought them out." She grunts as she lifts the bags to the counter. "I got your glue, too."

Rafferty adds half the green tea to the water and stirs with his hand. "What do you think?"

"I'm no expert," Fon says. "When I see money, all I look at is the numbers."

"Looks okay to me." He reaches over and untwists the cap on one of the big jugs of fabric softener from Fon's shopping bags and empties the entire bottle into the tub. "Let's just use one this time," he says. "Last batch got a little mushy."

"Fine," Fon says, looking down at the water. "Maybe there'll be a bottle I can take home."

"I'll trade it for the basket."

"Pretty expensive fabric softener," she says. She bends down and comes up with a large plastic laundry basket, which she gives to Rafferty. He upends it into the washer. Crisp, flat money flutters down onto the surface of the water, and Rafferty pushes it under and adds more, repeating the process until it's all in the tub. Fon takes the empty basket.

"I think we'll use the delicate cycle," he says, hearing the absurdity in the words. "It's faster." He is up to his elbows in water and money, so he says, "What time is it?"

"A little after two."

"We need more people," Rafferty says. He pushes "start" on the washing machine, dries his hands, and follows Fon into the living room.

Lek and three other women, all from Rose and Peachy's agency, sit on the floor around another laundry tub. The tub is blue plastic with square holes in the sides. Two of the women reach in and toss the money like a salad while the others aim hair dryers through the holes. The floor is a snake farm of extension cords. When Rafferty went into the kitchen to start the new load, the basket looked only half full. Now, with the bills drier and not clinging to each other, they almost reach the top edge. As the dry bills are blown to the top, one of the women gathers them and carries them to the couch, which is covered from one end to the other in loose, dried money, nearly a foot thick. Rafferty goes to it, picks up a double handful, crumples them, then lets them drop.

They look and feel a lot better. Not ready yet, but better.

"We're never going to finish at this rate," he says. "Who else can we call?"

As if in answer, someone knocks on the door. Rafferty waves the women into the kitchen, realizes there is nothing he can do about the money everywhere, and pulls the Glock. He opens the door an inch and sees Lieutenant Kosit. "Oh." He sticks the gun into his pants, behind his back. "It's you."

Kosit's eyes are red-rimmed, his face tight enough to have been freeze-dried. He peers past Rafferty and pulls his head back a fraction of an inch in surprise. "What are you doing?"

"Laundering money," Rafferty says. "To buy Noi back." He pulls the door open, but Kosit stands rooted where he is, and Rafferty's heart sinks. "News?"

"He's in intensive care," Kosit says. "The bullet hit the lung, but it also nicked a ventricle. If that tech hadn't been on top of Arthit's blood pressure, he would have bled to death internally."

"What do the doctors say?"

"They don't know shit. They're talking about shock, infection, a whole list of stuff that could kill him. But I'll get a call if anything changes."

"Come on in."

Across the hallway the elevator doors open, and Mrs. Pongsiri steps off, wearing a short black cocktail dress and carrying the world's smallest handbag, on the surface of which five or six sequins jostle for space. Her eyes go to Rafferty and then travel to Kosit's uniform, and she begins to smile. Then she sees the money spread over the couch, and the smile hardens into a mask. She says, "Oh, my."

From behind Rafferty someone squeals *"Anh!"* and he turns to see Fon grinning at Mrs. Pongsiri like a long-lost sister.

"Fon," Mrs. Pongsiri says in a voice Rafferty has never heard before: higher, softer, younger, the voice of the bars and clubs. She opens her arms like a soprano reaching for the top note. Fon shoves her way between Rafferty and Kosit, and the two women embrace. Mrs. Pongsiri kisses Fon on the cheek and squeezes her so hard that Fon lets out a little squeak. Holding Fon at arm's length, Mrs. Pongsiri looks back to the couch full of money and says, "But what in the world—"

Now the other women reappear. Lek and one other, whose name Rafferty doesn't know, give Mrs. Pongsiri wide, white smiles as they pick up their hair dryers and get back to work.

"You're . . . drying money?" Mrs. Pongsiri asks, the question wrinkling her forehead.

"We need to make it look old," Rafferty says. "So we washed it."

Mrs. Pongsiri blinks heavily, obviously sorting through, and rejecting, half a dozen questions. Finally she settles on the practical. "Don't you have a dryer?"

"Sure," Rafferty says, "but I think it'll make them too stiff."

Mrs. Pongsiri wearily shakes her head. *"Softener sheets,"* she says, as though speaking to a disappointing child. "Just throw them in with the money."

Kosit and Rafferty look at each other.

"I bought a box of them today," Mrs. Pongsiri says. "I'll be right back." She gets a new grip on her purse and bustles down the hall. As she unlocks her door, Rafferty hears her say, "Men."

———

KOSIT GIVES A disbelieving glance at the shirt cardboards Rafferty has glued together, looks at the suitcase and the bent coat hangers Rafferty plans to use for support, and says, "Never."

Through the open door to the living room, Rafferty hears the women talking. He feels like his battery died and corroded days ago, but the women are fully charged. For most of them, this is the first time they've worked their normal hours in months.

"Why not?" He and Kosit are sitting on the bed.

Kosit picks up the shirt boards. Rafferty's newly laundered shirts, stripped from the cardboard, litter the floor. "Too flexible," Kosit says, bending them. "Even glued together. You need it to be rigid. This stuff is heavy. And the lever won't work. Not enough pressure."

"Start with the boards. What can we do?"

"Can't add much weight," Kosit says, thinking. "What about those books in the living room?"

"Books are heavy," Rafferty says.

"The covers aren't. Get a bunch of hardbacks and some sort of cutter. Look." He frames a book cover in his hands and mimes placing them across the platform of shirt boards. "Overlap them," he says. "Crisscrossed. Glued on both sides, so they don't bend."

"That leaves the lever," Rafferty says.

"It leaves a lot of things," Kosit says. "The hinges on the suitcase, for example. You need to oil them so they're almost friction-free." He opens and closes the suitcase several times. "Too much resistance," he says.

"I've got oil. What about the lever?"

"I can fix the lever. But you need more . . ." Kosit searches for the word, then brings his hands slowly together and pulls them apart quickly.

Rafferty says, "Shit. Well, it's not the end of the world. I don't think I'll need this. It's just insurance."

Kosit sits back, looking doubtfully at the suitcase, at the mess they have made. Then his face clears, and he points at the mattress. His eyebrows come up in a question.

"Sure," Rafferty says. "If the next four or five hours go wrong, I'll never sleep on it again anyway."

He gets up and goes into the living room to get the books and an X-acto knife. The production line is in full swing. The dryer, with the last load in it, is running in the kitchen. Two women crumple or fold the bills and smooth them again. Another chooses one bill out of four or five and makes a small mark with a felt-tip, either black or red, like those used by banks. Fon has taken to writing random phone numbers with a ballpoint pen on every tenth or twelfth bill. She passes the bills on to Mrs. Pongsiri, who sorts the baht and the dollars into two stacks and smooths them again.

Suddenly Mrs. Pongsiri breaks into a laugh and then reaches over and swats Fon lightly on top of the head. The other girls gather round to look at the bill, and then they all laugh. Rafferty reaches for it and turns it over. It is an American hundred. In the slender margin at the edge, Fon has carefully written, *"Love you long time."*

Getting into the spirit, Mrs. Pongsiri says, "Roll up some of the American hundreds. Roll them very tightly and then unroll them again."

Kosit, framed in the doorway to the bedroom, eyes her narrowly for a moment and then says, "Good idea."

"Americans in my club," Mrs. Pongsiri says, hurrying the words. She has apparently just remembered that Kosit is a cop. "They do that all the time, and then they inhale something through it."

"Probably vitamin C," Kosit says. "I'm sure there are no drugs at your club."

"Very high-end," Mrs. Pongsiri agrees.

"What's the name of your club?" Kosit asks.

"It's called *Rempflxnblt,*" says Mrs. Pongsiri, sneezing most of the word into her palm. She presses an index finger beneath her nostrils. "Sorry. It's the perfume in the fabric softener."

"Mrs. Pongsiri my mama-san once," Fon says cheerfully in English. Mrs. Pongsiri blanches. "Same-same with Lek and Jah. Very good mama-san. Never hit girls, never take money."

"Almost never," Lek says, and the other women laugh again.

Lek is wrapping rubber bands around the stacks: ten thousand dollars per stack in American hundreds, one hundred bills in each stack of thousand-baht notes. She ran out of rubber bands ten minutes ago, and the women removed a remarkable variety of elastic loops from their hair. Mrs. Pongsiri traipsed down the hall a second time and came back with a box containing enough scrunchies to style a yeti. Rafferty is a little worried about the predominance of beauty products, but he figures if the stacks are mixed up enough, they won't be so conspicuous.

With a *thwack,* Lek snaps a bright pink scrunchie around a wad of thousand-baht notes, and Rafferty's cell phone shrills. Every eye in the room goes to him as he opens the phone and puts it to his ear.

"Coming up," Leung says. "With a surprise."

"What I don't need right now is a surprise."

"This is a surprise you'd rather have now than later. You might want to meet me in the hall." He hangs up.

"How much more?" Rafferty asks the women.

"Halfway done," Fon says. "We kept some to speed things up." The other women laugh, some more heartily than others.

"If you do," Rafferty says, "take the stuff on the coffee table. It may not be as pretty, but it's real." He pulls a dozen hardcover books of approximately the same size off the shelf and heads for the bedroom. He has just dropped them in front of Kosit, who is sitting on the bed, which has a long rip in it where the policeman worked out a spring, when the doorbell rings.

"Listen," Kosit says. "The bedsprings aren't enough."

"Well, Jesus," Rafferty says. He can barely focus on the problem. "Use anything."

Kosit shakes his head. "I don't know—"

"Use those," Rafferty says, pointing to the stun grenades hanging from Kosit's belt. "That ought to open things up."

Kosit tilts one up and lets it drop back. "I'm not sure. The pins are hard to pop. They take a good hard tug. I don't know if the lever—"

The doorbell rings again. "Please," Rafferty says. "Solve it." He goes back into the living room and opens the door, just enough to squeeze out into the hallway.

Leung stands there, water dripping off the end of his nose, a canvas bag hanging from his shoulder. The gun in his hand is pointed at the fat cop and the thin cop. *Pradya and Sriyat,* Rafferty thinks. The fat cop, Pradya, tries on a smile.

Rafferty looks at the three of them, and an overwhelming weariness seizes hold of him. He leans against the wall and closes his eyes for a moment, trying to find a way to make this new development work to his advantage. When he opens his eyes again, Pradya has given up on his smile. "You," Rafferty says to Sriyat. "Go back to Chu. Take your time, but go back. Tell him whatever you want. Tell him Leung caught you, I don't care. Tell him we kept Pradya." Sriyat doesn't even nod, just turns to ring for the elevator. "Do you still know which side you're on?" Rafferty asks.

Sriyat turns his head a quarter of the way, his mouth a taut line. "Not much choice," he says.

"Make sure you remember that," Rafferty says. To Pradya and Leung, he says, "Come on in. I'll try to find you someplace to sit."

41

The Deal Just Changed

V ery fucking cute," Rafferty says into the phone. "Sending those clowns after Ming Li."

"You changed the rules when you lied to me," Chu says.

"Oh, gosh," Rafferty says, "and we'd established such an atmosphere of trust." His eyes scan the room. The fat cop, Pradya, sits on the couch, head down, with Leung standing over him. The women paw through the rubies in the box, their eyes wide. Leung is watching their hands. Kosit is busy with the suitcase in the bedroom.

"You've been in contact with Frank," Chu accuses. "All along."

"No. Just the past eight hours or so. He called me with some news, and I didn't want to share it with you."

"What news?"

"Don't get excited about this. In the end you'll be happy about it."

"I'll decide what I'm happy about. What is it?"

"He sold your rubies."

"Yes," Chu says, dragging the word out. "I can see why you wouldn't want to tell me that. Just out of curiosity, how much did he get?"

"About a million four."

"Dollars, of course."

"Sure. Even with you on his tail, he's not going to sell them for a million and a half baht."

"He could have gotten more. I assume you have the money."

"I've got better than that. I've got the money and I've also got the rubies."

"You've got . . . you said he sold them."

"He did."

"Then how did you get them?"

"Violence," Rafferty says. Leung looks over at him and grins.

"You're better than he is," Chu says. "Better than he was in his prime."

"Don't make me blush. Here's the deal: The money evens things up. You have three items of Arthit's and mine, and I have three items for you. We're going to make one trade at a time. No promises, no IOUs, no payment for future delivery, no address left behind where we can find them. Cash for Noi, in the flesh. Rubies for Rose. Frank for Miaow."

Chu says, "Have you looked in the box?"

Careful, Rafferty thinks. "Frank popped the lid and showed me the stones. That's a lot of rubies."

"Didn't you go through it? After you got it back?"

"Why would I? I don't know anything about rubies. What am I going to do, weigh them one at a time?"

"Mmmm," Chu says.

Rafferty waits.

"I want Ming Li, too."

"Not part of the deal."

"The deal just changed."

Rafferty says, "Hold it. I need to think." He looks at Leung, whose eyes have returned to the women's hands. Pradya is frankly listening to the phone call, but he looks away when Rafferty catches him. "Buy her from me."

"Buy her? With what?"

"The rubies. Ming Li for the rubies." Now Leung is looking at him, and he's not grinning. Rafferty shakes his head.

"No," Chu says. "She's a bonus, for the trouble you've caused me."

"Half the rubies."

"You really are venal," Chu says, almost admiringly. "You're giving me your father and proposing to sell me your sister."

"It's a dysfunctional family."

"Two handfuls," Chu says. "In front of me. You can dip your hands into the box and bring up as many as you can hold. Put them in your pockets and give me the girl."

"Four."

"Two, and that's the end of it."

"Okay. Two."

"Send her to me now."

"No. Nothing gets traded on the basis of futures. No deferred transfers. Payment in one direction, person in the other. Right there, on the spot."

Chu says, "It sounds like you don't trust me."

"That's funny," Rafferty says. "The last person who said that to me was Arnold Prettyman."

Chu doesn't even hesitate. "What a peculiar name. Since we're both putting everything on the table, I'm assuming you have some safeguards in mind."

"Lots of them."

"I'm listening."

"You'll have your guys on hand, and I'll have my own. I'm keeping one of your guys with me—the fat one, Pradya, I kind of like him—and he takes charge of Frank. He's got a cell phone. He'll call you when we pick Frank up. You can even talk to Frank, if you want to make sure he's with us. I arrive with the money. You have someone bring out Noi. We swap, right there. Cash for Noi. The rubies and Frank—and Ming Li, I guess—are out of sight until they're needed. You can't shoot me or you lose everything else. I can't shoot you because you've still got Rose and Miaow, and your guy, Pradya, could pop Frank. With me?"

"So far."

"Then one of your people brings out Rose, and one of my people brings out the rubies."

"Who? Who are your people?"

"Only one of them has skills. The people who bring out your items will be girls from Rose's agency. Former go-go dancers." He can feel the women look up at him.

Chu laughs. "Go-go dancers? In costume?"

"They'll be in their underwear." Fon's mouth drops open. "Nowhere to put a weapon. Just wet girls."

"In my youth," Chu says, "I was partial to wet girls."

"I've looked at a few myself."

"What then?"

"Then it's Frank for Miaow and Ming Li for my share of the rubies."

"Very tidy. And when we've finished our exchanges?"

"My people will be out of sight, out of range. Sitting in a car with the engine running. You'll have everything, including Frank. You can have half a dozen guns on me, since shooting me won't get you anything back. We say good-bye, and you leave."

"Leaving is always the sticky part."

"So I've heard." He crosses his fingers. "What do you suggest?"

"I choose the place," Chu says instantly, and Rafferty relaxes. "I'll give you a general direction and call back a few minutes before you're due, to tell you exactly where you're going. Pradya will tell me where you are and who's with you when I call. I'll have people watching you arrive, just to make sure there aren't a dozen cops behind you. If I see anything I don't like, I kill the hostages, and you'll never lay eyes on me."

"*You* choose the place?"

"Of course."

"We could be walking into a setup."

"Why would I set you up? This is business. I'm not going to kill all these people if I don't have to. Bodies everywhere? That could come back to sting me. We Chinese come from villages, we live with hornets. We know better than to punch holes in the nest. I get what I want, you get what you want, and we shake hands. The hornets stay home."

"I'm not happy about you choosing the place."

"Think of it as an opportunity for greater understanding. Learning that you don't actually run the world can be a valuable lesson. Perhaps we should both consider this interaction a step toward enlightenment."

"Gee," Rafferty says. "How can I say no to that?"

"You can't," Chu says. He hangs up.

Rafferty folds the phone and says, "Let's pack the money."

AN HOUR LATER Lek says, "It's going to be cold."

"It was colder in the bar," Fon replies. "Didn't you bathe in the rain in your village when you were a kid? I remember waiting with my shampoo every time it got cloudy." She has sacrificed the rubber bands in her hair to wrap money, so she roots through Mrs. Pongsiri's box of scrunchies for a color she likes, a heavy twist of hair wrapped around her free hand. "Anyway, it's for Rose."

"Done," Kosit says, carrying the suitcase into the room. Judging from the slump in his right shoulder, it's heavy. "I only fastened one clasp because you're going to need a hand free. Just remember to put it down flat. Keep the handle toward Chu." He sets it carefully on the couch. "And if you pop the lever, don't look down at it."

"Is it going to work?"

"Fifty-fifty."

"Jesus. Couldn't you lie to me?"

"It's foolproof," Kosit says.

His cell phone rings.

"Kosit," he says, and he looks up at Rafferty, and then his eyes bounce away. "Yeah, yeah. What's he say?" He closes his eyes as though he is praying. "Fine," he says at last. "Thanks for the call."

Rafferty's forehead is suddenly wet. "What?"

"He's stable. They're still worried about shock and infection, but if he makes it through the night, he's got a chance." He wipes the back of his hand roughly over his mouth. "I'd kill for a beer."

"You don't have to exert yourself. Got some in the refrigerator."

"No. I'd pass out. I feel like I've been awake for a week."

"We'll have one later. Together. When this is over."

"With Arthit," Kosit says. "We'll all go—" he says, but he's cut off by his phone, which is ringing again. He pats his pockets frantically before realizing it's still in his hand. "Kosit," he says. He listens for a second and then says, "Fine." He folds it, looks at it like it just materialized, and puts it in his shirt pocket, tapping it once so he'll remember where he put it. "Car's downstairs," he says. "White Toyota, pulled out of the impound lot. No antennas, no fancy paint job. No super-duper ultra-beam halogen headlights. Looks like every other car in Bangkok."

Rafferty nods. "Ladies?"

For a moment he doesn't think they heard him. The women sit absolutely still as the silence stretches out. Then Fon reaches into the front of her T-shirt. When her hand comes out, it has her Buddhist amulet in it. She puts it between her palms, presses her hands together in a praying position, and raises them to her face. She bows her head. One by one the other women repeat her movements. Last of all, Mrs. Pongsiri fishes inside her silk blouse and brings out a golden amulet on a heavy chain. She brings her hands around it and lowers her head. They sit there, five women whose lives have been almost impossibly difficult, and offer their prayers for Rose, Miaow, and Noi.

Rafferty puts his hand on his own amulet, the one Rose gave him, and then he bolts from the room. He closes the bathroom door behind him and lets the sobs rise up and escape. It feels like they've been battering at the door for days. When he can control his breathing again, he throws cold water on his face, scrubs himself dry, and goes back into the living room. Fon, Lek, and Kosit are waiting at the front door, Kosit holding the suitcase. Leung stands behind Pradya, a cautionary hand on his shoulder.

Rafferty picks up the box of rubies and says, "Time for the swap meet."

42

They've All Got Their Little Hatchets

The chalkboard nailed to the wall says SPECIASL OF THE WEKE. Below the misspellings, which are hand-lettered in what looks like indelible paint, the board is blank.

"I hope that's not my week," Frank says.

Rafferty says, "We'll try to see that it isn't."

Ming Li sips a watery iced coffee and says, "How do you find these restaurants?" She puts the glass down, and the sound when it hits the table makes Pradya, seated across the restaurant with Leung, jump. Pradya is on the phone with Chu, letting him know they have Frank. His hand is cupped over the phone, but Leung has leaned forward to listen. He glances up at Rafferty and nods.

"I guess we're on," Frank says. His forehead is beaded with sweat. One leg jitters up and down beneath the table, providing a rhythm track to whatever is going through his head. He looks at the tabletop, dips a finger in the condensation at the bottom of his own glass, and begins to draw a series of wet loops, like a stretched spring. Ming Li watches his finger move, as intently as if he were writing a secret language only they can read, and Rafferty briefly wonders whether it is. Frank's hand is trembling, and he pulls it back and puts it in his lap.

Not surprisingly, given the hour, they are the only people in the restaurant, which is just off Khao San, a few blocks from the guesthouse. Fon and Lek are waiting in the car, chattering nervously. When the five of them came in, the waitress, who had been bent over a brightly colored book called *Let's English!* had gotten up and turned on the television. During the ten minutes they've been there, Steven Seagal has killed a dozen people with no apparent change of expression.

"Poke," Frank says. He is drawing loops again, and he waits until Rafferty looks over at him. "I'm sorry."

"I should be apologizing to you," Rafferty says. "You were right. If I hadn't brought Arnold into this, you'd probably be gone by now."

"I didn't mean that," Frank says, the words so soft that Rafferty's not sure he understood them. A series of grunts from the television is followed by a stitchery of gunfire from an automatic. No one bothers to look. "I meant for everything."

Ming Li has fixed an urgent stare on Poke, but Rafferty can't find a reply. Something Rose said goes through his mind, something about his having all those words in his head, but none of the ones he really needs.

"Just . . . you know," Frank says. "Whatever happens, I wanted to say that."

Rafferty says, "Thank you."

"Is this going to work?" Ming Li demands.

"I don't know." Rafferty picks up his own iced coffee and drains it. It's awful, but he needs the caffeine. "What I do know is that we have to try. I owe it to Arthit, I owe it to Rose and Miaow, and I guess I owe it to you. Chu's not going to quit. If you got up right now and walked out of here, he'd find you and it would all start over again."

"You're right," Frank says. "Chu's never given up on anything in his life."

"What haven't we thought of?" Ming Li asks.

"A hundred things," Rafferty says. "What if he just shoots us all as we come in? What if there are a dozen guys we don't know about? What if the place is booby-trapped?"

"He won't shoot us when we come in, and there won't be a booby trap," Frank says. "He won't do anything until he knows we've got everything he wants. He probably won't do anything until it's all in his hands. Chu is a lot of things, but he's not impulsive. It's taken him years to build all this—the rubies, the documents, the American identity. He needs this exit more than he needs anything else in the world. So as much as he wants to kill me, he'll wait. He'll wait until he's got everything."

"And then," Ming Li says, "he'll put your head on a spike."

A bleating sound cuts through the mayhem on the television, and Pradya opens his phone. He says something, hangs up, and leans over to Leung. Leung gets up and comes over to their table.

"Klong Toey," he says.

"He wants to kill Frank, and you're just handing him over," Ming Li says. She puts both hands on Rafferty's arm. "He's your father, and you're giving him away."

Rafferty gets up. "We're going to see if we can't make it a loan."

43

A World of Wind and Wet

They're barely inside the warehouse complex when Rafferty gets the first indication that things are going wrong.

"Keep coming," Chu says into the phone.

Blooming in the rain-dimmed headlights, directly in front of them, is a long wall of corrugated steel with an enormous red 3 on it.

"We're at three," Rafferty repeats.

"Yes, I heard you. Keep coming. Turn between two and one. I'm here."

"Fine," Rafferty says. "Coming." He leans forward, says to Leung, who is at the wheel, "Stop beside number two."

"Two?" Leung doesn't sound surprised, but it's close.

Rafferty presses his thumb over the phone's mouthpiece to mute it and says to Pradya, "You said three."

"Maybe he moved them," says the fat cop from the backseat. Something about his tone accelerates Rafferty's pulse.

He settles back against the upholstery, taking long, slow breaths and looking at alternatives. There aren't many, and he wishes he could be alone for a minute or two. They are packed so close together he feels like his thoughts are audible. The car, which had looked big enough when it was empty, smells of anxiety and wet cloth. They've had to open all the windows a few inches to keep them from steaming up. Frank and Ming Li share the front seat with Leung, and Rafferty is bookended by Fon and Lek. Beyond Lek, jammed up against the door, is the fat cop Pradya, his empty gun in his lap. Lek is muttering resentfully as she works her jeans down over her thighs, lifting herself from the seat to get them below her knees. Pradya is watching with more than professional interest.

Kosit is a minute or two away in his own car, with Elson beside him.

"We're at two," Leung announces, slowing.

"Turn the car around," Rafferty says. "I want it pointed at the exit." He hands Pradya the magazine for his automatic and says, "You can load it now." Then he reaches across Fon, yanks the door handle, and climbs over her into a world of wind and wet. As he starts to close the door, he feels Fon's hand on his arm.

"It'll be fine," she says.

He gives her a nod, suddenly on the edge of tears, and closes the door. Lifting his face to the rain, he opens his eyes wide, letting the fall of water wash them clean. He returns the cell phone to his ear and says, "We're here."

Chu says, "I'm waiting." Rafferty touches the Glock nestled into the small of his back and walks to the corner of the building.

The alleyway between the warehouses is wide enough for two trucks to pass each other, and about 120 feet long. Bars of yellow light stripe the asphalt as far as Rafferty can see through the rain, reflecting the bulbs set every ten or fifteen feet beneath the overhangs of the warehouse roofs. Rafferty has expected to be ankle-deep in water, but the entire area slopes down very slightly toward the river. Except for the occasional black puddle, which could be anywhere from an inch to a foot deep, there is almost no water underfoot.

Rafferty is trying to figure out whether the absence of water is good or bad when the rain eases for a moment, and he sees Chu, gleaming at him in a black rubber slicker that hangs almost to his feet. He is about sixty feet away. Chu lifts an arm and waves like someone in a home movie—*Hi there!*—and then the rain hammers down again, and Rafferty can barely make out his shape, just a vertical darkness drawing the eye like a cave behind a waterfall.

"Come on along," Chu says into the phone. "I want to get a look at you."

"This phone's going to short out," Rafferty says, moving forward. "It's too wet. I'm turning it off now."

"Up to you."

Rafferty's thumb finds the "disconnect" button and then, very quickly, he highlights the next number he will need. He slips the phone into a small Ziploc bag and puts it in his shirt pocket, buttons facing out. Instinctively he finds the "dial" button with his thumb. Then he does it again, walking all the time. He is about to do it yet again when Chu's form begins to solidify in front of him. Rafferty drops his hands to his sides and flexes his fingers repeatedly like a pianist about to tackle something difficult. They feel as stiff as sticks.

Ten feet away he stops and waits. Chu waves him closer, Asian style, palm and fingers down, but Rafferty shakes his head. A moment passes. Rafferty can feel something extending between him and Chu, something taut that pulsates like a high-voltage wire. Chu mutters irritably and trudges forward. Once Chu is moving, Rafferty continues toward him.

Chu is frailer than Rafferty imagined, and older. Somehow he had continued to see the Colonel Chu his father had described from all those years ago in Wang's room, not this papery retiree. The sudden image of Wang, stripped and shivering, being offered to dogs and horses, ignites a hot surge of fury. Rafferty damps it down as fast as he can, fearing it will travel the wire to Chu, and in fact Chu slows and regards him quizzically. But then he shakes his head again and smiles.

"You don't look like him." They are three feet apart.

"I thank my mother daily," Rafferty says.

Chu's face is a nest of creases, a topography of age folded into the skin around his eyes and mouth. His eyelids hang down at weary forty-five-degree angles, the eyes behind them as dry and hard as stone. His neck is two vertical ropes, the tendons taut beneath the skin. Deep grooves have been carved on either side of his mouth, and they deepen when he smiles. He is smiling now, a kind, grandfatherly, yellow-toothed smile that makes Rafferty wonder how much strength it would take to snap his neck. Beads of water glisten on the hairs sprouting from his mole.

"You're smaller than I thought you'd be," Rafferty says.

"Our fears always are," Chu says, "when we finally have the strength to look at them."

"I'll remember that."

A gust of wind catches Chu's slicker, billows it out, and snaps a corner up, throwing a spray of water at Rafferty. "This is a filthy city," Chu says. "I'm quite ready to leave it. I assume you have everything you owe me."

"And you?"

"I never go into a business meeting," Chu says, "without the currency I'll need. They're all here, a little wet but otherwise well. Eager to see you. Shall we begin?"

"Let's," Rafferty says. "I'm ready for you to leave Bangkok, too."

"First, though," Chu says, and he waves his hand. A man comes around the corner of the warehouse behind him. He carries an automatic weapon slung from his shoulder. When he gets closer, Rafferty sees a swollen upper lip, pulled high enough to reveal a broken tooth.

"This is Ping," Chu says. "He's going with you, just to see whom you've left around the corner."

Rafferty says, "The hell he is."

"Be reasonable. For all I know, you've got a car full of cops."

Rafferty looks at Ping. Ping sucks his tooth and winces.

"I thought you watched us come in."

"You may not have noticed," Chu says, "but visibility is limited. Ping is not negotiable. He takes a look or we both walk away right now."

"The gun stays here," Rafferty says.

"Fine," Chu says, too easily, and it causes Rafferty a twinge of discomfort. "Ping?"

Ping unshoulders the gun and passes it over to Chu. Rafferty steps forward, pats Ping down, extracts a small, flat automatic from under Ping's shirt, and holds it out. Chu looks at it but makes no move to take it.

"Think fast," Rafferty says. He flicks the safety and drops the gun to the asphalt. It lands with a clatter and a bounce. Chu takes a quick step back—a hop, really—and when his eyes come back, the grandfather is gone and there is murder in them.

"Don't worry," Rafferty says. "Nobody saw you jump except me. And old Ping here. Not much loss of face there." He turns to go and says, over his shoulder, "And if you're worried about Ping, you can always kill him later."

When they're ten or eleven yards from Chu, Rafferty says, "Have you thought about that? About him killing you later?"

"Shut up," Ping says, and then gasps. His tongue probes the tooth again.

"There must be something about me. Everybody tells me to shut up. How'd you break that tooth?"

No answer.

"Hard to break a front tooth like that. Usually it's a molar. Or did somebody else break it?"

Ping just slogs through the rain, but he brings a hand up to cover his mouth.

"You should have it looked at."

"I know."

"Of course, you may not need to get it looked at. You know how the triads cure a toothache? They amputate the head."

"She's just like you," Ping says. "Your daughter."

Rafferty looks at him quickly but can't find his voice to speak.

"Those pajamas," Ping says. He squints and puts the hand back over his mouth. "They've got bunnies all over them, and she acts like they're a suit of fucking armor. She even told *him* off. He went out and got her a milk shake or something, and she laid into him because it had melted."

The full weight of what he's doing—what he's trying to do—is suddenly pushing at Rafferty from all sides. He feels like a man walking the bottom of the ocean. The air and the darkness press in on him. His lungs are an inch deep. "Here we are," he says as they turn the corner.

Leung is standing by the car. He shades his eyes against the rain, sees Ping, and raises a hand, palm up, meaning, *What the fuck?* Rafferty says, "Get everybody out. Open the trunk. This is a paranoia check."

In a few moments, the car is empty. Fon and Lek, in bra and panties, huddle against the rain, which is hard enough to sting their bare skin. Ming Li and Leung face the car, their hands folded on their heads, while Pradya holds his gun—loaded now, Rafferty remembers—steady on Frank. Ping motions Rafferty to the trunk, where the suitcase and Chu's wooden box are stored. "Open them," he says.

"The suitcase," Rafferty says. "I don't know if I can close it again."

"Your problem, not mine."

"Fine. Be a hard-ass." He lifts the suitcase's latch, and the oiled lid pops up five or six inches as Rafferty holds his breath. Very carefully, he opens it the rest of the way and watches with some satisfaction as Ping's involuntary gasp sends him into a spasm of pain. Then Rafferty closes the suitcase gently and lifts the lid of the wooden box to display the rubies. "Okay?"

"Okay." The car sags suddenly as Fon and Lek scramble into it, ducking the rain. Ping pulls out his cell and dials. Chu takes his time picking it up. "It's fine," Ping says at last. "They've got everything, and no one is here who shouldn't be." The volume of the rain increases, and Ping says, "What?" He presses a palm against his free ear, screwing up his face to hear. "No. No weapons. Nothing obvious anyway." He listens for a moment and then tilts his chin at Pradya and hands him the phone.

Rafferty steps under the overhang of the warehouse roof and watches the sheet of water sliding over its edge. He is fighting for air.

"No problem," Pradya says into the phone. "Sure, sure he's here." He holds the phone out to Frank. "He wants to talk to you."

Frank snatches the phone as though he were planning to bite it in half. He puts his mouth to it and says, "I choose the people I talk to," and then shuts the phone and hands it back to the fat cop. "And fuck him," he adds.

Rafferty thinks, *Introductions over.* Forcing his mind to focus only on what he needs to do in this instant, he goes back to the trunk and lifts the suitcase out, holding it flat. He turns it carefully so the hinges are against his chest and Chu will be able to open it and see the money. To Ping he says, "Let's go."

He follows the man into the rain.

The bars of light on the asphalt again, the now-familiar landscape of looming warehouse walls, black sky, falling rain. Slowly the form of Chu emerges, shapeless and dark at first, then slender and almost frail, with the wind and rain lashing at him. Chu watches them approach, perfectly still except for the bottom of his slicker blowing around his legs.

Rafferty stops three feet away, lifts the suitcase an inch or two, someone presenting an infant to a priest. "Noi," he says.

Chu takes a step forward.

"Uh-uh," Rafferty says. "I see her first."

Chu raises two fingers to his lips, inserts them, and lets loose an ear-splitting whistle. Two people come around the far corner of Warehouse One. Rafferty keeps his eyes glued to Chu's until they are close enough to see clearly, and Chu raises a hand to stop them.

The thin cop, Sriyat, with Noi on his arm. She is bent in agony, one hand thrown up over her shoulder to hold her neck. Something kindles low in Rafferty's stomach.

"Your turn," Chu says.

Rafferty raises the top of the suitcase all the way, and Chu says, "Bring it."

When Rafferty has covered the space between them, Chu reaches into the suitcase and shoves aside the top few inches of loose bills, pulling out the ones beneath. Rafferty tries to keep his exhalation silent. He anticipated this. The real money, some of it wrapped, but quite a bit of it loose, is buried beneath a stratum of the laundered counterfeit bills. Chu rummages through the loose bills and removes five or six stacks, weighing them in his hands and then flipping through them, making sure there's nothing there except what should be there: no newsprint trimmed to size, no small bills slipped in among the big ones. He drops the packets and says, "More," and reaches this time completely through the top layers of money to bring up the stuff on the bottom, all of which is counterfeit. To Rafferty it still seems breathtakingly false, the color, despite all his efforts, too uniform, the edges too clean and straight. He smells the back-of-the-throat sweetness of fabric softener, but the wind is blowing toward him. A bright hair scrunchie, the color of a tangerine, circles the top stack in Chu's hand. Chu gives it a glance and a bemused snap, then drops it back into the suitcase.

Rafferty lowers the lid and puts the suitcase at Chu's feet. "I'll take her now."

Chu says, "Certainly." He waves Sriyat forward. They move slowly, Noi taking tiny steps as Rafferty's heart pounds angry fists on the inside of his chest. Hoping Fon is in position, he turns to gesture her to them and sees her, arms crossed and shoulders hunched against the cold, halfway to the end of the building. As she nears them, Chu registers her. He looks at her analytically and then brings his eyes, ancient and unsurprisable, to Rafferty. "You must have more charm than you've shown me," he says.

"Can the chat," Rafferty says. "Noi's got to lie down and get dry."

Fon is at his arm by now, returning Chu's interested appraisal with the kind of disdain that could freeze a bar customer at thirty feet. She is covered in goose bumps but not shivering, and Rafferty knows she is denying Chu any pleasure, however small, she can withhold. He wants to kiss her.

"Go with her, Noi," Rafferty says. "It's almost over."

"Poke," Noi says. Her voice is sandpaper on silk. "Is Arthit here?"

"Not yet," Rafferty says, surprised by the sudden spark in Chu's eyes, feeling that there's something wrong about it. He pushes it aside, forcing himself to stay focused on *this* moment, *this* exchange, the need to get Noi around the corner of that building and into that car. "We brought you some painkillers," he says.

"Arthit and I love you," Noi says in the same frayed voice, all strain and tendons. "Miaow and Rose are fine." Fon puts a sheltering arm around her and leads her slowly into the rain. Sriyat gives the suitcase a curious glance, puts one hand above his eyes to keep the rain out, and retreats, back the way he came.

Chu says, "One down." He is watching Fon's rear end. "If only I were younger."

"That would be nice," Rafferty says. "Maybe someone could kill you before you get to this point."

"There is no reason for this business to be any more unpleasant than necessary. We both want the same thing."

"Rose, now," Rafferty says.

Chu says, "Rubies."

Rafferty doesn't even look back this time, just raises a hand and brings it down again. Chu leans forward and says, "This one is prettier."

"If you want to see her up close, get Rose out here."

"Rose," Chu says. "Unusual name for a Thai girl."

Rafferty raises his hand again, the sign for Lek to stop. "Colonel

Chu. As you say, I have to do business with you, but I don't have to make small talk with you."

"You're mistaken, *laowai*. If I want to chat with you, you'll chat with me. If I want you to hop up and down on one leg and do bird-calls, you'll do that, too." He leans forward, close enough for Rafferty to smell the cigarettes on his breath. "You can walk away when we're done. Until then you do as I say."

Rafferty can't look at him, can't let the man see his eyes. "Speech over?"

"If I choose it to be."

"And do you choose it to be?"

"For the moment." He whistles again. Rafferty is powerless to keep his head down. He strains to see past Colonel Chu, to see through the rain. To catch a glimpse of Rose.

"She's coming," Chu says. "It's interesting. You have no feeling at all for one family, but you'll put your life on the line for the other one."

"What do you want, Chu? Do you want me to agree that it's interesting? Okay, it's interesting. It's fucking fascinating. A lot more fascinating than this conversation. Can we get on with it?"

"Occasionally," Chu says, "I think it's too interesting."

"I chose one family," Rafferty says. "I was stuck with the other one."

"Mmmm," Chu says. "Here she is."

Sriyat has both hands around Rose's upper arm, but she pulls it away and gives him a look that, Rafferty thinks, should dissolve him where he stands. Rafferty signals for Lek to come the rest of the way. "Your goddamn rubies," he says.

"Not all of them," Chu says. "Some of them will be yours soon." He watches Lek come. When she starts to hand Rafferty the box, he snaps his fingers, and she looks up, confused. "To *me*," Chu says.

"When Rose is here," Rafferty says.

Lek steps back, the box clutched to her bare stomach. Unlike Fon, she is shivering. And then Rose says, "Hello, Poke," as though she's just come back from an hour at the library, and a band around Rafferty's chest breaks, and he throws his arms around her.

They hold each other for the space of a dozen heartbeats, and then Rose disengages herself and says, "Miaow." She kisses Rafferty on the cheek and looks beyond him and says, "Hi, Lek." Lek smiles like a lighthouse in the rain, gives Rafferty the box without a glance at Chu's outstretched arms, and holds out a hand to Rose.

"Let's get you dry," Lek says. "In fact, let's get both of us dry." The two women turn and move off, toward the car at the far end.

Rafferty hands Chu the open box, and Chu reaches straight to the bottom and pulls out the envelope. He opens it and thumbs through the papers, then slips it into the pocket of his slicker. His eyes come up to Rafferty's. Rafferty is trying to look surprised at the envelope.

"A detail," Chu says. "Nothing important." He is running his fingers through the rubies. Cupping the box against his body with his left arm, he reaches inside the slicker with his right, and Rafferty puts a hand on his hip, as close to the gun as he can get it without giving it away, but Chu comes out with a jeweler's loupe and a small flashlight. He screws the loupe into his right eye, flicks on the light, and examines half a dozen stones, taking his time. Then he removes the loupe, drops it into the box, and says, "I'll do you the honor of not counting them." He puts his left hand back under the box.

"If you're short," Rafferty says, "you know where to find me." He turns to look over his shoulder at Rose and Lek, most of the way to the end of the warehouse by now, and sees someone a dozen steps behind them.

Sriyat.

"Where's he going?" he asks Chu.

"I have an exit to arrange," Chu says. "This is the time to arrange it."

Rose and Lek turn right, around the corner of Warehouse Two. Sriyat goes left, behind Warehouse One.

"Any more surprises?"

"Not from my end," Chu says. He is still holding the box of rubies, and Rafferty thinks, *Both hands busy.*

The thought must have shown in his face, because Chu says, "Now, now. We're doing so well."

"If you can see all that, how did you ever let Frank get away?"

Chu nods as though he's been waiting for the question. "This is a time of great opportunity. Expansion everywhere. New markets opening up. I took my eyes off him for too long. When the cat's away—"

"If I were you," Rafferty interrupts, "I'd stick with the canned Eastern wisdom, all those wheezes about enlightenment and confronting our fears, and leave the Western clichés to people with too much sense to use them."

"Let's not spoil things. I've actually enjoyed dealing with you. You have many characteristics I admire. You're devious, ingenious, energetic. You have a certain flair, which as far as I can see you're wasting completely." Chu eyes him speculatively, and then he laughs. "What I think you're doing," he says, "is stalling. Do I sense a little reluctance after all?"

"You have my daughter," Rafferty says. "I'd give you five copies of my father for her."

"One will do." Chu takes his open cell phone out of the pocket of his slicker and says to the fat cop, "Pradya. Bring him around."

"Tell Pradya to stop the moment he can see us," Rafferty says. "If he doesn't, I'll have him shot, and we'll see what happens after that."

Chu gives him the flicker of a smile and repeats Rafferty's command into the phone. Then he turns and shouts, "Come!"

The rain has lightened to the point where Rafferty can almost see the far corner of the warehouse. A form emerges, a larger form behind it. Like a color at three or four fathoms, shifted to the blue, Miaow's pajamas take what seems like an eternity to warm to pink, and when they do, Rafferty can't do anything about the catch of breath.

"A father," Chu says with considerable interest. "Selling a father."

The man grasping Miaow's neck is the one with the broken tooth. He steers her toward them and then stops, looking past them at something, and at the same moment Rafferty hears a shout behind him.

The fat cop is struggling with Ming Li, who has grabbed her father's arm and is pulling him back with all her strength. Her head whips back and forth in the rain, *No*, and her hair flies around her like snakes, suddenly frozen into sculpture by a flash of lightning. Chu says into the phone, "Point the gun at her, you idiot. I want both of them."

Pradya levels the gun at Ming Li's head, and she stops. One hand drops, and then the other, and all her strength deserts her, and she sinks to her knees at Frank's feet and cups her face in her hands.

"There's a lesson there," Chu says. "It's her father, after all. Pradya, bring her."

Rafferty says, "One at a time, remember?"

"I'm getting bored," Chu says. "Just take the rubies, and let's get it over with."

Rafferty shoots one more look at Ming Li, sees Pradya pulling her to her feet as Frank stands there, loose and empty, looking a century old. Rafferty dismisses the image and crouches down, sinking his hands into the loose stones in the box.

"In fact," Chu says above him, "we'll take them all."

The gun in his hand is aimed between Rafferty's eyes.

"I just can't make it work," Chu says, shaking his head. "I know that Western culture doesn't honor old people, and I know that you and your father have had problems. But no matter how hard I try, I can't believe that you actually intend to let me take him."

"Believe it." Rafferty looks over his shoulder again, sees Sriyat and two other men shepherd everyone around the corner. Fon and Lek are half dressed. Rose has her arm around Noi. Leung's hands are once again on top of his head. Sriyat and the two others have weapons trained on all of them.

"And even if I could believe it, there are all these *witnesses*," Chu says. "I can't leave them behind. So I'm afraid you'll all have to board the ship with us. A short sail, followed by a long sink. Except for Frank, of course. I have other plans for Frank."

"You forgot Arthit," Rafferty says. "You haven't got Arthit, and he knows everything."

"I have the hospital's name, the room number. A policeman of his rank gets shot, everyone knows."

Rafferty shifts a millimeter or two, centering his weight over his heels. "So what? Only cops can get anywhere near him."

"That's right," Chu says. "Only cops. And tonight he'll be visited by two he's not expecting."

"More information than I need," Rafferty says, just as Ming Li screams again, in anger this time, and beyond Chu he sees the man with the broken tooth pull a gun and shove Miaow violently to the pavement, and as she falls, there's another whiplash of lightning and a burst of wind, and Rafferty clamps his teeth tightly, closes his eyes, and presses down on the lever at the back of the suitcase.

He hears a little metallic click, not much louder than someone flicking a lighter, and opens his eyes to see the bottom of the suitcase pop up, maybe three inches, maybe four, and a few loose bills flutter up and get caught by the wind.

The barrel of Chu's gun touches the center of Rafferty's forehead, and he looks up to see Chu studying the suitcase quizzically. "What was that?" he asks. "Special effects?" And the pressure of the gun on Rafferty's forehead lessens slightly as Chu pulls back on the trigger.

And then it's as though the suitcase somehow contains all the light that's falling on the other side of the world, the bright side, and the light abruptly expands and escapes, cracking open the darkness with a dazzle that turns Chu stark white, followed by a deep, percussive boom, and suddenly the bottom of the suitcase is five feet in the air, and rubies and money are everywhere: rising against the rain, whirled and tossed by the wind, and pelted earthward by the weight of the falling water.

Chu was looking down when the bottom of the case exploded, and now he backs away, blinded, the hand without the gun in it clawing at his eyes, a shining-wet black figure in a downpour of water, money, and precious stones. Some of the money is plastered to Chu's slicker.

Rafferty hears two shots from behind and sees Chu trying desperately to focus his eyes just as a massive strobe of lightning freezes money, rain, and rubies in midair. Past Chu, Rafferty sees Miaow, flat on the pavement with Ping lying across her, the gun in his hand. Rafferty has his own gun out now, and he leaps across the suitcase and brings the gun up two-handed with everything he has, raking it across Chu's throat, trying to crush the larynx, then slamming it back against the man's cheekbone, and Chu's head whips around, taking his shoulders with it, the slicker billowing out like a magician's cloak. Rafferty is on his feet now, seizing Chu's gun hand at the wrist, grabbing his elbow, and bringing up a knee to break the arm across it.

Chu screams, pivots, yanks the broken arm back, and screams again as a bullet hisses through the rain, just missing his ear, and he freezes. Ping, still covering Miaow with his body, sights to fire again. Rafferty holds out a hand, palm up, to stop him, then kicks Chu's legs out from under him. Chu goes down, a slight, crumpled form in a wet black shroud, twisting in pain as money rains upon him.

Rafferty reaches down and takes Chu's gun and pats him for another. Chu hisses at him but doesn't move. Once he's satisfied that Chu has nothing else, Rafferty turns to see one of Chu's men flat on the ground, arms and legs splayed, and the other with his hands in the air. Pradya, Sriyat, and Leung all hold guns. Frank has Ming Li in his arms. Rose is half carrying Noi back to the car, with an over-the-shoulder look at Miaow.

Rafferty tosses Chu's gun a few yards away and pulls the Ziploc bag from his pocket. He removes the cell phone and pushes the "dial" button. It is answered on the first ring. He says, "Between Warehouses One and Two. Come now." He closes the phone, kicks Chu once, hard, in the area of the kidneys, just by way of letting off steam, and waves at Ping to bring Miaow. After an evaluative moment, Ping rolls off her, and Miaow gets up, her pink pajamas wet and filthy, and extends a hand to help Ping up. Ping stares at the hand for a second and then gives her an enormous broken-tooth grin, followed by an agonized grab at his mouth with his free hand. Miaow pats his arm and leads him, hand in hand, to Rafferty.

"This is Ping," she says. "I told him he wouldn't shoot us."

Rafferty picks Miaow up and hugs her so tightly she grunts. Her arms circle his neck. She says, "Is your father all right?"

"He's fine." He kisses the part in her hair, feeling like his heart will explode.

"That's good," Miaow says, pulling away. She hates being kissed on the head. She takes a sniff at herself, makes a face, and says, "I want a shower."

"If you want it," he says, putting her down, "you've got it." He turns to Ping. "Can you take her to the car?"

"I don't know," Ping says. "Miaow, can I take you to the car?"

"You're silly," Miaow says. She gives him her hand. As they walk away, Rafferty hears her say, "Does your tooth still hurt?"

Chu slowly rolls over until he is on his back. He is cradling his broken arm at the elbow. He says, "You're dead. All of you."

"Promises, promises." Cones of light sweep the alleyway, silhouetting Miaow and Ping in gold, and then the car is in sight. "You've got a full schedule for a while."

"You idiot," Chu says. "I'll be out in a week. There's nowhere in the world you can hide. And this time I'll make you watch people die."

The car slows to a halt a few feet away. Rafferty says, "That thing you said about how there's a valuable lesson in learning you don't run the world? I hope you meant it, because you're about to take a quantum leap in personal growth."

The car doors shut, and Elson stands over them. "Colonel Chu," he says, "I'm Richard Elson, United States Secret Service, and this is Lieutenant Kosit of the Bangkok Municipal Police. We're jointly taking you into custody on behalf of the Thai authorities and the government of the United States of America, on charges of counterfeiting, racketeering, kidnapping, and the murder of an American intelligence officer." Chu's mouth works, but nothing comes out. "Would you mind cuffing him, Lieutenant Kosit?"

"He's got a broken arm," Rafferty says.

"That's a terrible shame," Kosit says, grabbing it. Chu emits a high-pitched shriek as Kosit twists the arm behind him and fastens the cuffs.

"Jesus," Elson says, looking around. "We've got to pick up this money."

Kosit is still bent over Chu, and Rafferty tugs his sleeve. "Get some cops into Arthit's room," he says. He nudges Chu with the tip of his shoe. "This murderous old shit has sent some guys after him. And choose your men wisely, because the thugs he sent are cops."

Kosit gives Chu a look that does not suggest that the coming interrogation will be gentle. Then he moves a few feet away and pulls out his cell phone.

Elson shoves a hand under Rafferty's nose. There are eight or nine red stones in his palm, and his brow is wrinkled. "What the hell are these?"

"They're rubies, and they're all over the place," Rafferty says. "And just to keep things straight, they're not counterfeit and they belong to my father."

For a second, Elson is wearing his old face. "How does your father come to have a bucket of rubies?"

"Same as Peachy," Rafferty says. "He won them in a horse race."

44

Ping, Rose, Milk Shake, Tooth, Gun

In the middle of the wettest, warmest tangle of arms, legs, and hearts of his entire life, Rafferty is barely aware of the torrent of Thai coming from Miaow, perhaps two hundred words a minute, far too fast for him to catch more than a phrase or a name or two: *Ping, Rose, milk shake, tooth, gun.* All he can do is hold on, Rose on his right and Miaow on his left, but now they're a circle, and so Miaow is, as always, in the middle. Where she needs to be.

The circle opens to absorb Fon and Lek, both of them crying like children, and closes again. With the rain hammering down, the five of them squeeze together even more tightly, the two half-naked women no longer feeling the cold, and then the arms open a second time, and there is someone there who feels new, someone who *smells* new to Rafferty's heightened senses, and they wrap themselves around Ming Li. The sky cracks, a fork of lightning fingering its way down, followed by a sound like someone crumpling iron.

With the thunder, Poke feels Rose straighten, remove her arm from his shoulder, and pull away. He looks at her. With her other arm still around Miaow, she is gazing beyond him. Rafferty turns his head to see Frank. His father stands sideways to the group, not even sheltering from the rain. He faces back down the alley between the warehouses, where it all happened.

Something warm fills Rafferty's chest, and suddenly there are words in his mouth. And then he looks again at his father's profile, so familiar and so strange, a face he had thought was permanently turned away, and he can't say them. He swallows, so hard it feels as though he is forcing the words down.

Rose says, "Mr. Rafferty?"

Frank turns, and Rose raises the arm that had been around Rafferty, inviting him in. Frank stands there, not moving, until Rafferty steps aside, closer to Fon, expanding the space between him and Rose. Rafferty lifts his arm exactly as Rose has, the space between them wide and welcoming, and he hears something catch and break in Ming Li's throat. Slowly, like a man approaching a door he thinks will be locked, Frank joins the circle. It closes around him.

THE CAR IS even more crowded on the way out: Fon sits in Lek's lap and Ming Li in Frank's. Miaow has spread herself across both Rafferty's and Rose's laps, dead weight against them. She fell asleep the moment the car door slammed shut.

Leung is at the wheel. Noi is slumped against the front passenger door, next to Frank. Rafferty can hear her breath whistling in her throat.

With a last look back, Leung puts the car in gear and heads for the gates.

The silence in the car is a kind of warmth, a comforting insulation that makes the events of the last hour seem very distant, perhaps not even real. What's real *now* is a car jammed with people, bunched up against each other as though by choice, the steam of breath on window glass, the walls of the warehouses as they slide by in the headlights.

Frank suddenly sits upright and looks back, and Rafferty cranes his neck around, expecting the nightmare to reemerge: men with guns, Chu free somehow, looming out of the darkness with his slicker flapping around him, but he sees nothing. And then Frank begins to laugh.

"What?" Ming Li asks. "What is it?"

"Nothing important," Frank says, and then he laughs again. "I forgot my rubies."

45

White

He has been underground a long time. Stones push down on his chest. Some of them have been sharpened to points. Every time he breathes, he has to push the stones up with his chest to make room for the air. The air smells surprisingly of linoleum, alcohol, something unidentifiable that's as sweet and heavy as syrup, and, floating on top of all the other smells, a razor-sharp note of fresh linen.

The light comes closer. It seems to be finding its way by touch, spreading pale tendrils in all directions: forward, left and right, up and down, but always moving toward him. He waits, pushing up the stones with every half breath, watching the light extend itself toward him, now not so much smoke as a shining vine. When the vine reaches him, it will wrap itself around him, put down microscopic roots, fill him with light. Once he is charged with light, feels it surging tidally through his body until he is radiant with it, he will be able to lift the stones.

The *bum-BUM* noise has increased in frequency, faster now, and then faster still, until it begins to vibrate inside him, not unpleasantly but with the urgency of an indecipherable message. *Bum-BUM*, he thinks, pairs; what's so important about pairs? Pairs of drumbeats, pairs of breaths, pairs of people, pairs of numbers.

Pairs of numbers?

Something dims the light. Whatever it is, it's not between him and the light; it seems to be *behind* it somehow, throwing a shadow that travels down the vine like dirty water in a clear stream, and as the light thins and clouds, the stones feel heavier and sharper, and they grate against one another, a sand-gritty sound, less like stones than like . . . what? A room, he sees a room, and it's a terrible shade of green. It, too, smells of linoleum. Someone is with him, someone who doesn't like the sound of a shoe scraping over dirty—

A shoe. On linoleum.

Then the vine brightens again, blooming with light, and he opens one eye, just a crack, narrow as a blind drawn against the massed brightness of the day, to see a world of white. Close to him, only a foot or two away, is a white shape, white without outlines but brighter than the white beyond it, and it is moving. Moving parallel to him, away from his feet and toward his head, and he hears the scraping sound again, and then a whisper.

There is a second figure, this one brown, a brown he knows very well. A brown that makes him think for a second or half a second that he is looking at himself; he is out of his own body and looking at it as it moves across this white room, following the figure in white. He closes the eye, but the urgency of the tom-tom sound warns him to open it again, and he forces the lid up. The light floods into him and strengthens him, and he can focus.

A hospital room. White but for a darker rectangle where black is in the slow act of giving itself over to blue, with a note of orange bleeding upward, warming it from below. A window. Dawn? What dawn? How long has—

A doctor, dressed in white. Masked in white. Behind him a Bangkok policeman. Dawn through the window, the sharp pain of the stones on his chest, the smells, the sound of shoes on linoleum, a brilliantly clear sudden memory of a dark room, a big man, some kind of enormous, rib-caving punch to the chest, a slow fall. A girl in white.

White. The white-clad doctor, at the head of the bed now, reaching up. A gentle tug at the wrist, no more intense than a fly landing on it. The doctor has a clear plastic bag in one hand, filled with a liquid as transparent as water. In the other hand is a hypodermic syringe.

The policeman comes closer, watching the doctor. He is close enough for the man on the bed to see his face, a new face, a face he doesn't know, and to read the name tag on the uniform. The name tag says PETCHARA.

Arthit's eyes open wider as the doctor inserts the syringe into the top of the clear IV bag and pushes the plunger. Something—some tensing in his body—brings Petchara's eyes down to the bed, and he starts to speak, but Arthit rides a bolt of ten thousand volts of neural electricity to rip the intravenous needle from his own wrist and shove it into Petchara's thigh, while with his other hand he grabs the clear plastic bag and squeezes. Petchara leaps away, and Arthit lets the bag drop and sees the policeman stagger, dragging the bag with him, until his back hits the window where dawn is announcing itself, and finally it occurs to him to yank the needle. He stares at it in his hand, stares at the mostly empty bag, and then all his muscles let go, and he drops, loose-jointed and as awkward as a marionette, to the floor.

The doctor is already out the door when Arthit finds and pushes the big red button on the side of his bed. He can no longer hold his head up. His vision blurs and darkens at the edges, narrows, and the room disappears, leaving nothing but the rectangle of dawn, more orange now, framed by the window.

He sleeps.

46

Monsoon Christmas

F rank's a bonanza," Elson says. "Monsoon Christmas." He is seated comfortably on an uncomfortable chair as angular and uncompromising as he is, his black suit soaking up a surprising amount of the light streaming through the window behind him. The chair, just strips of black leather on a chromium frame, looks like he designed it. "Frank's the kind of gift that makes you wonder what you've been doing right all your life, why you deserve this. I mean, we're going to be able to dam up one major river of counterfeit into this awful country, without the North Koreans even knowing it, for a few months at least."

He bounces a couple of times in the uncomfortable chair, just out of enthusiasm. He's doing something with his mouth that might pass for a smile if the room was a little dimmer. "And it's extra-good we've got Frank, because Chu's not talking. And I mean not at all. On the other hand, we've got the other cop, the one who was dressed like a doctor, and he can't stop talking. He talks even when there's no one else in the room. Seems to think we're going to send him to Syria for interrogation." Elson rubs his hands together. "And there's all that fake *money*."

"For example," Rafferty says, "about Frank. What kind of things has he given you?"

"*Frank*," Elson says in the tone Miaow uses to say *chocolate*. "Well, Frank's just something that happens maybe once in a decade. He's given us fucking *flow charts* of the counterfeiting structure. A map of routes used to take money out of China, routes we can seal up. He's given us a bank in Harbin, China, owned by his former . . . um, company, that's a central distribution point, a bank we can crack into electronically. It'll let us put enough pressure on the North Koreans that the cash flow will dry up. No more cognac, no more new cars for the fat cats. It's probably enough to bring them back to the negotiating table."

"That's good," Rafferty says.

"And more. There's an American end, a sleeper who's been in place for almost twenty years, reporting directly to Chu. And he was *nowhere* on our radar."

"Irwin Lee," Rafferty says.

Elson's eyebrows go up. "Your radar is better than ours."

"Shucks," Rafferty says.

"Isn't it a wonderful name?" Elson says. He makes a frame with his hands and says the name into it. "Irwin Lee."

"Lee is one of the two most common Chinese names," Rafferty says, but Elson's enthusiasm tickles some obscure area of Rafferty's brain that specializes in obscure connections, and suddenly he's sitting bolt upright. "That's what this whole thing was about, isn't it?"

"What?" Elson asks.

"Irwin Lee. My father's going to be Irwin Lee, right?"

Elson looks disappointed, as though he's been deprived of his big surprise. "Nobody knows about Irwin Lee except Chu," he says. "It's a perfect fit. Lee has a twenty-year legend, one of the best I've ever seen. A house in Richmond, Virginia, that I can guarantee no triad member ever heard of. We're going to remove the current Irwin Lee and install your father. He'll live in Richmond and consult with us."

Rafferty leans forward. "What has Chu said about Frank?"

"About Frank? That's the one thing he'll talk about. Says he doesn't understand it, can't figure out why Frank betrayed him. They were friends, he says. Says he'd have made Frank his successor if Frank had been Chinese." He starts to add something and thinks better of it.

"What?" Rafferty demands.

"The, um, story about Chu insulting Frank's wife. I mentioned it as a way of suggesting why Frank's loyalty might be a little weak, and Chu said it never happened."

"Of course it didn't," Rafferty says. He can feel the blood rise in his face. "I can't believe I fell for it. You'd think, by now, I'd know. It's *always* about my father. Whatever it is, whatever is happening, it's always about my father."

"I'm not following you," Elson says.

"He took the goddamn box in the first place because he wanted to be Irwin Lee. The rubies were a bonus. All the stories about Chu being the worst thing since Grendel's mother were his way of justifying himself to me. His way of making sure I was on his side. He needed Chu either dead or put away forever, so he could be Irwin Lee. And I could help, so he sold me that line of crap."

Arthit says something that comes out as a croak, and Rafferty says, "Arthit. Don't try to talk."

But Arthit lowers a heavily bandaged hand—the doctors had to do a little emergency repair where he yanked out the intravenous line—and pushes a button that raises the top third of the bed to a forty-five-degree angle. As he comes up, he ages ten years; he has lost fifteen pounds in three days, and his face has slackened and droops downward as it comes toward vertical. His throat is as loose and rippled as a theater curtain. When he is upright, he reaches for a small carton of apple juice, sips it through a straw, closes his eyes for a moment to gather some strength, and says, "Dangerous. Chu . . . dangerous." The words are barely audible, not much louder than someone tearing paper.

"You bet he is," Elson says. "He's got fangs like a wolf spider. Your friend's right. Your father wanted you to be afraid of Chu, wanted you to realize how dangerous he was. He was doing you a favor."

"If you believe that, don't spend too much time with him," Rafferty says. "He'll have you nominating him for the Presidential Medal of Freedom."

"You're overreacting," Elson says.

"*Irwin Lee,*" Rafferty says, and he doesn't know whether to laugh or cry. "My father is going to be Irwin Lee. Do you know what Lee means?"

"No idea," Elson says.

"The character used to write it," Rafferty says, the sentence not coming easily, "is a tree over a child. It's an image of parental care."

"That's nice," Elson says. "I can't see the immediate usefulness of the information, but maybe something will come to me." He crosses his legs and looks approvingly at the shine on his shoe. "We're flying him back to America tomorrow. Get him out of here and put him somewhere safe. So we're going to have to take him away from you, just when you guys have sort of gotten together again."

"Take him today," Rafferty says. "That way I don't have to feed him dinner tonight."

Arthit says, "Poke." He puts a hand to his throat and tries to clear it. The effort obviously hurts. "He's . . . your father."

"Yeah, yeah, yeah."

"So anyway," Elson says, "he'll be leaving. And I won't forget that I owe you."

"Yes," Rafferty says with some vehemence. "You do."

"Well, don't get too comfortable with it." Elson turns and looks out the window, which opens onto a world of merciless sunlight. The monsoon has moved on, and it is so hot outside that the air-conditioning in the hospital room is producing a misty film of condensation on the inside of the glass. "You may have overachieved."

"That's the curse of talent," Rafferty says, still furious, and Arthit lets go with something that sounds like a toy steam engine releasing its first little puff. It's a laugh, Rafferty realizes, and in spite of everything he finds himself grinning at his friend so hard he feels like his face will split. Arthit has a hand pressed to his chest, damping down the pain of the laugh, but he laughs again. This one doubles him up, and when he sits upright again, he shakes his head and wipes the sweat off his brow and says, "Over . . ." He breathes. "Achieved . . ." He grabs another breath. "How?"

"Remember how I hated the monsoon?" Elson says to Rafferty. "Well, I hate this heat more. I hate everything about this climate. I hate the traffic here. I hate the food—it gives me the squirts, and they feel like lighter fluid. So what's my reward? I'm an *expert,* they say. I'm the guy with the map, they say. I'm being assigned here for a year."

Arthit, who has been sipping at the apple juice, suddenly spurts a substantial amount of it through his nostrils and into his lap. He bends forward, making the *puff-puff* sound again, and Rafferty takes the apple juice out of his hand and puts it on the tray, letting his free hand rest on his friend's shoulder.

To Elson he says, "I've got a great maid for you."

He's More Nervous Than You Are

Four hours later Rafferty opens the apartment door and finds himself in the Seven Dwarfs' cave. Little white lights create a rectangle of diamond sparkle to frame the evening sky, darkening through the sliding glass door. Small colored lights—rubies, emeralds, sapphires—have been strung to outline the inside of the front door. Looking around, focusing through the dazzle, he sees that his desk has been cleared and polished, that the dirt worn into the white leather hassock has been scrubbed away, that three new chairs have been crowded around the living-room table. A white candle flickers on his desk, and another gleams on the coffee table, beside a large crumpled plastic bag from Bangkok's new Book Tower.

The room smells like someone is cooking flowers.

And it is empty.

Going farther in, he sees a partial explanation for the fragrance of frying lilies. The counter between the living room and the kitchen is teeming with flowers, enough of them to create an optimistic send-off for a midlevel Mafia don. Beyond the flowers, on the kitchen side of the counter, is a sloping ziggurat of cookbooks, all open. Rafferty has never seen a cookbook in the apartment. He starts curiously toward them and remembers the Book Tower bag on the table. He gives the living room a second survey.

The door to the bedroom opens, and Rose comes in. She stops at the sight of him, so abruptly that for an instant he thinks she has failed to recognize him. Then her eyes clear, and she comes up to him and kisses his cheek, leaving a faint coolness behind. Rafferty touches it involuntarily and quickly pulls his hand away. Rose's upper lip is damp with perspiration.

This is practically a first. He has seen her weave through a crowded Bangkok sidewalk in the full glare of the sun, carrying Miaow's weight in plastic shopping bags, without popping a bead of moisture. When she does deign to perspire, it's always at the edge of her hairline. He resists the urge to check.

"How's Arthit?" she says, but her eyes are everywhere in the room.

"He's fine. He's amazingly fine."

He watches her hear the tone of his voice, her mind a mile away, and then put the words together. She gives him the smile that always puddles him where he stands. "That's wonderful. Noi must be so happy." Then her gaze wanders off again.

"Rose?"

Her eyes come to his, then slide down to take in his clothes. Her lower lip is suddenly between her teeth.

She says, "You have to get dressed."

He looks down at himself. "I am dressed. I've been outside and everything."

"I mean *dressed*." She tugs at his shirt and checks her fingers to make sure the color hasn't come off on them. "Your good clothes."

"I don't have any good clothes. Since when do we have cookbooks? Have I been complaining about the food?"

"Don't talk about the cookbooks," she says. "Never say 'cookbook' to me again." She goes past him into the kitchen, and he sees that she is dressed entirely in white linen: a flowing, midthigh something that he supposes is a blouse, over a pair of loose pleated slacks. The gold bracelet he gave her hangs on her left wrist. She starts slamming cookbooks closed. Without looking at him, she says, "Tell me you didn't forget."

"Of course I didn't forget," he says. "I just don't know why you need cookbooks."

"Oh, Poke," she says hopelessly. Then she stops, sparing the last couple of cookbooks in the stack, and stands still for a moment. Turning to him, she opens her arms. He's holding her in an instant, feeling the long arms wrap around him, feeling the cool dampness of her cheek against his, and then all there is in the world is the two of them, trying to press themselves into one.

"They'll be here in ten minutes," she says. "Your father and Ming Li."

"The place looks beautiful," he says. Then he says, "I need a beer."

"There isn't time."

"Please, Rose. I can actually drink beer while I get dressed." He opens the refrigerator and stares openmouthed. Every shelf is full of food: dishes, bowls, pans, even cups have been pressed into service and jammed any old way onto the shelves. "How many people are coming?"

"It's all terrible," Rose says. "I'm taking these books back tomorrow, every single one of them. I ordered steak from the Barbican. Your father will like steak. You always like steak."

"My father will love anything you cook," he says, finally locating a Singha and reaching over several dishes to get to it. "Anyway, you don't want to waste all this."

"We'll eat it tomorrow. After they leave."

"Rose," Rafferty says, popping the can. "My father isn't even going to taste anything. He's more nervous than you are."

"I'm not nervous," Rose says nervously. She steps around him and closes the refrigerator with the air of someone drawing a veil over a dicey past. "Your clothes are on the bed. I chose them. I got that stain off your slacks. And he'll love steak."

He knocks back half the beer. "Listen, I have to tell you something."

She's halfway out of the room, but she stops. "You mean now?"

"It's about Frank." And he tells her all of it, about how his father manipulated him, about Irwin Lee. When he is finished, she continues to look at him as though expecting more.

"And?" she finally says.

Rafferty looks at the tension in her body, and he thinks his heart will explode. "And I love you," he says, giving up. "More than I've ever been able to say."

"Then make me happy," she says, spinning the bracelet around her wrist like a twenty-four-karat hula hoop. "Get dressed."

THE DOORBELL RINGS as he is buttoning his shirt—one he's never seen before—and his stomach muscles tie themselves into an instant knot, but from the sound of Rose's voice it's the delivery from the Barbican. He hears the clatter of things being cleared away and wonders how many kilos of rare beef Rose ordered. He checks himself in the mirror, decides he's still relatively nice-looking, and suddenly thinks of Miaow.

The smiley face is on the door, but he knocks anyway.

"I'm home," Miaow says, and he opens the door.

She is sitting in front of her mirror, braiding her hair so tightly it looks painful. Her eyes meet his in the mirror. She regards him critically without turning and says, "You look nice. I picked out the shirt at the store."

"It's beautiful."

"It's okay," she says, eyeing it in the mirror.

"Are you all right?"

Now she does turn. She gives him a squint as though he's gone out of focus. "Why wouldn't I be?"

"Well, you know. . . . I mean, tonight is . . . It's the first . . . I mean, if you want to talk about it or anything . . ." She is still looking at him. "You know?" he adds.

"I got along with Ping," she says, "and he was going to shoot me. This won't be *that* hard."

"He's going to love you."

She purses her mouth and tugs it to one side. "Maybe. Maybe I'll love him, too. Maybe we'll start by just liking each other."

"You and Rose, the miracle girls," Rafferty says. "How can I be so lucky?"

"Beats me," Miaow says. "I put water on my hair. Does it look good?"

"You look beautiful."

"I hope so," she says. "It would be nice to be beautiful." She turns back to the mirror and studies herself. "They'll come soon. Go away now, okay?"

"I'm gone." He closes the door and, just for a moment, leans against the wall, every muscle in his body slack with love. "We're back," he says aloud. "We're all back."

WHEN THE DOORBELL rings again, Rose calls from the kitchen, "You."

Rafferty takes a breath deep enough to empty the room and opens the door. Frank stands there in an ancient, rumpled tweed sport coat, his right arm clamped rigidly to his body with three bottles of wine beneath it. Ming Li stands beside him, looking as cool and remote as ever, except that she has half of her father's left sleeve knotted in her fist. Her knuckles are paper white. Hanging upside down in her other hand, completely forgotten, is a bouquet of flowers.

Without thinking, Rafferty makes a move to shake his father's hand, sees a spark of something like panic in Frank's eyes, and has a sudden vision of him extending his hand and dropping the wine. So instead he pats his father on the shoulder and says, "Hello, Frank, Ming Li. Give you a hand with those?" and reaches for the bottles.

"*Poke,*" Rose says from behind him. He feels her hand on his arm and turns.

Tall and draped in white, she is framed by the colored lights behind her, the guardian spirit of an enchanted cave. Slowly she brings her hands together in a *wai*, raises them to her forehead, and says, "Hello, Father. Hello, sister. Welcome home."

And steps aside, her head slightly bowed, her hands still high. Frank glances quickly at Poke, licks his lips, and says, "Thank you, Rose." Without looking up, Ming Li tugs at the fabric of his sleeve, and Frank says, "Hello, son."

"Dad," Poke says, the word enormous in his throat. "Ming Li. Please come in."

As they come through the door, Ming Li gives him a smile that almost blinds him.

Note

If any government in the world today needs overthrowing, it's North Korea's. Everything in this book about the country's international counterfeiting activities is true. They pump out currency, cigarettes, and medications—including AIDS "drugs" that do nothing but make the victim retain water so he or she experiences a weight gain. And all of this is to provide a cash flow to enrich a few swine at the top of the pyramid.

A brilliant Stanford graduate thesis by Sheena Chestnut dubbed North Korea "the Sopranos State," and I recommend it to anyone who wants to know more. Chestnut reveals in considerable detail a nation whose foreign policy is based on thuggery.

The greediest thug, of course, is Kim Jong Il, recently revealed to be the biggest individual consumer of Hennessy Paradis cognac in the world. "Dear Leader" spends somewhere between $650,000 and $800,000 a year on this elite happy juice, which retails in Korea for $630 a bottle.

The average North Korean makes less than $900 each year. The country suffers periodic famines. Millions of North Korean children display the bloated bellies and stunted bone development associated with severe malnutrition. Meanwhile, the swollen cadres atop the power pyramid live in monarchical luxury.

The teensy (five-feet, two-inch) dictator also sends squads throughout the country to compel especially attractive women and girls, some still in junior high school, to serve in "joy brigades" that provide sexual companionship for ranking Communist Party officials.

The participation of the Chinese triads in North Korean counterfeiting scams is well documented, especially in Macau and the boomtown Special Economic Zones. Banks in Macau and Harbin have been identified by U.S. investigators as complicit in these schemes.

Acknowledgments

First thanks go to my agent, Bob Mecoy, who spotted several holes in this story from twelve thousand miles away, and to my editor at William Morrow, Marjorie Braman, who has read the book more often than I have and who reshaped it to make it leaner, meaner, and a lot faster.

The story was written in California, Thailand, Cambodia, and China. The people of Southeast Asia are famously hospitable, and I was well and warmly taken care of everywhere. As always, I wrote most of the book in coffeehouses. Thanks to the people at Lollicup in West Los Angeles and the Novel Café in Santa Monica; Coffee World in Bangkok; Mito Café and Coffee Language (great name) in Shenzhen and ChangPing, China; and, in Phnom Penh, the Foreign Correspondents' Club on the riverside and Black Canyon Coffee at Paragon Center.

A waitress at the Mito Café, Ah-Qiu, let me borrow her face so I could give it to Ming Li, and while I was at the Mito, my friend Randell Jackson told me about the ideogram for the name "Lee" that depicts a tree sheltering a child (李). Thanks to both of them.

Gratitude also to the people at Apple for the iPod, a boy's best friend when he's writing in a country where the local pop music is both ubiquitous and (to his ears) unendurable. This time out, Vienna Teng and Aimee Mann were indispensable, as were Bob Dylan (always), Rufus Wainwright (ditto), the phenomenal Fratellis, Emmylou Harris—who could sing in Latvian and still break my heart, Vince Gill, the criminally underrated BoDeans and Gin Blossoms, the Jaynetts (one record, but what a record), KT Tunstall, Kim Gun Mo, Puffy AmiYumi, the ever-essential Kinks, Los Lobos, Richard Thompson, Snow Patrol, and a bunch of others.

I've been remiss in not thanking Chris Lang and Maria Sandamela, who programmed and designed my Web site, www.timothyhallinan.com. They got the whole thing online, looking good, in about three weeks.

Marvin Klotz, Ph.D., showed me by example that it is possible to live a life centered on books and has told me more jokes than anyone else in my life. I've owed him a heartfelt thank-you for years.

And finally, overall inspiration for this book, as for all the others, was provided in more or less infinite amounts by my wife, Munyin Choy.